CONSTANT HEARSES

and Other Revolutionary Mysteries

EDWARD D. HOCH
(Photograph by Michael Culligan)

CONSTANT HEARSES

and Other Revolutionary Mysteries

Edward D. Hoch

Introduction by Brian Skupin

Crippen & Landru Publishers
Cincinnati, Ohio
2022

Cover Design by Gail Cross

ISBN (limited clothbound edition): 978-1-936363-63-6
ISBN (trade softcover edition): 978-1-936363-64-3

FIRST EDITION

*Printed in the United States of America
on recycled acid-free paper*

Jeffrey A. Marks, Publisher
Douglas G. Greene, Senior editor

Crippen & Landru Publishers
P. O. Box 532057
Cincinnati, OH 45253 USA

Email: info@crippenlandru.com
Web: www.crippenlandru.com

CONTENTS

INTRODUCTION

Edward D. Hoch, of Rochester, New York, was a celebrated mystery short story writer, award winner, and Mystery Writers of America Grand Master. He published his first story in 1955, and his last after his death in 2008. Hoch had nearly a thousand short stories published in his lifetime, and was best known for his many series detectives. Reader favorites include Dr. Sam Hawthorne, the New England physician investigating impossible crimes in the mid-twentieth century; Nick Velvet, a thief who only steals valueless items, and Captain Leopold, a policeman investigating homicides. But his best series may be the one he wrote about Alexander Swift, a civilian investigator for George Washington during America's Revolutionary War.

Swift is introduced in "The Hudson Chain", which takes place in 1778 as he travels on Washington's orders to West Point, on the Hudson River in New York State, to monitor the installation of a massive chain across the river to prevent British ships from using the strategic waterway. (This defensive chain was actually deployed during the war.) Swift discovers and fights a plot by the British to destroy the chain, and solves a murder along the way.

Although this sets the template for the rest of the stories (a commission by Washington or President Jefferson; an interesting event, often technological in nature, taking place in early American history; the results of Swift's investigation; and the solution of a murder) Hoch elevated the series starting with the third entry, "The Uninvited Guest."

Here Swift attends the wedding of Benedict Arnold as Washington's representative. As he becomes involved in a blackmail plot, he first begins to doubt the honesty of Arnold, the real-life general and one-time friend of Washington whose name would become synonymous with treachery. Over the course of the remaining stories Swift's suspicions grow, and although he is not always pitted directly against the traitor, Arnold's shadow always looms.

Hoch wrote other historical series incorporating real-life people, places, and events, notably those about Dr. Hawthorne and cowboy Ben Snow, but it's in the Swift series that he excels. The series follows a satisfying story arc, following the War and Arnold's place in it, and comes to a natural conclusion. In addition, while the inclusion of famous people and happenings in historical fiction can often be unnatural and awkward, Hoch was particularly deft in the Swift stories. He never seems to be inserting obvious authorial research without a narrative reason.

We know little of Alexander Swift's background when he's introduced in "The Hudson Chain" and don't learn much more. We don't know his profession, nor do we know how he is paid for his war work. He seems to be from New York City, and was married at one time. As the series progresses we learn more about his former wife, and the development of his new family life, but the focus is on the work he does and his battles with Arnold.

Hoch makes excellent use of actual technologies used during the war: the chain, an ingenious one-man submarine, codes, invisible ink, and other innovations which all fit well within the puzzle mystery framework. His legendary talents as a fair-play specialist, with all the clues needed to solve the mystery provided in plain sight for any enterprising reader to find, are on full display here.

Hoch is also, of course, celebrated for his locked room or impossible crime mysteries, and he included a borderline example in the Swift tales. In "The Sword of Colonel Ledyard" a British Loyalist is stabbed to death in a room apparently inaccessible to Swift and others being held prisoner across the hall.

Not borderline at all are the two impossibilities in Hoch's contemporary series about New York consulting detective Gideon Parrot, whose exploits are also included here. In "The Flying Fiend" a serial killer is cutting the throats of victims, and in one case the body is found on a beach in what seem to be impossible conditions. And in "Lady of the Impossible" an actress disappears, inexplicably, from a guarded room. Both stories, like all the Parrots, are complexly plotted, even for Hoch.

Clearly the first name Gideon (calling to mind Dr. Gideon Fell, one of impossible-crime specialist John Dickson Carr's two major detectives) and the last name Parrot (pronounced to rhyme with Poirot, one of Agatha Christie's two major detectives) are intended to evoke the Golden Age of detective fiction. The stories make use of many classic detective story tropes. Although they are certainly not parodies, these tales are unrealistic in almost every way, featuring fantastical crimes committed and solved with a minimum of practicality.

Readers may notice particular references to specific classic detective stories. For example, the setting used at the beginning of "The Man with Five

Faces" is recognizable to any reader of Conan Doyle. And Hoch is clearly putting his own spin on a couple of Christie's famous novels in two of the other tales, and perhaps he is also nodding to a mythical Carr title in a third. Readers with a fondness for the old days when detective story writers competed to find the next most ingenious solution will be delighted by Gideon Parrot.

As Parrot says in "Lady of the Impossible", they don't write them like this anymore.

Brian Skupin
New York City
January, 2022

THE HUDSON CHAIN

The rough mountain trails that connected West Point with the furnace and forge at Sterling Pond were still drifted with snow in spots, even though it was the end of March in this year of Our Lord 1778. Spurring his horse over the uncertain terrain, Alexander Swift was reminded again that the colonies fighting their war of independence had just suffered through one of the harshest winters of the century. General George Washington was still encamped at Valley Forge with his army, awaiting the arrival of spring, and word of their suffering had traveled north with the couriers who traversed the snowy countryside to keep open the lines of communication.

It was a twenty-five-mile ride over the mountains to Sterling, but Swift preferred it to the longer, if easier, route through Central Valley. His horse was well up to the mountain journey, which they'd already made a few times during breaks in the harsh winter. When the Sterling hearths themselves finally came into view, showering sparks by the edge of the great pond, the horse seemed to pick up speed for the final moments of the journey.

It was Chester Hayborne, the foreman, who came out to greet him. "Have you ridden up from Camp West Point?" he asked as Swift dismounted.

"I have. The day seemed right for it, and General Washington is nervous for word on the chain. He had hoped it would be in place by the first week of April."

"We will not miss that deadline by much. Come in, and I will show you our progress. How is the snow through the mountains?"

"Still deep in spots but quite passable. We will soon have this bloody winter behind us."

Hayborne was a man in his thirties, with muscles hardened from working at the forge. His face and arms were blackened by soot from the wood and charcoal used to heat the iron ore to a molten state. Alexander Swift followed him into the nearest of the buildings, feeling the intense heat as it flowed over his body in waves. Foundrymen were busy pounding red-hot bars of iron into shape, then bending them into links around a mandrel.

"Hot work," Swift remarked.

"The hottest. We welcome the cold winter here, even though there were days in recent months when the depth of the snow kept us from our labor. Here, look at what we have for George Washington's watch chain."

It was a name Swift had heard used before in referring to the gigantic chain being forged to stretch across the Hudson at West Point. It would have 750 giant links of two-inch-thick bar iron, with eight swivels and eighty clevises to yoke the sections of the chain together. Seeing the finished sections of nine links each, with a single clevis and pin, stretched out and ready for transport by ox sledges and water, he couldn't help but be impressed.

He tried to lift just one of the links. "In God's name, how much do these weigh?"

"The average weight is about one hundred fourteen pounds each, though we have one link that weighed in at one hundred thirty pounds. Each section of chain weighs more than half a ton. As you can see, they are formed from bar iron two inches square, with each link being about twelve inches wide by eighteen inches long. We trust it is much stronger than the chain at Fort Montgomery last year."

Alexander Swift still remembered General Washington's fury at that debacle, when the British outflanked the fort with an overland attack and then sailed up to the chain and filed away one link to break the barrier and open the river. Washington wanted the new chain to be strong enough to withstand a ramming by several of His Majesty's warships.

"When will you deliver it?" he asked the foreman.

"One of your officers, Colonel Clay, is here now working out the schedule."

The news surprised Swift. He had not seen Colonel Clay since arriving at West Point. He knew there was a feeling that as a civilian working directly for General Washington he'd come north to prepare reports critical of the garrison at Camp West Point. In truth, Washington only wanted the chain in position. He was not seeking to place blame.

"I should see the colonel," Swift said. "Take me to him."

Colonel Jeremy Clay was a Pennsylvania farmer who'd been one of the first to take up arms against the British. He was a gaunt man with sandy hair and the appearance of an outdoorsman. Swift had known him in New York before the British capture of the city in 1776. They found him in the foundry office going over the timetable for transporting the chain to West Point. He glanced up from the papers on the desk, showing a flicker of annoyance when he recognized Alexander.

"Ah, Swift, isn't it? I haven't seen you since before the hostilities began. You were getting married then. How's your wife?"

"She died," Swift replied without emotion.

"Oh. Sorry to hear that." He immediately dismissed the unpleasant thought. "Have you been in contact with General Washington?"

"I visited him at Valley Forge a fortnight ago."

"I know he is concerned about the chain, but you can assure him it will be solidly in place soon."

"How soon?" Swift asked.

"I told him you were working on it," Chester Hayborne said.

"I'll handle this now, Chester. You can leave us alone."

The foreman nodded and left them in the office.

"The chain was to be in place by next week," Alexander Swift said when they were alone.

"There will be a slight delay with no harm done. The winter weather is still with us and it will be another month before any skipper would be foolish enough to sail this far up the Hudson."

"Hayborne says the sections of chain are all but complete."

'That they are," Jeremy Clay confirmed. "The ironworks has been operating twenty-four hours a day for the past two months to fill the government order in record time. Sledges pulled by oxen will begin hauling the sections of chain down to the river tomorrow. The chain has eighty-four sections in all, which means eighty-four trips with the ox sledges. Then the chain will have to be assembled at a small foundry at the water's edge and floated down the river to West Point on pitch-covered log rafts. We'll have it in place, with its protective boom, within weeks."

Swift studied again the now-familiar chart of that portion of the Hudson, with its narrow S-shaped curve. He had to agree with General Washington that it was the most effective place to block the river, with gun positions able to target any ships approaching the chain. Still, "Do you think it will work, Clay? The one at Fort Montgomery—"

"This one is far thicker and stronger. The only problem might be its removal each fall and replacement the following spring. The frozen river would play havoc with the chain if we left it in place during the winter. Besides, the log platforms that buoy it up will need to be replaced each year to keep them afloat."

Swift nodded. "The General is resigned to that fact, and will issue the orders himself at the proper time each year. Is there any danger of Camp West Point and Fort Constitution across the river being outflanked as was Fort Montgomery?"

"Very little. Our main threat comes from Loyalist spies who are thick in the countryside."

"Spies? What could they do?"

"Keep the British advised of our progress." He reached into the deerskin knapsack at his side and brought forth a letter which he passed to Alexander.

"It seems to be a message from a daughter to her mother in New York," Swift said, skimming the lengthy letter.

"But look!" The colonel held the paper up to the light from the window and pointed out a number of tiny pinpricks. "These indicate certain letters which spell out the real message: *Rebels have six 32-pounders and twenty small cannon at Camp West Point. Chain across river in place by late April.*"

Swift could hardly believe his ears. He took back the letter and examined the pinpricks, spelling out each word. "Where did you find this?"

"In the pouch of a traveler trying to cross enemy lines north of New York. You can see it is dated March twenty-second, just last week."

"It seems there is a spy operating at West Point."

"Very likely. While this message did not get through, there will certainly be others."

"Do you think the British will attack the chain?"

Colonel Clay nodded. "At the first opportunity, if only because it is General Washington's personal project."

Alexander Swift made a decision. "I will remain at West Point until the chain is secure across the Hudson."

"Do what you wish, but the spy is my affair. When I find him I will enjoy watching him hanged from the nearest tree."

Camp West Point was a relatively small garrison, established to guard the river at this narrow bend. The British had long felt that the Hudson, with its passage into Canada via Lake George and Lake Champlain, was the key to splitting the Colonies. Only a year earlier Washington had said, "The importance of the Hudson River in the present contest, and the necessity of defending it, are subjects which have been so frequently and fully discussed, and are so well understood, that it is unnecessary to enlarge upon them. These facts at once appear when it is considered that the river runs through a whole state; that it is the only passage by which the enemy from New York, or any part of our coast, can ever hope to cooperate with an army from Canada; that the possession of it is indispensably essential to preserve the communication between the Eastern, Middle, and Southern States; and further, that upon its security, in a great measure, depend our chief supplies of flour for the subsistence of such forces as we may have occasion for in the course of the War."

Washington had tried other methods of blocking the river. The chain at Fort Montgomery had failed, as had the *chevaux-de-frise* at Fort Washington. These were a submerged shallow-water version of an old Dutch anti-cavalry device, using sunken timbers with projecting iron spears to puncture the hulls of the enemy's wooden ships. But the Hudson was too deep for them to be effective, and its powerful tides played havoc with the devices. Fire ships and fire rafts against enemy ships also proved ineffective and too easy to avoid.

Since he was not a military man, Swift did not stay at the camp itself, but at a small nearby settlement which had sprung up almost overnight to cater to the needs of the soldiers on duty at West Point and other nearby forts. On prior visits he'd stayed at a tavern called the Nugget of Gold. He returned there now and was pleased to see the same man behind the bar. Norb Flander was the owner of the place, a red-faced man in his fifties who'd worked at a tavern on Manhattan Island until the British came in '76. He'd moved north along the river like a great many others, finally pausing near West Point to build his own place. He'd bought an old barn for its wood, torn it down, and built the Nugget of Gold.

"Good to see you again, Mr. Swift," he said by way of greeting. "I got your room waiting for you. Want your usual rum?"

"That will be fine, Norb."

"I think the weather's finally beginning to warm up."

"It should. It's been a long winter."

A couple of off-duty soldiers from the camp were standing at the other end of the bar, but Swift didn't recognize them. He drank the rum down quickly and ordered another. After a bit more small talk he asked Flander, "You get many strangers around here?"

"Hardly at all. With the war going on, every stranger might be a Loyalist spy."

Swift sipped his second drink, having no intention of finishing it. "How's Molly? I don't see her around." Molly McVey was a barmaid who worked there occasionally. Swift had become friendly with her on his previous trips to the camp.

"Probably with one of the officers. You know how it is."

'Tell her I was asking for her." He left the rest of his drink and went around to his room at the back of the tavern.

He almost hoped Molly would visit him later, but finally he fell asleep alone.

The weather was damp and chilly during the first week in April, but ice was breaking up in the river. Alexander Swift watched it each day and thought about the great chain—George Washington's watch chain. On April 7, when half the chain had been assembled upstream, it was loaded on rafts of pitch-covered logs for the final leg of its journey to Camp West Point. Swift met Chester Hayborne and his crew at New Windsor, about fifteen miles upriver, where the chain-laden rafts were being launched.

"We'll keep them close to shore," the foreman told Swift. "If there is an accident we don't want to lose the chain in the deepest part of the river." He wore a sealskin jacket and cap as protection against the damp mist over the water, and watched carefully as his men poled the rafts along the shoreline.

"Colonel Clay is concerned about Tory spies," Swift told him. "Have you seen any strangers about?"

"Just the usual townsfolk. I've known them most of my life."

"Keep an eye out," Swift cautioned him.

"Are you in charge of the chain project now?"

"No, I'm just observing the progress for General Washington. Colonel Clay and Captain Machin are the military people in charge, and, of course, General McDougall." He was the senior officer in charge of all the highland posts. "When do you expect the remainder of the chain will be ready for us?"

The muscular foreman shrugged. "A week, ten days. No longer than that."

Alexander Swift nodded. "I'll be back then."

Returning to West Point, Swift found Captain Machin, the officer who had designed the chain and arranged for its construction, watching with Clay as the first half of it was made fast to the shoreline. "Soon it will be in place," Clay said happily. "If the enemy lets us alone two weeks longer, the job will be done."

Two nights later, as Alexander Swift drank with Norb Flander in the bar at the Nugget of Gold, he noticed a curly-haired stranger at one of the tables. "Who is that?" he asked Flander.

"A fur merchant named Rowland, down from Canada."

"Ever seen him before?"

Norb Flander shook his head. "He's new to these parts."

Swift picked up his drink and joined the man at the table, introducing himself. "Pleased to meet you," Rowland said, extending his hand. Up close, the mass of curly blond locks seemed almost too large for the man's head. Swift wondered if it might be a wig.

"Flander tells me you're a fur merchant from Canada."

"That's right."

"This is a dangerous place to sell your goods, in the midst of a revolution."

"I feel safe in this area," the man said. "Since the British defeat at Saratoga last October they have stayed away. The French in Canada are now support- ing your struggle."

"They stayed away only because of the harsh winter," Swift reasoned. "Now that spring is coming you will see their sails once more on the Hudson."

The merchant, who appeared not much older than Swift's own twenty- eight years, replied, "But your chain will stop them."

"Which chain would that be?" Swift asked innocently.

" 'Tis no secret in these parts. I see it lying down by the water's edge like some sun-basking serpent."

"It's not wise to pass such observations along to others," Swift warned him.

"I would not," the merchant assured him. He finished his drink and made a nervous exit from the tavern.

"Watch that one," Swift advised Norb Flander. "I do not like the look of him."

It was the following night when Molly McVey returned to West Point. Alexander saw her as soon as he walked into the Nugget of Gold. Oddly, she was standing by a table where the Canadian fur merchant, Rowland, sat whit- tling on a piece of wood, his left hand using a sharp hunting knife to carve out the shape of a rough wooden chain with three interlocked links. Swift watched him finish the task and pass it to Molly. "There you are. It's my gift to you," he told her with a smile.

"How clever you are!" She tucked it away in her dress and then seemed to notice Swift for the first time. "Hello, Alex. It's good to see you again." She was the only one, other than his wife, who had ever called him Alex.

"You've been away," he said.

She turned and said goodbye to the fur merchant, then followed Swift to a table near the opposite end of the bar. Norb Flander came over with a rum for him and a beer for Molly. "I was visiting a friend in Albany," she said. "How long have you been here?"

"Ten days."

Molly McVey was a slender, dark-haired woman with a creamy white complexion and a way of wearing dresses a bit tighter than the fashion allowed. She was probably a bit older than Swift. She was certainly wiser in many things. "You're looking good," she told him. "Most of my friends are pale and worn after this hard winter."

"I've made a few trips to Valley Forge through the deep snow in New Jersey. That ride will keep any man in shape."

"How is General Washington?"

"Vigorous and aching for combat. It's amazing how he's kept up the spirits of his troops through this winter, despite the terrible conditions and the death of so many from starvation."

"How long will he remain there?"

Alexander shrugged. "Perhaps till June if the British do not attack. He has Baron von Steuben with him, training and reorganizing the army."

"At least this winter is at an end," she said.

They had another drink and then he followed her up the creaking stairs to her room above the bar. When he looked back, the man named Rowland was carving out another of his little wooden chains.

He found himself drifting in and out of sleep until it was nearly dawn. At one point Molly said to him, "The chain is a big secret, isn't it?"

"We hope so, until it's in place. General Washington never mentions it directly in his letters."

She held up the wooden links that Rowland had given her. "Do you think the Canadian is a spy?"

"He could be."

And later, "Alex?"

"What is it, my love?"

"I heard something about you in Albany. People gossip, you know."

"What did you hear?"

"That your wife isn't dead at all. That she ran off with a British officer in New York."

He didn't answer, only lay there feeling the weight of the sheets. "Do you still love her?" Molly asked, but he didn't reply. Finally she asked, "If you found them, would you kill him?"

"Perhaps," he said, more to himself than to Molly.

"Would you kill her?"

He didn't answer. After a time he slept.

By April 16 the second half of the chain had been assembled at New Windsor. It was another damp day full of gray clouds and misty rain. When Alexander Swift reached the place, he saw Hayborne in the shallow water with his workers, trying to hoist a pair of giant links back onto their raft. Finally they succeeded and he came out of the water to dry off, fanning himself with his sealskin cap.

"That's hard work, Swift. Work for younger men than me."

"It'll soon be over."

The foreman shouted at his men to keep the rafts out of deep water as they began their journey downriver. Then he put the cap back on and strolled along with Alexander. "Over till the next job. They get harder in the summer with all that heat at the foundry."

Suddenly Swift saw someone on the hill above them. He recognized the mop of curly blond hair at once, even though he hadn't seen Rowland around for several days. "See that man? Do you know him?"

"I don't think so."

"Be careful. He may be a Tory spy."

"Glad you warned me."

Swift mounted up, preparing to ride back along the river, following the rafts in their progress downstream. Chester Hayborne disappeared from view among the pine trees, and he could no longer see Rowland anywhere. He'd ridden about fifty yards when some noise made him turn and look back. Hayborne had emerged from the trees and was walking along a raised bluff that commanded a good view of the river to the south. Perhaps he was checking the progress of the rafts, though the visibility through the mist had grown poorer.

Almost at once a second figure burst forth from the trees running after Hayborne. Swift recognized Rowland's curly blond hair at once, and saw the hunting knife in his raised right hand.

"Rowland! Don't!" Hayborne shouted, and turned to face his attacker.

The knife plunged in again and again, through the sealskin jacket. The foreman fell to the ground at the edge of the bluff even as Swift spurred his mount forward. Rowland pushed the body with his foot and it rolled off the edge of the bluff, falling a dozen feet to the water.

The current was swift at this point and Alexander saw the body turning over and over as it was swept along. He tried to reach it, urging his horse into the shallow water near shore, but the body was moving too fast, sweeping toward the river's center. The hat came off, bobbed a moment, and then vanished with the body. Chester Hayborne was gone, and his killer had vanished as well. There was no sign of Rowland among the trees.

Immediately upon his return Swift sought out Colonel Clay. He was not among the men working at the water's edge under the command of Captain Machin. "Where is Clay?" he asked the captain.

"I haven't seen him lately. Try his quarters."

Swift finally found him talking with Flander at the Nugget of Gold. He reported what had happened to Chester Hayborne. "You actually witnessed this murder?" he asked.

"I did, Colonel. Rowland stabbed him to death while I watched."

"Is there any possibility he might have survived?"

"None. I saw the body being swept away by the river."

"I don't believe I ever saw this man Rowland. Do we have an artist in the camp who might sketch him from your description?"

Norb Flander had been listening at the bar. "Molly's something of an artist, and she talked to him a couple of times. She could probably do it."

Norb found Molly in her room and brought her down. Her eyes moved from Swift to Clay while they explained what they needed. "You think he's a spy?" she repeated. Swift saw that she was fingering the little links of wooden chain as she spoke.

"And a murderer," Alexander added. "He killed Hayborne from the foundry."

"Why would he do that?"

"The British want to destroy the chain and make certain we can't replace it."

She went upstairs for her paper and sketching pencils. Swift had seen some of her drawings before, but he wondered about her ability to capture an accurate likeness of Rowland. Seated at the bar, she did a quick sketch and then began to fill in the shadings of the face and hair.

"Did you think he was wearing a wig?" Swift asked her.

"He could have been. If so, I'll have to draw him with it on because I never saw him any other way."

Flander peered over her shoulder, offering comments and suggestions. "I think the eyes are a little off, Molly. Weren't they a bit closer together?"

Alexander made suggestions too, based on his memory, and before long they had a passable likeness of the man who called himself Rowland. Colonel Clay took it and assured them it would be seen by every man at the camp. "I'll post it at mess," he promised.

"Let Molly make a copy," Flander suggested, "and I'll post it here at the bar as well."

Swift had personal doubts that it would do any good. If Rowland had been wearing a wig his appearance could be quite different already.

Two days later, on the twentieth, Captain Machin reported to General McDougall. Seventeen hundred feet of the great chain was ready for use, more than enough to cross the Hudson at West Point. They only needed to wait for favorable weather to fix it in place. On the slack tide of April 30, the weather finally broke. One end of the chain was made fast to a huge rock crib some ten feet high and eight feet wide, then slowly winched across the river to a similar crate filled with stone on the opposite bank. With both ends secure and the massive chain stapled to pine log rafts, the Hudson was finally effectively blocked.

"This is a great day," Swift told Colonel Clay as they stood on the shore surveying the scene.

"Tell that to General Washington. His wild dream has come true."

"I still wonder if a large ship, with a metal prow, might strike the chain at full sail and break it."

It was a thought that had obviously bothered the colonel as well. "The foundry is turning out a smaller chain for a boom. The work was slowed by the killing of Chester Hayborne but it proceeds at a good pace now." The boom, designed to float slightly downstream from the chain, was a series of foot-thick logs, fifteen feet long, spaced four feet apart and parallel to the water's flow, linked by sections of chain and iron bolts. The idea was that the boom would help absorb the shock of a ramming by an enemy warship, protecting the great chain from breaking. When the weather was favorable, loosely laid planks could turn the boom into a footbridge.

Swift spoke of it again that night with Molly. "It seems like a great deal of money for a chain across the river," she said. "And one man has died for it."

"Others may, too, if the British attempt to ram it."

"Is the Hudson that important?"

"It is our new nation's lifeline, as General Washington has pointed out many times. In the land east of the river there is no flour, to the west there is no meat. The two parts of our struggling nation have an absolute need for each other."

"When will the boom be in place?"

"In a few days, we hope."

"You'll be leaving then?"

"I expect so, yes."

"With Rowland still at large?"

"Colonel Clay and the others can deal with him, should he return. By now he's probably in Canada."

She fingered the chain of rough wood that Rowland had carved for her. "Where will you go next?"

"General Washington will have a place for me."

"You'd rather do this than serve in the regular army? If you're caught behind enemy lines, couldn't you be hanged as a spy?"

"I try to avoid enemy lines as much as possible."

"Don't you ever want to sneak into New York, to see her? Do you know where she is?"

"I know the street, I know the house. I can see her in my mind right now." He had turned away as he spoke.

Molly reached out to touch his face in the darkness. "Will I ever see you after you leave here?"

"I'm sure I'll be back. Washington will want periodic reports on his watch chain."

"It's different when you're here. This whole place is different. These few weeks have made everything else bearable."

"Sleep now," he told her softly. "I'm here. I won't be going away quite yet."

By the time the boom was finally in place, the hills of the Hudson Valley were alive with mayflowers. The harsh winter had been forgotten with the arrival of spring. Alexander took Molly for a walk on the plank bridge across the river, and she marveled at her first close look at the giant chain.

"It's enormous, Alex! Even seeing it on the shore didn't prepare me for this. It would hold back Caesar's army!"

"But will it hold back King George's navy? That is the question. They still command the Hudson south of Peekskill."

Back on shore she held tight to his arm. "You took me out there because you're leaving tomorrow, aren't you?"

"We each have work to do."

"My work can wait," she replied with a touch of bitterness. 'There are always soldiers to be comforted."

"Let us stop at the Nugget for a drink."

Norb Flander brought them their drinks and said, "We're all feeling better now that the boom is in place."

"Any sign of Rowland?"

The proprietor glanced back at Molly's sketch posted on the wall. "Not a bit. If he's been here he's a different person."

"He just might be that," Swift agreed, remembering the curly blond hair.

While she drank, Molly had taken out the carved wooden chain again and was playing with it. There were times when Swift wanted to take it from her and hurl it far away into the night. It was the gift of a spy and a murderer. Now, staring at it as if hypnotized, his mind suddenly cleared. "What is it?" she asked, noting the strange expression on his face.

"I've been a fool," he said.

"What—?"

"Flander, what night is the new moon this month?"

"Soon now. The night sky is already dark as pitch."

"But what night will it be darkest?"

"Thursday—two nights from now."

He nodded, then said to Molly, "I'll be staying through Thursday night."

The following day Alexander Swift spoke privately with Captain Machin, because the Hudson chain was ultimately his responsibility. Certain preparations were made, though he could see the captain thought him just a bit crazy.

He sat up Wednesday night watching the water, because he could not afford to be wrong. Once, after midnight, Molly came down to where he sat in the darkness. "Nothing's going to happen tonight," she said. "Come up to bed."

"I'll be up shortly. I suppose you're right. If the British were coming they'd be here by now."

On Thursday morning the chain still held, floating serenely on the unusually calm water. He went down to the boom and walked carefully across to the other side, watching for anything unusual. The chain was undamaged, exactly as it had been. When he reached the opposite side, at Fort Constitution, he inspected the large pile of wood he'd instructed Captain Machin to build on either shore. Then he walked back across the footbridge to the West Point side.

"You look worried," Norb Flander told him later when he stopped in the Nugget of Gold.

"Just apprehensive."

Norb poured him a drink. "Why do you think the British might attack tonight?"

"It's darkest with a new moon, and the current is moving slowly. If they're coming by night to try filing through a link as they did at Fort Montgomery, this is when they'll do it."

"But our chain is stronger."

"I hope so."

Even on the darkest night it was impossible to move a large British warship up the river without attracting attention. Progress would be slowed by the danger of running aground, and if spies tried to guide it from the riverbanks their torches would be seen from the forts. Swift knew the attack, if it came at all, would come by small boats sneaking silently up the river.

As it happened, it was Molly who spotted them first. It was just before midnight when she tugged on his sleeve. "Alex! There's something moving on the river!"

He saw it then, but couldn't make out what it was. "Stay here," he whispered. "I'm going out on the boom. If you hear a shot, have them light the fires."

He hurried onto the wooden footbridge, drawing a loaded flintlock pistol from his belt. If they were bent on cutting the chain—

Then he heard soft voices, and knew they were up ahead, climbing out of their boats and onto the boom. Some would be swimming under the boom to the chain itself. He aimed into the darkness ahead and fired the pistol. There was an immediate scurry and splashing as the men on the boom dove for safety. Then, behind him on the shore, a torch blazed and the pile of wood caught fire. The guards at Fort Constitution lit their bonfire as well.

Now suddenly the river was alive with light, the waters reflecting the twin fires growing by the minute into towers of flame. Swift saw now that there were two boats ahead, rowed upstream against the current. Men were in the water, dark figures whose faces reflected the red glow of the sky. Then he saw something that sent a chill through him. One of the swimmers was on the giant chain, clinging to a bobbing raft while he crammed a package inside a link.

Gunpowder.

They were trying to blow up the chain.

The man pulled out a long fuse and struck a large-headed friction match to light it. Swift hurled his single-shot pistol at him, missed, and leaped from the boom onto the nearest raft. From both shores came the scattered chatter of musket fire.

"Don't light it!" Alexander Swift warned.

The fuse sputtered into life. "You're too late," came the reply.

Swift leaped the four feet onto the adjoining raft and grabbed for the fuse. The other pulled out a hunting knife—the same one, surely—and raised it to strike.

"Not this time," Swift shouted. "No more killings, no more escapes." He went in under the knife and slammed the man down onto the giant chain. Then he grabbed for the fuse and pulled it free of the gunpowder.

There was more firing and an oarsman in one of the boats toppled into the water. The others swam to shore where soldiers were waiting. Colonel Clay and his men came running out with torches along the footbridge as Swift hauled up his prisoner.

"Here's your man!" Swift told them, and the torchlight fell on the face of the foundry foreman, Chester Hayborne.

When the Tory forces had been rounded up and the gunpowder bomb safely removed, Alexander Swift found himself with Colonel Clay and Captain Machin at the Nugget of Gold. Drinks were on the house, Flander said, and Molly served them.

"You knew it was Hayborne?" Colonel Clay asked, incredulous. "You knew he was still alive?"

Swift nodded. "See this little chain Molly has? I watched the stranger, Rowland, carve it with the knife in his left hand. That day on the river, the curly-haired man who stabbed Hayborne and pushed the body into the river struck with his right hand. When I remembered that the other night I was sure of one thing—the murderer had not been Rowland. Yet how was that possible? I myself heard Hayborne's voice shout out 'Rowland! Don't!' an instant before the stabbing. But then I remembered something else. That shouted plea came just *before* the man in the sealskin cap turned to confront his attacker! It was the attacker who shouted those words, not the victim. And if the attacker was not Rowland, it had to be Hayborne because I'd recognized his voice."

"Why would he shout out at all?" Clay wondered.

"To attract my attention, of course. He needed a witness to swear the victim had been Hayborne, and the killer Rowland. I should have been suspicious right away, because to my knowledge Hayborne didn't even know Rowland when he shouted the name. If you read over that intercepted secret message again you will see that it implies the spy has a knowledge of the great chain and its timing, yet is probably not someone stationed or living at West Point. Otherwise he or she would long ago have sent word on the number of cannons at the camp. It suggested that the spy might be a foundry worker who went to West Point only occasionally."

"Then Rowland came here to meet with Hayborne?"

"Exactly. By that time, however, I'd mentioned the possibility of spies. Hayborne was nervous and must have guessed his message had been intercepted. He decided to fake his death and make his way south to the British lines. Rowland afforded the perfect opportunity with that curly blond wig. Hayborne must have persuaded him to change clothes to avoid capture as a spy. Rowland donned the sealskin jacket and cap while Hayborne put on the wig and Rowland's coat. Then, after attracting my attention, Hayborne stabbed Rowland and pushed him into the Hudson. With the switched clothing and the poor visibility that day, he thought he could fool me. The body lost its cap, but since I'd never seen Rowland without his wig I still didn't recognize him. So far as I knew, the foreman was dead and Rowland had killed him. Hayborne was safe in assuming the body wouldn't be recovered from the swift-flowing river. He joined the British forces and led a raiding party back tonight to sever the chain with a gunpowder bomb, choosing a night they knew the sky would be at its darkest."

Clay finished his drink and stood up. "Chester Hayborne will be properly dealt with, and I will personally commend your actions to General McDougall and the Commander-in-Chief."

Swift shook his hand. "I leave in the morning for Valley Forge. Guard the chain, Colonel. Guard it well. Its links are holding this new nation together."

When he rode out at dawn the next day only Molly was there to see him, waving from her upstairs window at the Nugget of Gold.

KING GEORGE'S GOLD

It was shortly after the indecisive Battle of Monmouth, toward the end of June, in 1778, that Alexander Swift found himself once again in the company of General George Washington. The 46-year-old leader of the Continental Army showed few effects of his long winter at Valley Forge, though he regretted not having fared better during the recent New Jersey engagement.

"It's a pleasure to see you again, Swift," he said, taking Alexander's hand in his own. "You did a fine job defending our chain at West Point."

The Hudson chain, barring the river to British ships, was a favorite project of Washington's. Its efficacy in just a few short months was shown by the British attempt to destroy it and open the river once again to the Royal Navy.

"I only did what I had to," Swift said. As a civilian who often undertook special assignments for the army, his relationship with General Washington was somewhat special.

"At least it's one small victory for us this year."

"What news of Monmouth?"

"We should have won the battle. I made the error of shifting command from Lafayette to General Lee, and Lee let me down. I was forced to rebuke him publicly, on the battlefield. Lafayette and I slept together under a massive oak tree with our cloaks for covering, ready to attack at dawn, but by morning the British had slipped away."

"There will be other days, General."

"I feel the war is shifting to the south now. In my heart I wanted to retake New York by this summer. Ever since I allowed that city to fall to the British I have distrusted my own ability in the field."

"Things may not be as bleak as they seem," Swift tried to reassure him. "I have news from a spy in New York."

The general perked up at once. "Your wife?"

Alexander Swift felt a chill at the words. "No, she still lives with the British officer for whom she left me. I have had no word from her since our parting."

"Then what news have you?"

"A British frigate sank recently in the East River, a few miles north of the main harbor. It was carrying a cargo of gold valued at about a million American dollars. They will surely try to recover this gold for the war effort."

General Washington pondered his words. "Is there anything we can do to stop them?"

"One man alone might have a chance of slipping into the city."

Washington knew what he meant. "You'll be shot as a spy if they catch you."

"I'll take my chances. New York is my city and I've been away from it too long. Do I have your permission, General?"

Washington turned away. "I tell you nothing, but if you go and if you happen to see Amanda, give her my fondest regards." He had spoken the name of Alexander Swift's estranged wife.

Although early July marked the second anniversary of the colonies' declaration of independence from England, there were no celebrations in the city of New York. The British army was firmly entrenched in the city that clustered around the southern tip of Manhattan Island. Crossing the Hudson by night in a small boat, Swift could see the old Dutch windmill still silhouetted against the campfires.

No guards challenged him or even noticed him as he pulled the rowboat ashore. Wearing his ordinary civilian clothes, Swift walked east on Wall Street to the corner of Broadway where the ruins of Trinity Church still remained after a disastrous fire two years earlier. Here he had a decision to make, knowing he was only a few blocks from the place that had been home to him. But he knew that trying to see Amanda would be foolish. Her British soldier would no doubt be with her. He was a man Swift had sworn to kill, but not now, not this night. Not until he had completed his mission.

Instead he headed north along Broadway, braving the night streets on foot rather than risk renting a horse at a posthouse. Even at this late hour he was fairly certain that the man he sought would be at the waterfront around South Street. He found him after an hour's search, in the Blue Boar tavern near the East River.

"Feeney," he said, speaking the man's last name softly so as not to be overheard.

Michael Feeney turned with a grin, barely concealing the razor-sharp knife as he pulled it from his sleeve. "My God! Alexander! What brings you to New York?" The knife slipped back as quickly as it had appeared.

"I received your message about the sunken frigate."

Feeney nodded, his ruddy Irish complexion reflecting the glow of the oil lamps. "I knew that would interest you." He was a man in his mid thirties, perhaps a few years older than Alexander, who'd had the misfortune of starting a new life in the colonies just at the time that they revolted and declared their independence. Never a friend of the English, he continued to live and work among the loyalists while supplying his friend with information. He'd told Swift once that he considered himself more of a gossip than a spy, but they both knew the English would hang him in a minute if his activities were ever discovered.

Alexander Swift glanced around at the others in the dimly fit tavern. Most were obviously British seamen, part of the supply route from the mother country. He was sure none could overhear him as he asked, "Are they going to try raising it?"

"Believe me, they want that gold. The troops need food and supplies, more than can be shipped from England. The gold bullion on board the *Freetown* could keep the war going for years. My information is that the ship is resting on a ledge of rock just below the water's surface. If they can keep it from sinking any deeper, the gold can be removed with relative ease."

"What caused the *Freetown* to go down?" Swift asked, pouring himself a drink from the bottle the bartender had set down before him.

"A nor'easter hit just as she was coming into the river. Before they could get the sails furled it capsized her. My own opinion is that she must have been overloaded, though Captain Shay denies it."

"Not Randolph Shay?'

"None other! You know him, don't you?"

"We've met. He's the one who introduced Amanda to Major Jordan."

"Oh!"

Swift smiled ruefully. "I know. It was the beginning of bad times for my marriage."

"Will you try to see her while you're here?" Feeney asked.

"It would be a big mistake. If Major Jordan caught me I could be hanged as a spy—just like you. I have a feeling he'd like nothing better. It would save all the trouble of a divorce."

"What are you going to do about the *Freetown*?"

"Go look at it in the morning. Do you have an extra bed I could use?"

"Certainly. But be careful, Alexander."

At the first light of dawn, not long after five, Swift borrowed a horse from Feeney and rode north. He followed the familiar trail that hugged the shore of the East River, passing cultivated farmland and wooded areas before at last sighting the top of a mast protruding from the water. Almost at once he reined in his horse and took cover in the shelter of some pine trees. A pair of longboats moved out from shore toward the mast of the submerged frigate. There appeared to be six or eight men in each.

Swift cursed silently for arriving on the scene just a moment too late. He dismounted and dropped to the ground, crawling through the pine needles for a better view of the salvage operation. Behind him the horse whinnied a warning but he was too absorbed to understand. Suddenly a harsh voice spoke. "On your feet, laddie, before I poke you with me bayonet!"

"I was just—"

The British soldier jabbed him in the right buttock and Swift scrambled quickly to his feet. "That's better. You want to see what's going on, I'll give you a good view."

The first thing he saw as he was marched to the water's edge was a group of half a dozen British officers standing in a semicircle as they watched the progress of the longboats. The vessels were now tethered to the mast and two men from each boat dove into the water. They could stay under for a couple of minutes at most, and as each team surfaced a new team of divers replaced.

Alexander Swift suddenly realized that one of the six officers standing on the shore wore the uniform of a captain in the King's Navy. Swift had never seen him with a beard before, but it took him only a moment to recognize Captain Randolph Shay, commander of the sunken frigate *Freetown*.

Shay, for his part, stepped forward at once. "Alexander! Can that be you?"

"It is, Captain. I was out for an early morning canter when I noticed the unusual activity up here."

"I'd heard you had deserted the city when the rebels were forced to retreat two years ago."

To admit to that was to admit he was a spy. "No, no. I've been here all along. What are you doing here?"

Captain Shay gestured toward the river. "My ship went down in that nor'easter last week. We're trying to recover the cargo. I never knew a storm like that to hit this area in early July. It caught us with our sails fully rigged."

"Good luck with the recovery," Swift said, turning away. With a bit of luck he might be able to bluff his way out of this. But it was not a day for luck.

"Seize that man!" one of the army officers ordered. "He is a spy."

Alexander Swift whirled to face his accuser as firm hands gripped his arms. Though he'd only seen him twice before, he now recognized the face of the handsome major who stood with the others, pointing an accusing finger at his chest. "Major Jordan, isn't it? My regards to you, sir, and to Amanda, my wife. I trust she is in good health."

"He fled the city more than a year ago to be with Washington," Jordan announced. "I will testify against him."

At that moment he was interrupted by a shout from one of the boats. An officer in command of the recovery team was calling out to shore.

"What is it?" Captain Shay shouted in response. "Say again."

There is no gold on board here. The ship's hold is empty!"

Alexander Swift was taken back to British Army headquarters in lower Manhattan. He was questioned by a captain he'd never seen before and then left alone for more than an hour. Finally, when the door opened again, it was not the captain but Major Jack Jordan who entered. Seeing him in this room lit only by the morning sun, Swift could view him as Amanda might. He was handsome, certainly, but Swift's wife had never been one to be impressed merely by physical appearances. Perhaps there was something more, some sort of animal magnetism that Swift himself lacked. He'd been faithful during their time together, and even since their separation he'd found comfort only a few times in the arms of a barmaid named Molly who lived near the American garrison at West Point.

Staring now at this handsome British major, he spoke the words that had hovered in his mind since their meeting by the sunken frigate. "I always thought I'd kill you if we met again, Major."

"Killing a British officer is a hanging offense. But then, so is spying." He sat down across the table from Swift. "Amanda will be put through a great deal of torment as a result of your returning to New York, Swift."

"Release me and she need never know."

"Right now we have much larger problems than you. A valuable shipment of King George's gold has disappeared from that wrecked frigate."

"Someone simply got there first. I understand that looting wrecked ships for their cargo is not unknown along the English coast."

Major Jordan shook his head. "We had guards there ever since the wreck, day and night. No one went near it."

"Perhaps the bullion was removed earlier, on the high seas, and transferred to another ship."

"Such a thing would involve a major conspiracy of Captain Shay and the entire crew. It's out of the question."

Alexander Swift took a deep breath. "Release me and perhaps I can find the missing gold. I have a number of contacts on the waterfront."

Jordan snorted at the suggestion. "Find it for which side?"

"If I find it, you have my word that the gold will not go to the Continental Army."

This promise brought a laugh from Major Jordan. "The word of a man who has sworn to kill me?"

"What happened over my wife is another matter entirely. I will deal with that in due time. Right now you want your gold—"

"King George's gold," he corrected.

"—King George's gold. And I want my freedom."

Major Jordan stood up. "Let me discuss this with my superiors. I will return shortly."

Alexander Swift had a suspicion no superiors would hear of their conversation. Jordan had already decided on a course of action beyond British law. He had seen the flash of excitement in the man's eyes and could guess what it meant. He would be turned loose to find the missing gold, with Jordan's men close behind him. If he failed to find it, he could be killed for trying to escape. If by some miracle he found it, Jordan would take the gold himself and still kill him.

Major Jordan returned in thirty minutes and told him, "You will have twenty-four hours of freedom, carefully supervised. If you attempt to leave New York, you will be killed. If you attempt to contact any of Washington's spies, you will be killed. Find the missing bullion, deliver it to me, and I will guarantee your freedom."

"Fair enough," Swift replied, not believing him for a minute.

Jordan took a gold watch from his pocket and opened the cover. "Report back to me at eleven o'clock tomorrow morning."

"I have just one request. I would like to speak with Captain Randolph Shay if he's still in the building."

"That can be arranged. We are just completing our questioning of him. You may speak with him before he leaves."

There was more waiting until Swift was finally escorted to an upstairs office shortly after noon. Captain Shay sat at a desk looking tired and depressed. "Well, Swift! So even the enemy has an opportunity to question me now."

"We were friends at one time, Captain. I still don't consider us enemies, even though our countries may be at war."

"The rebellious colonies are not a country."

Swift ignored the remark and said, "I've agreed to help Major Jordan investigate the disappearance of cargo from your frigate. Tell me, did you observe the gold being loaded yourself?"

"Damned right, I did!" He chose a sheet of paper from the desk and passed it across to Alexander. "This is the *Freetown*'s manifest. She carried a sealed cargo of His Majesty's bullion in the hold. Gold ingots and bags of gold coins weighing the equivalent of three thousand pounds. A million in gold and we used it as ballast!"

"There was no interception or boarding on the high seas?"

Shay scoffed at the suggestion. "The *Freetown* was a heavily armed frigate, able to withstand any attack with a fusillade of cannonballs. Finest ship I ever commanded. Only the finest would be entrusted with the king's gold."

"But she went down in the East River."

"An act of God, certainly," the captain replied. "It was early morning and we had no warning of the storm. We'd sailed in through Long Island Sound and had turned into the East River at its northern end. There was a gust of wind when the storm hit and we went over like a straw man."

Swift glanced at the manifest. There was no doubt the gold had been loaded on board, just as there was no doubt the hold was now empty. Though the ship had gone over on its side as it took on water and sank, it was now resting almost upright—enough to show the top of its mainmast.

"Were any of your crew lost?"

"Eight able seamen drowned, good men all."

Alexander Swift nodded, getting to his feet and returning the manifest to Shay. "I may want to speak to some of your officers."

"They're available."

Swift left him alone in the room, thinking that he would not want to be Randolph Shay, facing probable court-martial for the loss of his warship and a fortune in gold.

He held his breath as he stepped outside and walked past the uniformed guards with their rifles held at port arms. No one challenged him. He was free for the moment.

Swift spent most of the afternoon shaking off two men dressed as seamen who'd started following him as soon as he left British headquarters. Finally he'd been forced to grab onto the side of a passing carriage and ride away unseen, leaving them standing in the center of the muddy street. He pictured Jordan's face when he learned that Alexander Swift had now disappeared along with King George's gold.

Once he was certain no one else was on his trail, he headed directly for South Street and the tavern where he knew Michael Feeney could be found in the late afternoon. The Irishman was off in his corner, and he raised a hand in greeting to Swift. "I had heard bad news about you, that you'd been taken by the British."

"All true, but I talked my way out of it. The next time I may not be so lucky."

"Some say the gold is gone."

"That it is. Their divers say the hold is empty."

"A curious turn of events."

"I've been set free until eleven tomorrow morning to find the gold."

Feeney merely grinned. "Like setting a fox to keep the geese."

"Look, I need your help."

"To get out of New York?"

"No, I can always steal a boat for that. Do you know a man named David Bushnell?"

His eyes narrowed to slits. "You're talking about one of Washington's secret weapons."

"I need him now, tonight if possible."

"He's not in the city. I think he's somewhere in New Jersey."

"Can you find him?"

"Not Bushnell himself, but I know Ezra Lee, an army sergeant who works with him. Their first missions failed, but they're anxious to try again."

"I might give them that chance."

"Can you be back here by ten o'clock?"

"Yes, and do your best, Michael. If you cannot find him by then, we must give it up."

It was dangerous for Swift to prowl the streets during the early evening hours, and even more dangerous to spend the time in a tavern or grogshop. British troops were everywhere, as were loyalists ready to report him if he was recognized. Strangely enough, the safest place for him was probably his wife's new home. Amanda may have cuckolded him, but she would never betray him to the British, not even to Jordan.

He had heard some time back that they were living together in a house on John Street, just off Broadway. The July evening was still bright with sunlight when he reached it, and he stood for a time in a doorway across the street, watching for any sign of movement. He was debating whether to risk approaching the front door when Amanda herself appeared, walking quickly along the road with an open parasol shielding her from the sun.

Even if it meant his capture, he had no choice but to approach her. "Amanda!"

She turned quickly at the sound of her name and the color drained from her face. She was as lovely as he remembered, with great green eyes like windows to her soul. "Alex! Don't you know they're looking for you? Jack says you betrayed his trust."

"I haven't yet. I'll be in his office tomorrow morning as promised."

"Come in. If you're seen on the street by his soldiers you might be shot."

"I hoped you'd let me stay until dark if Jordan isn't here."

She unlocked the door and led him into a small house that was better than the one they'd shared. "It belonged to a lawyer who fled the city," she explained. "Jack was able to get it for us."

"There was a time I said I'd kill him. And perhaps you too."

A smile played at her lips. She unbuttoned the neck of her blouse, baring her throat. "It's yours for the cutting if that's what you want."

Alexander sighed. "What happened to us, Amanda?"

"A revolution changed our lives."

"Do you really love the British that much?"

Her green eyes glistened. "I love Jack Jordan. That's the important thing. Don't tell me you haven't found someone to love since we parted!"

He ignored the question she wasn't quite asking. Instead he asked one of his own. "What will you do when the British lose the war, when Jordan is forced to return to England?"

"That's not going to—"

She was interrupted by a pounding on the front door. For an instant Swift feared he'd been tracked down by Major Jordan's men. "Don't open it!" he begged her.

"I must. It could be a message from Jack."

Swift ducked behind a drapery as she opened the door, revealing a middle-aged man with a dark, weathered complexion. "Please let me in!" he gasped. "I've been hurt."

Then he fell at her feet and they both saw the blood on the back of his shirt.

"He's dead," Swift told her after a moment's examination. "Stabbed in the back."

"But who is he? I've never seen him before," Amanda protested. "This isn't the jungle. Men aren't murdered on one's doorstep!"

"Apparently this one was." He glanced out at the stoop. There's a trail of blood on the steps but virtually none in the street. He was stabbed just as he reached here and started up the steps."

"He may have been looking for Jack, thinking he'd be home by now." She took a deep breath. "I must summon help. There are usually sentries on duty at Broadway."

"Do what you have to. I'll be gone when you return."

She lingered only a moment, casting a sideways glance at him, perhaps forming words in her mind that were left unspoken. Then she was out the door, leaving it ajar as she ran down the street seeking help.

Swift decided to exit through the back door, but he paused long enough to go through the dead man's pockets. He came quickly upon papers identifying him as one Roscoe Newcastle, naval lieutenant and first mate aboard the H.M.S. *Freetown*. He returned the papers to Newcastle's pocket and went quickly through the back door, crossing a small garden to Maiden Lane.

He had no idea why Lieutenant Newcastle had been murdered, but he was pretty certain it was connected to the disappearance of the gold from the sunken frigate. It was still too soon to meet Feeney back at the Blue Boar, so he roamed the waterfront for a couple of hours, watching schooners unloading supplies for the troops, until finally the fading light brought a halt till morning.

When he reached the tavern he found Feeney seated with a slender young man at his usual table. "This is Sergeant Ezra Lee of the Continental Army. Sergeant Lee, meet Alexander Swift, the personal representative of General Washington."

The young man smiled. "Pleased to meet you, sir."

"Feeney tells me you work with David Bushnell "

"That I do, sir. Took the *Turtle* into New York harbor all by myself and damned near sank a British warship."

"Not the *Freetown*?"

"No, sir. I had nothing to do with that."

"But you and Bushnell do have a vessel that can travel under water?" Swift asked.

"Yes, sir. Mr. Bushnell, he invented and built it. Calls it the *Turtle*. It's an egg-shaped craft propelled by screw-like devices operated by hand. You open a valve to admit sea water into a ballast tank. That causes it to sink. When you want to raise it again you empty the tank with a hand pump. Of course there's lead ballast in the bottom to keep it upright."

"Ballast," Swift repeated, trying to capture a thought that had flashed through his mind. "How long can the *Turtle* remain under water?"

"Only about thirty minutes because we have no underwater supply of oxygen. But we have a breathing tube we can use when the vessel is close to the water's surface. That way I was able to sneak into New York harbor."

"Why you and not Bushnell?"

"The man's an engineer, plenty of brains but not much strength in his arms. Look at these!" He held up his own well-muscled arms to demonstrate. "I had to propel the *Turtle* forward turning those screws by hand. That's hard work after the first few minutes. But I made it to the British warship Eagle, which was our target. I came in right next to the hull and started drilling a hole to attach a gunpowder bomb I carried with me. But a band of copper sheathing defeated me. The bomb bobbed to the surface and the time fuse exploded it harmlessly. The *Turtle* came up too, and I managed to escape with it. This was nearly two years ago and we've had two more failures since then. We could use a successful mission."

That was what Alexander Swift wanted to hear. "Can you take me to the wreck of the *Freetown?*"

"No, sir."

"Why not?"

"The *Turtle* is a one-man craft. There's no room for the two of us."

Swift cursed silently. Somehow he had to examine that ship. "Could I operate it myself?"

"With enough practice."

"We've got till dawn," he told the sergeant. "Can you teach me?"

"Let me see your arm." He felt Alexander's muscles. "Maybe," he answered, a bit dubiously.

"Where is it now?"

"Hidden north of Manhattan Island. Not too far from your wreck. You can come down the East River if your arms hold out."

"Let's do it."

Swift's first sight of the *Turtle* was anything but promising. It looked like a large egg with a pod of some sort fixed to its back and rudder and screws projecting in various directions. Its hull of oak staves was reinforced with iron bands to help withstand the water pressure. "What's the pod for?" he asked.

"The explosives. It's detachable once you fix it to the hull of a vessel."

"All right," Alexander said with some distaste. "Let's get it into the water and I'll climb inside."

Michael Feeney had come up the river with them, helping to row past the sentries in the darkness. The site of the sunken frigate was still under guard, and it was those guards Swift hoped to outwit by approaching the vessel underwater. Now Feeney helped Swift and Lee get the craft into the water. The two of them helped Swift clamber into the cramped quarters and Lee set about teaching him the use of the controls.

"You have lateral and vertical screw propellers that work by hand, and this rudder to steer with."

Feeney was holding a lantern to illuminate the scene and Swift had him shift it a bit so he had a better view of the controls as Sergeant Lee pointed them out. "What's this?"

"The hand pump to empty the ballast tank when you want to surface. This is a breathing tube, but you can only use it when the craft is partly above water. It closes automatically when the vessel is submerged."

"How do I see where I'm going?"

"There are small windows around the top, in this little dome. And the depth gauge and compass are marked with foxfire so they can be read in the dark."

Swift practiced in the dark, waiting for the first lightening of the eastern sky before setting forth. As he learned, the sergeant told him about David Bushnell. "He's a frail man, poor fellow, but a genius at mechanics. He could not afford to enter Yale until he was thirty-one, so it was seventeen seventy-five before he graduated. He and his brother built the *American Turtle*, as he first named it, during his final vacation and demonstrated it for Ben Franklin. In September of 'seventy-six, after the British drove Washington from the city, David decided to destroy Lord Howe's flagship, the *Eagle*, at anchor off Staten Island.

"He lacked the stamina to operate his submarine, as he calls it, himself. When his brother fell ill, I was enlisted for the mission. Sadly, I'd had too little training. This screw to attach the 150-pound powder charge to the ship hit a metal strap and failed to penetrate the wood. The submarine bobbed to the surface and as dawn broke a boatload of British sailors set off in pursuit. I set the bomb free and the timing mechanism blew it up, frightening the British. I escaped, but the mission was a failure."

"It was a good try," Swift assured him. He could see the first traces of dawn in the sky.

"I wish you better luck in your effort."

Swift asked a few more questions about screwing the bomb to its target and then set off shortly before dawn. It was hard work cranking the screws that propelled the vessel through the water. He kept the small portholes above the surface until finally the main mast of the sunken *Freetown* came into view. Then he let water into the ballast tank and submerged.

By the dawn's eerie light he found himself in a strange new world. The East River water was reasonably clear so he had a good view of the frigate itself, resting on a shelf of rock just beneath the water's surface. The big sails were mainly furled, with only a few of the smaller ones spread. The hold was open and enough morning sunlight penetrated to show him it was empty. He steered the *Turtle* around with difficulty, using the rudder and screw, trying to see what lay beyond the ledge on which the frigate rested. All he knew was that it seemed deep.

He steered in a little closer and used the drill mounted at the top of his craft. His first try was a failure, but within a half-hour he had attached the gunpowder bomb to the ship's side and set the clockwork mechanism needed to explode it.

Then it was a matter of getting away fast. He used both hands to operate the screw that drove the craft, and both were sore before he was far enough away to safely pump out the ballast and begin to rise. He looked back through a porthole just in time to see a fountain of water rise in the air and feel the shock waves from the blast. When the water settled, the main mast of the Freetown was no longer visible. On shore he could see guards scrambling for cover, not knowing what to expect next.

Alexander Swift was grinning as he headed back to the *Turtle's* hiding place. So far, it had been a successful morning.

At exactly eleven A.M. Swift rode up to British Army headquarters in New York and allowed a sentry on duty to take his horse. He was escorted into Major Jordan's office and sat waiting for some minutes before Amanda's lover appeared. "Well, Swift, I didn't expect to see you back here after your disappearance yesterday."

"I keep my word, sir."

"This whole business of the missing gold has taken a bad turn. Captain Shay's first mate, a Lieutenant Newcastle, was stabbed to death last night at my front door. Amanda was terrified, as you can imagine. We have no idea what he was doing there, but it seems it must be connected to the gold. I've just been speaking with Captain Shay about it. He came in this morning as soon as he heard."

Alexander nodded. "The situation seems clear to me, Major. If you are prepared to release me without charges I may be of some help in bringing this matter to a conclusion."

"You know where King George's gold is?"

"I believe so."

"What about the killing of Lieutenant Newcastle?"

"I believe one answer will explain both questions."

Suddenly the door of the room burst open. Captain Shay stood there, his face contorted in anger. "I have just been informed there has been an explosion aboard the *Freetown!* She has sunk further into the river!"

"What's that?" Jordan was on his feet. He whirled toward Swift. "Do you know anything about this?"

Alexander shrugged. "How could I?"

"Where is the gold?" the major challenged. "Tell me that!"

"Will I go free if I tell you?"

Jordan hesitated and then responded. "Yes."

"It is right where Captain Shay hid it."

Shay leaped at him with renewed fury. "I'll kill you, you meddling Yankee!"

Jordan shouted for the guards and the captain was quickly subdued.

"Take him away," the major ordered. "I'll deal with him after I hear from Mr. Swift."

Alexander resumed his seat. "Thank you, sir."

"Are you telling me that Captain Shay stole that cargo?"

"I am. He told us his ship was fully rigged when the storm hit, but why would it be so rigged sailing inland waters? I dived to examine it myself and discovered that he'd lied. The large sails were all furled as they should have been."

"Then what caused the ship to capsize?"

"My question exactly," Swift agreed. Then I remembered he also said the three thousand pounds of weight in gold ingots and coins was used as ballast on the voyage. A heavy cargo is often used as ballast to save the additional weight of lead ballast. But if that gold ballast had been moved during the voyage, taken above the water line, even above the main deck, the stability of the frigate would have been seriously compromised. A strong wind could have capsized the *Freetown* with very little effort. I'm certain that is what happened."

"Where could it be above the main deck?"

"I suspect in the captain's own cabin, and the first mate's. No crew members would dare venture in there."

"You're telling me that Captain Shay and Newcastle moved that gold out of the ship's hold and up to their own cabins? Three thousand pounds of it? Impossible!"

"It seems impossible when you state it like that. But gold is a very heavy metal. Two officers' cabins would easily hold it, though moving around in them might be difficult. As for carrying it up, they could do a little each day—a bag or two of coins, an ingot on every trip. One or two crew members might have helped. Perhaps they conveniently drowned in the storm. That was no doubt what frightened Newcastle enough to bring him to your door last night. Captain Shay caught up with him on your steps and silenced him."

Major Jordan made some quick notes. "If it happened like that, some of the surviving crew must have noticed something suspicious. But what would Shay have done when the ship docked without its cargo of gold."

"He could claim it was never loaded. By the time word got back to England he'd have found a way to smuggle the gold out of his cabin and onto shore. He'd be in the New World with a million in gold, vanished before you knew what happened."

Jordan's eyes narrowed. "You said you dived down to look at those sails. You could have placed a gunpowder charge at the same time."

"Don't you think it's more likely Captain Shay did that to cover up his crime? If the frigate was salvaged, the gold would surely have been found in his cabin. He'd rather have it at the bottom of the river."

Jordan took a deep breath. "Remain here," he said quietly as he left the office. It was a full half-hour before he returned.

"Well?" Alexander asked him.

"You did very well. Captain Shay has made a full confession, admitting he stole the gold and killed Newcastle to keep him from talking. The gold was carried up piece by piece and hidden in a spare ammunition locker near his cabin. The locker usually held extra cannonballs, which they dumped overboard to make room for the gold."

"Then I was wrong about the cabin."

"Yes, and he denies causing this morning's explosion on the sunken ship. We're looking into that."

"May I leave now?"

Jordan hesitated, then waved a hand in dismissal. "Be gone from here. I am a man of my word. The next time we meet, I may not be so generous."

"The next time we meet—" Alexander left the sentence unfinished as he walked out the door. There would be other times to settle their personal business. For now, he only wanted to get back to General Washington and report on the success of his mission.

THE UNINVITED GUEST

The spring of 1779 was an unusually quiet time for the American colonies in the midst of their war of revolution. Perhaps it was a result of the imperceptible merging of the seasons that year. Neither side in the struggle found it necessary to break camp and move out with the coming of spring because in truth there had been hardly a snow or frost since mid January.

General Washington and his wife Martha were with the troops at their winter quarters in Morristown, New Jersey, when Alexander Swift arrived there on April first in the company of Molly McVey. The camp itself consisted of sturdy huts and cabins, a far cry from the conditions at Valley Forge two winters earlier. And spring had indeed come early to the region, with buds already visible on the fruit trees.

"All is quiet," Washington said, greeting Swift with a firm handshake. The general was a tall man with big hands and feet. At age forty-seven his hair was still reddish-brown, and his large gray-blue eyes looked out from a pale face slightly marked by smallpox. "It is as if the war had gone away."

"The support of the French has been a great help," Alexander Swift replied. Indeed, since France had signed a treaty of aid with the revolting colonies and sent its fleet briefly into American waters the British had evacuated Philadelphia the previous year, leaving it to General Benedict Arnold to enter the city with a corps of Massachusetts troops. Arnold, wounded at Saratoga and unable to walk without support, had been made military commander of the capital. It was a post suitable for a wounded hero who was also an old friend of General Washington.

"And this would be Miss McVey?" Washington asked, extending his hand to the slender, dark-haired young woman at Swift's side.

"Excuse my rudeness. General Washington, may I present Miss Molly McVey, who was of great help to me at Camp West Point."

"A pleasure," the general said. "I have heard much about you, Miss McVey. Will you be living in this area?"

She blushed nicely. "I am traveling with Mr. Swift at the present time. I may be returning north soon."

"So might I," Washington responded, walking back to take a seat behind his desk. "In a month's time I plan to move north along the Hudson. I may set up headquarters at New Windsor, beyond West Point on the eastern bank."

"A wise move," Alexander Swift said. "It will bring you closer to the enemy activity."

"Meanwhile, I have a particular assignment of a social nature for you—for both of you, as a matter of fact."

"A social nature?" Swift could not imagine what the general had in mind. Until now his special assignments as a civilian had involved informal action against the British, sometimes as a spy.

"Two old friends, General Benedict Arnold and Miss Peggy Shippen, are to be married in one week's time. I cannot attend personally, but I would like you to represent me and take a gift from Martha and me."

"So Arnold is marrying again!" Swift knew the wounded hero only slightly, but was interested in the news. Benedict Arnold was a widower with three half-grown sons. "He must be nearly forty."

"Thirty-eight, I believe," Washington said. "Peggy is much younger, of course, not quite eighteen. She is the daughter of Judge Edward Shippen, a prominent Quaker and something of a Loyalist, I do believe. I've known her since she was a child."

"They remained in Philadelphia during the British occupation?"

The general nodded. "And I daresay Peggy waltzed with British officers. Young women her age can be terrible flirts. I visited the city this past winter and saw them all, including Arnold. These are difficult times for him. He harbors some bitterness at others being promoted ahead of him. When our rebel troops reentered the city, Arnold placed Philadelphia under martial law. Shopkeepers resented that. As you know, Arnold has since resigned his post. But a faithless friend of mine, Joseph Reed, now president of the state's Supreme Executive Council, has actually brought charges of malfeasance against him, and Congress is considering the matter." He lowered his voice slightly. "I must admit, Alexander, that when I visited Philadelphia this past winter I found the general living in a grand style of which I could not approve."

"How is his leg?"

"Not good. He needs help standing upright, and four men must assist him in and out of his coach. Still, he claims to be improving. Certainly young Peggy sees some improvement, but then love is blind."

"Where will next week's wedding be held?"

"At the Shippen home in Philadelphia. It will be a quiet ceremony, and I am sorry I cannot be there. Will you go? You can both attend as my representatives."

Alexander Swift glanced at Molly. He could see that the suggestion intrigued her. The social world of a Philadelphia wedding was a long way from the tavern at West Point where she was employed. "Certainly," he told General Washington. "We would consider it a great honor."

Washington had sent a message ahead to inform the family that Swift and a guest would be attending in his place. Arrangements were made for Alexander and Molly to arrive the evening preceding the wedding and spend two nights with Major Cutler, an aide to Benedict Arnold.

Cutler proved to be a slender, taciturn man in his early thirties, about Swift's age, who also would be attending the following day's ceremony. His wife, Louisa, was more talkative. She was a plain but lively woman a few years younger than her husband. Molly liked her at once, and the two fell into a lengthy conversation following dinner.

Swift and Major Cutler stepped outside for a cigar, but the major still said very little. "How is Arnold's leg mending?"

"Better."

"Does he still need support for standing and walking?"

Cutler drew on his cigar. "Sometimes he tries hopping about. He'll probably use his cane at the wedding."

"Do you think the British are gone from this city for good?"

"I think so."

"It was a great victory for our side."

The slender officer shrugged. "They pulled out, we came in."

Later, when they were beneath the covers of the great feather bed in Cutler's guest room, Molly spoke quietly to Alexander Swift. "Louisa Cutler told me some interesting things about Benedict Arnold while you and the major were enjoying your cigars."

"I'm sure it was more interesting than our conversation."

"She said Peggy Shippen's brother was arrested as a Tory sympathizer, and most of their rich friends are not really loyal to America. Peggy herself was courted by Major John André, a British officer, and wore a lock of his hair in a locket on her necklace. More than that, Louisa hinted at Arnold's extravagant living and illegal business partnerships."

Swift wasn't surprised at the latter. "Washington mentioned something about charges of malfeasance being brought against him." He considered the situation as he drifted into sleep. Washington was an old friend of General Arnold. Perhaps he'd had more than one reason for sending a representative to the wedding in his place, especially a representative like Swift who'd handled special assignments in the past.

Washington's gift to the bride and groom was a silver sugar bowl and creamer fashioned by Paul Revere. It seemed a fitting wedding present, linking these patriots who had fought the British from the beginning. If Arnold was marrying into a family of Tory sympathizers, Swift felt sure he could hold his own against them.

They left their horses at the Cutler house the following morning and the two couples traveled by carriage to the Shippen family home, the box containing Washington's gift on the floor at their feet. It was Thursday, the eighth of April, four days after Easter, and the Philadelphia streets were bright with springtime. In the front yard of the Shippen home the apple trees were blossoming weeks ahead of schedule.

It was to be a quiet ceremony, with only the family and a few friends and neighbors in attendance. The minister was a solemn Church of England gentleman who stood apart with Judge Shippen. Swift introduced himself and Molly, expressing General Washington's regrets and presenting the gift he had sent. Judge Shippen, in turn, introduced Peggy's mother, brother, and two older sisters, as well as Arnold's boys. The guests milled around the large parlor speaking with family members, and Swift counted about two dozen people in all. He walked over to where a broad-shouldered General Arnold sat in full dress uniform, awaiting the appearance of his bride.

"I'm Alexander Swift. You probably don't remember me, sir."

Arnold's stern hawkish features turned toward him, the blue eyes seeming out of place in such a swarthy face. When he stood with the help of a thick walking stick he was shorter than Swift remembered. "You're General Washington's man."

"That's correct. He is sorry he could not be here in person. Both he and Martha send their regrets and promise they will visit you both at their earliest opportunity."

A man in formal clothes had begun to play a harpsichord, and all conversation ceased. Suddenly the bride appeared on her father's arm. Peggy Shippen, twenty years younger than Arnold, had the blossoming freshness of a young girl in springtime, a slim blue-eyed beauty who seemed totally in control of the moment. Her hair was piled high on her head in an elaborate European style and she wore a flowing white wedding gown. As the minister stood by, Judge Shippen delivered her to Benedict Arnold. For a moment Swift was reminded of his own marriage, which ended with the coming of the revolution when he left New York while his wife Amanda stayed on with a British officer.

Arnold stood with some difficulty at Peggy's side, supported by his cane, while the minister read the vows, concluding with, "I now pronounce you man and wife." The happy couple kissed while the small audience applauded.

Some bottles of French champagne were produced and servants filled glasses for the guests to toast the new husband and wife. Following the toast, Swift noticed for the first time a tall, angular man whose clothes seemed a bit loose. He sipped the champagne as he moved about the parlor; stopping first at one group and then another. No one seemed to acknowledge his presence until her finally reached the Cutlers and Molly. Major Cutler and his wife said a few words to him and he set his champagne glass on a table momentarily to take something from his pocket to show them. Swift turned as General Arnold approached with his bride. Across the room he spotted Molly conversing with a woman guest.

"Mr. Swift, I have the pleasure of introducing my bride, Peggy."

Seeing her close up, Swift was struck again by her youthful beauty. "I wish you both every happiness," he said. "General Washington was quite disappointed that he was unable to attend."

"Tell him we missed him," Peggy Arnold said, her voice soft and melodious.

When they'd finished making their rounds of the guests, Arnold signaled for quiet. He thanked everyone for coming and then, announced that as a wedding gift to his bride he had purchased Mount Pleasant, a large Philadelphia estate on the banks of the Schuylkill River. It had a hundred acres of gardens and orchards, and Peggy seemed to glow with pleasure at the news.

"How can he afford such a place?" Swift wondered, speaking to the Cutlers a few minutes later.

As usual Major Cutler said little, but Louisa lowered her voice and told them, "I hear that he is deeply in debt with loans from moneylenders. He has borrowed on his house in New Haven and pledged the back salary and commissions he hopes to obtain from the Congress."

Swift was troubled by the news. He knew Washington would not be pleased.

Others were proposing toasts now, and the lanky man in the ill-fitting suit stepped forward to raise his glass. "To the Sons of Liberty!" he announced, speaking the name of a patriotic society, originally secret but now disbanded. "To Sam Adams and Paul Revere!"

He took a long drink from his glass as someone else started to propose a toast. Then, barely a moment later, he uttered a sharp cry and doubled over, clutching his stomach. Swift stared at him, frozen to the spot like everyone else. The man seemed to fold in half, then topple slowly to the floor.

A doctor emerged from among the guests, a neighbor of the Shippens named Caleb Wade. He was a big man with long white hair, though his face was not especially old. He quickly knelt by the body, feeling for a pulse.

"This man is very sick," he announced after a moment's examination. "Can we get him to a bed?" Several of the men came forward to help carry the stricken man upstairs. By now he seemed almost unconscious struggling to breathe.

"Who is he?" Swift asked Major Cutler. "I saw you speaking with him earlier."

For a moment Cutler looked blank. "Did you?"

"Of course, dear," his wife reminded him. "He was the odd man who came up to us and started talking. Remember? We were wondering if he was a friend of the bride or the groom."

"What was he talking about?"

"Just the wedding," Louisa Cutler replied. "He took out a little drawing of an animal to show us. I thought it very odd."

"It was a deer," Molly McVey verified. "A female deer. I said it was nice and he gave it to me."

General Arnold came up to them then, much distressed. "Do any of you know that man? I've spoken to the judge and his wife and he wasn't on their guest list. They assumed he was a friend of mine."

"We spoke to him," Cutler replied, "but we don't know who he is."

"I had better see to him," Swift decided. "Is it all right if I go upstairs?"

"Of course," Arnold said. "Dr. Wade is still with him."

He found the doctor in the bedroom of one of Peggy's sisters, at the top of the stairs. He was bending over his patient but he straightened up as Swift entered. "Can he speak, Doctor?"

"I'm afraid he's passed away, just a moment ago."

Alexander Swift stared down at the body, suddenly smaller in its ill-fitting garments. "Did he say anything before he died?"

"Just one word. It sounded like *dough*, or perhaps *do*, as in music."

Swift remembered the drawing the man had shown to Molly and the Cutlers. "Could it have been *doe*, a female deer?"

"I suppose so."

"We'd better go tell Judge Shippen and General Arnold that he's dead."

The death of the uninvited guest cast a pall over the wedding party. While arrangements were made for the removal of the body, Alexander Swift again separated Benedict Arnold from his bride. "I think we should talk about what happened, General. Washington will want a full report when I return."

They were in the judge's library at the rear of the house, looking out on a sloping yard with more apple trees in bloom. "I never saw the man before," Arnold insisted. "I have found no one who invited him." As he spoke his hand went to his injured leg, massaging it as if to drive away the pain.

"Could he have been someone to whom you owed money?"

"Certainly not!" The question seemed to offend him. He stood up, leaning heavily on his walking stick. "If you will excuse me, I must rejoin my bride. We have nothing more to discuss."

Swift helped him out the door but did not follow immediately. The body was being removed under the supervision of Dr. Wade. The rest of the wedding party had gone outside while the grisly task was performed. Swift caught the doctor's eye and motioned him into the library.

"Would you care to speculate as to the cause of death, Doctor? Could it have been a heart attack?"

"Certainly not that. The stomach cramps, together with his death within such a short time, suggest a poison of some sort."

"Do you mean the man took his own life?"

"Either that or someone took it for him."

The festivities had been dampened by the death of the unknown man, but once the body was removed the family seemed determined to make the best of it. Before long there were more toasts to the bride and groom, and with a final round of goodbyes the happy couple went off in a carriage for a bit of privacy. "He's a real American," Judge Shippen remarked. "My daughter is lucky to have him for a husband. That's a beautiful estate he's bought for her."

Later, as the party was breaking up, Swift asked Major Cutler about his brief conversation with the dead man. "He showed you a drawing of a female deer, and Dr. Wade thinks his final word might have been *doe*. Would that have any meaning to you?"

"None at all."

Swift and Molly walked to the carriage with the Cutlers and the major instructed the driver to take them home. On the way the conversation was mainly about the wedding, with only a passing reference to the dead stranger. It wasn't until they were alone in their bedroom at the Cutler house that Swift reminded Molly of the drawing she'd said the unknown man gave her.

"I have it here, but it is hardly a work of art."

He took the small sheet of stiff paper which she'd rolled into a tube and slid up the sleeve of her dress. It was not an original pencil sketch, he saw at once, but a printed copy. The deer seemed to be prancing through some underbrush. On the back a name was written, very small: *John Slate*. It was followed by the words *Penn House Inn*.

"Do you think that's the artist or our uninvited guest?" Molly wondered.

"I don't know," he admitted. "But it gives me something to work on."

"To work on? General Washington sent us to attend a wedding, nothing more!"

"He told me Judge Shippen has Loyalist sympathies. If that's the case, a killing at his home on the very day of his daughter's wedding to an American general—could be important."

Molly thought it over. "Most likely he was simply an old beau of Peggy's and she didn't want to admit it."

"Wouldn't her father know him if that was the case? Certainly he'd be a familiar figure at the balls she attended." He looked again at the back of the picture. "Where is Penn House Inn?"

"It's here in the city, down near the waterfront. Did you see me speak to that girl at the wedding? We worked together briefly in Albany. She told me she's a waitress at Penn House."

"Strange that she was invited to such a small wedding." He tapped a finger thoughtfully on the drawing. "Of course there's another possibility."

"What's that?"

"She might have come with the man who was killed. Did you notice her after his collapse?"

"No," she admitted, "but I wasn't really looking for her."

"What's her name?"

"She calls herself Persia Tolliver."

"Suppose we pay a visit to Penn House Inn."

Alexander and Molly excused themselves, telling the Cutlers they wanted to see a bit of the city before they headed home the following day. Molly had changed into a riding costume and they set out in early afternoon, heading their horses toward the Delaware River. "I never expected to be in Philadelphia," she confessed. "A few days away from the tavern at West Point seemed a good enough idea. I should have known nothing is ever simple with you, Alex."

"If this man Slate, or whatever his name was, is a murder victim, Washington will want the details. Philadelphia is full of Loyalists, and they seem to be getting closer to Benedict Arnold all the time."

"I don't like your getting involved in these things. You could have been shot as a spy when the British captured you in New York last year."

"Washington needed me there," he said simply. It was something they'd talked little about.

"You saw your wife in New York."

"*And* her British lover," he emphasized. "There is no love lost between us."

Molly rode silently for a time, until at last they came to a large three-story building that displayed the sign *Penn House Inn*. They dismounted and went inside.

"You have rooms for the night?" Swift asked the innkeeper, a bearded man with sly eyes.

"That we have! Our rates are posted on the wall."

"I'm looking for John Slate. Is he staying with you?"

"Slate? We may have had someone by that name, but he is no longer with us."

"What did he look like? Lanky, with ill-fitting clothes?"

"Perhaps."

Molly could see his mounting frustration and she asked a question of her own. "Is Persia Tolliver working today?"

The sly eyes shifted. "You know Persia?"

"An old friend. I saw her this morning at a wedding and she told me she was working here."

He nodded. "I expect her soon. She's due in at two o'clock."

They waited at a table in the bar and presently the young woman Swift had glimpsed at the wedding came through the door from the kitchen. She had changed out of the dress she'd worn to the wedding and she carried a bar rag, ready for work. Molly stood up and addressed her. "Hello, Persia. My friend wanted to meet you. This is Alexander Swift."

She shook her head, a look of fear shooting across her face. "I don't know anything about what happened."

Swift tried to keep his voice low and nonthreatening. "Were you invited to the wedding, Persia?"

"I know the family. Peggy's brother comes in here sometimes." Up close she was older than he'd thought, easily into her thirties. Her pale blond hair was already showing some gray.

"So you decided to attend the wedding and take John Slate with you."

"Who?" she asked.

"Don't play games. The tall thin man who had to borrow a wedding garment that was a poor fit. The man who was poisoned, Persia."

"Yes," she agreed. "It was a bit loose, wasn't it? He got it from the cook here, just before we left for the wedding. But what's this about poison?"

"You know he's dead, don't you?"

Her eyes widened a bit. "I slipped out after he fell down. I thought he was drunk and they'd find out we weren't invited. I didn't know he'd been poisoned."

"Who was he?" Molly asked.

Persia Tolliver sighed and made a sour face. "You had it right. His name was John Slate, or at least he told me it was. He'd been here at the inn for three or four days. He told me a lady friend had information that would make him rich. When I mentioned knowing Peggy Shippen's brother he insisted we must attend the wedding."

"Her brother didn't recognize you?"

She blushed a bit. "I didn't really know him. I only waited on him once. His father approached us before the ceremony and I said we were friends of General Arnold."

"He showed us a drawing of a female deer," Molly said. She took it from her pocket. "What does it mean?"

"I have no idea."

"His name was written on the back, along with the name of this inn," Swift told her. "It was meant as a message, an address where he could be reached."

"I know nothing about it," she insisted.

"This city was under martial law," he reminded her, "and the army retains a great deal of power here. You could be imprisoned as a spy."

She snorted. "For what? For spying on a wedding?"

"Are John Slate's belongings still here at Penn House?"

"I suppose so. They'd be up in his room."

"The innkeeper said he'd left."

"Morris? He probably heard of Slate's death and hopes to keep his possessions for himself."

"Could you get a key to his room?"

Persia frowned at the question. "Are you trying to get me in trouble?"

"John Slate was murdered. We're trying to keep you out of trouble."

She thought about that, wiping the table with her rag. "I've got a key," she said finally. "I'll take you up there."

She disappeared into the kitchen and returned after a moment, nodding for them to follow her. They went up the stairs quickly while the innkeeper was busy with his ledgers. She stopped at the third door on the left and inserted a long slender key into the lock. The room was somewhat drab, with a big brass bed as its major feature. Persia went immediately to a closet and opened the door. A jacket, pants, and shirt hung there.

"These are uniform pants," Swift said at once, examining them closely. "Was he in the Continental Army?"

"I know next to nothing about John Slate. He appeared at Penn House on Easter Sunday morning and took a room for several nights. I had some drinks with him after my work was done, and came up here a few times because he was lonely. I guess he was in the army for a while."

"What did he talk about?" Molly asked.

"Not about himself. Nothing about himself. He asked about Benedict Arnold and his officers. When he found out I knew Peggy's brother he insisted we go to the wedding, even though we weren't invited. I was crazy to agree to it, but he said he had to see somebody to get his money."

While they continued talking, Swift went quickly through the few clothes in the closet. He found nothing, nor was there anything of interest in the leather saddlebags on the closet floor, other than a paper confirming that John Slate had indeed served in Washington's Continental Army as a private.

He was about to abandon his search when he noticed a small sheet of paper on a writing desk near the window. It was a duplicate of the printed drawing of the deer Slate had produced at the wedding.

There was a small cast-iron stove in the room for heating purposes, and Swift noticed a few scraps of paper waiting to be burnt. He picked them up and saw at once that it was a letter, or the draft of one. The date and salutation were missing, but after piecing the rest together he was able to read it: *This is your second warning. I know your secret. Leave one thousand pounds at Penn House—*

Something after that had been crossed out, and then he'd torn it up and probably started over. There could be no doubt it was, the beginning of a blackmail letter, threatening someone with exposure. Probably it had been written that very morning, before the wedding, since the stove would have been lit the previous night to take away the chill. Even with the early spring that year, the Philadelphia nights could be cool in early April.

John Slate had written that note in the morning, knowing he was to attend Arnold's wedding with Persia Tolliver. It seemed likely that the blackmail message was meant for someone who would also be attending the wedding. Had he delivered it, and had that caused his death?

Molly paused in her examination of the room to peer over his shoulder at the assembled pieces of torn paper. "It is certainly not a suicide note," she observed.

"No," he readily agreed. "If John Slate was contemplating suicide he would hardly be hatching a blackmail scheme. It seems likely that the person being blackmailed acted quickly to remove the threat."

"That quickly, Alex? Who would carry a vial of poison with them, especially to a wedding?"

It was a logical question and he had no immediate answer for it. Something was stirring in his memory, though. Something—

"Didn't General Arnold own a pharmacy and bookstore in New Haven before the war?"

"I don't know, Alex. I know nothing about his early days."

"A pharmacist, even a former one, might be a source for poisons."

"But he must have sold the store long ago."

Swift shook his head. "I believe he left it in the care of his sister."

"Certainly you can't imagine he might have poisoned a guest at his own wedding."

"Anything is possible."

"But what was the meaning of the drawing? How would Arnold be linked to a female deer?"

He'd forgotten about the picture of the doe. "Tell me exactly what happened when John Slate approached your group with that illustration."

"As I remember it, he said something about the wedding and then took some papers from an inside pocket. He showed us the drawing of the doe and asked if any of us had ever seen it before. Louisa said she had not, and passed it to her husband. When it was my turn I admired it and he said I could have it, that he possessed more copies."

Swift turned to Persia Tolliver, hovering near the door as if waiting a chance to escape. "Thank you for your help here. We'll be on our way."

"You won't tell them I was at the wedding, will you? I had nothing to do with his death."

"You will be kept out of it if at all possible," Swift assured her.

John Slate's body had been taken to an undertaker frequently used by the Continental Army in Philadelphia. Swift and Molly rode there from Penn House Inn, arriving around four o'clock. After a brief conversation the undertaker took them into his office and showed them the contents of the dead man's pockets. "Nothing unusual here, as you can see. A money purse with a few coins, a handkerchief, a key."

Alexander Swift picked it up. "That's to his room at the inn. You found no letter or message of any sort?"

"Nothing like that."

He thanked the man and they returned to their horses. "What do you think, Alex?" Molly asked.

"Assuming he wrote a final version of that letter, it seems that he managed to deliver it to someone at the wedding. He and Persia went nowhere else."

"How would Slate even know who would be at the wedding? It was a small, private affair."

"Exactly! Think about it, Molly. Who would he know with certainty would be attending? The bride and groom, and the bride's family. I think we can rule out Arnold's children by his previous marriage. They're hardly old enough to have a secret of interest to a blackmailer. And his sister is still in New England. But there is one other person who would certainly be at the wedding—Major Cutler, Arnold's personal aide."

"Cutler!"

"I'm sure I'm right, Molly, and I want to confront him with it. Can you get his wife out of the house on some pretext this evening?"

"I'll try, but I can't believe that Cutler—"

"That's who Slate spoke with. That's who he showed the drawing to."

"True enough," she agreed.

"All I have to do is trace the poison to him."

"Do you think General Arnold got it for him?"

"There's one other possibility. The Shippens' neighbor, Dr. Wade."

After a light supper Molly suggested a walk by the river, and Louisa Cutler agreed, though it was already growing dark outside. When they were alone, Swift lit one of Major Cutler's cigars and said, "This has been a full day. At least Arnold and his bride will be relaxing now."

"And most enjoyably so," Cutler agreed with a little chuckle. "Peggy is a lovely young woman." He opened a bottle of French brandy and filled their glasses.

Swift put down the cigar after a few puffs and cleared his throat. "I've spent a few hours this afternoon looking into the death of that strange fellow at the wedding."

"Oh? Have you learned anything?"

"Quite a bit. The man's name was indeed John Slate and he had a room at the Penn House Inn. He came to the wedding uninvited, in the company of a waitress at the inn named Persia Tolliver. She exited quickly after his collapse."

"What was his purpose in attending?"

"The man was a blackmailer," Swift told him. "He came to deliver a second blackmail note to someone he knew would be present. Because of his ill-fitting clothes, he attracted my attention from the outset. Though he approached several groups, yours was the first party he spoke to, and the first he showed the drawing of the deer. I believe, Major Cutler, that you were the object of the blackmail, and that you eliminated the threat immediately by poisoning the man's drink when he set it on the table next to you."

"You're very observant." The major smiled slightly. "Where did I obtain this poison, and how did I happen to bring it with me to General Arnold's wedding?"

"You obtained it from the Shippens' neighbor, Dr. Wade, with the excuse that you needed to kill some rats in the house."

"I see you have spoken to him. We do have rats and Wade gave me some poison for them. But I never killed this man Slate or anyone else, except in battle!"

Alexander Swift smiled slightly as there came a knocking on the front door. "I asked Dr. Wade to come over here after supper. That should be him now."

The portly physician was shown in by a servant. He shook hands with Swift and Cutler and took a seat. "Now how can I be of service, gentlemen?"

It was Major Cutler who took up the conversation. "Mr. Swift believes that I poisoned that man today with the dosage you provided for the killing of our house rats."

"Well—" The doctor seemed suddenly embarrassed. "He asked if I had ever provided you with poison and I remembered that instance last month. I certainly cast no suspicion in your direction, Major."

Swift took from his waistcoat pocket the pieces of the note he'd found in John Slate's room, plus the folded picture of the deer. "This is my proof of a blackmail plot, gentlemen. It was the motive for the crime."

"What motive is this?" Major Cutler demanded. "This picture of a doe means nothing."

But it was Dr. Wade who spoke again. "Doe was the dying man's last word. I didn't see this picture until now so I didn't connect the two. This is the symbol of D.O.E., a Loyalist secret society that is the antithesis of the Sons of Liberty."

"D.O.E.?"

The doctor nodded. "The Daughters of England."

And in a flash Swift realized his terrible mistake. He had sent Molly off in the darkness with a murderess.

It was almost dark by the time Molly and Louisa Cutler reached the river, which was swollen with spring rains. Louisa was as talkative as ever, chattering on about life in Philadelphia since the British withdrawal. "It's certainly nice to taste French brandy and champagne again," she enthused. "And that Lafayette! Why, he's little more than a boy!"

"He is three years older than General Arnold's new bride," Molly pointed out.

"Well, she's just a child too! I do hope she doesn't ruin the general with her extravagant ways."

"The man who was poisoned at the wedding—John Slate—apparently came there to blackmail someone. Do you think it could have been Peggy?"

"I doubt it. We never saw her until she entered on the judge's arm, and following the ceremony she was clinging to General Arnold the whole time. When could he have slipped her his note?"

Molly felt an instant chill down her spine and stopped walking. "Louisa," she said carefully, "how did you know about the blackmail note? I never mentioned a note."

"Isn't that what blackmailers usually send? The word itself implies mail."

Everything was falling into place for Molly. "When Slate approached us at the wedding it wasn't to give a message to your husband. You were the one he was after. He handed the drawing of the doe to you first, and the folded note would have been underneath. It was you who dropped the poison into his glass, not your husband."

"Oh, I don't think anyone would believe that," Louisa said. She reached out to grab Molly's arm. "Come on, let me help you. It's treacherous along the river in the dark."

Molly shook her off. "You'd had a prior threat and prepared yourself with a vial of poison. You saw your chance and you took it. What is your secret, Louisa? Does your husband know it?"

Now the woman grabbed both her arms, dragging her toward the water. "My secret is that I am loyal to the mother country, loyal to England. If that is a crime for which I can be blackmailed, so be it! There are plenty of others like me, including Arnold's wife. What you win on the battlefield may be lost in the bedroom."

The earth went out from under Molly's feet and she grabbed at the woman's sleeve, pulling her down too. Then she felt a strong arm grip her waist just as her feet hit the water, pulling her up and free. It was Alex, come from somewhere in the dark like a charging animal.

Louisa Cutler screamed once from the darkened water, and then she was swept away.

"She killed that man," Molly gasped, trying to catch her breath.

"I know," Swift said. "I figured it out just too late."

"It was soon enough for me."

"She belonged to a secret society called the Daughters of England. Slate found out from one of his lady friends and tried to blackmail her. She obtained some poison her husband was using to kill rats, and when Slate appeared at the wedding with a second warning she slipped it into his drink when he set it down to take out the picture.

"That's when he passed her the note. After the first message she was expecting him at any time.

"We'd better get back and tell Cutler what's happened. An accidental drowning perhaps"

"Alex, right at the end she said Arnold's wife was involved too. Can we believe that?"

He breathed a sigh. "Perhaps General Washington should not be told of this until we are certain. The war is not yet won. There are dangerous days ahead."

DUEL AT DAWN

George Washington, looming tall and stately in his gold-braided general's uniform, turned from the window overlooking the liberty pole at his Bergen County headquarters and said, "Invisible ink, Mr. Swift. It was known to Ovid as far back as the first century B.C. He suggested writing in new milk, which became visible when touched with coal dust."

Alexander Swift held up the vial Washington had given him. "This hardly looks like new milk, sir, though I will grant you it is white."

"These vials were obtained from Sir James Jay, John's brother, in England. He's a London physician, and after innumerable experiments he perfected a superior form of invisible ink, better than anything the British have." He reached into his desk drawer for a second vial of clear liquid. "I keep the counterpart here. When I wet your letter with a fine brush dipped in this liquid it renders the message visible. Write just a few lines in black ink to allay their suspicions and then write your invisible message on the blank portion of the sheet."

Alexander Swift smiled slightly. "And where will I be writing from, General?"

"I thought you knew. I want you to make another trip into New York City."

This was in late August of 1780 and New York was still in the hands of the British. Word had just reached them of a defeat for Washington's southern army in South Carolina, where Cornwallis had routed General Gates at Camden. Earlier in the year, troops from Massachusetts had mutinied over terms of enlistment, and those from Connecticut had done the same over pay and rations. These were trying times, testing Washington's will and skill. He had shuffled commanders and placed General Benedict Arnold in charge of the garrison at West Point, and he had used the civilian Alexander Swift as both spy and surrogate in a number of instances.

But to Swift's ears the news of another venture through the British lines to New York was no sweet music. His former wife still lived there, married to a British officer, and they'd crossed paths on his last visit. That had almost cost Swift his life. "A great many people in New York know me by sight," he told the general.

"There's no one else I can send," Washington said. Swift could see his teeth were bothering him, as they sometimes did.

"What is happening there of such great import?"

"I must know whether the British plan to evacuate the city soon or if they will keep the army there. This will be best known by their preparations of wagons and horses. Are the wagons being repaired, the horses reshod? Are they being collected together for an evacuation? Are the European merchants selling off their goods and packing up? I am concerned especially about Coffin, who keeps a large dry-goods store to supply the officers and army. Inquire also if the fleet from Cork has arrived yet, and how many provisions they carry."

"A big job!"

"I am relying on you," Washington said. "Use the invisible ink and send a letter in care of the Culpers."

Swift knew it to be a safe address maintained by people using the code name Culper. Washington relied on them to pass any letters along to him at once. "It's that urgent?" he asked. "You can't wait until I return from New York?"

"If you learn anything I must know it at once. I cannot take the chance—"

"That I might be captured?"

Washington's eyes met his. "It is always a consideration."

It was more than two years since Alexander Swift had last crossed the Hudson by night in a small boat. That had been July of '78, and it was also the last time he'd laid eyes on his estranged wife Amanda. Word had reached him last year that their divorce was final, and she had married Major Jack Jordan, the British officer with whom she'd been living.

The sentries along the shore were notoriously lax, especially on a cloudy or moonless night, and Swift's night vision had always been good enough to be guided by the old windmill, a reminder of pre-British days when the city was still New Amsterdam. He beached the boat without difficulty in a wooded grove about a mile north of the docks, taking care to hide it well in the underbrush. It would probably be his only way back to the New Jersey shore.

He was dressed in the clothing of a dock worker, and he dozed on the shore till the first hint of dawn. Then, his shoes still muddy from the marshy shoreline, he ventured along the streets. Only the southern end of Manhattan Island had the look of a city, with a population of some 25,000 people. To the north it was still farmland. He headed south, moving along the streets unnoticed, passing a morning patrol of King George's soldiers without incident. It took him a half-hour to reach his destination and he stopped along the way for a bit of breakfast with the dock workers. A few minutes' conversation answered one of Washington's questions. The fleet from Cork had been sighted off the tip of Long Island and was expected to dock in two days' time, when the tides were right.

Coffin & Anderson's Dry Goods was one of the city's larger businesses. Swift had met Coffin once in the days before the commencement of hostilities, but this day, as he entered the store shortly after eight o'clock, he was more interested in one of the clerks, a former sailor named Edgar Jamison. The man walked with a limp, the result of an accident that had ended his days at sea. Swift spotted him at once, unwinding a roll of muslin for a woman customer. When Jamison had completed the transaction, Swift strolled over to ask a casual question and the man recognized him at once.

"Well, if it isn't Alexander Swift!"

He smiled at Jamison. "Not so loud! Some of your customers might recognize the name."

"What have you done, sneaked through the British lines?"

"Let's just say I'm here unofficially. How have you been, old friend?"

"Good, most days. The dampness bothers my leg. How is life across the river?"

"Never dull!"

Jamison's weathered face turned somber. "You know Amanda has remarried?"

"I heard that."

"She still shops here on occasion. A lovely woman."

"She always was." Swift fell silent for a moment, then changed the subject. "How has business been? Is Coffin keeping up the stock?"

"Oh yes. If anything, the British are buying more supplies from us."

That was not the news Washington wanted to hear. "I am glad for your sake that the job seems safe. Perhaps we can meet for a beer some night."

"Fine by me. How long will you be here?"

"I don't know."

Edgar Jamison nodded. "Watch out for yourself."

"I will."

Among Amanda's women friends had been one named Elizabeth Short, whose family ran a large livery stable on Wall Street. Swift headed there next, making his way through streets that seemed more crowded with British soldiers than during his last visit. As the August sun rose higher, the day grew warmer, and he could smell the odors of the stable a full block away.

Swift realized he was taking a risk going there, but it was the best possible source for the information Washington required. Before he was even in front of the place he spotted Elizabeth, tall and blond, with a mass of curls at the back of her head. They seemed in stark contrast to the trousers she wore like a man.

She was washing out one of the carriages and at first she didn't recognize him. He had to remind himself that they hadn't seen each other since the English seized the city in '76 and it became a Loyalist stronghold. "Hello, Elizabeth. Don't you have someone to do your scrubbing for you?"

She squinted into the sun, still not knowing him, and then it seemed to come to her. "Alexander? Alexander Swift? Oh my God!" She looked as if she had seen a ghost.

"I'm sorry to startle you like this."

"Amanda—" she began and then stopped, not knowing how to continue.

"I know about it."

"She and Major Jordan seem very happy." She twisted her hands uncomfortably. "She told me she saw you once, a couple of years back. Are you here to see her again?"

He gave her the best smile he could muster. "No, I came to see you, Elizabeth."

"What for?" She seemed genuinely puzzled.

"Is your father around?"

She lowered her eyes. "Papa died last year."

"I'm sorry to hear that. He was a nice man."

"I'm running the livery now, until my brother gets back."

Her voice had dropped to a mere whisper at the end and Swift guessed what that meant. "Tom is fighting with the Loyalists?"

"Yes. He had no choice. To oppose the English would have meant the loss of the business."

"It was a difficult decision for all of us," he reminded her. "If I had stayed in the city I might have won Amanda back."

"She says you have a woman at West Point."

"Molly. She works at the garrison there," he confirmed. "She has been a great comfort to me."

"We all need that. Now why did you come to see me?"

"I was wondering how your business has been. You were doing a great deal of work for the English officers."

"We still do." A wisp of long blond hair had strayed over her face and she tucked it back in place. "If General Washington wins, I hope we'll be shoeing his horses too."

"Has the shoeing business shown any increase of late? Have your employees been repairing any English carriages?"

Her eyes narrowed as she weighed his questions. "I see," she said after a moment. "You're here as a spy."

"I never use that word."

"You'd better go now, Alexander. I have nothing to tell you."

"All right," Swift said. "Next time you see Amanda, tell her hello for me."

"I expect she and Major Jordan will be in New York for a long time," Elizabeth said, turning back toward the livery stable with her pail and scrub brush.

It wasn't until later that it occurred to him she might have been sending a secret message of her own, telling him the English had no plans for evacuating New York.

Late that morning, seated at a corner table in the old City Tavern, Swift wrote a few quick lines to Culper, Jr., commenting on New York's warm weather and the hope that the rebels would lay down their arms before another winter. Then he withdrew the vial of white ink from its hiding place beneath his shirt and carefully began to fill the rest of the page with invisible writing. "711," he wrote, the code for General Washington, "*Corks bobbing on water until Thursday's tide. No other movement here.*" When it had dried sufficiently he sealed the letter and took it to a nearby post office. There were few of them around, but Ben Franklin had made great strides since the Continental Congress set up a postal system independent of England in 1775. If the censors didn't delay it, his letter should be in Washington's hands within days.

In the early afternoon Swift headed for the tip of Manhattan Island, where another friend named Mandrone ran a seamen's shop. In the past he had sold uniforms and ship's gear to British officers, and he was in a position to know of any plans for an evacuation of the city, especially by ship. The place was as Swift remembered it, a small crowded shop with a fine view of the harbor.

Felix Mandrone had lost a few pounds and a great deal of hair since Swift last saw him. At that moment he was demonstrating the thrusting power of an officer's sword to a potential customer, but as his eyes fell on his new visitor he seemed to lose interest in the sale. As soon as they were alone he hurried over to embrace Swift. "Alexander! I heard that you were back. What have you done, man?"

"Done? Nothing. How could you have heard I was back? I have been here less than twelve hours."

"Already the soldiers are searching for you. My boy just brought me the news."

A chill ran down Swift's spine. "What news?"

"About Amanda's husband, Major Jordan. He's been killed in a duel."

Felix Mandrone could offer few details about the killing, except that Jordan's body had been found in a field north of Canal Street, in an area sometimes used for duels. He had been shot once in the chest, and there was an unfired pistol by his side. "When did they find him?" Swift asked.

"The farmer who owns the field came out just after dawn. He hadn't seen or heard a thing, but there were carriage tracks near the body. The dead man was wearing his major's uniform and the English identified him right away."

"Why are they searching for me?"

Mandrone shrugged. "Somebody saw you, that man Jamison from the dry-goods store where the officers go. He told them you were in there right after eight o'clock."

Swift glanced nervously out the door, searching for English soldiers. "Thank you for the warning, old friend. Don't mention my visit here."

"If you need a boat to take you across after dark—"

"I'll remember your offer."

Swift had only one destination in mind when he departed from Mandrone's shop and headed north. It was the most dangerous place in New York for him to be at that moment, but there was no avoiding it. He had to see Amanda, whether she needed him or not.

His former wife and Major Jordan had a house on John Street, just off Broadway, where he'd secretly visited her two years earlier on a previous mission. He found the place without difficulty, but was unprepared for the carriages and visitors arriving at her door. The news of her husband's tragedy had spread fast among their friends. As he watched from a doorway down the block, Elizabeth Short appeared on the front steps, returning to her carriage, where a driver waited. An English officer Swift didn't know was arriving on horseback at the same time. He had a scar on his left cheek that might have come from a duel. Removing a package from his saddlebag, he took it up to the door with him. Swift circled the block and cut through a small back garden, entering the house through a rear door he'd observed on his previous visit.

From the kitchen he could hear the conversation in the parlor, and he prayed no servant would appear to discover him. "—so good of you to come, Captain Redding. This terrible thing—I'm still in shock."

"Do you have any family, anyone you could go to?"

"No family, but Miss Short has offered to stay with me the next few nights. Are you conducting the investigation, Captain? What can you tell me?"

"I wanted to ask what you could tell me. The place where Jack was found is notorious for illegal dueling. Another officer was killed there just two months ago. Often the duels are fought with swords, but this was with pistols."

"They say his weapon hadn't been fired."

"That's correct," Captain Redding confirmed. "He'd taken a single shot in the chest, burning a hole in his uniform jacket, but there was virtually no blood. You'll be relieved to know his face seemed at peace, without pain." There was silence for a moment and then the officer said, "This is the unfired weapon that was at his side. Did it belong to him?"

"A flintlock dueling pistol? He never owned such a thing!" Then she back-tracked a bit. "At least, not to my knowledge."

"What about enemies? Excuse me for asking, but were there rivals for your hand?"

"My former husband was Jack's only rival."

"We have information that Alexander Swift has been seen in the city this very day."

"I doubt if that's true. Even so, dueling was never his way of settling things. Alexander is much more a man of action. He would use his fists before a dueling pistol."

"Just one more question, Mrs. Jordan. Do you own a carriage?"

"We have a small one, yes. Right now it's having a wheel repaired."

"There were tracks of a single carriage in the damp grass by your husband's body. We found no other tracks. It appears both men, and their seconds, traveled together in the same carriage."

"Why didn't they report what happened?"

"Because a killing in a duel is murder under English common law, even though it's not yet a court-martial offense in our army."

"You believe Jack was killed by a fellow officer?"

"In all likelihood." He gave a small cough.

There was the sound of her moving about. Even now, four years after their marriage ended, he could still picture the nuances of her movement in his mind. "Could I get you some tea, Captain?"

"I cannot impose upon your grief, madam, but a bit of water would refresh me before I leave."

Amanda came through the door of the kitchen before he could move or hide. Her eyes widened at the sight of him and she opened her mouth as if to call for help. He held up his hand, imploring her to silence. She hesitated, then walked quietly to the pump and filled a glass with water.

He listened while she returned to the parlor with the water, but she did not betray his presence. After a bit more conversation Captain Redding took his leave. Swift peered around the kitchen door. "May I come out now?"

"What are you doing here, Alex?" his former wife asked. "Is it true that you killed Jack?" She was not yet in mourning, wearing instead a dark green gown that would be suitable for afternoon calls.

"Of course not! You know better than that, Amanda. I would never fight a duel."

She could still light up a room with a flash from her deep green eyes. For a moment he remembered why he had loved her, and why he had lost her. "Not even for me?" she asked with a seductive smile.

"You hardly seem the grieving widow," he observed. "The last time I visited, you were deeply in love with him."

"I made a mistake, not my first nor my last. I would hazard a guess that the duel was fought by an angry husband seeking satisfaction."

"I'm sorry. I had no idea Jack was that sort."

"Nor had I! There were times these past few months when I might have shot him myself." Her eyes blurred with sudden tears, not for her husband but for herself.

He wanted to take her in his arms and comfort her, but he did not. There was no telling where such a move might lead. "What husband might have been most likely to fight a duel with him?" Swift asked, keeping his distance.

"I do not know. One night recently I found long blond hairs on his uniform jacket."

"And the dueling pistol Captain Redding showed you just now?"

"I never saw it before. I'm certain Jack never owned it."

"Then it belonged to the other party in the duel. Or to their seconds."

She reached out to touch his arm. "Alex, you must flee this city. There are those who think you are the most likely person to have shot him."

"Do you believe that?"

She turned away. "No, but everything's confused right now."

The knocker on her front door sounded again. "That will be another friend come to pay respects."

She nodded. "You had better slip out the back. My cook will return from shopping soon and she mustn't find you here."

He said simply, "Goodbye, Amanda." Then he was gone, as she hurried to answer the door.

It may have been his imagination, but there seemed to be more patrols of English soldiers in the streets as he made his way across lower Manhattan. The original plan had been for him to remain in the city for some days, gathering what further information he could about possible troop movements. Now that plan had changed, and it seemed best to hide until dark and then row back across the Hudson River to the New Jersey side.

Heading north beyond the docks, toward the place where he'd left the rowboat, he found himself once again in the area of Coffin & Anderson's Dry Goods store, where he'd encountered Edgar Jamison that morning. If Jamison was indeed the man who'd reported him to the British, he was someone to avoid at all costs.

As the afternoon drifted into evening Swift found a small public house that served food. While he ate he thought about Amanda's husband. There was a time when his hatred of Jack Jordan might have led to violence, but that hatred had died long ago. He had Molly up at West Point now. Amanda would always be a fond memory, but no longer someone to fight duels over.

He tried to imagine Jordan standing at dawn with his back to his opponent while someone counted off the traditional ten paces. Jordan walking forward, the dueling pistol pointed toward the sky. Jordan turning, aiming, and then being struck in the chest by his opponent's shot.

But he couldn't see it.

He couldn't see it because something was wrong with the picture.

Swift was still puzzling it out as he headed for the boat after eating. The day had turned cloudy with a threat of rain, and dusk was settling in fast. He hoped the waves beginning to churn on the river wouldn't prevent his crossing. Quickly he crossed the muddy stretch of shoreline and began pulling the boat from its hiding place.

"Do not move, Mr. Swift," a sharp voice commanded from behind him, "or you are a dead man!"

He stood perfectly still and waited until Captain Redding stepped into his line of vision. The officer held a flintlock pistol aimed at Swift's chest. "How did you find the boat, Captain?"

"That was not difficult. A man named Jamison reported seeing you in his shop early this morning. He said there was dried red mud on your boots. River mud. We found your earlier footprints leading away from the boat. I've had men watching the area since afternoon. I was lucky enough to be here myself when you returned."

"If you think I killed Captain Jordan, you're wrong."

"We'll see. I've visited his widow twice today and learned a great deal of useful information. Certainly you had a strong motive for killing him. I've just come from there now—her friend Miss Short is staying the night—and I expect to finish my investigation before the funeral. Regardless of whether or not I can prove your involvement, Mr. Swift, you will be hanged as a spy."

Swift could see two soldiers with muskets standing at a distance. Even if he might have disarmed Redding, there was little chance he could outrun two musket balls. "Let me offer you a bargain, Captain. Give me my boat and a half-hour's start before you come after me. In return I'll give you Major Jordan's killer."

The Englishman laughed at the idea. "I have you, Mr. Swift, and there's no reason I should let you go. Finding the duelist who shot Major Jordan is only a matter of time. Sooner or later one of their seconds will talk about it."

"If it was a duel. Suppose it was something else?"

The officer frowned, uncertain now. "What do you mean?'

"Promise me freedom and take me to the Jordan house. I will show you the murderer."

It took some convincing, but finally Captain Redding procured a horse for him and Swift set off with the Englishman. Two soldiers brought up the rear, leaving Swift to wonder whether the bargain they'd struck would really be honored. Back on John Street, with the coming of twilight, no carriage waited before Amanda's door. If she was spending the night, Elizabeth Short would have sent her driver back to the stable with her vehicle.

It was she who answered Captain Redding's knock. "You're back again," she said, a bit surprised, and then saw Swift with his guards. "What is—?"

"We have come to see Mrs. Jordan," Redding said quite formally. "Please announce us."

Amanda hurried out of the parlor to greet them. She was still wearing the dark green dress she'd had on earlier, but she seemed to have recovered her composure somewhat. "Alex, what is this? Have they arrested you?"

"The captain is very close to it. I have to persuade him otherwise, and I think I can do that."

Amanda led the captain and Swift into the parlor while Elizabeth brought up the rear. The guards remained by the parlor doors. Swift took a seat facing the others and started right in. "Amanda, I don't believe your husband was shot in a duel. The only evidence for it, really, is the place where the body was found and the unfired pistol by his side. The evidence against a duel is much stronger. Major Jordan was shot once in the chest, but at so close a range that his uniform was burnt around the wound. Certainly that was not from twenty, or even ten, paces away."

"Perhaps the other man cheated," Elizabeth suggested, "and fired before the full ten paces were counted off."

"Then the wound would have been in Jordan's back and not his chest. There's something else too. I heard you say earlier, Captain, that there was virtually no blood. Usually there is considerable bleeding from a chest wound. The implication seems obvious. Not only was Jordan not killed in a duel, but he was not killed where the body was found. The body was transported there in the carriage that left its track in the damp grass. After all, it's hardly likely that both principals and seconds would arrive in a single carriage. Nor is it likely that a dueling pistol would have been left at the scene if the deed was to remain secret. Its absence from its mate would have been readily noticed. No, Captain, there was no duel. Jordan was shot at close range sometime during the night and his body transported by carriage to the infamous dueling grounds at which it was found."

"Then I might have killed him myself," Amanda said in barely a whisper.

"But you did not. You told me yourself your carriage was having a wheel repaired. But you also told me of Jordan's unpleasant affairs with other women. Since it was not a duel, the killer is not necessarily a man. It could have been a spurned lover—a woman with long blond hair like the hairs you found on his uniform jacket."

Only Swift was prepared for what happened next. Elizabeth Short bolted from her chair and ran toward the tall casement windows at the back of the parlor. But Swift was too quick for her. He was on her, gripping her about the waist, before she was halfway there.

Amanda stared with unbelieving eyes. "Elizabeth? Elizabeth and Jack?"

"I'm afraid it's true," Swift told her as Captain Redding took charge of the prisoner.

"But how did you know?"

"This morning when I stopped by her livery stable she was scrubbing out one of the carriages. I thought it was odd she didn't have an employee doing it, and she seemed almost frightened by my sudden appearance. Of course, it was the carriage she'd used to transport Jordan's body, and she was scrubbing out the blood. It was not a task she could assign to her stable boy or carriage driver."

Elizabeth turned toward Amanda, her face twisted in a grimace of pain. "He said he was leaving you and I believed him. When he backed out and decided to stay with you, I just went for the pistol and shot him."

Amanda's hands were covering her face, no longer able to look at her friend.

A few minutes later, Captain Redding said, "I'll keep my part of the bargain. You'll be escorted to your boat, Swift. But if you're still within sight of shore after thirty minutes my men will fire at you."

"Fair enough. I hope the clouds have made it a moonless night."

It was Amanda who came to the door as he was leaving, asking if she might have a private word with him. Redding nodded and said, "Two minutes only."

She stood very close and whispered the words in his ear. "This is for all of Jack's betrayals. Now I'm betraying him. The British have an American traitor at West Point. I don't know who, but warn General Washington if you can."

Alexander Swift nodded once and hurried off into the night.

THE BROKEN CHAIN

The secret intelligence report that the British might have an American traitor at West Point had caused General Washington to send Alexander Swift hurrying back there in early September of 1780. Since August third, Major General Benedict Arnold had been in command at West Point, establishing his headquarters at Robinson House, a confiscated private residence on the east bank of the Hudson.

Arriving at the fort's familiar ramparts after an all-night ride through enemy lines, Swift could barely make out the two-story Robinson House through the morning mist on the Hudson. The first friendly face he saw was that of Major Jasper, an old-timer who'd fought with Washington during the French and Indian War and was now the chief legal officer at the fort. Jasper knew Swift only as one of the traders and fur merchants who frequented the area, and who'd played an important part in saving Washington's Hudson chain two years earlier. But perhaps he suspected more.

"How are things going here, Major?" Swift asked after they'd exchanged the usual amenities.

Jasper shrugged. "General Arnold's making a great many changes. You won't like what's happening to that chain you saved from the British attack."

Alexander Swift frowned at the words. Saving the Hudson chain had been one of his main accomplishments. "What do you mean?"

"One of the center links was damaged and the general feared it was coming apart. He ordered it removed, to be repaired or replaced."

The great chain across the Hudson at West Point had been placed there by order of General Washington, to keep British ships from sailing up the river. It was a serious matter if the chain had been removed without Washington's knowledge. "The blacksmiths will take weeks at that job," said Swift. "How is the river to be blocked in the meantime?"

"The great chain is held together by a strand of rope," Major Jasper muttered. "A loaded ship could easily snap it."

"Has any officer complained about this?"

"You don't complain to General Arnold. He sent four hundred men on a detail to cut wood at Fishkill, even though his second in command, Colonel Lamb, warned that he was compromising the safety of the fort. We would be better served by completing the fort's western wall before we worry about wood for a winter we may never live to see."

"Is it really that bad?"

"It is. You must believe me."

Swift nodded. "I know Benedict Arnold. I was at his wedding. I will row across the river and call on him tomorrow."

A short distance from the fort itself was a small settlement serving the needs of the troops. On his visits Swift had always taken a room at a tavern called the Nugget of Gold. After his wife Amanda left him for a British officer, he'd developed a close friendship with Molly McVey, a waitress at the tavern. She'd traveled with him more than once, and had been his companion at Benedict Arnold's wedding in Philadelphia the previous year. Molly was a slender, dark-haired young woman, a year or two older than Swift, with a milk-white complexion and a way of handling herself among the denizens of an army fort.

"How was New York?" she asked as she placed a schooner of beer on the table in front of him. She knew of his undercover missions for General Washington, which had taken him into the British-occupied city on a couple of occasions.

"Good." He kept his voice low. "The people grow restless. There are rumors of a British pullout."

"Did you see your former wife?" It was a question he'd known she would ask.

"Yes. The British officer she married is dead now."

Molly drew a sharp breath. "And she wants you back."

"At this point Amanda doesn't know what she wants, or even which side she's on." He said no more. Only General Washington had been informed that Amanda was the source of the secret intelligence about a traitor at West Point.

"Will you be staying the night?" Molly asked as she moved on to the next table.

"I have my usual room."

Later that night, when they were alone, he asked her about the Hudson chain. "It's true," she replied. "General Arnold himself ordered the link removed and repaired. Everyone knows the rope holding the two parts together is useless."

"Why would he do such a thing?" Swift wondered.

"Ever since I met him in Philadelphia I've thought him a strange man, walking with his stick like some wounded beast."

"That wound was suffered at Saratoga, fighting for our freedom. His horse was shot out from under him and shattered his leg when it fell."

"Some who've visited him at Robinson House say he uses the living room for his office, and with a spy glass on his desk he can observe activity at West Point."

"He controls an area of some sixty square miles. It's not surprising that he would want to keep a close eye on it." Swift realized he was being defensive of Benedict Arnold, perhaps overly defensive. He did not want to tell Molly there might be a traitor at West Point, and he especially didn't want to tell her the information had come from Amanda.

At the first light of dawn Swift took a rowboat across the river to Robinson House. It was an easy journey because the estate, confiscated from Colonel Robinson when he went over to the British side, lay slightly south of West Point and he was able to travel with the current. It was only in the final stage that he had to pull in to shore, aiming for a small dock below the high bluff of Robinson House. Arnold had an old whaleboat secured there, with a crew of six at his constant disposal to ferry him quickly to West Point or other destinations on the river.

Swift announced his presence and one of the men escorted him up the steep path to the house. He'd never been there before, and was surprised at the wild and gloomy setting of the two-story home, nestled among rocks and wooded ravines in the desolate Hudson Highlands. He doubted if there was another house within a mile. The living room which now served as Arnold's headquarters was a large square area with a fieldstone fireplace and oak ceiling beams, opening onto a terrace and garden.

General Arnold sat at his desk, working by candlelight since the bright morning sun had not yet reached the windows that faced west. His left leg was out straight in front of him and the thick walking stick was close at hand. On the desk was the powerful spy glass Molly had mentioned.

"Good to see you again, Mr. Swift," he said, extending his hand in greeting. "Pardon me for not rising."

"Excuse me for interrupting your work. Is Mrs. Arnold well?"

"Quite well, thank you. She is arranging to come here from Philadelphia with the baby within the week. My aide, Major Franks, has already been dispatched to escort her."

"I had heard you had a son."

Arnold nodded. "He'll grow into a fine lad. But tell me, did Washington send you?"

"He asked that I return to West Point and pay my respects to you while I was here." Washington had left it to Swift's discretion whether or not to advise Arnold of the report of a traitor. The news of the broken chain was bothersome and for the time being he decided to say nothing about a traitor. The chain itself was another matter, however.

"I'm always glad to see you," Arnold told him. "I've only been here for a month, but Peggy and I will soon be settled in with two of my aides and a few servants. This is a charming house with a fine view of the Hudson and West Point."

"I can see that."

"How is the river flowing this morning?"

"Moderately, I would say. I understand there has been a problem with the chain."

"A weak link, but it will soon be repaired. I know that is Washington's personal project, and I will see to it."

"In the meantime the chain is useless against the British."

Arnold smiled slyly, shifting his leg to a more comfortable position. "But they do not know that, nor will they, until the chain is once more whole."

"I take a special interest in it because once before I saved it from destruction."

"I understand that, and you have been a great help to General Washington. Your efforts will not go unrewarded."

They talked a bit longer, and when Swift was ready to depart Arnold suggested that one of the whaleboat crew could row him across the river. "I can manage it," Swift told him. "But thank you for the offer."

As he hurried down the path to his own boat, he wondered if there wasn't something just a bit sinister in Arnold's offer of the oarsman. At the dock, a muscular sailor named Pierre repeated the offer, but Swift once more declined. Instead he rowed himself upriver to the giant chain and examined it for himself. It was as Major Jasper and Molly had said. The chain was tied together with a simple rope, no stronger than a cobweb against the thrust of a heavy sailing ship.

Norb Flander, a red-faced man in his fifties, had opened the Nugget of Gold after fleeing the British occupation of New York City four years earlier.

Alexander Swift had passed many an hour in conversation with him at the bar of his tavern, especially on those occasions when Molly was away.

"Come have a beer with us, Alex," he called out as Swift returned to the Nugget of Gold just after noon that day.

Flander's drinking companion was Nathan Irving, a traveling sutler who set up his tent near army posts and sold provisions to the soldiers. Swift knew him slightly and greeted him with a handshake. "What are you selling these days, Nathan?"

"Horses," came the reply. The short, bearded man grinned, showing the gap of a missing front tooth. "I go right to the top now, no more selling tobacco and powder horns to the troops. I have an agreement to sell fifty horses right here at West Point."

"Where are you getting fifty horses?" Swift wondered.

"Up in Canada. I'm bringing them down next week. I figure you can use them here. Rumor is that the British warship *Vulture* is moving slowly up the river."

"Where?" Swift asked, trying to make it a casual question.

"South of Dobbs Ferry."

"That's far enough away."

Norb Flander brought more beer from his bar. "This one is on me," he said. "I saw you out on the river earlier, Alex. What were you up to?"

"I rowed across to pay my respects to General Arnold."

They chatted for a time about the progress of the war against the British. Then, promptly at one o'clock, Molly came down from her room to start her afternoon shift, cleaning off the tables and sweeping the floor. "You gents will have to move," she told them. "I've work to do here. That includes you, Norb."

He chuckled. "Nothing like the hired help ordering me about! What say you to a game of cards, gentlemen?"

But Swift and Irving both had other things on their mind. Irving had to meet with Major Jasper to conclude the sale of the horses, and Swift wanted to check on Jasper's report that four hundred troops had been sent to Fishkill, some twenty-five miles away, to cut wood for the winter. He found Sergeant Driscoll, the fort's top enlisted man, at his desk at headquarters.

"Well, Alex, I heard you were back," he said in his familiar gravelly voice. He was a bulky man in his fifties, with a weather-beaten face and a reputation of having been an Indian fighter in his younger days. "What are you up to on this trip?"

Swift gave him a wink. "I had to sneak into New York to visit some lady friends."

"I wouldn't be surprised at anything you do, but I wish you'd do it in the Continental Army like the rest of us."

"I can get killed just as quickly out of uniform," he assured the sergeant. "I'm here for some information. Is it true that General Arnold sent four hundred troops to Fishkill to cut wood?"

Sergeant Driscoll studied his face before responding. Then he asked, "Why do you want to know?"

"The word is that the great chain is under repair and a British warship, the *Vulture*, is sailing north on the Hudson. It seems a bad time for so many men to be away from the fort."

"Two hundred men were already chopping wood," the sergeant said. "General Arnold doubled the number to finish the task more quickly."

"That seems a sensible course to follow," Swift agreed. "And perhaps it would be, were it not for the damaged chain and the *Vulture* under sail."

Driscoll seemed to have more to say, but his reluctance got the better of him. "Look here, Alex, will you be at the Nugget of Gold tonight?"

"I can arrange it."

The gravel-voiced sergeant grinned. "I'll let you buy me a beer and we can talk some more."

The Nugget of Gold always filled rapidly after the officers and enlisted men went off duty at the end of the day. There was very little else for them to do except drink or gamble, and the Nugget provided an opportunity for either vice. Norb Flander employed two barmaids who had rooms upstairs. Molly refused to become too friendly with the customers, turning them away with a gentle but firm hand. This was not always true of Willow Reece. That evening when Swift arrived he saw that all of Molly's tables were already full so he sat at the bar, a long plank supported by barrels, and ordered a tankard of ale from Willow, a half-breed Iroquois woman whose dark beauty made her popular with the soldiers.

"Looks like a busy night, Willow," he told her as she filled his tankard.

"Always is, around payday."

There was no sign of Sergeant Driscoll, but he saw that Flander had started a card game at a corner table. Paydays for the Continental Army were an uncertain thing at best, but apparently this month the money had come through. A little later in the evening Major Jasper came in, looking for

Irving, the horse dealer. Norb Flander called over from the corner card table, "He'll be here, Major. If he's in town he never misses a game on payday. Sit down and have a beer. We need a fourth for whist." Everyone knew that Flander's whist games always evolved into Dummy or a variation known as Boston which allowed betting on the result.

Molly was as busy as the other barmaid and Swift only had a brief opportunity to speak with her, agreeing to see her upstairs after the Nugget closed. He had another ale but the place was getting noisy and he could feel a headache coming on. He retreated to his room and locked the door, planning to rest for a half-hour before returning to see Sergeant Driscoll.

The rooms at the Nugget of Gold had space for little more than a bed, a wash bowl, and a curtained-off section for hanging clothing. A chamber pot was provided under the bed. The facilities were bare but adequate for his visits. He glanced around at them as he sat on the bed and felt the room begin to spin. Stretching out on the bed, eyes tightly closed, he could still hear the faint sounds from the tavern below. Then a cloud seemed to settle on him like fog over the Hudson.

The next thing he knew, Molly was shaking him awake. "Alex, Alex! What happened?" she whispered.

"What?" He struggled to regain his senses. "What time is it?" He realized there was something sticky in his hand. He focused his eyes on a hunting knife, its blade covered with blood. "My God! What's happened?"

Molly leaned toward him and rested her hands on his chest, saying very quietly, "Willow's body is on the floor. She's been stabbed."

He sat up in bed, trying to clear his thoughts. He could see Willow's body now by the lamp that Molly held, but he still couldn't believe it. "I only dozed off for a minute," he insisted. "I was waiting for you."

"What time did you come up here?"

"Around ten, I think."

"It's after midnight now."

He turned to her with pleading eyes. "You can't believe I did this."

"Of course not! But someone wants it to look like you did. We have to get her out of here before—"

But already it was too late for that. The door was pushed open by Norb Flander. "What happened here, Alex?" he asked, ignoring Molly's presence. "I heard a woman scream."

"I think I was knocked out or drugged somehow. Molly found me just now."

Major Jasper crowded into the room behind Flander. He knelt by the body and then stood up. "What time did Willow leave work?" he asked.

It was Molly who answered. "About an hour ago. She said she wasn't feeling well and I told her to go to bed. The crowd downstairs had thinned and I knew I could handle the rest."

"Did you notice anyone follow her upstairs?"

"No," Molly admitted. "But I wouldn't be likely to."

Major Jasper turned to Swift. "I'm sorry, Alex, but this woman has been murdered in your room. I'll have to take you to the fort for further questioning."

He had little choice. While he got a jacket from behind the curtain, Molly said to him, "I'll see what I can find out. Don't worry."

He waited until he was alone with Major Jasper, being escorted down the hill to the fort, before he spoke. "You know I didn't kill that girl. Someone is trying to frame me."

"Why should they do that?" the officer asked.

"Because I've been asking too many questions since I returned here yesterday. About that broken chain and the detachment of soldiers chopping wood at Fishkill. It's not just that chain of iron that's broken. It's the chain of loyalty holding the Confederation together. If there is a traitor here at West Point, he wants me silenced."

"Then why didn't he simply kill you instead of Willow?"

"A good question." He remembered the oarsman Pierre's offer to row him back to West Point from Arnold's headquarters that morning. "Perhaps he tried to, and failed. Or perhaps he needs to discredit me first in General Washington's eyes."

After some preliminary questioning Swift was taken to the guardhouse and locked in a cell. He knew there was little chance of further sleep that night, though his head was not yet clear. The arrival of Molly just after dawn was a welcome sight. "I brought you some food," she said. "The guards all know me."

"Is there any news?"

She glanced around, making certain no one could overhear the conversation, and produced a small package from the folds of her skirt. "After Jasper left with you and they took away her body, I sneaked into Willow's room. The same key opens all the doors. Hidden in one of her drawers I found these dried herbs labeled for different purposes. One was to rouse men's passions. Another was to put them to sleep. I saw her serving you tankards of ale last night. She could easily have slipped these ground-up herbs into the tankard."

"And she wasn't trying to rouse my passions. Good work, Molly!"

She slipped the package between the bars and he dropped it into his pocket.

"But who put her up to it?"

"The same person who killed her, obviously. No one else would have known what she was doing. He probably paid her to drug my ale and told her to be in my room at a certain time. He met her there and stabbed her, then left the bloody knife in my hand."

"But who?" she repeated.

"Do you know an oarsman named Pierre? Right now he's assigned to General Arnold's whaleboat."

"I know the man. I wouldn't trust him."

"Was he at the Nugget last night?"

"I didn't see him, but the place was crowded. He might have come in the back entrance and sneaked upstairs before I noticed."

"Try to find out if he was friendly with Willow." He realized his suspicions of Pierre were based on nothing more than the look on the man's face when he offered to row him across the river. Still, it was the only suspicion he had. He'd spoken to Arnold about the broken chain, and someone could have observed him later rowing up to it in his boat. He remembered the powerful spy glass on Arnold's desk, and the windows with their view of the river.

"I'll do what I can," Molly promised. Their hands touched briefly through the bars and then she was gone.

The morning dragged on for Alexander Swift, and it was ten o'clock before Major Jasper summoned him for more questioning. He sat quietly across the desk while the older man glanced through some papers. Then Jasper lifted his head and asked, "Do you still think someone is trying to frame you for this?"

"I'm convinced of it. I never would have taken Willow Reece to my room. I'm sure you know I have a close relationship with Molly McVey."

"Close enough to make her jealous if she found Willow in your room?"

"Do you think Molly killed her?" Swift's anger was beginning to boil over. Until now he had considered Jasper a friend.

"It's just a possibility."

"No, it isn't a possibility! I went up to my room around ten and passed out on the bed, probably because of something Willow slipped into my ale. Molly told me Willow said she was feeling ill and went upstairs around eleven. Molly couldn't have followed her up because she was the only one left to wait on customers. Even Norb Flander, her boss, was busy with a card game."

"But she was there when you woke up."

"By that time the blood on the knife was sticky, almost dry. Willow must have been killed closer to eleven, right after she came up to my room. Did you notice anyone go upstairs around that time?"

Major Jasper frowned. "No one. I'd been waiting for Nathan Irving, the horse trader, and he finally came in about that time. We were finishing up our business."

"Who was in the card game with Flander?"

"Let's see—there was Sergeant Driscoll and two of the cooks. I don't know their names. I watched them playing Boston and Dummy for a while before Irving showed up." He smiled suddenly. "Who's doing the questioning here?"

"You are, Major. I just thought I could help you out."

"Now it's my turn. Is there anything else you want to tell me?"

"What do you mean?"

"A guard saw Molly McVey slip you a small package when she visited you this morning. She brought you food too but you slipped this package into your pocket."

He didn't know which side Major Jasper was on, but he was in a spot where he had to trust someone. He took the package of dried herbs from his pocket and handed it over. "Molly found them in Willow's room. I think she drugged my ale with this one."

Jasper sighed and poured out a bit of the herb on his desk. "You know, I think I believe you, Alex. You weren't going to show this to me, were you?"

"Not yet. I have to get out of here, Major. I believe West Point to be in grave danger." His mind seemed clear for the first time since the previous night. "I might even be able to show you Willow's real killer."

"Keep talking."

Swift did, and finally the major stood up. "I'm taking a chance. We're going to leave here and walk back up to the Nugget of Gold. Who knows what might happen on the way? You might even escape."

"Or be shot."

"That, too," the major conceded. "I think it depends on how much we trust one another."

A few minutes later they left the stockade together and started up the hill. Major Jasper had his hand on the loaded flintlock pistol in his belt.

It was still morning and the Nugget of Gold was all but deserted. There was no one at the bar and only Sergeant Driscoll sat at one of the tables, chatting with Norb Flander. Both men seemed surprised when Alexander Swift entered alone. "Did you break out of the stockade?" Flander asked with a smile.

"Something like that. You're the man I wanted to see last night, Sergeant. Sorry we didn't get together."

"They said you'd gone upstairs."

"I had to lie down for a bit," Swift said. "Can we talk now?"

"Sure. I just came over, hoping you'd be here."

Flander left them alone, returning to his task of washing out the glasses and mugs from the previous night. While he was busy with his work Swift told the sergeant, "Yesterday we were talking about the British warship *Vulture*. Is she planning an attack on West Point?"

"No, not from what I hear."

"What, then?"

"I don't know, exactly. She's said to be carrying some mysterious passenger, but for what purpose, no one knows."

"Interesting. I believe that's something General Washington should know about. I'll be riding out in the morning to contact him."

He rose and shook the sergeant's hand, ending their conversation. Waving a greeting to Norb Flander, he headed for the stairs. He unlocked the door to his room and stretched out on the bed, much as he'd done the night before. Within minutes he heard someone at the lock, and the door began to open.

"Come in, Norb," he said. "I've been expecting you."

The proprietor of the Nugget stepped inside. In one hand he held a hunting knife, the twin to the one that had killed Willow. "You have to understand this is war, Alex. It is nothing personal."

He lunged at Swift on the bed, but suddenly Major Jasper appeared from behind the curtain, grabbing his arm. "No more killings, Norb. The war is over for you."

Norb Flander sat down on the bed and covered his face. "How did you—?"

It was Major Jasper who answered him. "Alex persuaded me on the way over here that you could be the guilty man. We found Sergeant Driscoll and sent him in ahead of us. Then Alex went in to have his conversation with Driscoll, just loud enough for you to overhear, while I slipped in through the back door and came up here to his room. If you were guilty, we thought you'd try to keep Alex from contacting General Washington."

Sergeant Driscoll had joined them, standing against the door in the event Flander tried to escape. "But you wonder how I knew it was you," Alexander said to the innkeeper. I'll tell you how I knew. It had to be Willow who drugged me with those Indian herbs. They were in her room and she was the one who served me the ale. Then she came to my room, either arriving with her killer or meeting him there. In either event, there were two people in on the plot, and we can assume the other person urged her to drug me. It had to be someone who could persuade Willow to take part in this. Her employer seemed a likely person."

"But why would he kill her?" Driscoll asked.

"It was important to someone that I be removed from the scene. I was snooping around, asking the wrong questions. Willow was killed so I could be framed for her murder and locked up in the stockade. She was merely a pawn to be sacrificed. It was Flander who arrived at my room with Major Jasper, claiming he'd heard a woman scream. But that would have been impossible. Willow and Molly were the only women here, and Willow had been dead nearly an hour by that time. Her blood on the knife was almost dry. Molly was there, but I awakened to her whispers. She was purposely keeping her voice low, certainly not screaming."

"But Norb was playing cards with us the whole time!" the sergeant objected.

Alexander Swift shook his head. "I don't think so. One of the games you mentioned playing was Dummy, a three-handed variation of whist. As the name implies, it is played with a dummy. When Flander was dummy he could have wandered over to the bar or to the outhouse, then easily gone upstairs from there. He was always in charge of the games and I'm sure he suggested which ones would be played."

"Did someone put you up to this?" Major Jasper asked Flander.

"There are things you have to do for your country," the innkeeper answered.

"For the British?"

"For your country."

Molly appeared then, running up the stairs to Swift's room. She paused, staring at them, and seemed to know everything from their faces.

Later, as Alexander Swift sat alone on a parade-ground bench, Major Jasper came to him. "We've learned a little, not much. The warship *Vulture* rests at anchor carrying a British officer, Major John André. He is waiting to make contact with someone here at West Point. Flander would not give us the name."

In the afternoon light Swift could just make out the house on the hill across the river. "Never mind. I believe I know the name."

"Will you tell General Washington?"

"It is a grave accusation. I must have proof. And I must have it quickly, within the week."

"What happens then?" Jasper asked.

"General Arnold's wife and son will arrive here from Philadelphia."

VULTURE IN THE MIST

Benedict Arnold's wife Peggy had been with him at Robinson House, across the river from West Point and about two miles below it, for some days when Alexander Swift saw her for the first time at the fort, standing alone in the September sunlight. He had been a guest at their wedding in Philadelphia, representing General Washington, and it was the first time he'd seen her since then.

"You're looking as lovely as ever, Peggy," he told her. "When did you arrive?"

She was slim and blond, a blue-eyed beauty not yet nineteen when the thirty-eight-year-old Arnold wooed and married her in Philadelphia a year and a half earlier. Now she was a mother with a new baby son, caught up in something she barely understood. "I reached Joshua Smith's house outside Haverstraw last week," she told him, "and General Arnold met me there."

"It's good to see you again," Swift said, though he hardly meant it. Peggy's presence meant that Arnold need not worry about her safety if he was indeed the traitor about to deliver West Point to the British. And their meeting place at Joshua Smiths house was further reason for suspicion. Smith seemed a loyal but somewhat gullible young man given to empty chatter. He would believe anything Arnold told him. Washington had little use for the man, though on occasion necessity forced him to stay overnight at the Smith house.

"This is my first visit to West Point. It's lovely seeing the river from here."

"A commanding view, in more ways than one."

She pointed out toward the water, "And that is the famous Hudson chain?"

Swift nodded. "Put there to keep the British from sailing upriver. Your husband found a damaged link which is presently being replaced at the mill."

She turned to smile at him. "I never thought I'd be a general's wife."

He saw her husband, his hawklike face turned toward the sky, hobbling on his bad leg up from the garrison. "I'd better let you go join the General," he said waving to Arnold as he headed in the opposite direction. Chatting with Peggy was one thing but he was reluctant just then to confront the man he suspected of plotting treason. As a civilian who undertook special assignments for General Washington, Swift was certain to be considered a spy by Arnold.

Instead, Swift walked over to the Nugget of Gold, the inn where he stayed when he was at West Point. Molly McVey was a waitress in the tavern there, a woman who'd given him much comfort when his wife left him for a British officer in New York City. She was in there now, tending to the bar, and he knew she'd been watching him through the window. "I saw you with Peggy Arnold. She's put on some weight since the wedding."

Swift smiled slightly. "She's had a baby since the wedding."

"She has extravagant ways."

"So has Arnold. It may be his downfall. He is so deeply in debt that he may be seeking money from the British."

A sutler named Horace Flexman, who sold all manner of supplies at the fort, entered the tavern at that point and they ceased their conversation. A bit later, when Molly had been relieved by the regular bartender, she signaled Swift to follow her upstairs to her room. "I've heard something that may interest you," she told him.

"What's that?" He knew at once that her invitation had no amorous intent.

"As you know, General Arnold has a crew of six bargemen on duty at all times, with a whaleboat docked down the hill from Robinson House. They stand by on two twelve-hour shifts. Jed Buckins, in charge of one crew, was in here drinking late last night. After his tongue was loosened he told me they'd rowed the general downriver a week ago Sunday, the tenth. He stayed overnight at Joshua Smith's house and early in the Monday morning mist continued downstream almost as far as Dobbs Ferry. He had the bargemen row very close to the *Vulture*, a British ship accompanied by three gunboats, but they had no flag of truce. As the whaleboat approached, the gunboats opened fire. One shot struck an oar blade and shattered it. Arnold ordered the bargemen to retreat and pull into a nearby cove. Some of our soldiers met him there, and he immediately wrote a letter for delivery to General Washington, claiming—as he also told the bargemen and the soldiers—that he'd been inspecting beacons along the river when fired upon. Buckins believes that wasn't true, that he was planning to board the *Vulture* for a meeting of some sort and was angry at being fired upon and then seen by our troops."

Swift found the story both interesting and alarming. If Buckins was right, Arnold had actually planned to meet with the enemy, only somehow the plans went afoul. Today was Thursday, the twenty-first, and he wondered if the meeting had actually taken place by now. Somehow he had to find out. Washington himself was due to arrive for a visit this weekend. If his suspicions were correct, West Point could be in British hands by then.

"Do you know any of the other bargemen besides Jed Buckins?" he asked.

"Most of them come in for an ale when they're off duty. They work in shifts, of course, six men at a time. They transport General Arnold between West Point and his residence across the river, as well as up and down the river on inspection trips."

"Write down as many names as you can remember," he suggested, handing her a piece of paper.

"Some I just know by sight, others by nicknames. These four I'm sure of. They're buddies of Jed's. There's one more on the crew but I don't know his name. He doesn't come in here."

Swift glanced at the names she'd written: Samuel Fain, Red Heron, Jonathan Springwater, and Martin Cheever. He knew Fain and Heron fairly well, but the other two he knew by sight only. "I'll talk to them," he said. 'If you learn anything else let me know at once."

As Swift was leaving the Nugget of Gold he spotted the sutler, Flexman, ahead on the path. He caught up with the man and engaged him in conversation.

"I know you sell fishing gear and the like. What about oars?"

"Oars?" He grinned at Swift. "You and the lady thinking about taking a moonlight canoe trip?"

"I was thinking of larger oars, ones for General Arnolds' whale-boats. Do you handle anything that big?"

"Don't tell me another one has broken! I just supplied one last week and that's all I had in my stock."

"Who came to you for it?"

"One of the general's bargemen, Springwater by name."

"Did he say how his oar had been damaged?"

"Hit a submerged rock, I guess. He left it on the shore somewhere."

Swift knew that it would have taken more than a submerged rock to splinter a heavy whaleboat oar. "Have you seen Springwater at the fort today?" he asked.

"He's around somewhere. His crew works the night and early morning hours."

"Do you know the others?"

The sutler shook his head. "Only Springwater by name. I've seen the others around."

"Keep your eyes and ears open. There may be some sort of plot afoot. General Washington will pay well for any information you can supply."

"I'll remember that," Flexman promised.

Alexander Swift thanked him and continued along a path rutted by cannon wheels to the garrison headquarters, where coded messages from General Washington, delivered by courier, sometimes awaited him. There was one such letter today and he hurried back to his room to decode it. The message was dated the previous Monday, the eighteenth, and read: *While crossing the river by ferry this morning in the company of Arnold and Lafayette, I observed the enemy warship* Vulture *anchored off Tellers Point. Do you have knowledge of why it is so dangerously far up the Hudson?*

Alexander Swift took a deep breath. Washington had been in Arnold's company only four days ago, obviously still placing his trust in the man. But the more important news was that the *Vulture* had sailed north from Dobbs Ferry to Tellers Point, within sight of Joshua Smith's house.

Realizing that he must learn more about Arnold's attempt to board the *Vulture*, Swift headed for the dock where bargemen often congregated when not on duty. He recognized Red Heron at once, a slender red-haired man with squinty eyes and a pale complexion. Not even rowing on the river had brought much color to his face, and his eyebrows were so light that they seemed nonexistent.

"How are you, Red?" he asked. "Still working with the night crew?"

"That I am, Alex. We get in a lot of slumber time in our tent over at Robinson House. The general doesn't travel much after dark, though Buckins tells me we may be rowing this night."

Swift kept the conversation casual, shifting to the weather. "Do you think it will be a bad winter?"

Red Heron shrugged. "Not as bad as three winters ago at Valley Forge."

"You were there with Washington?"

"I was there. Lost a toe to frostbite. The general still remembers me, always has a kind word when he sees me."

"It was a bad time," Swift agreed. He glanced at the other men chatting in groups along the river's edge. "Have you seen Jed Buckins today?"

"He's probably still asleep. They were playing hazard with dice most of the night while the rest of us were trying to sleep."

"Who was Buckins playing with?"

"The Indian, Onquoit."

Swift remembered now that Onquoit, a member of the Seneca tribe, was the sixth member of the whaleboat crew. That was why he did not frequent the tavern with the others. It was not too surprising to find an Indian among the soldiers at the West Point garrison since George Washington's first military mentor had been an Iroquois chief known as the Half-King. "The six of you are close, aren't you?"

"I guess so. We work together, sleep in the same tent, bathe in the river together."

"What do you think of Benedict Arnold?"

Heron shrugged. "He's the general. I do what he says."

Swift walked on, searching for others in Jed Buckins's crew. The other whaleboat was docked slightly downriver on the other side, by Robinson House, a good indication that the day crew had rowed Arnold and Peggy back home. The rambling two-story mansion also housed two of Arnold's aides, Colonel Varick and Major Franks, but they rarely used the boat unless accompanying General Arnold.

There was a sudden burst of laughter from near the blockhouse overlooking the Hudson, and Swift spotted two of the bargemen, Cheever and Fain, talking with some of the other soldiers. He strode up the embankment to join them. Cheever was a rough-looking man with a scarred face, which he'd acquired as a seaman aboard one of the British merchant ships. Fain was very young and handsome, popular with the women in the area. When he saw Swift approaching he said, "I hear General Washington will be visiting us on the weekend."

Many of the soldiers knew of Swift's close connection with Washington, but he tried to keep the relationship vague. "So they say," he replied. "Have you seen Springwater around or is he still asleep?"

It was the scarred Cheever who replied. "He's up. I saw him heading for the Nugget of Gold."

Swift found the oarsman at the bar in the Nugget. Molly wasn't in sight as he rested next to Springwater and ordered an ale. "I hear you had an accident with an oar last week."

Springwater was a man in his forties with a weathered face and a deep scowl. "Where'd you hear that?"

"One of the sutlers mentioned selling an oar."

"Yeah, that would be Flexman. I don't know what happened. Hit a rock or something. Maybe a shark bit it off." He was still scowling but there was a bit of humor in his gray eyes.

"Someone said you might have had a run-in with the British navy."

"His eyes narrowed. "You hear a lot, Mr. Swift."

"Just talk." He realized he would get no further information from Springwater, but he already had all the confirmation he needed. Washington would be interested in the true facts behind Arnold's account of the shooting.

Swift spent the night with Molly, listening to the soldiers singing in the tavern below. In the early morning he walked along the river for a time. The mist was still too thick for him to see down to Robinson House on the other shore, so he was not certain if the whaleboat had returned from its nighttime journey. Later, as he headed over to the fort, he came upon Molly, hurrying along the path. "Alex, I've been looking for you," she told him. "That sutler, Flexman, left a message for you. He said it was important." She produced an envelope with the sutler's business seal on the back.

He opened it at once and read the message. *Swift–I have news for you. Gen. Arnold overnight at Smith's house, met secretly with British major, John André by name. I am in danger. Meet me at one on far side of Crazy Creek–H. Flexman.*

"Is it important?" she asked.

"Very important. I must go to meet him."

Crazy Creek was well named, a wide but shallow stream, rarely more than a foot deep, that followed a twisting path through the woods before emptying into the Hudson just south of West Point. When he reached it, Swift removed his boots and stockings and waded across, keeping as dry as possible. It was a few minutes after one o'clock, but he saw no sign of the sutler. Then he heard a gasping wheeze and found Flexman doubled up behind a bush. His hands were trying vainly to stanch the flow of blood from a gaping chest wound. A bloody bayonet lay nearby.

He knelt by the dying man's side. "Flexman, it's Swift! Who did this to you?"

"Arnold's oarsman. I followed them by canoe last night . . . saw Arnold meet with André near Smith's house. Overheard them. Link removed from Hudson chain. . . ."

"I know that. What else did you hear?"

"British warships will break through chain Monday morning. Arnold will surrender West Point at noon."

"Good God! Where is André now, back on board the *Vulture*?"

Flexman shook his head. "Shore battery fired on *Vulture*, drove it downriver. André . . . stranded at Smith's house."

"How will he—?" Swift started to ask, but suddenly a gush of blood choked off Flexman's words. He died before he could speak again.

Swift got to his feet, trembling with frustration. Here was solid evidence of Arnold's treason at last, but the only witness to it was dead. He covered his eyes in a silent prayer for the sutler, then searched for evidence of the crime. Flexman's boots were dry, which meant that he'd carried them and had time to put them back on before the killer struck. Over toward the creek Swift came upon a recent bootprint in the damp soil, partly filled with water. It seemed about the size of his own, but it was impossible to measure with any accuracy.

He could not involve himself by reporting the killing and arousing Arnold's suspicions of him. It would be left for someone else to find the dead man, perhaps days or weeks from now. He recrossed the creek, wiped his feet, and put his stockings and boots back on. Then he gave some thought to Major André's situation. If the man was trapped at Smith's house as the sutler had said, then he had not yet been able to return to New York with timing for the attack on West Point.

Yet General Arnold surely would have arranged some way for him to get back. Assuming the *Vulture* had retreated as far south as Dobbs Ferry, what would be the most likely course for Arnold to follow? He would issue a safe-conduct pass. André, wearing civilian clothes, could pass through the American lines and rejoin the *Vulture* at Dobbs Ferry for the trip to New York. He would carry on his person Arnold's secret report with its timing for the attack. Signing the pass would implicate Arnold, of course, but by Monday noon all would be revealed in any event.

Friday night and much of Saturday passed uneventfully as the body of the sutler remained undiscovered. Swift could not move until he knew with some certainty what had happened to Major André. He sought out the Seneca Indian, Onquoit, as the oarsman most likely to tell him something of value, but the man spoke very little. Yes, they had been out Thursday night with General Arnold, and they had returned Friday morning from Smith's house. But nothing unusual had occurred. Swift was hesitant about revealing too much to the Seneca, for fear that he might be Flexman's murderer. There was little doubt in his mind that at least one of the six bargemen was an agent of Arnold's, and may have been carrying out Arnold's orders when he bayoneted Flexman.

By Saturday evening the mood of the garrison had undergone a subtle change that even Molly commented upon, "The troops seem ill at ease tonight," she told Swift. "There's been no singing all evening and that's unusual, especially for a Saturday."

When Swift encountered one of Arnold's aides, Major Franks, that evening the reason became clear. He'd occasionally chatted with the foppish young man at the Nugget of Gold and now the major told him, "There's something brewing that I don't understand and can't find out. All I can say is, look out!"

"What's the trouble?"

"That man Joshua Smith appeared at Robinson House this afternoon with some sort of important news for the general. They went into Arnold's private office and closed the door. Neither Colonel Varick nor myself has ever fully trusted Smith. I overheard a snatch of conversation between the two, something about Smith guiding some person through enemy lines. Then he stayed for dinner and got into a shouting match with Colonel Varick and myself."

"Over what?"

"He tried to say the Continental dollar was virtually worthless and I called him a scoundrel. Mrs. Arnold was so upset she left the table and went upstairs. I departed soon after and told the general I would tender my resignation. Whatever is going on with that man Smith, I don't like it. General Arnold is far too friendly with him. I hope to speak directly to General Washington when he arrives at Robinson House tomorrow."

Swift pondered what he'd heard. "Why did you call Smith a scoundrel?"

It took Franks a moment to respond. "Colonel Varick received a letter from New York this morning. It contained information that the man is suspected of being a double agent, selling information to both sides and using his house as a secret meeting place for traitors to our cause."

"Those are serious charges."

"Most serious," Major Franks agreed. "I fear for General Arnold's reputation if he continues meeting with the man."

"You and Varick have not warned him of this?"

"He seems quite content dealing with Smith. He would hear nothing said against him."

Later, when he was alone, Swift stood on the shore gazing through the darkness in the direction of Robinson House. If this Major André had successfully made it back to British headquarters in New York, enemy warships might be sailing up the Hudson by this time Sunday night, prepared to take over West Point on Monday morning. Washington was on his way here, but his exact location was unknown. An attack on Monday morning might even capture him along with West Point. Swift had to do something, but what?

Early on Sunday morning he arranged to be at dockside when the night crew of bargemen completed their shift and returned to West Point while the day shift replaced them in their own boat. Having spoken with everyone but Jed Buckins, he sought out the crew leader, who'd first told Molly the story of the splintered oar."

"Jed," he called out. "How is the river today?"

"Misty coming across, but the sun will soon clear it off. You're up early, aren't you?"

"I hoped we could have a few words before you turn in for some sleep."

Buckins squinted at him. "What about?"

"Your visits downriver with General Arnold."

"I got nothing to say about that."

"I understand British ships fired on you earlier this month."

"A full report of that was dispatched to General Washington."

"But I don't think Washington knows Arnold was attempting to board the *Vulture* when the shooting started."

Buckins cursed and spat on the ground. "That Molly told you, didn't she? I should have known better than to loosen my tongue around her."

"There are bad things happening here," Swift warned. "You don't want to be on the wrong side."

"Watch your own self, Mr. Swift. General Arnold holds the winning hand here."

"We'll see."

Later that Sunday Swift found Molly busy waiting on tables at the Nugget of Gold. The place was crowded, but he saw none of the bargemen nor either of Arnold's aides. "What time do you finish?" he asked her.

"They'll all be out of here before midnight. Why do you ask?"

"I have to ask a favor of you, Molly. I see no other way around it. There is no one else I can trust. Washington is on his way to Robinson House, and I'm afraid he's riding into a British trap. He must be warned before he reaches there tonight or tomorrow morning. If I row you across the river, could you wait for him on the trail? He'll have a large party of aides and soldiers so you cannot miss him. Deliver this letter into his hands. He knows you and will act on this information."

She stared at the letter in his hand. "What does it say?"

"That I have information General Arnold is a traitor, prepared to deliver West Point into British hands at noon tomorrow."

"My God! Are they on their way?"

"Their warships should be sailing up the Hudson right now, and the chain with its missing link will not stop them. I'd go to meet Washington myself but I must remain here and try to contact what few officers I can trust. If I guess wrong and am arrested, at least you can still warn him."

She hesitated only a moment. "I'll get off work and come with you now," she decided. "You can rely on me, Alex."

"You may have to give up a night's sleep if Washington is late."

"That's little price to pay."

She changed into dark clothing and they hurried through the gathering darkness to the river's edge where there were always boatmen to ferry soldiers and civilians across. A powerful man named Eiger, well known to Swift, rowed them across for his usual fee. On the other side, just below the Robinson House dock, Molly left the boat with Swift's letter safely stowed in her bodice.

He held her for a moment and they kissed. "I'll come for you in the morning," he told her. "The trail Washington's party will take is just at the top of this hill."

He gave a final wave from the boat as she disappeared from view.

Alexander Swift spent much of the night in conversations with the few officers he thought he could trust. He relied especially on those who'd expressed concern when Arnold removed a link from the Hudson chain, supposedly because it was damaged, and others who questioned the wisdom of Arnold's dispatching a large company of soldiers to cut firewood for the coming winter. Both actions seemed to weaken West Point's defenses, making it more vulnerable to attack.

As dawn approached he had a half-dozen men in key positions, ready to act at the first sign of an attack. If the sutler's information was correct, it would hardly be enough, but it might give Washington time to act. As for General Arnold, no one was brave enough to move against him on the basis of Swift's dubious evidence.

At the first sign of daylight, Swift was at the dock again, peering through the mist toward Robinson House. The second whaleboat and its day shift had departed earlier to relieve the night men, but there was no evidence of the night shift's return. It was impossible to see across the river but, after a time, one of the boats appeared. It was Washington's party, with the general himself standing in the prow as he must have done when he crossed the Delaware a few years earlier.

"Mr. Swift!" he called by way of greeting. "A friendly face at last! Is General Arnold here?"

"I sent Molly McVey to intercept you with a message. Didn't she—?"

"I have seen nothing of her," Washington said, stepping ashore. His aide, Colonel Alexander Hamilton, and the Marquis de Lafayette accompanied him, along with the oarsmen from the day shift. "I arrived at Robinson House to find that Arnold had left not thirty minutes earlier to prepare for my arrival here. Peggy Arnold had retired to her bed."

"General Washington, I fear that a British attack may be under way shortly."

Before he could say more, Hamilton handed Washington a dispatch, apparently received by courier as their boat was leaving the other side. "General, you must read this at once!"

As Washington read the document his face turned ashen and he trembled with emotion. "Arnold has betrayed us!" he cried out. "Whom can we trust now?"

"I sent Molly to warn you," Swift told him. "What news is there?"

Washington read further, glancing at the message's enclosures. "The British Major André was stopped and searched by some of our irregulars near Tarrytown on Saturday. He was wearing civilian clothes and carrying an official pass in Arnold's handwriting. In his boot they found secret papers and a battle plan for an attack on West Point this morning. The handwriting matched Arnold's on the pass. After being taken into custody, André revealed his true identity as a British officer and pleaded that he was not a spy but was merely trying to return to the British lines."

The boatman named Eiger, who'd taken Swift and Molly across the Hudson the previous night, had pulled into the dock and came running up to their group. "Mr. Swift, sir," he spouted out, "I was on the river and I saw General Arnold headed downstream. He had Miss Molly with him and when I pulled near he waved two pistols and warned me away."

"He's headed for the *Vulture*," Swift said with certainty. "And he's taken Molly as a hostage. One of the oarsmen must have spotted her waiting in the woods." He turned to Washington. "I must go after her, General. She was on a mission for me when this happened."

Washington shook his head. "If an attack may be imminent, I can spare no men."

"I'll go alone if I can have this whaleboat and crew of oarsmen. Nothing else will get me there in time."

"Take it," Washington said. "This man can row us back to Robinson House."

"Happy to do it, General," Eiger responded.

The general turned to Hamilton. "Order the immediate arrest of Joshua Smith, and have Major André brought to me at Robinson House under heavy guard. And place Major Franks and Colonel Varick under house arrest."

Within minutes, Alexander Swift was on the river, his fate and future in the hands of eight men he barely knew. Ahead lay the *Vulture*, Benedict Arnold, Molly, and a murderer.

They were nearly to Teller's Point before the sails of the *Vulture* became visible through the morning mist. Swift had raised a white flag on a stick, procured by one of the oarsmen before they shoved off. He prayed the British would see it before they opened fire as they had done with Arnold's boat two weeks earlier. Luck was with him. The gunboats remained silent when he approached, and a rope ladder was slung over the side as he reached the warship He climbed on board, but the soldiers waved his boat away.

"My name is Alexander Swift," he told the British officer who met him at the top of the ladder. "I request to see General Benedict Arnold at once."

He was kept waiting under guard for a few minutes until the officer returned. "Come with me," he was told. "General Arnold will see you."

The ship was at anchor for the moment, gently swaying with the current.

Swift followed the officer below decks to the captain's cabin. Benedict Arnold was seated at a table there, just completing a letter. At least, Swift thought, he's had the decency to remove his uniform jacket.

He glanced up as Swift entered. "I'm sorry we must meet under such dire circumstances," Arnold addressed him, putting down his quill pen.

"Where is Molly McVey?"

"I assure you she has come to no harm. She is being held on board with my crew of oarsmen, all of whom declined to come over to the Loyalist side."

"Why did you take her?"

"She was found in the woods last night carrying a letter to General Washington. The letter implied treason on my part, and it was signed by you."

"Treason it is this day," Swift reminded him. "Release these people and throw yourself on Washington's mercy."

"It is far too late for that." He held up the letter he'd been writing. "I have just completed a letter to him. I will read you the gist of it. *On board the Vulture, 25 September 1780. To His Excellency General Washington.*" He read a lengthy paragraph regarding the unhappy contest between Great Britain and the Colonies, and then continued, "*I have no favor to ask for myself . . . but from the known humanity of your Excellency, I am induced to ask your protection for Mrs. Arnold. . . . I beg she may be permitted to return to her friends in Philadelphia, or to come to me, as she may choose.*" In a postscript, he added, "*In justice to the gentlemen of my family, Colonel Varick and Major Franks, I think myself in honor bound to declare that they, as well as Joshua Smith Esq. (whom I know is suspected), are totally ignorant of any transactions of mine that they had reason to believe were injurious to the public.*"

Swift had listened to the reading of the letter with a stony expression. "How does this concern me?"

"I want you to take it back to General Washington, deliver it into his hands. Now that I am safe on board the *Vulture* I will release Molly McVey to you as well." He nodded toward the officer who had accompanied Swift, and the man disappeared into the depths of the ship.

"Major André never reached the British lines with your message," Swift told him,

"I know that. I fled when word of his arrest reached me."

"West Point is still in our hands. You have betrayed your country for nothing."

"I will fight on the British side now. We will bring down the rebellion."

The officer reappeared with Molly. Her wrists were chained in front of her, I'm sorry, Alex," she said when she saw him. "I was caught off guard."

"Unlock her chains," Benedict Arnold said, and it was done. Then he told Swift, "You may take my letter to General Washington and leave with Miss McVey. The boat that brought you is still waiting nearby."

"There's one more thing—the six bargemen in the crew that brought you. I believe one of them has been working for you and killed the sutler Horace Flexman near West Point on Friday."

Arnold smiled slightly. "Can you name which man you suspect?"

"I believe so. Will you surrender him if I can prove his guilt?"

He considered that for a moment. "I will do so to show my good faith, in hopes that Washington will agree to Peggy's freedom."

Presently, Arnold's six bargemen were brought up in chains and Alexander Swift faced them, letting his eyes rest on each in turn as he spoke. "Jed Buckins, Samuel Fain, Jonathan Springwater, Red Heron, Onquoit, and Martin Cheever. I know you all to some extent, and I know that one of you stabbed Horace Flexman with a bayonet on Friday afternoon near Crazy Creek, and left him to die there."

The men quickly protested their innocence, all but the Indian Onquoit, who remained silent. "Get on with it," Arnold told Swift, growing impatient. "Present your proof, if you have any."

"Very well." He turned toward Arnold. "I happened upon the sutler as he was dying from his wound. I had to remove my boots and stockings to wade across Crazy Creek, as had Flexman, since his boots were dry. He lived long enough to tell me it was one of your bargemen who'd stabbed him."

"There are twelve in all," Arnold pointed out.

"But the other six would have been on duty at one in the afternoon. It had to be one of these six, probably not Springwater, since Flexman knew him by name. Probably not Onquoit either, or Flexman would have referred to him as the Indian. It was likely that the killer could be found among the remaining four: Buckins, Fain, Heron, or Cheever. Then, by the creek, I found a bootmark in the wet sand. It could not have been made by the victim, whose boots were dry, and I had also removed my boots. It was most likely the bootprint of the killer, who had followed Flexman to the meeting place. Why had he soaked a good pair of boots by wading across the wide but shallow creek with them on, especially since the damp boots could have been evidence against him if he was stopped on the way back? Only one likely explanation comes to mind. He knew he might leave prints in the damp soil by the creek's edge, and he couldn't risk doing that. Removing his boots and stockings and leaving a bare footprint in the wet sand would have immediately identified him. Why? Because the killer of Horace Flexman had only nine toes!"

Red Heron tried to lunge forward but the chains held him. "Sure, that's me. I told you I lost a toe to frostbite. But maybe some of the others did too!"

Swift shook his head. "I'll admit I knew nothing of the others' feet, but you did, Heron. You said you slept with them and bathed in the river with them. If even one other crewman was missing a similar toe, you could have safely crossed the creek in your bare feet. You couldn't know Flexman would live long enough to partly identify his killer, but you still couldn't risk leaving that telltale footprint."

Red Heron turned his fury on Arnold. "You can't give me over to him! I killed the sutler because he spied on your meeting with Major André!"

Arnold seemed suddenly weighed down with fatigue. "Take him," he told Swift. "Take him and the girl. But deliver my letter to Washington. He must allow Peggy her freedom."

"I'll do what I can," Swift promised and turned away. He would not shake hands with the traitor.

Major John André was tried by court-martial at Tappan on September thirtieth and sentenced to death. Washington hoped to trade the young officer to the British in exchange for Benedict Arnold, but when that failed André was hanged as a spy on October second.

Peggy Arnold was allowed to rejoin her family in Philadelphia, but public outrage at Arnold's treason ran so high that the Executive Council of Pennsylvania confiscated his estate and ordered Peggy to leave the city within two weeks. She had no choice but to join Arnold in New York City in November.

As for Arnold himself, he became an officer in the British army and that winter led a force of raiders against Richmond in the south. But that is another story.

THE SWORD OF COLONEL LEDYARD

General Washington was standing with his hands clasped behind him, deep in thought, when Alexander Swift entered his quarters at the encampment near Staten Island. It was early September in 1781, nearly a year since Benedict Arnold's treasonous attempt to surrender West Point to the British.

"You wished to see me, General?" he asked, announcing his arrival.

"Alexander, yes. You've served us well in the past and I find I must call upon you again. As you know, Benedict Arnold is now a brigadier general in the British army. He caused us no end of grief with his incursion into Virginia last December and now he is on the move again. I have information that he returned to New York in June and is preparing for a new operation."

Swift had not seen Arnold since the morning he confronted him on board the British ship *Vulture*, following the traitor's flight to avoid capture at West Point. He had never expected to cross paths with the man again. His voice may have betrayed his apprehension as he asked, "What sort of operation?"

Washington gestured toward a map of the area. "I came here with every intention of mounting an attack on New York, to drive the British from the city once and for all. After reconnoitering the ground, I have concluded we could not succeed against the superior enemy forces. Instead I have decided to move south with my army and attempt to engage Cornwallis in Virginia. We march in two days' time."

"Where does Arnold figure in all this?"

"I have received secret intelligence that he will mount an expedition somewhere in Connecticut in hope of diverting a portion of my army from the campaign in Virginia. I cannot spare any troops and still go up against Cornwallis, even with promised help from the French. You must do what you can to learn Arnold's plans and warn the Connecticut militia."

"Where will he strike?"

Washington shook his head sadly. "I have no idea."

In his heart, Alexander Swift had hoped that Washington would at last be able to free New York from British occupation. Since early in the war, Swift's private life had been a jumble, with a former wife living in New York under

British rule and his passionate love, Molly, awaiting him at West Point. Though Amanda had left him for a British officer, now dead, he still felt some obligation toward her so long as the British held the city.

Now his mission for General Washington would take him away again, and he rode up to West Point to tell Molly. She worked at a tavern called the Nugget of Gold and lived in an upstairs room where he often spent some time. He'd brought with him a map of Connecticut that he studied while they ate. "I believe he will attack by sea," he told Molly. "But where?"

"Someplace he knows well," she suggested. "Isn't Arnold from there?"

He tried to remember. "I believe you're right. Before the war he had a bookstore in New Haven. But I don't think he grew up there."

"They must have his records at the fort."

She was right, of course. In the morning he walked down the hill to Fort West Point and quickly learned that Benedict Arnold had been born and raised near New London, about fifty miles east of New Haven. "I think that's it," he told Molly later. "I believe he's planning to lead an assault on New London."

"Would he really attack his boyhood home? Against his former neighbors, even his schoolmates?"

"He hates America so much, that's exactly what he would do."

"Will you go there, Alex?"

Swift nodded. "I have to warn them if I can."

"It's no more than guesswork."

"Washington's intelligence is that he's headed for Connecticut. I think New London is the most likely place. The town is an important port for privateers and has a large quantity of military stores."

They ferried him across the Hudson at West Point and he rode on to the east toward the Connecticut border. He reckoned the journey at close to 150 miles, and knew he'd have to stop somewhere overnight. The following morning he continued on, and the city of New London came into view shortly after noon. It was the fifth day of September.

Swift stopped first at Fort Trumbull on the west bank of the Thames River. Trumbull, facing the harbor, was defended by a captain and a company of twenty-four men. Swift warned of the possibility of an attack and then continued on. Fort Griswold, on the eastern side of the river, had more men, nearly 150 in all, under the command of Lieutenant Colonel William Ledyard. Its square fortification, with twelve-foot stone walls surrounded by a ditch and a line of pointed spikes, seemed to be safe from attack, but Swift knew it would not stop Arnold for long.

"Colonel Ledyard," he said, extending his hand as he was ushered into the man's presence. They'd met once before at Washington's encampment. "I bring you word from General Washington."

"News reaches me that he is moving south," Ledyard said. He was a young-ish man in full uniform, with a sword at his side. "Is that true?"

"It is, but he fears the traitor Benedict Arnold, now a British commander, may launch an attack in this area to force the general to commit part of his army here."

"I believe we can handle ourselves," the colonel replied, but Swift could see that the news troubled him.

"I have been riding much of the day. May I spend the night here?"

"Certainly. You will dine with my wife and my officers tonight."

There were five officers at Fort Griswold in addition to Colonel Ledyard, and they seemed to be seated by seniority around the dinner table. Major Sullivan's hair was turning gray and he was probably older than the colonel. There were two captains, Rolph and Dunwiddy, both youngish men with dark hair. The remaining two were lieutenants, the sandy-haired Fox and the stocky Yates, both of whom seemed a bit nervous at Swift's presence.

The chair to Ledyard's right was empty, and while they awaited the arrival of his wife the colonel passed on Alexander Swift's news. "We don't know that Arnold will attack here, but if he's heading for Connecticut this could be a logical target, given his familiarity with the city. The troops must be on alert at all times."

Major Sullivan raised a tactical question but all such conversation ceased as Emily Ledyard joined them at the table and every man stood up. She was a striking woman with deep brown eyes and a long, swanlike neck. When she took the seat next to her husband it was as if a queen had entered their company. "Darling, this is Alexander Swift, on a special mission for General Washington," Ledyard explained. "Mr. Swift, my wife Emily."

"How do you do," he said with a slight bow of his head. "It's a pleasure to meet you."

"But not under the best of circumstances," she replied, "in the midst of a revolution." Her eyes sparkled and she pushed a stray hair away from them. "Will we have trouble here at Fort Griswold?"

"I trust not, Mrs. Ledyard. We are doing everything we can to prevent it."

"Will there be reinforcements?"

"We can hope so. They have been promised."

She could only sigh. "The war has been difficult for everyone. William and I used to go rock climbing in Vermont each summer. Now we stay here and wait for an attack I pray will never come."

Her husband turned to Captain Rolph. "Is the nine-pounder in position?" he asked, referring to the cannon that was one of the fort's major weapons of defense.

"It is, Colonel."

"We should be safe for the night. Even Arnold would wait for daylight to attack."

"Arnold?" his wife repeated. "Would that be the traitor Benedict Arnold?"

"The same. But Mr. Swift has no real evidence that he will attack New London."

As the food was served, the conversation drifted into other matters. Mrs. Ledyard was the only woman at the fort, staying there occasionally while maintaining her home in the city. Captain Dunwiddy had actually been born in England rather than the colonies, but came to America with his family at an early age. All of them had one thing in common, a fierce loyalty to their cause and a belief that they must remain free from British rule.

Dinner ended with a toast to General Washington, proposed by Colonel Ledyard.

Early the following morning, Lieutenant Yates came running to Swift's room to tell him that British troops had landed under cover of darkness and were attacking on both sides of the harbor. Though he'd been warning against the possibility, the news that it was actually happening still surprised Swift. He hurried up to the parapet to view the situation. The British had indeed landed, with what appeared to be a full division of redcoats on either side of the river. Both of the American forts were greatly outnumbered, facing some 1,700 enemy troops, with British ships anchored offshore already bombarding the town with their cannon. Swift could see that four companies on the west bank of the Thames were being detached to attack Fort Trumbull.

"That officer seems to be leading the main force," Yates said, handing his spyglass to Swift.

Focusing the small telescope on the central British column, he immediately recognized the officer at its head. "It's General Arnold, just as I'd feared." Even as they watched, Arnold's troops overran a small redoubt and pressed on toward the town. The division on the east side of the river immediately moved forward toward Fort Griswold. During the terrible hour that followed, the British commander, announcing himself as Lieutenant Colonel Eyre, called upon the fort to surrender, but Colonel Ledyard quickly refused. Eyre then divided his forces and launched an attack on two sides of the fort simultaneously. The outnumbered garrison at Griswold returned heavy fire, and from his observation point Swift saw the British colonel go down.

"Get me a weapon," he told Yates, who passed him the musket of one of their dead soldiers.

The attacking forces came on a second time, making a lodgment in the defensive ditch and tearing down a section of the pointed stakes. They were briefly repulsed, but on the third try they mounted each other's shoulders and succeeded in climbing over the parapet. The fort's nine-pound cannon took its toll, but in the end even the stubborn defense of the garrison was no match for the superior numbers of the attacking force. Major Sullivan received a fatal bayonet thrust from a British soldier and Swift could almost see the fighting spirit drain from Colonel Ledyard's body. The walls had been breached and surrender was the only option.

Ledyard called upon his men to cease fire. Then he drew his sword and held it out, hilt first. "I wish to surrender Fort Griswold to your senior officer."

With Eyre dead it took them a moment to locate Lieutenant Colonel Potter, an officer from the New Jersey Volunteers who'd been fighting on the Loyalist side. "Do you wish to surrender, sir?" he asked Ledyard.

"I do, sir. Here is my sword."

Potter accepted the sword and immediately plunged it into Ledyard's chest.

Swift sprang forward at the sight of it, but a pair of British soldiers held him back. He and the remaining officers were confined to the colonel's quarters, where Emily Ledyard was overcome with grief at the terrible news. They heard shouts and screams from below as Potter instructed his men to finish the job with muskets and bayonets. In the end, almost the entire garrison was dead or wounded. The two captains, two lieutenants, and Swift were the only survivors other than Ledyard's widow, and Colonel Potter announced they would be dealt with personally by General Arnold.

"Is that the man who killed my husband?" Emily Ledyard asked when Potter had left the room.

"It is," Lieutenant Fox confirmed. "I saw it myself and I shall never forget the brutality of the act."

She brooded over that fact for some time, and when she spoke again she said, "I want you to kill him for what he did to William."

"Me?" Fox responded, wide-eyed at the request.

"Any of you. All of you."

Captain Rolph exchanged glances with the others and said, "Any of us would gladly lay down our lives for you, Mrs. Ledyard, but what you are asking is virtually impossible. If any of us were to challenge Colonel Potter to a duel I am certain he would run us through on the spot, as he did your husband."

"I am not suggesting a duel," she told them. "I am suggesting that one of you four, my husband's trusted officers, take revenge for his death by killing Colonel Potter by any means possible."

They exchanged glances again, and this time it was Dunwiddy who spoke. "I am willing to do it."

"And I!" Captain Rolph agreed. The lieutenants, Fox and Yates, joined in.

Alexander Swift stepped forward. "Not so fast! What you're suggesting will only get you all killed."

"We're dead men anyway," Dunwiddy argued, "as soon as General Arnold gets here."

"Perhaps not. I know Arnold. He can be reasoned with."

But Colonel Ledyard's widow was beyond the point of reasoning. "You four officers may draw straws for the honor of killing him," she announced. "That way none of us will know who actually does the deed." There was a broom standing in a corner of the room and perhaps that had given her the idea. She went to it at once and pulled out the straws, then broke one of them in half. She arranged them behind her back, like a half-remembered child's game, then held them out to the officers.

"Take one."

"Mrs. Ledyard . . . Emily," Captain Rolph implored her.

"Take one!"

Each of the officers did so, hiding their straws and consulting them in private. "There now," she said with relief. "I expect it should be done tonight. The morning may be too late."

They remained confined for the night in the late colonel's quarters, which consisted of two rooms on the top floor of the fort. Emily slept, or tried to sleep, in the bedroom. Swift and the four officers occupied the outer parlor, with two armed guards just outside the closed door. Colonel Potter, satisfied that the fort was secure, had taken an empty room across the hall.

Swift had expected General Arnold to arrive at the fort that evening, but he'd been busy securing their positions in the town and ordering its destruction. Churches, stores, and private homes were set aflame as the enemy troops ran through the streets with firebrands held high. The courthouse and jail were burned, along with the shipyards and dozens of vessels. At one point Emily called them into her bedroom and they watched from the balcony as New London and the adjoining town of Groton on the east bank were going up in flames. A warehouse stocked with gunpowder exploded and the town was showered with a hail of fire. British ships continued to ride at anchor in the harbor, a sign that the troops probably would be embarking once the destruction was complete.

It was shortly after dawn when Arnold turned his attention to Fort Griswold, coming over with two aides to survey the damage. He had summoned Colonel Potter and while waiting for his arrival Arnold visited the quarters where the officers and Mrs. Ledyard were being held. When he recognized Alexander Swift he was taken aback.

"Swift, can that be you? What are you doing here?"

"Trying to stay one step ahead of you, General. Are you responsible for the butchery that took place here yesterday?"

"Like all British officers, I have orders to put down the rebellion at any cost. Exactly what are you referring—?"

One of Arnold's aides burst into the room. "General, come quickly! Someone has killed Colonel Potter!"

Even Swift was startled by the news, and his first reaction was that someone else had beaten their man to the task. There was no way one of the four officers could have gotten free to kill Potter. All of them had been confined to the room with him, and he was certain none could have left without his knowledge.

Leaving them under guard, Arnold hurried away with his aide. It was a quarter-hour later when he returned, and now he summoned Swift into an adjoining room. "Tell me what this is all about," the general demanded. "Which one of you killed him?"

"We are prisoners here! If someone killed Colonel Potter it had to be one of his own men."

Arnold opened his clenched fist and dropped a gold button on the table. "This came from an American officer's uniform. I found it near his body."

"There may be other officers—"

"Ledyard and Major Sullivan are both dead, as you know. The button came from one of those four."

Swift continued staring at the button. "How was Colonel Potter killed?"

"Run through with a sword. His men say it's the same one he used to kill Ledyard."

"Yes," Swift agreed, half to himself. "It would be."

"I've seen some of your work in solving crimes of this sort. Your reasoning was quite impressive during our last meeting on board the *Vulture*."

"Frankly, General, I have no desire to solve the killing of Colonel Potter. Such a man is better off dead."

Arnold smiled unpleasantly. "Then I must offer you an incentive. We sail from here at the high tide, shortly before noon. I will hang the killer of Colonel Potter in the courtyard before we depart. If the killer has not been identified by that time, I will hang all four officers, and you and Mrs. Ledyard along with them."

When he returned to the others, Swift's first action was to examine the uniform coats of the four officers. None of them was missing a button. He explained the situation to them, without urging a confession by the guilty party. The men exchanged glances but said nothing. It was Emily Ledyard, coming out of the bedroom in her robe, who overheard the conversation and joined in.

"Whichever of you performed this heroic act, you have my undying gratitude. It is entirely your choice if you wish to admit to the act. If you do not, I am prepared to die with the rest of you."

Captain Rolph took the lead in the discussion. "One of us is guilty and only one of us should be punished if it comes to that. Why should six people die instead of one?"

"Do we really believe Arnold would release the other five?" Fox countered. "We are all doomed no matter what happens."

"He might let Mrs. Ledyard and Mr. Swift go," Dunwiddy reasoned. "They are noncombatants."

But Swift shook his head. "Mrs. Ledyard perhaps, but not me. Arnold knows me to be an agent of General Washington."

"We have a bigger problem here," Lieutenant Yates pointed out "We were under guard all night. How could any of us have left this room to kill Potter?"

Alexander Swift nodded. "I've already considered that. We have chamber pots in the rooms so no one was allowed to leave for any purpose. Mrs. Ledyard's bedroom opens only onto this room. As for myself, I was awake much of the night and was not aware of anyone leaving. Certainly the guards at the door would have prevented it."

"What will you do?" Emily asked him. "There's so little time."

"I'll see if I can examine the room where it happened. If someone else killed him they might have left a clue other than this gold button."

General Arnold, busy deciding what loot from the town could be taken with them, paid scant attention to his request, directing an officer to escort him to the room. In Arnold's eyes, Alexander Swift was already a dead man. A tall, lean officer, Captain Smithfield, took him to the room where Colonel Potter's body still lay sprawled among the blood-soaked sheets. It was across the hall from Emily Ledyard's room and a duplicate of it, reached only through an outer room whose door would have been opposite their own.

"The two guards at your door had a perfect view of the only entrance," Smithfield told him. "They swear no one entered or left either room."

"Tell that to General Arnold." He lifted a corner of the sheet and, peered beneath it. "What happened to the sword?"

"The general took it."

Swift walked out on the balcony and looked down at the harbor. Redcoat soldiers were carrying loot from the burning town down to their boats. Soon they would be gone. He turned back to the room. There was nothing here, no clue as to which of the four officers had drawn the short straw. "Will this fort be destroyed too?"

"I believe so. A cannon has been brought up to fire at the walls."

Swift returned to the room where the others waited. Emily had gone into the bedroom to dress. Fox was nervously pacing the floors while Yates and Rolph played a card game. When he told them he'd come up with nothing, it was Captain Dunwiddy who spoke. "I will tell them I killed Major Potter."

"Did you?"

"No, but then at least there's a chance for the rest of you. I would have killed him, if I'd drawn the short straw."

"There's no chance for us," Yates argued. "Our only way out is if we can work together and overpower the guards."

Swift had been considering the same possibility. But with this scheme they would need the help of Ledyard's widow. The door to the bedroom was closed and he knocked gently on it. "Come in," she said.

Emily was dressed in black for mourning. She was tying a bow at her neck as he entered. "If they're going to hang me they can hang me like this," she told him.

"I don't want anyone to hang. There might be a way for us to escape. It's a long chance but I think it may be worth a try."

"Tell me."

"You hide in the closet. I'll go out and tell the guards you've jumped from the balcony. When they come running in to see, we'll overpower them or push them off. If there aren't too many other guards downstairs we might have a fighting chance."

"All right," she quickly agreed. "I'll do it."

He outlined his plan to the four officers. "Any action seems better than nothing," Yates said. "I've been in favor of fighting right along. Let's give it a try."

When he was sure Emily was well hidden he opened the door. "Come quickly," he told the soldiers. "Mrs. Ledyard has jumped from the balcony!"

The first guard rushed in, but the second one remained in the doorway with his musket covering them. Swift was unable to follow the first man into the bedroom. Then they heard a shout and a scream as the first guard went off the balcony, and he knew Emily Ledyard had done their work for them. She appeared in the doorway, magnificent in her black gown, and the second guard shot her through the heart.

They could waste no more time. Captain Rolph flattened the guard with his fist before he could reload, and Swift paused only to be certain Emily was dead. Then he followed the others down the stone steps and out of the fort. Three guards on duty near the entrance had run over to examine the body of their fallen comrade, and by the time they spotted the fleeing Americans it was too late. Only one managed to get off a shot, high of its mark. Then Swift's party was into the woods east of the fort.

"Keep running," he urged the men. "If they decide to come after us we could still be in trouble."

Soon they worked their way back toward the shore and found a spot where they could observe the British ships. Already, boats full of redcoats were heading back, and other troops lined the beaches. General Arnold's raid was over, and they were safe.

They remained hidden until all the ships had sailed, then returned to the smoldering town to do what they could for the survivors. It was some time later, toward the end of the day, when Lieutenant Fox thought to ask, "Which one of us killed the Colonel? Who drew the short straw?"

The four men looked at each other and then at Alexander Swift. He had the answer for them. "There was no short straw. Emily Ledyard herself murdered the man who killed her husband."

"How is that possible?" Yates asked. "There was no way out of her room except through the parlor where the five of us were being held, and past a door with two armed guards."

"She didn't pass through our room," Swift explained. "She passed over it. At dinner two nights ago she mentioned that she and her husband went rock climbing in Vermont. We were on the top floor with a balcony outside her room. The room across the hall where we knew Colonel Potter slept was identical. A rock climber would have no trouble boosting herself from the balcony railing to the fort's battlements, and down again on the other side."

"But we drew straws!" Dunwiddy protested.

"Emily did that simply to shift suspicion from herself. She knew none of you could get out to kill Potter during the night, so she kept the short straw herself and presented you with four identical straws from which to draw. It couldn't have been anyone else, really. She dropped that gold uniform button to implicate one of you, perhaps planning to pull one off a jacket if given the chance. But when none of your buttons was missing I knew it could only have come from one of her husband's uniforms, which would have been there in the bedroom closet."

"She was a brave woman," Captain Rolph said. "We owe her our freedom, our lives."

Benedict Arnold's raid on New London was the last battle of the war in the north. It did not deter Washington from his march to Virginia, where he trapped Cornwallis at Yorktown. Just six weeks after New London, Cornwallis laid down his arms and surrendered an army of seven thousand British troops. Perhaps he had heard about Colonel Ledyard's sword. When the moment came to surrender his own sword to General Washington, Cornwallis pleaded illness and sent an aide with the sword instead. It was accepted and then immediately returned.

Although the official treaty of independence was still two years off, the American Revolution had ended. Somehow, though, Alexander Swift felt he had not yet seen the end of Benedict Arnold.

ST. JOHN AND THE DRAGON

The years following the conclusion of the Revolutionary War had been good ones for Alexander Swift. His former wife had remarried for a second time in New York City, and Swift himself had finally married Molly McVey in a joyous ceremony at West Point. Their first son had been born a year later. He had remained close to General Washington, and in 1785, when Washington was named president of the Potomac Navigation Company, he'd hired Swift as one of his assistants.

The company had been chartered by Virginia and Maryland to build a canal and road system linking the Potomac and Ohio rivers, but it soon became clear to Swift that his duties extended well beyond this. His special assignments for the General were to continue. Thus it was not surprising that in the summer of 1787 Washington summoned him into the State House in Philadelphia, where the new nation's constitutional convention had begun. It was a hot and humid summer in the city and he arrived for his appointment in time to see Benjamin Franklin, age 81 and president of Pennsylvania's Supreme Executive Council being carried in a sedan chair borne by trustee convicts. A crowd of spectators cheered his arrival and Swift slipped unnoticed into the building.

George Washington was awaiting his arrival in a second-floor office. "It is good to see you again, Alex."

"And you, too, General."

"I had feared you might grow fat and lazy at that desk job with the Potomac."

"They keep me busy, sir."

"Good, good." He cleared his throat, getting to the point of the meeting. "Alex, I want you to go to Canada for me."

"Certainly, General. What is the purpose of my mission?"

"Our old nemesis Benedict Arnold is back on this side of the ocean."

Following the British surrender at Yorktown, Arnold had fled to England, where his wife, Peggy, had joined him soon thereafter. Swift heard that they had two children now, and that Arnold had pleaded with George III to be placed in command of an army to retake the colonies. The king had finally agreed, but Parliament wanted no part of it and the idea died.

"He's in Canada?"

Washington nodded. "He and his family are in St. John, a thriving community in New Brunswick, not sixty miles across the border from the Maine territory claimed by Massachusetts. Following the British surrender, thousands of Loyalists fled to St. John. Its population increased so quickly that it has been incorporated as Canada's first city. Now Arnold has gone there to open a trading post. Somehow I cannot imagine that scoundrel engaged in a legitimate enterprise. He is up to something, and we must know what it is."

Swift nodded. "I will do what I can to find out," he promised. That night, when he told Molly that Washington was sending him on a special assignment to Canada, she looked unhappy. "I thought the war was over, Alex."

"So did I."

Swift allowed his beard to grow for a few days, hoping it would alter his appearance somewhat. Then, carrying a minimum of supplies in a saddlebag, he traveled on foot through the Maine woods to the vaguely defined border with Canada. He camped out for one night under a starry sky planning to complete his journey the following day. In the morning he came to a dirt road which according to Washington's careful instructions, should lead him into St. John.

Before long he was lucky to encounter a farmer bringing a load of corn to market in his wagon. "Need a ride, mister?" he called down as he was passing Swift.

"I could use one. You heading for St. John?"

"Sure am!" He held out his hand to help Swift up. "I'm Richard Hanson."

"Alex Smith. Glad to meet you."

Hanson was a handsome young man, barely past thirty, dressed in farm clothes with pants tucked into his boots. An old straw hat shielded his face from the sun, but Swift could see that it was already taking on a weathered look. "You looking for work?"

"I am. Know of any?"

"Nothing special, but St. John is growing since it became a city. Lots of new businesses and new people. I work the farm with the wife and kids, and we can hardly keep up with the demand."

They topped a rise and the tall masts of distant sailing ships came into view. "It looks as if they've got quite a port there."

"The Bay of Fundy is one of the best in the world, but the sailors say it's a treacherous one. Because of the way the channels funnel water into the harbor, they have tremendous tides, sometimes forty feet or more in the spring. I've talked with ships' captains who've never seen anything like it."

"Isn't it dangerous for the ships at anchor?"

"The bay is deep enough for safety, so long as they're careful. But those tides are something to face twice a day. They have a sea wall to protect against storm surges. As if that wasn't enough, these last two months there have been reports of a sea serpent or dragon in the bay."

"Really?"

"Well, only a few sailors have seen it, usually after a night of drinking in the taverns. I haven't been convinced."

They were coming into the city itself, and Hanson pulled on the reins to slow the horses down a bit. There were rows of wooden or stone buildings on either side of the road, one or two stories high, and further along Swift could see the steeples of three churches towering over them. Their wagon crossed a bridge over a narrow strait and they entered the main shopping area close to a public market that was Hanson's destination.

"You will notice the water on two sides of us," the farmer said. "The city could be well defended against attack from the former colonies. Perhaps that is one reason so many Loyalists fled here." He brought the wagon to a stop. "Shall I drop you here at the dock? The ships are often hiring crewmen for the return voyage to England."

Swift shrugged. "This is as good a place as any. Tell me, is there a nearby inn where I could stay?"

"The *Schooner*, just down the road. See Juliette and tell her I sent you. I deliver fresh eggs from the farm every morning and that is one of my stops."

"What about jobs here in the city? There must be some trading companies with all this shipping activity."

"You see that new warehouse up on the hill? A man named Arnold just built it this spring. He came from London but he talks like you. It's the West Indies Trading Company. He might need help."

Swift thanked him and jumped down from the wagon. Hanson backed into position at the market and began to unload his corn.

Walking along the harbor road, past the tall ships at the end of their long piers, Swift wondered what had attracted Benedict Arnold to a place like this. Could he hope to organize these Loyalists from the colonies for an invasion? Halfway down the block he stopped in a general store that seemed to sell everything from cheesecloth to muskets. He was buying some tobacco when he heard a half-remembered feminine voice telling a clerk, "You do not need to wrap it. My driver will carry it to the carriage."

It was a voice he could never forget. Peggy Shippen. Peggy Arnold. The traitor's wife.

Alexander Swift retreated quickly from the store before she saw him. He took up a position across the road and watched while a slim man with a stringy black beard carried her purchases to a waiting carriage. Then Peggy appeared, looking as attractive as he remembered her, but with her hair cut shorter. How old would she be now? Twenty-six? The driver helped her into the carriage. "Thank you, Pierre," she told him, and they rode off.

Watching her like that, he remembered her wedding day in Philadelphia on the verge of her eighteenth birthday. He'd been there as General Washington's representative, and a joyous occasion it had been. Now so much had changed for them all. He walked along quickly after the carriage, watching it turn up the hill toward the trading company. A man came out to greet them, walking with a limp and even at that distance he recognized Benedict Arnold.

Still carrying his possessions in the saddlebag, Swift thought about renting a horse but decided he probably wouldn't need one. Instead he walked back in the other direction until he found the *Schooner Inn*. It was a two-story gabled house with a little porch overlooking the harbor. He went in and found an attractive young woman in a gray blouse and long skirt working at a desk before a painting of a schooner under full sail.

She greeted him with a smile and a distinct French accent. "Hello. May I help you?"

"I am looking for a place to stay. Mr. Hanson suggested I try here."

"Richard, yes! I know him very well. He delivers our eggs. How long would you be staying?"

"A few days, maybe more."

"I will need three nights in advance. Here's your key. Room number six at the top of the stairs. I serve breakfast in the morning. When you go out, leave the key at my desk."

"Do you work day and night?"

"One of our guests, Mrs. Meadows, helps me out in the evening. I'm usually here the rest of the time if you need anything. My name is Juliette." She glanced at the saddlebag he was carrying. "Do you have a horse?"

"I had to sell it. I thought of renting one but decided I should get a job first. If I end up on a sailing ship a horse would not be of much use."

"True enough."

The room was clean and pleasant enough, with a soft bed, a pitcher and bowl, and a commode in one corner. The window provided an excellent view of the harbor, though Arnold's warehouse was just out of sight. He unpacked his saddlebag, washed up, and went back downstairs. It was almost time for supper.

"Enjoy your stay," Juliette told him.

"I hope to. Do you run this place all by yourself?"

She nodded. "My father died two years ago and left it to my brother and me. We could have sold it, but I wanted an adventure so I moved here from Montreal. He's still there."

"Someone told me there's been a sea serpent or something like it in the harbor recently."

She laughed. "Seen only by sailors at midnight after too much beer and rum. You have nothing to fear."

"It's safe for swimming, then?"

"So long as you're aware of the tides. They turn very swiftly here. One of our new arrivals, Mrs. Arnold, swims frequently. She even had a bathing-machine sent from England."

He filed that fact away for later. "Is her husband the man with the trading post on the hill?"

"Yes. I know little about them, but they have two lovely children."

At the door he thought of one more question. "Where is a good place to eat?"

"The *Fundy Tavern*, about a mile down the road."

"I will try it on your recommendation," he told her with a smile.

The *Fundy* was in a row of bars and taverns facing the docks and obviously popular with seamen. One of the ships, a brigantine named *King George II*, was newly arrived in port and was still being unloaded of its cargo. Swift found a table and ordered a fish dinner from the menu board.

Presently a bearded seaman joined him. "Mind if I eat with you, laddie?"

"Not at all. Sit down."

The man was about Swift's age, with powerful muscles and a sailor's weathered face. "Name is Cotton Wayne," he said, extending his hand.

"Alex Smith. Are you off one of the ships?"

The seaman nodded. "The *George*, that brigantine. Just made port today."

"This seems like a busy place."

Wayne nodded. "It is. More cargo coming in than going out, though. Mostly machinery from England. This is my third trip since winter. These folks need everything. On the last trip we even sold some of our lead ballast."

"Have you seen the dragon that's supposed to be in the harbor?"

"That devil tide is enough of a dragon for me."

They chatted about England and the sea, and after a leisurely supper that lasted until dark Swift suggested they walk down the sea wall steps to the beach. "How far up does the water come?" he wanted to know.

"All the way to this sea wall at high tide."

They were on a direct line with Arnold's warehouse up the hill. Ahead of them in the surf, bathed in the light of a nearly full moon, Swift could see a wooden structure that looked for all the world like an outhouse on wheels. "What is that?" he asked.

"A bathing-machine. They're popular on English beaches but you don't often see them over here. A woman had that shipped over this summer. They can change their clothes in there and step directly into the water without being seen in their swimming attire. It's rolled down and positioned wherever you want it."

He remembered Juliette mentioning that Peggy Arnold had one. Obviously this was it. The evening tide was rising fast and Swift stopped to remove his boots before wading out for a look at the front of the structure. It had a new wide door in place, firmly closed with a heavy padlock.

They strolled back to the harbor road and parted. He noticed that Wayne headed for the next tavern down the line, but Swift didn't join him. There was too much to think about.

He was starting back up the road to the *Schooner Inn* when someone stepped out of the shadows to intercept him. He froze when he recognized Peggy Arnold's carriage driver. "You're new around here."

"I'm passing through. Name's Alex Smith. Who are you?"

"Pierre," the slim man replied. "I heard you in the *Fundy* earlier, asking about the dragon."

"Are the stories true?"

"True enough. He's out there."

"I would like to see this dragon or serpent or whatever he is.

Pierre eyed him slyly. "For ten pounds I would show him to you."

"Ten pounds is a great deal of money. Let me think about it. Where can I find you?"

"I usually eat supper at the Fundy."

"Very well. I might take up your offer when I get some money."

Pierre slouched off into the night and Swift continued on his way. As he reached the stone walk leading into the *Schooner Inn* he saw Juliette coming out, her long skirt sweeping the ground. "Good evening, Mr. Smith."

"Good evening. Are you going out this late?"

"Only for my nightly walk on the beach. I like to see the tide rush in, and feel my toes in the sand."

"It sounds ideal. May I join you?"

She smiled sadly. "I'm afraid not. I really treasure this time alone every evening. But Mrs. Meadows is inside. She'll give you your key."

He entered the inn to be greeted by a pleasant white-haired woman who reminded him just a bit of General Washington's wife, Martha. "Good evening, I'm Mrs. Meadows. Are you a guest here?"

Swift nodded. "Alex Smith, room six."

She handed him the key. "Have a pleasant night."

Upstairs, gazing at the harbor, he could just make out Juliette's tall figure striding across the sand as the tide rushed in.

In the morning he was awakened early by sounds of conversation at the foot of the stairs. When he went down he found Juliette in excited conversation with Hanson, the egg farmer, and Mrs. Meadows. "I saw the dragon last night," she told Swift. "It was right off-shore in the moonlight. I wouldn't have believed it!"

"What did it look like?"

"The head wasn't too large and it was close not the water, covered with waves much of the time. What I saw of it I could not be a sure of the color, but it might have been dark green. I watched it for a minute or two and then it disappeared."

"And you hadn't been drinking?" Hanson asked with a smile.

She shifted his basket of eggs as if she might throw one at him. "I hadn't a drop. Mr. Smith saw me leaving on his way in. He will vouch for my sobriety."

"I do," Swift answered sincerely.

"Then it seems we have a real witness to the dragon at last." Hanson scratched his head. "What do we do now? Organize the townspeople to go hunting for it?"

"First we have breakfast," Juliette announced, holding up the fresh eggs. Hanson went on to make the rest of his deliveries and Swift accompanied

Mrs. Meadows into the little dining room. She proved to be an interesting breakfast companion, telling him of her younger days accompanying her late husband on fur-trading journeys among the Eskimos.

After breakfast he walked down to the docks and watched the ships taking on cargo for their return voyages. Then he walked a few blocks away from the harbor and circled around the back of Arnold's warehouse. There was no great activity, and only a few men were visible. He saw no sign of Peggy's carriage or her driver. In the afternoon he boarded a couple of the ships, going through the motions of seeking employment, always making sure no one would really hire him.

That evening he dined again with Cotton Wayne, who was disturbed that their return trip would be delayed while they awaited a cargo of lumber that hadn't yet arrived. "The woman at the *Schooner Inn* saw the dragon last night," Swift told him at one point.

"I heard that. I suppose something must be out there."

"Do you think it's really a dragon?"

The seaman shrugged. "With these tides, most anything could get swept into the Bay of Fundy from the deepest parts of the ocean."

There was no sign of Pierre at the tavern that night. Later, when Wayne had departed, Swift made his way down the sea wall steps to the damp sand. As the rising tide drew closer he stood in the darkness against the wall and watched for the dragon. It never came, nor did anyone else. From time to time he could hear people on the road above him on the lookout for it, too, but all were disappointed.

Swift watched the rising waters creep up the side of Peggy's bathing-machine until the whole thing was under water. He was forced to retreat a bit up the stone steps as the tide lapped at his boots. He stayed until midnight, when the tide began retreating as quickly as it had come. There was no dragon tonight.

He went back to his room, accepting the key from a drowsy Mrs. Meadows.

This time it was her scream that awakened him. He was surprised to see that it was already dawn, that he had slept some five hours. He hurried to the top of the stairs and called down. "What happened?"

It was the farmer Hanson but he had no eggs in his hand. "I was starting my deliveries and I saw something out by the water. I stopped my wagon and ran down to have a look. It was Juliette. She's dead! She's been cut and clawed by something."

Swift dressed quickly and followed him out of the inn, hurrying along the sea wall to the nearest steps. The morning tide was beginning to turn, gathering power for its assault on the beach. Mrs. Meadows had composed herself enough to follow, and some of the early-rising sailors were about, too. He saw Cotton Wayne observing them from the top of the sea wall before starting down. Already they could make out the body in the shallow water, turned slowly as the incoming waves lapped at it.

Swift came upon Hanson's footprints, firmly embedded in the damp sand, and followed them straight to the body. The tracks stopped a few feet away and then started back. Ignoring the water, Swift gripped the body under the arms and pulled it up away from the waves. He uncovered Juliette's torso and legs, revealing the wounds Hanson had described. There were gouges and cuts, and three parallel red lines that looked like claw marks. He guessed she had been dead for some hours. "The dragon!" someone in the gathering crowd said with a gasp. Perhaps the worst thing for Swift was the stray band of seaweed entangled in her toes, a touch that seemed out of place on a corpse. He glanced around in the water, searching for clues, but found nothing.

The city constable was informed, and within an hour the body had been removed. A watchman was assigned to keep a lookout for the dragon and sound an alarm if it was seen. "She shouldn't have gone out there again," Hanson said as he and Swift walked back to his wagon and its patient horses. He sorted through the baskets of eggs, tossing aside a rusty rake and a pair of shoes. "Would you like some eggs?" Hanson asked. "I doubt if Mrs. Meadows will be preparing breakfast."

"No, thanks. I will get something at one of the taverns." Swift noticed a small barrel in the back of the wagon with everything else. "What's that?"

"Gunpowder," Hanson replied. "I use it to blast out tree stumps on the farm."

"Where do you buy it?"

"At the general store, along with everything else. If you ever try using any, though, be sure you have a long fuse. It can be very dangerous."

The farmer went on his way. Swift ate breakfast alone, trying not to think of Juliette's dead body and what he had done wrong. Might she still have been alive if he hadn't come to St John?

Then he spotted Pierre, passing by the window of the tavern. He abandoned the remains of his breakfast and ran out after the slim man. "Pierre!"

Peggy's carriage driver turned, seeming not to recognize Swift for a moment. Then he asked, "What do you want?"

"To see the dragon. I have the ten pounds."

"Things have happened. It may be too late now."

"I have twenty pounds. Ten now and another ten when you take me there."

He thought about it, then said, "Not now. Maybe tonight."

"Where and when?"

"The sea wall steps on this end. Nine o'clock, just after dark."

"I'll be there."

"Give me ten now."

Swift handed him the currency, wondering if he'd ever see the man again. Men like Pierre had been known to do crazy things with that much money. His only hope was that the second ten would prove even more tempting.

Next he went to the general store, where he made some purchases. He spent the afternoon in his room, writing out a detailed report to General Washington, telling him everything he'd found and just what it meant. If something happened to him, he hoped this report might find its way back to Philadelphia.

That evening he ate another meal at the *Fundy*, then walked around a bit until it was time to meet Pierre at the top of the steps at nine o'clock. "This can be very dangerous," the slim man told him. "Give me the other ten pounds."

"Here." Swift passed it over.

"Come quickly, but first take off your boots. We will have to wade in the surf."

Swift did as he was told and then followed the man across the damp sand. Once more the tide was turning, rising so quickly that removing his boots and rolling up his pant legs did little good. Pierre was headed for the bathing-machine, and by the time they reached it the tide was up to their thighs.

"In here," he said, directing Swift to the door of the little structure. Swift went up the three wooden steps, noticed the padlock was off the door, and opened it.

There was the dragon, as promised. It was a large egg-shaped device made of oak staves reinforced with iron bands, filling the entire inside of the bathing-machine. On its top had been affixed the carefully carved wooden head of a dragon, painted sea-green. Around its base, lead ballast had been piled to keep the structure from rising with the tide.

Suddenly Pierre's hands collided with his back, sending him toppling forward. He hit against the wooden egg just as the man slammed the door shut. Swift heard the padlock snap closed. "Pierre! What is this? Open up!"

"With the compliments of Benedict Arnold!" the man shouted through the door "Enjoy your last minutes on earth. The bathing-machine will be completely under the tidal water in less than a half-hour."

Then there was silence, except for the increased pounding of the surf. Swift hit the door with his shoulder but it didn't budge. He remembered it was new, of a special width to allow the Dragon inside. He felt dampness on his feet and saw that the water was rising through the cracks between the floorboards. Picking up the oil lamp, he held it to the ceiling. The wood charred a bit but was too saturated with water to catch fire.

All right, he thought calmly. There is a way out of this.

This Dragon was merely a British copy of the *Turtle*, the one-man submarine he'd once piloted around New York Harbor when the British were in command of the city. He was not surprised that they were experimenting with it, and that Benedict Arnold had brought it here to St. John for testing. Certainly the enormous tidal changes in the Bay of Fundy made it the perfect place to test an underwater craft.

He'd suspected something like this ever since the seaman Cotton Wayne told him of someone buying the lead ballast from one of the sailing ships. Lead ballast was necessary for submarines, and the bathing-machine itself needed it to keep from floating off while the Dragon was out in the open water. Swift had watched that bathing-machine remain steady the previous night as the tidal water rose above it, and he knew then that it must contain something heavy.

But now it was time for action. The carved dragon's head on top of the submarine, no doubt put there to frighten or mislead anyone who saw it in the water, could be his salvation. In earlier days, when armies used battering rams against fortified positions, there was sometimes an actual ram's head carved onto the business end of the device. He was hoping the dragon's head would serve the same purpose, and he was about to find out. The water was almost to his waist.

Quickly he opened the hatch of the one-man submarine climbed inside with the lamp, and closed it against the rising water. It was a tighter fit than the American original but he was relieved to find that the controls were very similar to the *Turtle* built by David Bushnell. He could only imagine what harm the British could do to the fledgling American navy with a fleet of these, traveling underwater to attach explosive charges to the hulls of ships.

As with the *Turtle*, lateral and vertical screw propellers, operated by hand, propelled the Dragon. There was also a hand-operated rudder, and small portholes near the top of the vessel. A valve was opened to admit sea water into a ballast tank causing the craft to sink. When raising it, the ballast tank was emptied with a hand pump. Lead ballast in the bottom kept it upright. Swift knew the closed compartment held only enough oxygen for about thirty minutes, though there was also a breathing tube for when the craft was close to the surface.

He waited until the water level rose well above the Dragon's portholes and opened the valve to admit the sea water. Then he closed it and started working the hand pump as fast as he could. He quickly realized that his vision of the dragon's head battering through the roof of the bathing-machine was a futile one. The submarine rose slowly, but with virtually no force at all. It nudged the wooden roof and rested there. He took it down for one more try, trying not to panic.

This time the underwater craft rose a bit faster. It hit the roof with more force and the wood separated into two parts on hinges that swung open to the night sky. Of course! They couldn't take it out the door every time they wanted to test it. The operator simply sat in the Dragon until the tide was high enough and then rose right through the roof of the bathing-machine. That was why they'd needed the ballast to keep the bathing-machine in one place, so the submarine could return the same way.

The strong tidal waters were tossing the Dragon around a bit, and he was anxious to settle down in one piece. Working the screw propellers he headed for shallow water, finally settling down safely in the shadow of some rocks where the Dragon could pass unnoticed for a time. He climbed out and hurried to an outcropping in the sea wall where he'd hidden the supplies he bought earlier.

The barrel of gunpowder went into the Dragon, with the long fuse Hanson had recommended. He lit the fuse and hurried up the sea wall steps to the road. Pierre was having a casual drink at the *Fundy* bar with a couple of seamen. The color drained from his face when Swift walked in.

His hand grabbed the neck of a bottle, but Swift was faster. His left fist drove deep into Pierre's gut, and when the man doubled over Swift floored him with a right uppercut. Just then the sound of the explosion reached their ears. Pierre, still groggy, rolled over on the floor. "What was that?"

"The demise of your Dragon. I was told to use a long fuse."

Swift didn't know exactly what to expect the following morning at the *Schooner Inn*. He'd been awake much of the night, seated in a chair facing the door waiting for Pierre or perhaps Benedict Arnold himself to walk through it. When neither one had come by dawn, he washed and changed his clothes, preparing to leave after breakfast. Downstairs he found Mrs. Meadows very much in charge, whipping up eggs with the help of the farmer Hanson.

"I have written to Juliette's brother," she explained, "telling him I will keep the inn open until he arrives. That is the least I can do for the poor man."

Alexander Swift nodded. The time was not yet right to say any more. Instead he turned to Hanson. "Will you be heading back to your farm after breakfast?"

"I will. All the eggs are delivered."

"I am returning to Maine," Swift told him. "I'll ride with you that far."

But before he could leave, Mrs. Meadows brought him word that a young woman had arrived alone in a carriage to see him. Puzzled as to who it could be, Swift walked out to the entrance hall.

And faced Peggy Arnold.

"Hello, Alex," she said.

"Peggy! It's been many years—"

"I recognized you at the store the other day. I had to tell my husband."

"He sent Pierre to kill me last night."

"I didn't know that until later. I did not want this, any of it. But he is my husband. Pierre came with us from England. He has been testing the Dragon in the tidal waters two or three nights each week."

"Why did you come here this morning?"

"When you blew up the submarine last night it infuriated Benedict. He has ordered Pierre to kill you at any cost."

"You do not owe me a warning."

"Not you personally, perhaps, but I know you come here on behalf of General Washington. My home is in England now, and I will never return to America. But I owe something to my homeland. Leave St. John at once, and may God bless your new nation."

"Thank you, Peggy."

Within a half-hour he was on the road with Hanson heading home. The morning sky was bright, with a refreshing breeze off the bay. "We have had a nice summer," the farmer said. "But for Juliette's tragic death, it would have been a perfect summer."

"I have to ask you about that, Hanson."

"Ask me?"

"Why did you kill her?"

"I didn't! It was that man Pierre, wasn't it?"

"It was you," Swift insisted. "It couldn't have been anyone else. You see, Juliette claimed she went walking along the beach every evening. On the night she was killed I was down there until mid-night. She never came. You said you spotted her body in the morning and ran out to it. But your footprints were firm and deep in the sand, not running footprints at all. The prints stopped a few feet from the body, yet you described her wounds—wounds I couldn't even see until I had uncovered her. Later, when you were rearranging the eggs in the back of this wagon, I saw a rake with what appeared to be rust spots on it. I now think that was dried blood, and that the rake made those clawlike scratches on her side. There was a pair of shoes back there, too. You wear boots, but Juliette was barefoot when we found her body. I remember the seaweed on her toes, and there was no sign of her shoes or anything else near the body. Those shoes were hers, weren't they? She was with you in this wagon when she was supposed to be walking on the beach. You killed her here, then used the rake to simulate claw marks. It was her sighting of the supposed dragon that gave you the idea. You carried the body down there after midnight, choosing a route where the retreating tide would wash away your prints. Yesterday morning when you came in with your eggs, the body was still out there so you walked down and pretended to find it."

Hanson was silent for a full minute. When he finally spoke, it was almost to himself. "I have a wife and family who love me. I must have been mad to get involved with Juliette. And then I couldn't break it off. I knew that as long as she was alive I could never stay away from her."

"You killed her because you loved her?"

"Because I loved her too much. I strangled her, and then made the cuts on her body, hoping that sea creature would be blamed."

While they talked, a rider had overtaken the wagon. Swift saw that it was Pierre, come to fulfill Arnold's orders. "Stop the wagon!" he shouted. "I only want the American."

As Hanson slowed the wagon to a stop, Pierre drew a flintlock pistol from his belt and aimed it at Swift. That was when Hanson acted. For a reason Swift would never fully understand, he threw himself off the wagon seat and onto Pierre just as the pistol fired. Both men hit the ground together, grappling for the gun. Hanson wrenched it away from Pierre and brought it down hard on the bearded man's head. Pierre sagged to one side and didn't move. Only then did Swift realize that the man's single shot had hit Hanson in the chest.

He knelt over the dying farmer, unable to stanch the flow of blood from his wound. "Pierre is dead," he said. "You saved my life."

"Don't—" Hanson gasped. "Don't tell my wife about—"

"I won't," Swift promised.

The city constable was not one to ask too many questions. He recorded the incident as an attempted robbery, and neither Arnold nor Peggy disputed that. When Alexander Swift left St. John for the second time, after attending Hanson's funeral with his widow and children, Arnold was nowhere to be seen.

A few years later Swift learned that Arnold's warehouse had been destroyed in a mysterious fire. He and his family returned to England. By that time George Washington had taken office as the new nation's first president. Swift asked him about the fire once, but Washington only smiled and said nothing.

CONSTANT HEARSES

During George Washington's second term as President of the United States, it was not uncommon for Alexander Swift to visit him at Mount Vernon. The plantation, situated atop a hill overlooking the Potomac River, was always a lively place. On this sunny afternoon in late October of 1793, he found the President on the second floor of his round barn where horses sometimes walked in circles, threshing wheat.

"Isn't it a bit late in the season for threshing, Mr. President?" he asked.

"Alex! How good it is to see you! Stay by the stairs. I'm coming right down." When they reached the barn's main floor, he answered Swift's question. "The threshing season is over, but there is always the cleanup in preparation for winter. Tell me, how goes progress on the Patowmack Canal?"

In the years following the Revolution, Washington had become president of the Potomac Navigation Company, hiring Swift as one of his assistants. After his election to the highest office in the new nation, Washington had resigned from the canal company, but Swift stayed on. He lived with his wife Molly and their eight-year-old son in Maryland. President Washington still took an interest in the canal company and asked about its progress whenever they were together.

"Progress is slow," he admitted, "but we're coming along."

"Will I live to see it completed?"

"I don't know that either of us will," Swift answered with a smile. "But we're certainly trying. I hope our new capital in the District of Columbia is finished sooner than the canal."

"I hope so, too. I laid the cornerstone for the Capitol building on a sunny day a few weeks ago, but the President's House still has only a foundation. I will never live there."

"If you are elected to a third term . . ."

Washington held up his hand. "No, no! Tell me, how are Molly and George?"

"Fine, sir, both of them." Washington had been especially pleased when they named their son after him.

The President turned serious as they walked toward the house. "I have summoned you here on an important matter."

"Not Benedict Arnold again?"

"Not directly, though there may be some connection. He's back in London with his family, and not faring too well, from what I hear. There is, at the moment, a much more immediate problem. I'm sure you are aware of what is happening in Philadelphia."

"The plague of yellow fever? The newspaper accounts are terrible."

Washington nodded. "It started among the sailors and grog sellers on the waterfront back in August. Poor Hamilton almost died of it, and many in the government are stricken. When I agreed to move the capital from New York to Philadelphia, I never dreamed of anything like this happening. I left the city as planned on September tenth, to spend time here until Congress reconvenes on December second. Now I am seriously considering moving the session to Germantown or some other location. Alex, we have nearly five thousand known dead in a city of fifty-five thousand. And they died a horrible death, with that yellowish skin color and black vomit. I saw many of them myself before I came here in September."

They'd entered the big house and Martha Washington greeted Swift warmly. She was a small woman, barely five feet tall with dark hair and a gentle manner. "It is good to see you again, Alex," she said, inquiring about his wife and son.

"Patsy," Washington asked, for that was what he caller her, "could Joshua bring us some tea on the back porch?"

"I'll see to it at once."

Seated next to the President in one of the rocking chairs overlooking the Potomac, Swift felt at peace with the world. He knew however, that the President had summoned him for a serious purpose. "I want to help however I can, sir, but of course I am not a medical man. I know nothing of the disease or how it is spread."

"Nor does anyone else, although there is a feeling that the French colonists who fled Haiti in late July might have brought it with them to our shores. Certainly it has been a bad summer in our nation's capital. Philadelphia has been hotter, drier, and dustier than anyone can remember, with an amazing number of flies and mosquitos adding to the discomfort. Only now is there some relief with the coming of a light frost, but still the death toll from the fever climbs." He was silent for a moment, and then added, "One of our Pennsylvania congressmen died of it just two weeks ago."

"Who would that be?"

"Clayton Emory. Did you know him?"

"I don't believe so."

Washington sighed. "Here is the problem, Swift, and what I am about to tell you must go no further."

"Certainly not."

"Emory was fifty-eight years old and a widower. He lived alone in a small row house that was filled with papers from his military service and from various positions he held in the colonial government. Last week, when members of his family started to clean the house out, they made a surprising discovery in one of the boxes—a large quantity of British currency, all in five-pound notes drawn on the Bank of England."

"How much is a large quantity?"

"Seventy-eight envelopes of one hundred notes each. Thirty-nine thousand pounds in all."

"That's a great deal of money."

"A small fortune," Washington agreed. "I take only twenty-five thousand dollars a year, hardly enough for the expenses incurred while serving as President. That is a bit over six thousand pounds. The money hidden in Emory's house is more than I will collect during my first six years in office."

"Are these banknotes still legal currency?"

"They are in England."

"Where did they come from?" Swift asked, taking a sip of tea.

"I want you to find out. The family notified the Treasury Department of their find, and with Hamilton still in a weakened condition I was contacted directly by post."

"You mentioned this might involve Benedict Arnold indirectly. What did you mean by that?"

Washington closed his eyes for a moment, then said, "Before West Point, when Arnold was still military governor of Philadelphia, Emory served under him, I ask myself if it is possible Emory, too, was a traitor, receiving money from Arnold."

Swift sat up straighter in his chair. "Do you believe that?"

"No, not really. But I want you to find a better explanation for me. What was he doing with all that hidden British currency, twelve years after the war ended?"

It was Alexander Swift's first visit to the new nation's capital since Washington's reelection to a second term. With construction in the District of Columbia moving slowly, the President and Congress would have to endure Philadelphia for another few years. Right now, with the yellow fever still raging and the city's streets almost empty, Swift felt a chill of apprehension. He was aware that until recently even some post riders refused to enter the city. He'd faced death many times, during the Revolution and after, but always from a human foe.

Washington had suggested he go first to the dead man's home, one of the row houses along Chestnut Street, not far from City Hall and the State House, and within blocks of the President's own residence. When he reached the house, he noticed a handbill affixed to a tree near the street. It was a poem titled "Pestilence," and had been written by Philip Freneau, editor of the *National Gazette*. The first stanza read:

Hot, dry winds forever blowing,
Dead men to the grave-yards going:
    Constant hearses,
    Funeral verses;
Oh! What plagues–there is no knowing!

As he read through the rest of it, a wagon trundled by. From the stench of it, he knew there were bodies beneath the canvas covering. Constant hearses, indeed.

Tying his horse to a hitching post, he rapped smartly on the closed door. After a few moments it was opened by a young woman who wore a gauze scarf across her mouth and nose. "There has been death here," she told him. "You'd best be gone."

Quickly he introduced himself. "I am Alexander Swift, sent here as a special representative of President Washington."

"Oh!" She stepped aside. "Come in, then, if you dare. The yellow-fever germs might still be loose. We don't know how it's spread."

"You are . . . ?"

"Oh, sorry! I'm Amanda Emory, the congressman's granddaughter. Here, wrap this gauze around your face. It might offer some protection."

She was a pert young woman with blond curls, perhaps still in her late teens. He took the gauze as she had instructed, though he doubted that it offered much in the way of protection. "I didn't realize he had a granddaughter this grown up. Your father must be Jonathan Emory."

"Yes, he is. He, too, had the fever, but he is resting now and seems better."

"It was you who found the hidden money?"

She nodded. He followed her into the small bedroom at the rear of the house. Wooden boxes full of papers were stacked on the floor, apparently in an attempt to organize them for ultimate removal. While she showed him the closet he started to sit on the dead man's bed and then thought better of it. The bedclothes had been removed, but the mattress was old and soiled with the scent of death. "It was right here, in this box. My father was very ill at the time and I could not ask him what to do."

"Who is your family doctor?"

"It was Dr. Shippen until he fled the city at the end of August," she replied with a trace of bitterness in her voice. "He was one of the best doctors at Pennsylvania Hospital. Since my grandfather fell ill in mid-October we've had Dr. Bradley."

Swift nodded. Benedict Arnold's wife was Peggy Shippen. Her father was a judge and the doctor was a cousin. Swift remembered him faintly from Arnold's wedding, which he'd attended as Washington's representative. He would be in his late fifties now, and obviously not the bravest of men. "I've heard of Bradley," he told her. "I understand he's a good man."

"Not good enough to save my grandfather, but perhaps no one would have been. In those last days I was here as often as I could be, cleaning up his vomit, trying to make him as comfortable as possible. I pray Dr. Bradley can do better with my father's illness."

"You have no fear for yourself?"

"What good would it do? The fever is all around us, everywhere along the waterfront and in the eastern half of the city. You either flee or pray, those are the only two options."

"President Washington is concerned about the convening of Congress in a few weeks. It may be moved to Germantown."

"The frosts have helped a bit," she told him. "In a few weeks the worst might be over."

"I have heard the summer was bad."

She put a hand to her forehead. "The heat, the mosquitos everywhere, I don't know how anyone survived it. They have tried everything to stamp it out, even firing cannons in the streets of the city in the belief that gunpowder could combat the disease. There is little solace to be found, even in religion. All but one of our Catholic priests and many of our ministers have been infected themselves."

"Tell me about the money."

"My father was in no shape to clean out the house, and my mother has been tending to him night and day. I told them I would get a start on it, clearing out those boxes of old papers from his closet. It was there I found the five-pound notes, in seventy-eight envelopes. I brought my mother over the next morning to see them, and she was fearful we would be arrested if we did not report our discovery. Mother contacted a clerk at the Treasury Department, one of the few not suffering from the yellow fever, and brought the money to him."

Swift nodded. "With Secretary Hamilton still weak from the fever, President Washington was notified directly."

"I—I cannot believe my grandfather would be involved in anything criminal or treasonous."

"We have no reason to believe he was so involved," Swift replied, trying to reassure her. "You did the correct thing by turning in the money immediately, but now I must speak with your father. Is he well enough to receive me?"

"He seems better today. Let me close up here and I will take you to him."

The Emory house was but a few blocks away, on Ninth Street, and Swift walked there with Amanda Emory, leading his horse behind him. "The yellow fever has changed this city so much," she told him. "Sometimes we feel the rest of the nation has cut us off completely. People here stay indoors and avoid contact even with their closest neighbors. A man next-door to us died of the fever and was buried before we ever knew it. We only learned of my grandfather's death because Dr. Bradley had been calling on him daily and I always arranged to be there when he came, to let him in. That day we arrived together and went inside to find Grandfather dead."

At the Emory house they found that the doctor had arrived to minister to Amanda's father. Bradley was a slim man whose dour expression seemed to mirror the everyday horrors he was witnessing. "Jonathan is progressing well," he told Amanda, motioning toward her father, who was seated in a rocking chair with a pillow behind him. "I wish I could say the same for my other patients."

Alexander Swift introduced himself. "The President is especially interested in the death of Congressman Emory. Can you tell me anything about it, Doctor?"

"He lingered for weeks, which gave me some hope that we might save him. I visited daily, and the ladies looked after him in the evenings. When the end came, it surprised me by its suddenness."

"I was there during the day when the doctor came, and Mother and I went there at dinnertime, at least until my father, too, fell ill with the disease.

Then I went alone," Amanda explained. "It was terrible for Grandfather, being by himself overnight, but there was no space for him at Pennsylvania Hospital or anywhere else. We did the best we could."

Swift turned his attention to the dead man's son. "How are you coming along?"

Jonathan Emory, a man still in his late thirties, nodded and, gave a weak smile. "Better than my father, I hope. Abby and Amanda had me to nurse as well as him. But I will pull through. I know I will. Already there is talk that I may fill my father's congressional seat until next year's election."

"You must get back on your feet before you make any plans," the doctor told him, and his daughter quickly agreed.

Abby Emory came downstairs at that moment. "You should have told me we had a visitor, Amanda." Though probably still in her thirties, the woman was pale and gaunt.

"I am reluctant to intrude at such a time," Swift said. "President Washington is most concerned about the large quantity of banknotes found in Congressman Emory's home. Can any of you offer an explanation?"

"What's this?" Doctor Bradley asked.

"Nothing that need concern you," Abby Emory said. "Let me show you out, Doctor."

"I'm sorry," Swift apologized when the doctor had departed. "I assumed he knew about it."

Jonathan Emory sat up a bit straighter in his chair. "He is not the family friend that Dr. Shippen was. Unfortunately, Shippen fled the city at his first opportunity. Dr. Bradley took over his files and his patients. We must content ourselves with him. It is scandalous that so few doctors remained here after the outbreak."

"You all must know Dr. Shippen's relationship to the young Peggy Shippen who married the traitor Benedict Arnold. Some members of the Shippen family were Loyalists opposed to the Revolution. It is possible one of them, perhaps even Dr. Shippen himself, attempted to bribe the congressman."

"Impossible!" Jonathan Emory told him with a trace of anger in his voice. "No one was more loyal to the new nation than my father."

"Have you any other explanation for all this money in British currency?"

"No," he admitted, then turned to his wife. "Do you think Crouchman might know?"

"Well . . ." She hesitated, considering the idea.

"Who is Crouchman?" Swift asked.

"He was on Clayton's congressional staff," Abby Emory explained. "Houghton Crouchman. He used to call on him a few nights a week, even when Congress wasn't in session. But we've heard nothing from him since my father-in-law's death. We sent a message to him by runner and received no reply. For all we know he might be stricken with the yellow fever himself."

"Can you give me his address?"

She produced a number on Vine Street, some distance away. Swift took his leave, promising to inform them if he learned anything.

The ride to Vine Street was anything but pleasant. Whenever a wagon passed him bound for the cemetery, the odor from it made Swift's horse rear up in fright. Though the air was cooler and clearer now, the city was still awaiting the killing frost that everyone prayed would bring an end to the suffering. On Vine Street a few people were out, one woman in front of the house where Crouchman resided. When Swift asked after Congressman Emory's staff assistant, the woman informed him that Mrs. Crouchman had been a recent victim of the yellow fever and Crouchman himself had not been seen in a couple of days.

Swift went up the steps and tried the door. It was the sort that needed a key to lock or unlock it, but it swung open when he pressed down on the latch and pushed.

The inside parlor was neat and formal, as befitting a congressman's aide. "Mr. Crouchman," he called out, but no one answered. The house appeared to be empty. He made his way through the downstairs rooms and decided that Crouchman had probably fled the city following the death of his wife.

Still, there were some pieces of moldy bread on the kitchen table that did not jibe with the neatness in the other rooms. Swift doubted that Crouchman would have left it like this. He went out to the hall and climbed the stairs to the second floor. He saw at once that the master bedroom was occupied. A man was bundled up with blankets in the bed, his eyes closed. "Mr. Crouchman?" he said again.

As he moved closer to the bed he saw the yellow skin, and realized that the man was dead, struck down by the same terrible plague that had taken his wife. The bedclothes around his neck were dark with dried blood, Swift assumed it was from the hemorrhaging that often accompanied the disease, and he braced himself as he carefully lifted the blanket. Then he saw that Crouchman's throat had been savagely cut.

Someone had taken the trouble to murder a dying man.

Swift wanted desperately to relay the news to President Washington, but the mail out of the city was only just returning to some form of normalcy. For all he knew, the President might already be riding north to inspect Germantown as a possible site for the congressional session. He went instead to the high constable's office, identified himself as the President's representative, and reported the discovery of the slain man. He knew there was unlikely to be any sort of investigation. At a time when thousands were dying, little notice would be taken of a murder victim who would have died anyway in a matter of days.

Swift returned to the Emory household and told Jonathan, Abby, and their daughter Amanda what he'd discovered. He was a bit surprised to find Jonathan Emory out of his rocking chair and moving around the house. "I am feeling much better today," he said. "The worst of it seems to be over. But I cannot understand about poor Crouchman. He was not the sort to make enemies. Is there any possibility he killed himself in despair over his illness?"

Swift shook his head. "His arms were beneath the blanket, and there was no weapon. Someone did it to him, someone who couldn't risk letting the disease run its course."

"How long had he been dead?" Amanda asked.

"I'm not a good judge of that, but certainly no more than a couple of days. A neighbor saw him recently."

She let out her breath. "That's a relief."

He could almost read her thoughts. "You feared your grandfather might be somehow involved."

"The money. I don't know what to think." She shook her head as if trying to clear it. "Crouchman was on my grandfather's staff. If any money was given to him, Crouchman might have known about it."

"That's nonsense!" her father stormed. "Your grandfather never took a bribe from anyone! He was an honest man, one of our new nation's true patriots. You have to believe that, Mr. Swift."

"Still, Crouchman's death might well be linked to the money. Did your father have other staff members with whom I could speak?"

Emory exchanged glances with his wife, and it was she who answered. "There is no harm in saying it. Since his wife's death two years ago, Clayton has been friendly with a woman named Mrs. Langtree. So far as we know, they are good friends only. She is not a staff member, of course, but if you can find her you might speak with her."

"Do you think the money might have belonged to her?"

"I doubt it. Her husband was a minister before he died. It's not an occupation that brings in a great deal of money, certainly not in British pounds."

"Where might I find her?"

"We have no idea," her husband answered. "We haven't seen the woman in months."

"I heard she was helping out at the Pennsylvania Hospital," Amanda said.

Once again Swift ventured into the streets, as the sun began to dip low on the western horizon. The Pennsylvania Hospital was located on Eighth Street in a park area between Spruce and Pine. Usually peaceful, it had come to represent all the pain and hopelessness of the city. Since it was overcrowded, present inmates had to be protected by barring the admission of lonely or homeless people who had no one left to care for them. The blocks around the hospital were crowded with these poor souls. Some lay dying in doorways and alleys, without hope.

The man at the admissions desk told him that Mrs. Langtree was somewhere in the hospital, but he knew not where. It took Swift a half-hour to find her, ministering to plague-ridden children in one of the hospital wards. "My name is Alex Swift," he told her as she stood up at the sound of her name. "President Washington has asked me to look into the circumstances surrounding the unfortunate death of Congressman Emory."

She was an attractive woman in her forties, with bags under her eyes testifying to many sleepless nights tending the sick. "I can tell you as much about this poor child as I can about the congressman. The yellow fever is no respecter of age or class."

"You were friendly with him before he died?"

"Yes," she admitted. "We were two lonely people who enjoyed each other's company. There was nothing untoward about it."

"I'm sure not. Might I ask you about his finances? Did he have a quantity of cash on hand?"

She soothed the sick child's brow with a damp cloth, taking a moment before she answered. "I don't understand your question, Mr. Swift. Clayton was not a wealthy man. He'd had some business success in his younger days, but lately he was devoting himself to his duties in the Congress."

"Let me be frank with you, Mrs. Langtree. A quantity of British currency was found among his papers after his death. Did you have any knowledge of this?"

"Certainly not! If you are implying that he was somehow in league with the British Loyalists, you are quite mistaken. No one was more loyal to our new nation than Clayton."

"Might a member of his congressional staff, such as Houghton Crouchman, have knowledge of it?"

"I assure you there is nothing to have knowledge of! Certainly Crouchman was a valued assistant, and he called on Clayton during his illness. I understand he himself has now fallen ill with the disease."

"Worse than that. His body was found earlier this day."

She closed her eyes for a moment, perhaps in silent prayer. "Is there no end to this plague? Must it destroy our entire city?"

"Crouchman suffered from the yellow fever, but that was not what killed him. His throat was cut as he lay in his bed."

"Who would do such a ghastly thing?"

"I do not know," Swift admitted, "But my task is to find out. I know that some city residents do not bother to lock their doors at night. Was Crouchman one of those?"

"No. I visited him with Clayton on more than one occasion and his door was always locked."

"I understand that Dr. Shippen was Clayton's physician."

She nodded. "And Crouchman's, too, until the good doctor fled the city."

"What can you tell me about Shippen?"

The ill child had fallen into a peaceful sleep, and Mrs. Langtree felt she could leave him. "Let us walk for a bit, Mr. Swift, and I will tell you what little I know. Dr. Shippen is a highly regarded physician and medical educator. During the Revolution he was chief of the medical department of the Continental Army."

"A man beyond reproach until he fled the city in the face of the plague."

"Well, not quite beyond reproach. His predecessor in the position charged him with bad faith, and he was later court-martialed for financial irregularities in office. However, he was acquitted of the charges."

"Yet he tended to members of Congress?"

"There was no solid proof of wrongdoing against him, and he was always a good doctor."

"His cousin Peggy married Benedict Arnold."

"I know that. They are in England now."

"And Shippen fled the city in late August?"

"After a meeting of physicians on August twenty-fifth. He has not yet returned."

Swift was grateful for her help. "You have been of great assistance. Please continue with the fine work you're doing here."

"I am only trying to keep them alive."

Night had fallen on the plague-ridden city. Riding through the almost deserted streets, Swift could feel a decided chill in the air. There would be a frost this night, perhaps a killing one. It was hard for him to believe that he had been there only a single day, moving through these dangerous streets, encountering the healthy and the dying and the dead.

The hospital office had told him that Dr. Bradley had gone home for the night. When Swift showed his warrant from President Washington, they gave him the doctor's address. It proved to be a modest home on Beech Street, near the Schuylkill River and well away from the worst plague areas.

It was the doctor himself who answered the door, looking grim. "I have worked all day, sir. I cannot go on another call tonight, no matter the circumstances."

"We met earlier," Swift reminded him. "At the Emory house."

"Oh yes. Mr. Swift?"

"Alexander Swift. May I come in?"

"Certainly. I am alone here. My wife and children have been sent to the country until the plague passes. Please have a seat."

"I must tell you that another of your patients has succumbed, Houghton Crouchman, assistant to Congressman Emory."

"I am indeed sorry to hear that. He was a good man, as was Emory himself. May I offer you a bit of wine?"

"Thank you, no. I have come on a matter of government business."

"And what would that be?"

"The matter of seventy-eight envelopes of British currency found among the papers of the late Clayton Emory."

Dr. Bradley showed surprise. "Is that so? Where did they come from?"

"From the British, almost certainly. Otherwise the money would have been in some form of colonial or United States currency. But it was the number of separate envelopes that told me what I really wanted to know."

"Seventy-eight? What does that tell you?"

"Separate envelopes, separate payments. Seventy-eight payments of five hundred pounds each. Our Revolution began with the battles of Lexington and Concord, and Paul Revere's ride, in April, seventeen seventy-five. It ended, for all practical purposes, with Cornwallis's surrender at Yorktown in October of seventeen eighty-one, seventy-eight months later."

"The British were paying someone a monthly fee—"

"A large monthly fee, which ended only after the situation became hopeless with the surrender. An agent, a spy, a traitor, call him what you will."

"And this money went to Clayton Emory?"

Swift shook his head. "No, for two reasons. First, the British would hardly be paying that sort of money, month after month, to someone who was a mere private soldier in the Continental Army. And second, Emory was not in a position financially to merely let those envelopes pile up. He would have found a way to spend the money, at least in the beginning when Philadelphia was still in British hands."

"Then who did these payments go to?"

"Most likely it was Dr. Shippen. He held the important position of chief of the medical department with the Continental Army, he wouldn't have had to spend the money immediately because of his other income, and he came from a family of known Loyalists. He'd also been in trouble before, and was acquitted at a court-martial."

Dr. Bradley expressed puzzlement over that. "But if the money went to Shippen, how did it end up in Clayton Emory's closet?"

"I believe you put it there, Bradley, just as I believe you murdered Houghton Crouchman."

"That's insane!" the doctor sputtered.

"Is it? If we agree that Shippen received the money originally, someone had to take it to Emory's house, someone who knew he'd be too sick to go rummaging through his boxes and accidentally find it. Could it have been Shippen himself? No, because he fled from the city in late August, and Emory wasn't stricken with the fever until October. But who else might have come across the envelopes full of money, no doubt hidden somewhere in Shippen's own files? You, Dr. Bradley, who took over Shippen's files and patients after he fled. Once you'd discovered it, you surmised that the money was gained illicitly and determined to have it for yourself. When Shippen discovered it missing he could hardly report it to the authorities without implicating himself. Yet you couldn't take a chance on hiding it here, where some member of your family might discover it. So you took it, perhaps a dozen envelopes at a time, to Clayton Emory's home. You'd seen the boxes of papers stacked in his closet and you knew it was a perfect temporary hiding place. Even though his granddaughter was usually present when you called, it was easy enough to hide the envelopes while she was out of the room and Emory was dozing. Only he died unexpectedly. You told me yourself you were surprised by the suddenness of his death. You had no chance to remove the money when you and Amanda discovered his body, and soon after that she found the money herself. I had already deduced this much before you admitted a few minutes ago that you knew the money was in Emory's closet. The family hadn't mentioned the money's location in your presence. You could only have known because you put it there."

"What has any of this to do with Crouchman's killing?"

"I believe he found out about you somehow. You were treating him, too, and you feared he might say something about the money before he died. You couldn't take that chance. His front door was unlocked although he always locked it. The killer didn't enter with a key or he would have relocked the door as he departed.

"I asked myself why a sick man, living alone, in bed much of the time, would leave his front door unlocked, and the answer came to me at once. It was so his doctor could enter and minister to him."

Dr. Bradley's face twisted in despair. "He called on Emory one day while I was in the closet. He saw nothing, but I feared when he heard about the money he would remember that. It wasn't really murder. He had only days to live anyway."

"That will be for a jury to decide."

He stared down at the floor, then lifted his gaze to Swift. "Do you see the yellow in my eyes, and on my skin? These are symptoms of the fever. A jury of the Lord has already convicted me."

Bradley was one of the last to die, some weeks later. Early Sunday morning, November tenth, President Washington rode alone into the city from Germantown. Alexander Swift met him and they rode together through the clean and quiet streets of Philadelphia. The first heavy frosts of winter still hung in the air.

"It is clear," Washington decided. "The air seems healthy now. The Congress will convene here as scheduled."

"The frost has done it," Swift observed. "The mosquitos are all dead and many of the birds have departed."

"And thanks to you, the mystery of Congressman Emory's hidden money has been solved."

Swift nodded. "It is ironic that Dr. Shippen, the cause of it all, will return to his former position at the hospital, while Dr. Bradley, who stayed to help the dying, is paying with his life."

"Bradley is guilty, too," the President reminded him. "And at least Shippen has lost all seventy-eight months of his ill-gotten wealth. He will not be retiring to England as he no doubt planned."

"We can only hope that the yellow fever will not come upon us again."

"Someday there will be a cure," Washington predicted. "There are better days coming, for Philadelphia and for the nation."

THE ORCHARD OF CAGED BIRDS

I t was in late November of 1793, shortly after the abatement of the yellow-fever plague in Philadelphia, that Alexander Swift returned home to his wife and son in Maryland. Molly had prepared a special dinner for them, as she always did when he returned from a journey, and after they sent young George up to bed they sat talking before the fire.

"That plague could have killed you," she said. "Sometimes you take terrible risks, Alex. Your feud with Benedict Arnold has become an obsession with you."

"Arnold was nowhere near Philadelphia. He's in London with his family."

"I know you'll never forgive him for his treasonous actions at West Point."

Swift nodded. "It's hard to believe we were once friends, or that he was a hero at the battle of Saratoga."

"What was he like back then, Alex? You never talk about it."

He smiled. "I don't like to bore you with the years when I was married to Amanda." Swift's first wife had left him for a British officer when the Revolution broke out. The officer was later killed, but Amanda had married for a third time and was living a good life in New York.

"Go ahead," she urged. "Bore me."

"Well, there was one incident at Saratoga that certainly wasn't boring. As you know, the British under Burgoyne moved south from Canada in an attempt to link up with Sir Henry Clinton's forces advancing north along the Hudson. If they'd succeeded, the New England colonies would have been cut off from the rest of the Union and our Revolution might well have failed. General Gates was dispatched to take command of the army at Saratoga and Arnold was sent under him with reinforcements from the main American army. As a captain, Arnold had fought bravely during the early months of the war. In the spring of 'seventy-five he began a bitter rivalry with Ethan Allen, the commander of Vermont's Green Mountain Boys. The two men were given joint command of an attack on Fort Ticonderoga, a British arsenal on the eastern shore of Lake Champlain. The attack was successful but their dispute continued. When Arnold returned home to New Haven he learned that his first wife had died, leaving their three young sons in the care of his sister."

"I had forgotten that Peggy was his second wife."

Swift nodded. "Perhaps his first wife's death changed him. He grew more daring, and in July of 'seventy-five he persuaded General Washington to put him in charge of an overland expedition against Quebec. In late September, leading eleven hundred men on a six-week march, he started out. It was a terrible journey, through swamps and bad weather, and by the time they reached the Canadian city the cold rains of November were falling. Only six hundred of his men were still able to fight. They camped across the river from the city for more than a month before finally attacking in a snowstorm on New Year's Eve. The attack was beaten back, and Arnold was wounded in the leg. He remained at the camp with his men for several months, hoping for reinforcements, but finally retreated in June of 'seventy-six. All this, of course, was before our Declaration of Independence, and before the colonies were truly united in revolution."

Molly smiled at him. "You are a great history professor, but tell me about Saratoga."

"Well, Arnold was a brigadier general by then, but a dispute over some missing expense vouchers may have delayed his elevation to major general. He fought like a tiger at every opportunity, leading volunteers against the redcoats when his native Connecticut was threatened in April of 'seventy-seven. His horse was shot out from under him but he drew his pistol and shot a redcoat trying to take him prisoner. A few days later, the Continental Congress commissioned him as a major general."

"Alex, Saratoga," Molly reminded him again.

"Saratoga. By late summer of that year, Burgoyne's army was heading south, attempting to join up with General Clinton's men at Albany and cut the colonies in two. Arnold begged to launch an attack on Burgoyne, but General Gates preferred to cut his supply lines first. He discounted reports that General Clinton was sailing up the Hudson. In early October I rode north, skirting the British lines, to find out the truth. . . ."

It didn't take long to establish that British ships from New York were on the move, but they were only at Peekskill, still some distance from Albany. Swift rode on, avoiding the British, until he was north of Albany, approaching Saratoga. He found General Gates's encampment without difficulty, identified himself through a safe-conduct pass from Washington, and asked to see Benedict Arnold.

The general was in his tent, staring bleakly at a map of the area, when Swift entered. He was thirty-nine at the time, a broad-shouldered man of great strength and self-confidence. "Alexander Swift!" he exclaimed, standing to shake his hand. "What brings you this far north?"

"A mission for General Washington, sir. He wishes to know the true nature of the situation here."

Arnold motioned toward the map. "Burgoyne's army is almost upon us. They are moving slowly and we have fought back well, but their losses have been few. Our men are in retreat and General Gates does nothing. He fears that spies report our troop movements to the English. I swear to you, Swift, there have been times recently when I have questioned whether this is a war worth fighting."

"You can't mean that!"

Benedict Arnold stared up at him. "Does General Washington know that Gates has relieved me of my command?"

His words took Swift by surprise. "I'm sure he does not. What has happened here?"

"Over the next rise, a few miles away, is a place called Freeman's farm. When Gates would not move against the redcoats there, I took matters into my own hands. I spearheaded an attack on the farm two weeks ago. Though we inflicted a grievous blow to Burgoyne and forced him to retreat, Gates was furious. I offered to resign and Gates quickly accepted. I was to leave here and head back to Washington's troops in Philadelphia."

"But you have stayed."

"I am reluctant to leave. Burgoyne is advancing again, and Gates is doing little to stop him. He sends a few men to cautiously harass the British while staying well away from the fighting himself. I believe another attack at Freeman's farm, or at Bemis Heights overlooking it, could surprise Burgoyne and force him back. I am prepared to lead such an attack, with or without General Gates's approval."

Swift could sense Arnold's impatience all too well, yet he tried to forestall any rash action. "Let me do a bit of scouting first," he suggested.

"If you're caught you could be shot or hanged as a spy."

"I'll risk that. Give me a map of the area."

Arnold produced one from the papers on his table. "This is Freeman's farm, just west of the Hudson. Bemis Heights is south of it, and we are further south, right here along the river."

"So approach from the east is blocked by the river," Swift mused. "What about the west side?"

"That is the Meuse farm. It's a strange place and we've kept our distance from it."

"Strange in what way?"

"They don't seem to do much farming, but an orchard by the house has birdcages hanging in the trees. There are birds of every sort, close to a hundred, and they set up a terrible cry when anyone approaches."

"Like watchdogs."

"I suppose so, yes," Arnold agreed. "But it seems very odd."

"Have you spoken to the farm's owner?"

"No. There is a woman who is often seen at the place. I call her the bird lady. She keeps her distance from both sides. The front lines are very fluid there. We send out our patrols and so does Burgoyne."

Swift nodded. "I'll set out in the morning. Don't do anything rash until I return."

The red-coated British troops were easy to spot, the darker uniforms of their Hessian allies were more difficult, and the Indians Burgoyne employed were almost invisible in the woods. The Indians were good fighters, but there were occasional barbarous atrocities when they attacked a farm. Burgoyne tried to prevent the outrages, but Swift knew they were having the effect of turning more of the colonists against the British.

Swift rode in a wide circle to avoid them all, catching a distant hint of bells, and came upon the Meuse farm from the west. He approached an apple orchard, not realizing until too late that it was the orchard of the caged birds. They set up a clatter that might have been heard a mile away. He dismounted at once, leading his horse slowly in hopes of calming them down. The caged birds were of all sorts, many of them doves and pigeons but including a few bluebirds, robins, and cardinals. There were even a couple of parrots sharing a large cage. In all, he counted fifty cages in the orchard, most holding two birds each.

"Who are you?" a woman's voice called out from the porch of the farmhouse.

"A mere traveler," Swift told her, seeing the musket she held pointed at him. He doubted if she could fire accurately at that range but he wasn't about to find out.

"There is a war on. There are armies just over the next hill."

"Then perhaps it is wise that I stop here and continue after dark."

"No. That would not be wise." She lifted the gun to her shoulder.

"Why do you keep all those birds in the orchard?"

"To confound people like yourself who ask the question. Tell me, sir, are you a Rebel or a Loyalist?"

"I am an American, name of Alexander Swift, from New York." He strode a bit closer with his horse while they talked, and now he had a clearer view of her face. He guessed her to be in her twenties, with dark hair pulled back in a bun, a few wisps of it falling over her face. It was a gentle face, Swift decided, and he hoped she wouldn't squeeze the trigger. Holding his hands up, he dropped the reins of the horse and strode toward her.

She lowered the weapon as he approached. "You're a brave man, sir."

"Do you have a name?" he asked.

"Selma."

"Selma Meuse?"

She shook her head. "Selma O'Hara. Mr. Meuse is inside. Would you like to see him?"

Something was wrong. Swift realized that her face was pale and beaded with sweat. Behind him, the birds still chattered. "Yes," he answered. "It would be a pleasure to meet him."

"I said see him, not meet him."

She led the way into the parlor and stood aside as Swift entered. A bald man was seated at the dining room table, his head thrown back. An Indian tomahawk was embedded in his skull.

Swift tensed immediately, fearful he'd been led into a British trap, but the young woman had put down her weapon. "I found him like this a few minutes ago," she said. "He was my uncle. Uncle Franz." Though her voice was firm, he could see that she was trembling a bit. He checked the dead man's hands for some sort of defensive wounds but there were none. Apparently he'd been killed without warning, and the body was still warm.

"Did you live here with him?"

She shook her head. "He was alone since his wife died. I rode over here every few days to see if he needed anything."

"Who are you?"

"I told you. Selma O'Hara."

"From the next farm?"

"Until it became a battlefield. My folks moved into town and I've been staying with neighbors so I could watch over Uncle Franz." She glanced quickly at his body and then away.

"Have there been Indian attacks here before?"

She shook her head. "I have heard stories that the redcoats are employing Indians, but I have witnessed nothing like this."

"If your uncle lived here alone why didn't you stay here rather than with a neighbor?"

"The birds," she said simply. "They make such noise when they get to chattering. I couldn't stand living here. He would spend his days tending to them, feeding them, and cleaning out their cages. It was the only thing he lived for."

"I will notify General Gates's men of this atrocity. They will send a burial detail."

"Thank you," she said. "I didn't know what I was going to do."

"What about the birds?"

"I'll feed and water them today. Then I might have to turn them loose."

Something was bothering Swift and he paused to look again at the body of Franz Meuse. "Would an Indian warrior leave his tomahawk in the head of his victim?" he wondered. "Wouldn't he take it with him, to be used again?"

"It was meant to terrify us," the young woman said. "To make us flee from our homes."

"Perhaps. In any event, you're not safe here. The Indian attack may have been a prelude to an encircling maneuver by Burgoyne. I can escort you back to General Gates's camp where you'll be safe."

"Then you are not a mere traveler as you proclaimed."

"In wartime, truth is often the first casualty," he told her. "Gather up your things."

"The birds—"

"Release them. I'll help you."

"All right. I have nothing else here. My horse is outside."

They went down the lines of cages, opening the little doors. Some birds took flight at once, others hovered for a time in the shelter of their cages. "What did he do in the bad weather?" Swift asked.

"Brought them into the barn, but there was not really room for all these cages. Happily these days have been warm and dry for early October. He took good care of them, cleaning their cages and feeding them even though they often bloodied his fingers with their pecking. These parrots live a long time. They might have been older than he was." On the last line of trees she stopped before one of the final cages. "I should take this pair of rock doves to remember him by."

"Go ahead."

She lowered the cage and carried it to her horse. Swift mounted up and led the way through the woods to General Gates's encampment.

A half-hour later, they passed through the picket of soldiers guarding the American camp and he delivered her to the tent where other women were staying. Swift went alone to see General Gates. "Alexander Swift, sir, reporting on a reconnaissance mission."

Gates was a British general who'd resigned his commission in 1772 to cross the Atlantic and settle in Virginia, where he became a friend of Washington. He was one of the few American generals who'd seen service in a regular army, and Swift knew that Washington valued him highly. He was of medium height with slightly stooped shoulders that made him appear older than his fifty years. Some said he was a better politician than a general, and the previous December he'd campaigned hard with the Continental Congress to be appointed commander of the northern army. Following an Indian attack and the brutal killing of a young farm woman, he was chosen for the position.

"I understand you had a meeting with General Arnold this morning," he said without waiting for Swift's report. "He has been relieved of his command."

"I know that, sir, which is why I've come to you with my report. A farmer named Franz Meuse has been killed by an Indian tomahawk. I found the body at his house."

Gates frowned at the news. "The Meuse farm is just west of the Freeman place, and it is well known that the British have enlisted the Indians to help them. I have a report on my desk that a peddler known as Foxy Foley is missing in the same area and may have stumbled upon an Indian war party. How long had Meuse been dead?"

"Less than an hour, I think. The body was still warm. His niece found him shortly before my arrival. Could you send a burial detail over there?"

"Not today. It could be a trap of some sort. But I will note it."

"The man had an apple orchard with caged birds hanging from the trees."

Gates nodded. "One of my scouts reported that. It seems very strange."

"His niece and I released them since there was no one to care for them."

"All right, Swift. Thank you for the report. If you see General Arnold, tell him he is no longer welcome here."

"I will convey your message, General."

He left the tent and crossed to the other end of the camp where he found Arnold drilling his troops. Presently the drill ended and the general came over to stand by him. "Where have you been, Swift?"

As they walked back toward Arnold's tent, Alex quickly told him of Franz Meuse's murder. "The tomahawk seems to indicate he was killed by Indians."

"You sound as if you're not certain," Arnold remarked.

"There were no signs that he'd put up a struggle. And if an Indian killed him, would he have left the tomahawk in the wound? Would an Indian war party have left all those birds hanging in their cages without taking some for food?"

Benedict Arnold pondered this. "You say there was a woman at the house."

"A niece, Selma O'Hara. She may be the bird lady you mentioned earlier. I brought her back with me to protect her."

"Where is she?"

"In the tent with the other women." Swift did not inquire about the others. He knew some might be wives following their husbands to the battlefield, while others might be mere camp followers or prostitutes. This close to the battle scenes, all were risking their lives. As they reached Arnold's tent Swift added, "General Gates gave me a message for you. He said you are no longer welcome here."

It was those unfortunate words that changed Benedict Arnold and perhaps the course of the war. "No man shall keep me in my tent today!" he cried. "I am tired of Gates's halfway measures." He went inside and buckled on his sword.

"What are you doing?" Swift asked.

"Leading the attack!" Arnold told him. Mounting his horse, he rode through the camp calling to his men. Many seemed ready to follow him gladly, though he had no right to command or give orders. Swift stood by helplessly and watched, knowing he was witnessing some sort of history.

Gates was out of his tent, shouting to his troops, but Arnold cried, "Victory or death!" and rode on.

"Major Armstrong, stop him!" Gates ordered a nearby officer. Armstrong mounted up and took off in pursuit, but it was immediately obvious that Arnold and his band of men would not be overtaken. He led the way two miles north to the redoubt on Bemis Heights, where the English Colonel Breymann protected Burgoyne's main column as it advanced again toward Freeman's farm. Arnold gathered up three more regiments along the way, but at first they were repulsed.

Back at Gates's camp, all was in an uproar. One of the camp followers, a husky young woman named Clare, came running up to Swift, demanding to know where her fiancé Major Armstrong had gone off to. "General Gates sent him after Arnold," Swift told her.

"He'll be killed!" she sobbed, sitting down in the dust to cry. "He'll be killed and I'll never see him again!"

Swift tried to comfort her. "I'm sure he'll be all right. Don't you have any other friends in the area?"

"I only know Mr. Meuse, and now he's dead, too. They say the Indians killed him."

That caught Swift's attention. He helped her to her feet and dried her tears. "Did you ever visit his farm, with his apple orchard full of birdcages?"

"Y-yes, I went there every week after his wife died. Sometimes, if it looked stormy, I helped him carry the cages into the barn."

"Was he always at home?"

"No, he often rode around the countryside watching the progress of the rebel armies. But then last week we had a terrible fight. He accused me of stealing his money and slapped me. I got angry, and we tussled. I pulled his hair and bit him but he threw me out and told me not to come back."

"Did he have any weapons around his house?"

"I saw a musket, but all the farmers have those."

"No tomahawk?"

She shook her head. "Nothing like that"

"Did you know his niece, Selma O'Hara?"

She nodded. "I recognized her in the tent when I saw the birdcage. She was at the house once when I came. I heard her telling the other women that the Indians killed him."

"Did you speak with her?"

The woman shook her head. "I stayed out of her way. She might have thought I killed him."

"You might have had more of a motive than the Indians," Swift pointed out.

"Sure, we fought and he threw me out, but I didn't come back with a tomahawk and kill him. He wouldn't have let me in the house, certainly not with a weapon in my hand."

Swift left her and entered the women's tent. He found Selma easily by the birdcage above her bunk. She was talking with one of the other women but came over to Swift as soon as she saw him. "What news of Arnold?" she asked. "They say he rode out of here with a detachment of men, bound for battle. General Gates is in a fury."

"I know that, but it's about all I know."

Ignoring all military conventions, exercising command without authority, Benedict Arnold took charge of whatever brigades or regiments he came across. Like a madman he flourished his sword and charged into the thick of battle. British cannons fell to the Americans and were turned on Burgoyne's troops. General Gates saw none of it, for he had remained at his headquarters throughout the battle.

It was at this moment of victory that a British bullet found its mark and killed Arnold's horse. His left leg was broken beneath the falling beast. The enemy was in retreat but Arnold had to be carried from the field of battle.

It was about this time that a detachment of Gates's men, miles from the action, came upon a man who identified himself as the missing peddler Foxy Foley. His packhorse, with gently ringing bells, was loaded with Indian trinkets, headdresses, and weapons, and he was only too happy to receive an escort back to the American camp. "If they'd ever found me peddling those Indian things they'd have killed me," he told the officers at Gates's headquarters while Swift stood by listening. Foxy was a hairy middle-aged man and perhaps it was the hair that had earned him his nickname.

"A farmer named Franz Meuse was killed by Indians," Swift told him. "Did you travel near his farm?"

The hairy man turned to stare at him. "I don't think so. I'm new in this area."

"You'd remember it if you had. He had an apple orchard with birdcages hanging from the trees."

"Whatever for?" the peddler asked.

Before Swift could answer, there was a fresh disturbance from the other side of camp. "General Arnold's been wounded!" someone shouted, and several men came running.

"I'll be back!" Swift told the peddler and broke into a run himself.

He pushed his way through the ring of men around the canvas litter. Benedict Arnold's face was twisted in pain, and Swift could see the bone protruding from his crushed left leg. "My God, Swift," he gasped when he saw Alex. "It's the same leg that took a musket ball at Quebec!"

"Just lie still. The doctor is on the way."

It was Major Armstrong himself who attested to Arnold's courage. "This man was a hero today. I saw him break through the British lines, leading his men without a thought for his own safety. He completely routed Burgoyne's troops at Bemis Heights, riding blindly into the crossfire with sword outstretched."

"Go tell General Gates that," Swift suggested. "This may be the perfect time to throw his troops into a full-scale assault."

The rest of the day was filled with activity. The encampment was fully alive for the first time since his arrival the previous day. The men were preparing for battle and the women were caring for the wounded. Though the sun was low in the west everyone felt sure Gates would order a full-scale attack by dawn. Already there were the occasional sounds of musket fire in the distance.

Swift saw Selma O'Hara making a purchase from the peddler and he followed her into the tent. "What did you buy?" he asked.

"This scarf." She held up a long wool cloth.

"Ready for winter?"

Selma laughed. "Not yet. I bought this to wrap around the birdcage so they would sleep instead of chattering all night. Even their coos can be annoying."

He watched her return to the tent and then went in search of Major Armstrong. The young officer was inspecting his men's muskets to be sure they were ready for battle. "Their red coats make them easy targets," he was saying, "even in the woods. Make every shot count."

"Major Armstrong, may I have a word with you?"

The officer frowned at the interruption by a civilian. "Mr. Swift, I am preoccupied."

"It is a matter of utmost importance which will only take a moment of your time."

"And what would that be, pray tell?"

Swift lowered his voice so the others wouldn't hear. "Who are the best shots in your regiment?"

"I have two men who are quite good."

"I need them both."

"You need them? My dear sir, I obey only the commands of General Gates."

Swift looked at the sun sinking toward the horizon and knew he had no time to waste. "Listen carefully, Major. You have these men's lives in your hands."

A bit later, with occasional musket fire still to be heard, Alexander Swift sought out Foxy Foley again. The peddler was packing his gear, ready to be on his way. "You'd best head south tomorrow," Swift advised.

"I know that."

"I told you about the farmer with the birdcages. Is that the sort of thing you might sell?"

"Birdcages? No. They're too big for me to handle, even with my packhorse. I couldn't take more than two a trip, and I only get up this way every few months. It would take me years to deliver fifty cages."

"I'd suggest you stay the night," Swift said. "I will speak to Major Armstrong about letting you sleep in one of the tents."

"Thank you," the peddler said, obviously pleased.

Swift walked across the campgrounds and entered the women's tent. Some were already asleep and he went first to Clare's cot to be sure she was all right. "I'm awake," she said, stirring a bit as he approached. "I heard musket fire."

"Everything is all right now," he assured her. "You can go to sleep."

He crossed to the other side of the tent, where Selma O'Hara's birdcage was delicately wrapped in its woolen scarf. "No cooing," he observed. "That scarf has done its job."

She nodded. "They are sleeping soundly."

"This is a trick of legerdemain I learned from a famous magician," Swift said, and before she could move he grabbed an end of the scarf and yanked it from the cage. The cooing doves had vanished.

"What happened to them?" she asked in alarm.

"I fear they're both dead," he told her with a sense of regret. "I had them shot out of the sky before they could carry your urgent message to General Burgoyne."

Selma tried to bolt from the tent but Swift held her fast until Major Armstrong and his men arrived. "Take her into custody," Swift told him. "I'll explain everything."

"You'd better do that. I have to report all this to General Gates."

A bit later, by the lantern light in Armstrong's tent, Alexander Swift started talking. "We have to go back to the killing at Meuse's farm."

"You're telling me the young woman killed her uncle with a tomahawk?" the major asked.

"No, as a matter of fact I doubt if she killed anyone. To drive a weapon like a tomahawk into a man's skull like that takes a good deal of strength. What I'm saying is that the dead man is not Franz Meuse, and obviously she must have known that."

"Not Meuse! How—?"

"Selma showed very little emotion after finding her supposed uncle brutally murdered. More important, the dead man was bald. A woman in our camp, who claims to be your fiancée Clare—"

Major Armstrong snorted at that. "She is nothing of the sort!"

"In any event, Clare frequented the Meuse farm and told me she recently fought with Franz Meuse, pulling his hair. And the dead man's hands were without wounds, though Selma told me the birds pecked at Meuse's fingers, often drawing blood. No hair and no hand wounds. But if the dead man wasn't Meuse, why did Selma lie about it? The answer, of course, is those birds. Why did Meuse keep them in his orchard?"

"Because there were too many to fit in the house," Armstrong suggested.

"And why were there so many, and of so many different types? To hide the fact that many of them were rock doves, better known as pigeons. In Europe pigeons have been used for centuries to carry messages tied to their legs, homing in on their destination in a matter of minutes. I was suspicious of this when I remembered Arnold telling me General Gates feared that spies were reporting on our troop movements. Franz Meuse was an English spy who reported by carrier pigeon back to Burgoyne's headquarters camp. From there a rider could be dispatched to the front lines with news of our positions. I was suspicious of Selma's part in this, but I had to catch her in the act. Her only reason for bringing those two pigeons along was to warn Burgoyne one more time. She launched both pigeons with the same message of our impending attack, certain that at least one would get through. I saw her get the scarf from the peddler. When she wrapped it around the cage it wasn't to quiet the birds, but to hide the fact that they were gone. Happily I'd already persuaded you to have two marksmen watching for them."

"But who was the murdered man at Meuse's farm?"

"The peddler, Foxy Foley. Meuse himself killed him shortly before I arrived. He escaped through the back while Selma kept me busy out front. I thought I heard distant bells, like the bells on Foxy Foley's packhorse, as I approached the farm. We know Foley traded in Indian weapons among other things. He might have been showing Meuse an authentic tomahawk when he happened to question the pigeons in their cages. Perhaps he'd even noticed tiny message tubes attached to some of their legs. Meuse killed him and took his packhorse as a means of escaping, leaving Selma to send a final message to Burgoyne."

"Then she wasn't his niece?"

"I doubt it. She's not talking, but that woman Clare should be more than willing to identify the man calling himself Foxy Foley as the supposedly dead Franz Meuse."

She was, and he surrendered without a struggle.

Two days later the British had retreated to the heights above Saratoga, but Burgoyne paused there too long. Without the messages from his spy, his escape route to the north was cut off and the troops found themselves completely encircled by the Americans. On the morning of October 17th, Burgoyne surrendered. America had its first great victory of the Revolution.

Molly had listened with rapt attention to Alex's story. When he finished she asked, "What happened to Meuse and Selma?"

"He admitted the killing and both of them were tried as spies by a military court. Meuse was hanged and Selma was sent to prison. The crime was pretty much as I'd described it to Major Armstrong. While Meuse was examining the tomahawk, Foxy Foley made some comment about pigeons carrying messages. Meuse killed him, hoping Indians would be blamed, and when I arrived on the scene he escaped with the packhorse, planning to avoid detection until he could join up with Burgoyne's men. If Selma hadn't brought those pigeons along to our camp I might not have realized what was going on."

"And Benedict Arnold? He was a hero after all."

"At Saratoga, he certainly was. To this day he limps as the result of his leg wound. But something changed him. Money, perhaps, and a greedy second wife. In any event, he won the battle at Saratoga but almost lost the war for us with his treachery at West Point."

"Is there good and bad in every man?"

"Perhaps. I would like to think that Arnold now regrets those crimes against his country. If we ever meet again, I will ask him."

PAUL REVERE'S BELL

It was the spring of 1794, a time when British seizures of American ships in the Caribbean was becoming a major problem. Alexander Swift had arrived in Philadelphia to report to President Washington on continued progress with the Patowmack Canal, but he found that Washington had other things on his mind.

"It is always good to see you, Alexander," he said, offering a firm handshake. "I hope your wife and son are well."

"Very well, sir. And this city seems back to normal following the yellow-fever scourge."

Washington nodded. "It's difficult to remember how bad it was just six months ago. Now our attention is given over to foreign matters. The British are disrupting our trade with the West Indies. Jefferson wanted us to be firm with them, to retaliate in kind, but since he resigned as Secretary of State our policy has foundered a bit. My new Secretary, Edmund Randolph, is no Jefferson. Nonetheless, I am resisting retaliation and will send Chief Justice John Jay to London in hope of averting war. Our country is too young to risk another clash with the British."

"Is there anything I can do?" Alexander asked, more out of habit than anything else.

President Washington eyed him for a moment, perhaps remembering all his earlier assignments, in the days of Benedict Arnold. "There is one thing," he said slowly. "You can go to Boston and see about Paul Revere's bell."

Boston in 1794 was the third-largest city in the United States, with a population approaching 19,000. Built on a somewhat isolated peninsula connected to the rest of the state by a narrow strip of land called Boston Neck, it was the center of the universe for the new nation's first immigrants. Though he was approaching his sixtieth birthday, Paul Revere remained the acknowledged leader of the city's artisans, with his own foundry on Lime Street near the tip of North Boston and a silversmith shop on Anne Street.

He received Alexander Swift on a cool May morning in his little office at the foundry, a place that brought back memories for Swift of the one north of West Point where the fabled Hudson Chain had been forged during the war years. "Sometimes I think Boston is a city of rope," he told Swift after being complimented on the foundry. "From the earliest days there have been cordage factories here for the shipyards. Ropewalks, they call them. I have always dealt in sturdier stuff."

Paul Revere was a stout, dignified man with hair that was turning white and the beginning of a jowled appearance to his face. Swift wanted to ask him if he still rode horseback a great deal, but the remark might have seemed flippant. Instead he said, "President Washington tells me you have recently begun casting bells."

"So I have, Mr. Swift. Sit down and let us take tea together. I cannot believe the President sent you to Boston to talk about my bells. I should never have informed him of my misgivings."

An employee named Rossiter brought them a pot of tea and two cups, and Swift remarked, "You seem to have a good relationship with your workers."

"I pay them well and treat them like human beings. I know I could hire men for less, but they wouldn't be loyal like my people. John Rossiter has been with me for twenty years."

"Tell me about these bells."

"It came about in an interesting manner," Revere said, warming to the subject. "Two years ago, the bell on our church—the bell that hung on the famous Old North Church until British troops took the building down for firewood—cracked and could not be rung. There was talk of shipping it to England to be recast, but none of the church leaders wanted to do that. At our meeting, mellowed by some bottles of fine Madeira, I not only agreed to be one of thirty-five contributors to the cost of restoring the bell but also offered to recast it."

"Had you ever recast a bell before?" Swift asked, sipping his tea and thinking wistfully of that fine Madeira.

"Never," Paul Revere admitted. "In fact, very few bells have been cast in America. The most famous, of course, is the Liberty Bell. But I knew there was a bell foundry in Abington and I sought help from them. I must admit that that first bell was harsh and shrill, but I am getting better at it. I am even running small advertisements in area newspapers. My goal now is to craft a bell for every steeple in New England."

"A noble but difficult task. The President tells me you have already run into unexpected problems."

Revere sighed. "Only in Washington's mind. Some of these bells weigh up to eight hundred pounds, and as each one is finished now I cart it from the foundry to my own backyard a few blocks away on Charter Street. In the presence of a committee of church deacons and donors, and a group of neighborhood children, I sound the bell for the first time with a hammer. Should the tone be unacceptable, I will buy back the old metal. I must tell you, Mr. Swift, what the bell sounds like is largely a matter of luck. Still, my customers are usually pleased."

"Then what is the problem?"

He took a sip of tea before responding. "My latest bell, and my largest thus far, is bound for Quebec. A delegation of Canadians will arrive tomorrow to hear it rung for the first time. Somehow the President is concerned their trip might be part of a British plot."

Swift chuckled at the idea but said, "Perhaps he fears our old nemesis Benedict Arnold may sneak back into the country as part of your Canadian group."

"In a nation this young, I suppose he must always be vigilant."

"Certainly Arnold and others have tried to persuade George the Third to launch an attack on us, and the recent harassment of our West Indies shipping trade is troublesome. But from all reports, the British Parliament is loath to undertake any formal action against us."

"What does President Washington want of you?"

"Only that I remain here until the bell is safely delivered to the Canadians and they depart. He didn't feel it proper to send the militia—"

"I'm glad of that! Armed guards might give churchmen the wrong impression."

"You are one of the true heroes of the revolution," Swift reminded him. "It is always possible that the British might wish to assassinate you."

Revere laughed at the idea. "I hardly think they'd consider me a threat at my age. If they came again, someone younger than me would have to spread the alarm. But come to my house Thursday, by all means! Another set of ears is invaluable in judging the tone of the bell. We plan to cart it over there around eleven in the morning, and to sound it for the first time at noon."

"I will be there on Thursday," Swift promised, "and accompany the bell on its brief journey." But he couldn't help wondering what had prompted the President to send him on this mission. Was it simply uneasiness with the Canadian delegation, or something else?

It was years since Alexander Swift had visited Boston, and he was encouraged by the way the city at last was beginning to shake off its postwar decline.

Its trade with London and the West Indies had all but collapsed after the Revolution, and both the British and the French harassed the ships that did put to sea. There was talk in Philadelphia of forming a United States Navy to protect the ships, but in that spring of '94 it was only talk. Still, the rope-walks and foundries and fish markets were busy, and traffic in the port was gradually increasing.

Revere had arranged for Swift to stay with a neighbor, Mrs. Patrick, in her pleasant little house on Charter Street. She proved to be a formidable widow with graying hair and a keen sense of the world around her. "You can call me Betsy," she informed Swift when he arrived at her house. "Like the flag woman. It's a very patriotic name."

"It is indeed," he agreed. "You must feel a part of history, being a neighbor to Paul Revere."

"Well, I wasn't yet his neighbor when he and Dawes made their famous rides. In fact, he still owns the house on North Square, but he rented this one a few years back to be closer to his foundry. He's a proper sort and Rachel is a dear wife, ten years younger than Paul. They've had eight children, though only five survived their infancy. He had eight by his first wife, too, and it killed her."

Somehow this was more than Swift needed to know. "He'll be ringing a new bell on Thursday."

Betsy Patrick sighed. "Paul is a good friend, but those darn bells really have started to annoy me. My dear husband, when he was alive, used to dread each new one. He would hear the cart trundling down Charter Street shortly before noon, and we both knew it was another bell on the way. The children know it, too. They flock around, as do the neighbors. These days he's turning out the bells so fast there's at least one a month."

"Did your husband fight in the war?"

"He was a Minuteman," she answered proudly. "He fought at Lexington and Concord."

"The militia was our savior in those early days. People like your husband and Paul Revere and the rest made this nation possible. Certainly you can put up with the single gong of a bell once a month."

"It's not a single gong, though. Sometimes the buyers want several strokes to be certain the bell is sound. When I hear them coming now I stay in my house and play the spinet to try to muffle the sound."

After dinner, Swift insisted Betsy Patrick play a few selections on her spinet. She was quite good, and he listened for nearly an hour before retiring early. He missed his wife and child, as he always did when traveling, but sleep came quickly to him.

Revere had arranged for dinner the following evening with his Canadian guests, and he sent a message inviting Swift to join them. The meal was at the Revere home, with his wife, Rachel, serving food for the six of them. She was a jovial, smart-looking woman with an oval facial contour that men seemed to admire. Swift thought her nose a bit long, and concluded that she was handsome rather than beautiful. Though some of their children still lived at home, she fed them separately before joining their guests at the table.

They were six in all, the Reveres and Swift, plus three delegates from the church in Quebec. One was a woman, Mrs. Southworth, a pale, attractive lady in her thirties who was introduced as the church's organist. Then there was Rollo Blake, a parishioner, and the Reverend Douglas Hayes, the church's rector. Revere introduced Alexander Swift as a personal representative of President Washington, which seemed to impress them immensely.

Swift was seated next to Mrs. Southworth, who wanted to hear all about the President. After a few minutes he managed to shift the conversation to church organs. "Was yours built in Canada?" he asked.

"No, no. The good organs all come from Europe. Ours was brought over on a brig from Germany. We thought it would never arrive. Now our church is almost complete. We lack only Mr. Revere's bell for our tower."

"How have you traveled to Boston?" he asked, curious as to the problem of transporting the bell back to Canada.

"It has been an arduous journey in Mr. Blake's wagon, now parked in Mr. Revere's yard. He was kind enough to send our horses to a stable down the street. Tomorrow the bell will be transferred to our wagon and we will carry it back with us, but it is not the most comfortable method of travel."

"We are almost three hundred miles north of here," Rollo Blake explained. "We stopped overnight at a Vermont inn, a charming place."

"You should come this way in autumn for the change of seasons. I'm told the colors of the foliage are less vivid in Canada."

"We're close enough to the Vermont border that it makes little difference. I often visit Boston, and on one of my previous trips I learned that Mr. Revere was now casting church bells. I communicated the news to Reverend Hayes and he was most enthusiastic."

"Indeed I was," the minister agreed. Hayes was a bit younger than Rollo Blake, probably still in his forties. He was quite slender, with a pale complexion.

"How do you happen to have business here?" Swift asked the older man. "Is trade increasing between our countries?"

"It is, and as a former resident of the Massachusetts Colony, I am always pleased to return here." He smiled slightly. "I confess I was one of the Loyalists who fled to Canada when your Revolution succeeded."

"We have put all that behind us," Revere told him. "We hope to be friends with our neighbors to the north, and with George the Third, too, for that matter."

"With the revolution in France, all monarchies are shaky these days. However, I believe the king will endure."

Mrs. Revere's dinner was a tasty mix of traditional Boston dishes, and her guests thoroughly enjoyed it. Following another hour of pleasant conversation, with cigars for the men, the Canadian visitors departed, promising to return before noon for delivery of the bell.

"They seem very nice," Rachel Revere commented. "Mr. Blake looks familiar."

"He said he travels here on occasion. You may have seen him in North Square," her husband suggested.

"And how are you getting on with our neighbor, Mrs. Patrick?" Rachel asked, directing her attention to Swift.

"She is a charming woman, very talkative. I thank you for arranging the accommodation." He took out his pocket watch. "Now I believe I must return there, before the poor woman shuts the door on me. I will see you both on the morrow."

Like many residences in the city, Paul Revere's Charter Street house sat flush with the sidewalk and had no front yard. Swift and the Canadians passed through a gate in the wall to reach a yard at the rear where Rachel maintained a small garden. The gate also provided entrance for the bell, which arrived on a wagon driven by Revere's assistant, John Rossiter. As soon as the neighborhood children saw its approach, they ran to meet it, crowding into the backyard to such an extent that Revere himself had to order them back.

Mrs. Southworth, Mr. Blake, and the Reverend Hayes were all caught up in the rush of children. The big bell, forged from a mixture of copper and tin, with some zinc and lead as well, remained on the wagon, hanging from a crossbeam. Its clapper had not yet been attached. Rossiter climbed onto the bed of the wagon and handed Revere a hammer with which the first blow would be struck. Around them there was silent anticipation.

"This is it," Revere announced. "The first ringing of a new church bell." All eyes were on him as he lifted the hammer above his head to bring it down. Then, suddenly, there was the sound of a gunshot and the ping of something hitting the bell. Swift's first thought was that one of the older children had fired at the bell, but then he saw Rollo Blake fall to the ground clutching his chest.

"He's been shot!" Rossiter yelled. "He's bleeding!"

Blake made an effort to lift himself from the ground, but it was too much for him. He dropped back and lay still. Reverend Hayes turned him over, to reveal even more blood. "Rollo! Rollo!" Then his face seemed to crumple. "May God have mercy! He's dead."

The children were hustled away, retreating to the street where they crowded around the gate fighting for the best view. But the uproar brought neighbors, including Mrs. Patrick, to the scene. "What happened?" she asked Swift. "It sounded like a shot."

"It was a shot. Someone killed Rollo Blake, one of the Canadians."

"But who would do that?"

"Some would-be patriot, I fear," Paul Revere told her. "The man was a British loyalist who had fled to Canada."

Boston law-enforcement officers were summoned to the scene. Though they wore no uniforms and carried no guns, they were the first such force in the new nation, predating the Revolution by several decades. Swift was unimpressed by the two men who arrived to take charge, and their main action was to search everyone in the crowd for a weapon. No one had seen anything, and no weapons were produced.

"It could have been one of the older children," Mrs. Southworth suggested.

Swift knew that was a possibility. He went out to the street to speak with those who were still there, well aware that a guilty child might have fled when the law officers arrived. One boy, taller than the rest and probably around seventeen, seemed nervous. "What is your name, son?" Swift asked.

"Gerber, sir." The youth was already edging away.

Swift gripped his shoulder with a firm hand. "Do you know anything about this shooting?"

"No, sir."

"Did you see anyone with a flintlock pistol? Perhaps someone was trying to ring the bell with it and hit that man by accident."

"I don't know anything," he whined, trying to break free.

"Do you own a flintlock?"

"No, no!"

"Then why are you so nervous?"

"I knew him. I seen him around."

"The dead man? Rollo Blake?"

"I didn't know his name, but I seen him down the street at the *Pig and Whistle* a couple of times."

"When was this?" Swift wanted to know.

"Back last fall and winter."

"Was he with anyone?"

"Don't know. Le' me go!"

"Something must have made you notice him."

Revere's assistant, John Rossiter, had joined them on the sidewalk. "What's the trouble here?"

"This boy claims to have seen the victim in the neighborhood last year."

"Sure, didn't Mr. Revere tell you? That's how we got the job. Mr. Blake came down here occasionally on business and heard about our bell casting."

Now Swift remembered Rollo Blake mentioning his frequent trips at dinner the previous night, but he was still surprised to learn the dead man had been a patron of the local pub. Perhaps he had made an enemy there.

"Do you ever go to the *Pig and Whistle*, John?"

"Been in the place a few times. Never saw him there, though."

Swift wished there was some way to convey the news of the killing to President Washington in Philadelphia, but a courier would take two days by horse. He couldn't help feeling that Washington's motive in sending him to Boston might have had something to do with Blake's presence in the city. But if that was the case, the President must have learned of the planned visit from Paul Revere.

Swift released his grip on young Gerber's shoulder. Revere was the one he had to speak with.

Once the official investigation had wound down and Blake's body had been removed, Revere turned his attention to the bell. The fatal flintlock ball had passed through Blake's body, apparently from back to front, with the back wound being higher than the front. Then it had hit the bell near the bottom of the rim. Revere examined the tiny dent and proclaimed it almost invisible to the eye, which in truth it was. "A bit of buffing should remove it entirely," he assured Reverend Hayes and Mrs. Southworth.

"When will we hear it rung?" she asked.

"There is no time like the present." So saying, Revere picked up the hammer and swung it at the bell. It gave off a deep mellow tone that brought a smile to Mrs. Southworth's face.

"A fine sound, don't you think?" she asked Reverend Hayes.

"Glorious! I only wish Rollo were here to experience this moment."

Revere reached the hammer inside the bell and struck it about where the clapper would hit. The sound seemed to resonate even more. "That should bring your worshipers in," he said.

The minister smiled. "We'll take it," he said, shaking Revere's hand.

"But how will we get it back home without Mr. Blake to drive the wagon?" Mrs. Southworth wondered.

At Revere's side, John Rossiter cleared his throat. "If Mr. Revere allows it, I could drive that wagon up to Quebec for you. I know how to handle a good team of horses. I can trail my own mount behind the wagon and ride him back."

Reverend Hayes seemed to sigh with relief. "Mr. Revere, if you would allow it, this would be of great help to us. Managing a team of horses pulling a heavy load such a long distance might be more than I could handle."

Revere thought about it. "Today is Thursday. Best to stay overnight and get a good morning start. Three days up would be Monday, three days back would be Thursday."

"Or Wednesday night," his assistant replied. "A lone horse and rider will make better time than a heavily loaded wagon with three passengers."

"Very well," Revere agreed. "But be careful. I cannot afford to lose you."

His workmen transferred the bell to Blake's wagon, and arrangements were made to wrap his body in protective sailcloth for the journey home. It was agreed that the travelers would spend one more night in Boston before starting out. "Perhaps it is fitting that Rollo accompany Mr. Revere's bell to its new home," Mrs. Southworth commented.

When they were alone, Swift asked Revere if he had contacted Washington about selling the bell to the Quebec church. "I sent him a message, but he had no problem with it," Revere said.

Yet the whole thing bothered Swift. Later that night, back at Mrs. Patrick's, he asked her about Revere's yard. "That fence wouldn't keep anyone out if they wanted to get in. Are there ever any prowlers over there?"

"Once in a while. Just last night I saw a couple of people from my bedroom window, moving around in the dark. The moon wasn't bright enough to see who they were. Neighborhood kids, I suppose. I called out from the window and shooed them away."

"Was it always like that, or just since Mr. Revere rented the house?"

"My husband died in 'ninety. It was quieter in those days. Our neighbors were an elderly couple who went to bed at dusk every night. The place is livelier with Mr. Revere and his family and I don't resent that. He's a great national hero."

After supper, she played the spinet for a time, filling the house with the rousing sound of "Yankee Doodle." Swift applauded at the end. "I don't think I've ever heard that played on a spinet," he told her.

"It's one of my favorites." She closed the keyboard and stood up. "I'm going to bed now. I don't like to disturb the neighbors by playing after dark. I'll have breakfast for you in the morning."

"I regret being such a bother. I promise to be gone by tomorrow night."

"You're no bother at all. It's good having a man around the house for a few days."

After she'd gone up to her room, Swift sat by the lamplight for some time. Rollo Blake's murderer, seemingly invisible to their eyes, must have had a motive. He rejected the idea that a youngster might have fired a pistol at the bell and hit Blake by mistake. Blake was an occasional visitor to the city and might have made enemies. If that was the case, he should check out the *Pig and Whistle*, the local pub where he'd been seen.

The streets were not quite dark when he left Betsy Patrick's house, strolling along Charter Street toward the pub. He passed the fish market, and ahead he could see the glow of lamps in the pub window. There were a half-dozen customers at the bar. He ordered a beer, and when the bartender brought it he said, "I hear somebody shot Rollo Blake. Did you know him?"

He wiped up some of the spilled beer. "Not by name. They tell me he came here when he was in town."

Swift glanced at the other customers. "Any of his friends here now?"

The bartender called down to the end. "Smitty, you knew that Blake chap, didn't you?"

A young man with long blond hair, who appeared to be in his early twenties, answered. "I had a beer with him last night. Who wants to know?"

Swift moved down the bar to his side. "I'm Alexander Swift. I was there when he was shot this noon."

"Don't know anything about that, just what people are saying."

"How about his wagon?"

Smitty shrugged and said nothing. He wasn't the talkative sort. Swift finished his beer in silence. He was about to leave when the youth spoke up. "Why'd you ask that?"

"What?"

"About the wagon."

"They're not able to get it back to Quebec without Blake. I understand one of Paul Revere's assistants will be driving it up."

"They looking to hire a driver? Plenty of young gents around here could use the money. Me, for one."

"I believe it's been taken care of, Smitty."

Swift left him at the bar and went out into the night street. A few people were on the sidewalk, but they ignored him. The city had once had a reputation for street fighting and even now as he hurried back to Betsy Patrick's house he could not help but imagine he was being followed.

All seemed quiet at the Patrick and Revere houses, but he could see that the gate to the Revere yard was ajar. He entered, using the moonlight to guide him to Blake's wagon. The heavy bell was in place for the return trip, and in the morning a team of fresh horses would be brought from the stable. Swift felt around the bell and the wagon itself, finally dropping to his knees to examine the underside of the wagon. Something was there, something—

The intruder was upon him before he heard a sound, wrestling him flat on the ground and striking his shoulder with some sort of club. They rolled over in the dirt, with Swift aware only that he was fighting a younger, stronger man who wanted to harm him. The attacker managed to straddle him and Swift turned his head as the club descended again, just missing him. He unseated the man and toppled him to the ground, following up on his momentary advantage to wrestle the club from him. The assailant scurried away in the dark, spiderlike, and Swift had only a quick glimpse of him in a sudden beam of moonlight as he got to his feet and ran.

He couldn't be sure, but it looked like Gerber, the tall lad who'd been at the scene of Blake's killing earlier.

Swift took a deep breath and went back under the wagon, keeping the confiscated club handy for defense. There were four wooden barrels strapped to the underside, but without a light he could not identify what they were. Frustrated, he returned to the house and lit one of Betsy Patrick's candles. Checking the yard and street to make certain his would-be assailant had not come back, Swift ducked under the wagon once more and held the candle up to the barrels. He saw the words *Poudre à Canon* and froze. It was a full five seconds before he had the wits to blow out the candle flame.

Rachel Revere came to the door in response to his knocking. She carried an oil lamp and was obviously frightened to be awakened in the middle of the night. Swift apologized and told her he must speak to her husband at once.

"What is it, Rachel?" Revere called out, coming down the stairs in his nightshirt.

Swift quickly explained the reason for awakening them. "There are barrels of gunpowder attached to the bottom of Blake's wagon. They could blow up the entire house."

Revere's face was grim. "I'll get dressed immediately."

With an oil lamp on the ground a safe distance away, Revere examined the four barrels and carefully freed them from their bindings. Swift helped him carry them a safe distance from the house. "That should do it," he said with relief.

"We'll remove it in the morning. I thank you for your warning, Alexander."

"Someone jumped me while I was searching the wagon. I believe it was one of the youths who were here yesterday. Mrs. Patrick said she'd chased some away the previous night."

"The markings on these barrels are French," Revere observed. "They were smuggled in from Quebec."

"But why? Certainly there is no shortage of gunpowder here."

"I fear it was meant for a bomb. It is nearly two centuries since the Gunpowder Plot to blow up Parliament, but British loyalists may have been planning something similar here. Boston is our state's capital and the cradle of revolution."

"Do you think those Canadians planned this?"

"I doubt if the minister or Mrs. Southworth was involved. About Mr. Blake I cannot say. He was an admitted loyalist who fled to Canada when the Revolution began."

"We must question Reverend Hayes and Mrs. Southworth about this."

"Of course," Revere agreed.

"Meantime, I'll try to locate the youth who assaulted me."

At sunrise he walked down to the fish market, carrying the club he'd retrieved from his assailant. The previous day's catches were being sorted and priced while early shoppers began to drift in. One man holding a three-foot-long cod seemed familiar and Swift remembered him from the *Pig and Whistle*.

"Smitty, isn't it?"

The blond-haired youth recognized him at once. "Looking for that driver, are you?"

"No, looking for a kid named Gerber. Younger than you, tall, maybe seventeen or eighteen."

"I know who you mean. Hasty Gerber. Don't hire him to drive your wagon. He's a knacker."

"What's that?"

"He kills stray animals and sells their carcasses to rendering works. It's a loathsome occupation."

"Does he use a club like this?" Swift held up the weapon.

Smitty nodded. "Looks like one he carried."

"Where do I find him?"

"Down by the docks if he's not still asleep. Sometimes he helps unload boats at Hitchbourn Wharf."

Following directions, Swift walked south to Fish Street and then west for several blocks to the wharf. He suspected Gerber's height would make him easy to spot, and he was right. The youth was standing with some others as Swift approached. He saw him coming, saw the club dangling from his right hand, and took off down the pier. It was a dead end for him, but he didn't seem to realize it till Swift had him cornered.

"I just wanted to return your club," he told the youth. "You might need it to kill a stray dog or two."

Hasty Gerber looked frightened. "I wasn't trying to kill you last night."

"I know. You came there for the gunpowder. Now you're going to tell me who you're working for, or I'll do a little knacking myself."

Some of the others on the pier had gathered around, but no one came to Gerber's aid. "All right!" he pleaded, pushing out with his open palms. "Don't hit me!"

Swift gripped him by the shoulder as he had on their first meeting. "Did you kill Rollo Blake?"

"What? You're crazy! I never did it. I was just after those barrels of gunpowder."

"Come along. You're going to tell us all about that."

In the presence of Paul Revere and a law-enforcement officer, Hasty Gerber told how he and another youth had been hired by Rollo Blake to sneak into Revere's garden after dark and remove the four barrels from under the wagon. A neighbor had heard them the first time and frightened them off. After that, the other lad had wanted no part of it. Gerber had returned alone last night and encountered Swift. The law officer listened to it all and promised to pursue the investigation.

"It was all Blake's doing, of course," Swift remarked when he was alone with Revere. "He suggested the church purchase a bell from you so he'd have an excuse to cross the border with his wagon. The border guards had no reason to search it carefully with a minister and two parishioners on board."

"All right," Revere agreed, "but why did this Gerber youth try to steal the gunpowder last night, after he knew Blake was dead?"

"Just to have it for himself," Swift answered.

"Do you think he killed Blake for that purpose?"

"I don't know. When I grabbed him on the street just after the shooting he had no pistol with him."

But he wasn't satisfied. At ten o'clock, when Reverend Hayes and Mrs. Southworth arrived to begin their journey back to Quebec, he still wasn't satisfied. He stood in Revere's yard, near where Blake had fallen, and imagined where the killer might have stood. The sun had come out, bathing the city in the first real warmth of spring.

Betsy Patrick came out on her back porch and called to him. "I've made some lemonade if you'd like a glass."

"That would taste good about now." He went up the steps and she handed him a glass. He pulled up a chair to join her.

"I see John Rossiter has arrived," she said, filling his glass from her pitcher.

"He's volunteered to drive the wagon back to Quebec. Reverend Hayes was uncertain he could manage it with that heavy bell on board."

"Will you be leaving today as planned, Mr. Swift?"

Swift nodded. "I only came here at the behest of President Washington."

"He was concerned about Rollo Blake?"

"I believe so, yes. Now that Blake is dead and the bell is on its way to Canada, my work here is finished."

"What about Blake's killing?"

"That may have to go unsolved, at least by me. That is, unless you feel the need to confess."

Her eyes shot up, suddenly full of fear. "What do you mean?"

"You killed him, Betsy. You shot him from your bedroom window with your husband's musket."

"How could you know that?" she demanded. "Did you see me do it?"

"No, but the angle of the bullet, entering high on his back and exiting lower down at the front, indicated he was shot from above. This would explain why none of us saw a weapon. You'd told me your bedroom window overlooked Revere's yard when you yelled at the intruders two nights ago. You also told me you played the spinet to drown out the sound of the bells, but there was no spinet to be heard yesterday morning because you were at the upstairs window."

"Why would I shoot Rollo Blake?"

"You know the true motive better than I do. You told me that Revere's ringing of each new bell annoyed your husband, but Revere didn't cast his first bell until seventeen ninety-two. Your husband died in seventeen ninety. Who was this person annoyed by the ringing of the bells, someone you equated in your mind with your husband? I contend it was Rollo Blake, a frequent visitor to Boston and to the *Pig and Whistle* pub just down the street. His face was even familiar to Rachel Revere. Visiting your house was how he learned of Revere's bells and how he devised his plan for smuggling gunpowder into the city. He even told you about that, didn't he?"

She'd put down her glass of lemonade and was staring across the yard at the wagon as the horses were hitched up. "Sometimes, after he'd been drinking, he got crazy. He talked about blowing up our State House. I wrote President Washington an anonymous letter warning about it, but he did nothing."

He did something, Swift wanted to say. *He sent me.* Instead he said, "So you shot Rollo."

"There was no other way to stop him. When I saw them trying to retrieve something from that wagon, I knew he was going through with his plan. He was a bad man, Mr. Swift, in more ways than one."

"I suspected from the beginning that he was killed by a musket rather than a pistol, because the ball passed through the body with enough force to ring that bell. But no one standing near the victim could have hidden a musket under their clothing and fired it without being seen. I thought about that just now, and remembered the angle of the shot."

"What will you do about it?" she asked.

"I will report back to President Washington that the situation was dealt with by a patriot named Betsy. Thank you for the lemonade."

She smiled, perhaps with relief, as he got to his feet. "Tell me one thing, Mr. Swift. How did you know my husband had a musket?"

"Madam, you told me yourself he was a Minuteman. And I'm sure he was a brave one."

THE BARBER'S TOE

It was with a certain sadness that Alexander Swift called upon President Washington for possibly the last time in September of 1796. He'd seen little of the President in recent months, and Washington's decision not to seek a third term had set off a flurry of activity among both the Federalists and the Democratic-Republicans.

"It is a delight to see you again, Alex," the President said, greeting him with a firm handshake in the presidential office in Philadelphia. The date was September nineteenth, and he was about to depart for a few weeks at Mount Vernon. "How are Molly and young George?"

"Fine, sir, both of them. I was greatly moved by your Farewell Address in this morning's newspaper, though I'm sorry to learn of your decision not to seek a third term. Now you will never reside in the new presidential mansion in the District of Columbia."

Washington smiled sadly. "I leave that honor to my successor. Our new nation does not need another monarchy. Two terms are enough. Adams and Jefferson can battle it out."

"I understand that John Adams has not been happy in his role as your Vice President."

"He has complained to his wife, Abigail, that it is the most insignificant office man ever conceived, and I suppose there is some truth to that. But our nation is still young. I trust that in future generations the office will become more meaningful. Adams has another problem right now. As I understand it, someone from his past has threatened his life. He is quite concerned, and we have no official means of protecting him. I suggested you might be able to help."

"Of course," Alex said at once. "I'll do what I can."

"It would only be temporary. I suspect the threat will pass after the election."

"You can't think Jefferson's people are behind this."

Washington shook his head. "No, no—of course not. This is something far in the past. It is a bizarre story, but it is best you hear it from him."

A meeting had been arranged with Adams for the following day. The Vice President was a small man, especially when compared to President

Washington, and he had a small office. His round face was set off by tufts of gray hair on either side of a balding head.

"How is your campaign going?" Alex asked after they exchanged pleasantries.

"It is just getting started, but I fear the Federalists are losing power, at least in New York. Jefferson's Democratic-Republicans are gaining on us. It will be a very close vote." He seemed a bit weary as he spoke, looking all of his sixty years. "Since presidential candidates do not run for office with vice presidential candidates of their own choosing, it is possible that Jefferson and I might have to take office together as President and Vice President—if we are the two top vote-getters. But whoever wins, the country must come to grips with the increased naval threat from France and Britain. I feel we should avoid war with France at all costs."

"President Washington said you were having a problem."

"Yes, yes. A minor thing," he said, dismissing it with a wave of his hand. "But he felt you might be of service to me. This all happened eighteen years ago, in March of seventeen seventy-eight, when I was aboard the frigate *Boston*, en route to France on a diplomatic mission for the Continental Congress. It was a long, rough voyage and I was seasick part of the time. We encountered and captured a British warship and had run-ins with the French as well. We had on board a French barber whose name I have forgotten, if I ever knew it. During one skirmish off the coast of Spain he tried to go below deck, contrary to orders. He scuffled with a sentinel and the man cut off the barber's left big toe with his cutlass. For a brief time, there was ill will with the other Frenchmen on board, but we managed to calm them."

"How has this event come back to trouble you?"

"The barber, apparently a man named Pierre Facon, is living in New York. Last week, after rumors of Washington's impending retirement began to circulate and I let my candidacy be known, I received this threatening message. It was hand-delivered to my office by a street urchin."

Alex took the message and read it. The handwriting was crabbed, difficult to decipher, and seemed to be in a combination of French and English. The writer accused Adams of having ordered the sentinel to cut off his toe, causing him to go through life with a painful limp. He ended the message with a promise of vengeance unless he was paid an unspecified sum of money.

"The maiming happened during a scuffle," Adams insisted. "It was not deliberate."

"In any event, why would he blame you, a mere passenger on the ship? It was not as if you were under arms."

"It is a fact that I was carrying a musket at the time. I sometimes aided our forces by firing at enemy ships during an engagement. This barber may have objected to my actions. It is difficult to remember after so many years."

Alex turned over the message, seeking an address. There seemed to be none, although the letter had been written on the back of a handbill for a boardinghouse on New York's Greenwich Street. He knew the city well, having lived there with his first wife at the start of the Revolution. "I could go to New York if you wish, and try to find this fellow."

"It would put me deeply in your debt if you could remove this threat. With the election looming, Abigail is already concerned for my safety. Offer the man money if he is in need of it."

"I know it was eighteen years ago, but do you have any recollection of this Pierre Facon's appearance?"

"A tall man, as I remember. Taller than me, at least. He'd be middle-aged by now. I hadn't thought of him in years, didn't even remember his name."

"I doubt if you're in any real danger," Alex told the Vice President. "But I will attempt to find this French barber and deal with him."

Adams seemed alarmed at his words. "I don't want the poor man harmed."

Alex laughed. "I am not a violent man, sir, as I'm sure the President has told you. During the war it was something else, but now I prefer peaceful resolutions to problems wherever possible."

"When will you leave for New York?"

"Tomorrow. Perhaps a good conversation with Pierre Facon will settle the matter."

It had been some years since Alexander Swift last visited New York. The nation's capital had moved to a more central location in Philadelphia, and the city on the Hudson brought back unpleasant memories of his first wife, Amanda. She'd left him for a British officer, Major Jack Jordan, and when he was subsequently killed she'd married for a third time. Now a happily married husband and father himself, Alex had no desire to seek her out. He knew she now lived not far from Greenwich Street and he hoped their paths would not cross.

The coach had brought him to the ferry in New Jersey, and Alex crossed the Hudson River to land at the Cortlandt Street dock in late afternoon. It was only a few blocks up Greenwich Street to the Ring boardinghouse, the place advertised on the handbill in his pocket. It was a large house with three stories plus an attic, and could probably accommodate more than a dozen boarders at a time. A wooden canopy stretched forward across the wide sidewalk to a street with a convenient water pump at the corner.

Alex carried a saddlebag with a few necessities in it. When he stopped at the desk inside the door, a middle-aged woman glanced up from her ledger and said, "I'm Mrs. Ring. Are you looking for a room?"

"I was to meet someone here. I'm not certain I have the right place."

"What's his name?" Her tone was almost indifferent, as if she didn't care whether he stayed or left.

"Pierre Facon."

"No one here by that name."

"A Frenchman, middle-aged, walks with a limp."

"Can't help you," she said, returning to her ledger.

"He might work as a barber."

"There is a barber down in the next block," she admitted. "He would be closed now, though."

"Is that a place where you left this handbill?" he asked, showing her the printed side.

"It might have been."

Alex took a room for the night, deciding it was useless to continue the search before morning. He paid in advance and she gave him a key, directing him to Room Seven on the second floor. The bed was lumpy and uncomfortable but he had slept on worse. Mostly he missed the pleasure of sleeping with Molly in their own bed back home.

Alex was up early, breakfasting on the meager fare offered by Mrs. Ring before venturing onto the street. The boardinghouse was quite close to the docks, and even at an early hour there were seamen about, some returning to their ships after a night in town. He spotted the striped barber pole in the next block and headed in that direction. The shop with its sign *Dijon Barber* was already open at eight in the morning, with a customer in the chair. A gold-headed cane stood against the wall by the customer's coat.

The barber motioned him to have a seat, but instead he asked, "Is there a Pierre Facon who works here?"

The barber, a grizzled man in his forties with at least one gold tooth, shook his head. "I'm Matthew Dijon. I cut hair as well as he does."

"I'm sure you do. Where can I find him?"

"Ask Meg Wycliff. Sometimes she takes him in."

"Doesn't he work at a barbershop?" Alex was noticing some of Mrs. Ring's handbills on a shelf next to the door. Facon had picked one up somewhere to write his note to Adams.

Matthew kept the scissors flying as he answered. "Works for me off and on, when he feels like it. If you find him, tell him I could use an extra hand for a few days while the ships are in."

"Where can I find this Meg Wycliff?"

The barber glanced at his wall clock. "If she's up yet she'd likely be having breakfast with Prester Gamecock at the *Purple Seal*."

"Who?"

"You're new around the docks," Matthew remarked. "That's the name he uses. Prester Gamecock deals in fighting cocks. Everyone bets with him." He finished with the customer, who paid him, grabbed his coat from a hook, and hurried out to the street.

Alex thanked the barber and went on his way, thinking about Prester Gamecock. He decided he'd been away from the city too long—or not long enough.

He did know the *Purple Seal*, though, a long-time hangout for sailors off the merchant ships. It was only a few blocks down the street, near the dock where a large fishing schooner lay at anchor. He entered the place casually, well aware that his city clothing immediately set him apart from these dock-dwellers out for a morning's food and drink. He stopped a barmaid carrying two tankards of ale and asked, "Is Prester Gamecock here yet?"

Her lips tightened into a grim line as she motioned toward a back booth. Alex saw a large man with a mottled face, wearing a blue bandanna around his head. He was seated with a dark-haired, green-eyed young woman who might have been twenty or a bit younger. He must have overheard Alex's question because his head came up slowly until their eyes met. "Looking for me?" he asked in a rasping voice that seemed to go with his face.

"Looking for Meg Wycliff. They said she might be with you."

He placed his arm possessively around the dark-haired woman. "How much is she worth to you?"

"I only want to talk," Alex said, slipping into the other side of the booth. "You are Meg Wycliff?"

"I am," she announced with some pride.

"My name is Alexander Swift and I come from our nation's capital. I'm seeking a friend of yours, the French barber named Pierre Facon."

The woman and man exchanged quick glances. "I know him. He has not been seen lately," she replied.

"Why do you seek him?" the man called Gamecock wanted to know.

Remembering John Adams' offer of money, he said, "I might be able to help him if he's in financial difficulties."

"He is that!" Meg Wycliff confirmed. "Are you a friend?"

"I've never met him, but I bring a message from someone who has, our Vice President. Could you tell me where I might find him?"

It was Prester Gamecock who answered. "We see him on occasion. Perhaps even tonight. I have a prize cock fighting at the Men's Sporting Parlor in the Bowery, and that usually attracts him."

"I may come there," Alex told them. "Where is it located?"

"In Patsy Hearn's Five Points grogshop. Anyone can direct you to it."

Alex spent the remainder of the morning searching the dock area and nearby boardinghouses for Facon, without success. Gamecock and Meg Wycliff seemed to be the only leads he had. He prowled the city's center, stopping to inspect the stocks and whipping posts as well as the nearby gallows designed to resemble a Chinese pagoda. Hanging, he knew, was still the punishment for burglary, arson, and forgery, as well as for murder. Further along he encountered a pair of pigs running wild in the street. Perhaps pigs, like people, were enjoying their freedom from British rule.

By afternoon his travels around the city had extended east to John Street, where he knew Amanda and her present husband resided. He was not especially surprised to recognize her entering a greengrocer's halfway down the block. Avoiding an encounter would have been easy enough, but he realized that he wanted to see her again after all, to learn how her life had been.

She did not notice him in the shop until he spoke. "It is a bit late in the season for the best greens, Amanda."

She looked up, startled, and relaxed only when she recognized him. "Alex! What brings you to New York?" She was still a handsome woman, even with the bits of gray creeping into her hair.

"I'm here on business, just for a day or two. I recognized you entering the shop and thought I'd say hello."

Her face had relaxed now into the smile he remembered. "It's good to see you again. Are you happy?"

"Very much so. Molly and I have a fine twelve-year-old son named George."

"After Washington."

"Of course. We were married at West Point and Washington attended the ceremony. How about you?"

"Roland is a master tanner. He sells leather to shoemakers in the city. I help with his bookkeeping. We entertain at dinner and keep quite busy." A thought occurred to her. "I'd like you to meet him. Would you be free for dinner tonight, Alex?"

He smiled. "Roland might not appreciate meeting your former husband. Besides, I have an engagement tonight, in the Five Points neighborhood."

"That place is a slum, infested with Irish immigrants!"

"It's business. I'm certain no harm will come to me."

"Alex—"

"Next time. Perhaps Molly and I can dine with you next time. It was good seeing you, Amanda." He turned and left her in the shop.

The Men's Sporting Parlor was in the rear of Patsy Hearn's grogshop, and Alex found a place to sit on the pine planks that ran around a sunken pit some fifteen feet square. Admission was a mere twenty-five cents, and the man next to him explained that it had cost more before the opposition to bearbaiting had ended that practice in many places. Now there were only the cocks to fight, and an occasional battle between rats and trained terriers. All the events were good for wagering, and Alex joined in by betting a dollar on a ruffled rooster that looked as if it had survived a few previous battles.

He didn't notice Prester Gamecock until the end of the first match. Alex's cock had triumphed and a one-eyed sailor brought him his winnings. As he looked up he saw the large man with the blue bandanna seated across the arena from him, along with Meg Wycliff and another man. There were five matches scheduled that night, and when the last of them ended with an explosion of blood and feathers, Alex made his way around the pit to join Gamecock's party.

"Did you have some winners, Mr. Swift?" the woman asked

"I won on the first match and quit while I was ahead. How often are these fights held?"

"Whenever we have enough cocks," the large man answered. "Once a week, sometimes twice."

The crowd around them had cleared out, and a black man was spreading sawdust over the bloodstained pit. Alex's gaze had drifted to the third member of their party and Meg Wycliff announced, "This is Pierre Facon, the man you've been looking for."

"Mr. Facon?" Alex asked, extending his hand.

"Yes, that is me," the man agreed. He spoke English with only a trace of a French accent. He was fairly tall, but seemed a bit young to have been working on shipboard eighteen years earlier.

"Did you work as a barber aboard the frigate Boston in seventeen seventy-eight?"

"I did, sir. Those were proud days, fighting alongside the Americans."

Alex glanced at the others and decided the rest of the conversation should be between Facon and himself. He thanked Gamecock and the woman for their help and went off with the Frenchman to the front of the grogshop. Once they were seated he ordered two tankards of ale and told the man, "I've been sent here by Vice President Adams."

"I assumed as much."

"You wrote him about the events on board the Boston."

"Yes," he agreed.

"Your letter could be seen as a threat against the Vice President."

"I didn't mean it as a threat," he replied, suddenly ill at ease. "I just felt I should get some money for what happened."

"You must realize the Vice President was not responsible for your injury."

"He owes me something," Facon insisted. "He might be the next President."

"As a Frenchman, that should please you. Adams opposes a war with France over the maritime incidents."

"Aye, he is not a bad man."

"Are you working? I spoke with Matthew, the barber down on Greenwich Street. He said he could use you for a few days."

Facon smiled and shook his head. "I made some money tonight on the cocks and I expect some more from Mr. Adams. I don't need his job, though he has been kind to a fellow countryman."

"You'd better tell him you won't be in."

"I'll leave a note on his door tonight. What about the money?"

"Meet me for breakfast tomorrow at Mrs. Ring's boardinghouse. Perhaps I can help you out, if you promise to cease annoying the Vice President."

"Mrs. Ring's," he repeated with a smile. "I'll be there. About eight?"

"Fine."

Back in his room at the boardinghouse, Alex considered how much he could reasonably offer the man the following morning. Adams had given him a free rein, but he did not want the exchange of money to seem like any sort of payoff or bribe to keep quiet. The Vice President had done nothing wrong, and any payment must be of a compassionate nature only.

In the morning he decided on an appropriate sum and went downstairs a little before eight to await the arrival of Pierre Facon. But it was Meg Wycliff who appeared at the boardinghouse door, her face twisted with grief. "You must come," she told him. "Pierre has been murdered!"

Alex quickly followed her down Greenwich almost as far as Liberty Street. "What happened?" he asked as they walked. "Who killed him?"

"We don't know. He spent the night at a bawdy house."

She led him to a two-story frame dwelling with shuttered windows. They went up the front steps to the door where a stout older woman waited.

"No police!" she told Meg. "I told you no police."

"He's not police. He's from the government. Alex, this is Mrs. Blithe. She owns this place."

"Where is Facon?" he asked.

"This way." The stout woman led them to a second-floor hallway. Girls in nightdresses, barely past school age, clustered by an open doorway until she shooed them away. Facon's body lay inside and blood from a head wound had turned the rug crimson. He was wearing one-piece underwear and his feet were bare. He had ten toes.

"What happened to him?" Alex asked.

Mrs. Blithe shook her head. "I don't know. He was in here with one of my girls and she went down the hall to wash up. She swears he wasn't alone for more than five minutes. She heard a thump and came back to find him like this."

"His skull was crushed by a hard blow," Alex said, glancing around for any possible weapon. Nothing likely was visible "You must know who was up here at the time, Mrs. Blithe."

"This early in the morning most of the girls are asleep. Anyone could walk in the front door."

He motioned toward the body. "Is it common for customers to spend the night?"

"Sometimes, if they come late. This man had no wife."

"Pierre Facon? Was that his name?"

Mrs. Blithe shrugged. "It was the name he used. Down on the docks nobody asks many questions."

"Where's the girl he was with?" Alex asked.

She glanced around, finally summoning one of them. "Estelle, come here! Tell this man what happened."

Estelle was a bit older than the others, with squinty eyes and a hard mouth. "He came in after midnight," she told them. "After a while he just fell asleep, so I let him be."

"Was he a regular customer of yours?"

"I guess you could say that," she admitted. "He always came to me if I wasn't busy."

"Then someone looking for him might have come to your room."

"Maybe," she admitted with some reluctance.

"Did he ever talk about his past, about his days at sea?"

Estelle's eyes squinted even more. "He was a barber, not a sailor. What would he be doing at sea?"

"How about enemies? Did he seem fearful of anyone?"

She thought about it. "That man Gamecock. Everyone's afraid of him. He's the one should have gotten killed."

"I thought they were friends."

"Nobody's his friend. The girls all fear him, and the men hate him because he takes their money. Some say he even fixes the cockfights, feeding small amounts of belladonna to some of the birds to sicken them."

Alex considered the possibilities. "Could he have gotten in here his morning without being seen?"

"Of course he could! And anyone who happened to see him would be afraid to say so."

Meg Wycliff had followed him upstairs and tugged at his arm. "You're endangering these people with your questions! Facon is dead. Whatever you came here for, it's over."

"Perhaps. Where can I find Gamecock now?"

"Sleeping, probably. He sleeps late, especially on the mornings after a cockfight."

"Where?"

She took a deep breath. "If I told you, he'd kill me."

"All right. Tell me this—where is the real Pierre Facon?"

"What? In there, on the floor. What do you mean?"

"This man isn't Facon and I think you know it. When you and Gamecock heard I was looking for him, offering money on behalf of the Vice President, you found someone to pass off as Facon in hopes of making an easy profit.

Only I happen to know that the real Facon is missing the big toe on his left foot, and that body on the floor has all its toes."

"And I happen to know he's the real Pierre Facon, and there's no business with missing toes. I've known him all my life."

"The barber, Matthew, said you took him in sometimes."

"I took him in because he was my half-brother."

In the downstairs parlor, while Mrs. Blithe poured them tea, Meg Wycliff told her story. "My mother was married to a French trader named Victor Facon. He fought with the colonists against the British and was killed at Trenton in 'seventy-six. Their son, Pierre, was twelve at the time."

Alex remembered thinking he'd seemed a bit young to have been aboard the *Boston* in 'seventy-eight. "And your mother remarried?"

She nodded. "The following year, to a man named Peter Wycliff, and I came along soon afterward. They moved west to Ohio a few years ago, but I stayed here with Pierre."

"He was a barber by trade?"

"He worked at the shop with Matthew Dijon for a time, but he was always looking for something else, something that would bring him big money. I think that's why he wrote the letter to John Adams."

"Then you knew about the letter?"

"Not immediately. When you came looking for me yesterday he told me what he'd done."

"He was never on board the ship with Adams?"

"Never on board anything bigger than the fishing boats around the harbor. In seventeen seventy-eight he was only fourteen, still living at home. He told me how he helped take care of me as a baby."

"Did you ever hear this story before about a toe being cut off?"

"Never."

"What about you? Were you here when he was killed?"

Her face reddened at his question. "I am not a strumpet, in spite of anything you might have heard. Mrs. Blithe sent someone for me as soon as she saw the body. I remembered Pierre telling me you'd be at Mrs. Ring's boardinghouse and I came for you at once."

"All right, I believe you. Now tell me where I can find Prester Gamecock."

"If I know him, he'll be collecting his winnings from last night's match. You might find him in any of the shops along the river."

The police, always a bit reluctant to deal with bawdy houses, had at last arrived on the scene. Alex managed to slip away, and if any of the officers noticed his exit they no doubt took him for a shy customer eager to avoid questioning. He made his way over to the river and stopped in all the likely shops, asking after the man he sought. But if any of them knew the name Prester Gamecock they were reluctant to admit it. By the time he reached the *Purple Seal* they told him Gamecock had been there and gone.

Gazing down Greenwich Street, he saw the familiar barber pole at the Dijon shop. It was as good a place as any to try next, and it was a fortunate choice. Alex peered through the window and saw Gamecock collecting some coins from the barber. He opened the door and went in to join them. There were no customers, and no coats or canes by the wall hooks.

"Do you have business with me?" Gamecock asked, obviously annoyed at his presence.

The barber moved off to one side, as if fearful of being caught in the middle. "Pierre Facon was killed this morning at Mrs. Blithe's house," Alex said.

"Interesting," the large man said, weighing the coins he'd just received in the palm of his hand. "You'll need a new assistant," he told Matthew.

"Who might have wanted him dead?" Alex asked them.

The barber shrugged. "He probably got rough with one of Mrs. Blithe's girls and she whacked him. Wouldn't be the first time."

Alex turned to Gamecock, who had started for the door. "What do you think?"

"I never judge people. There is enough of a challenge in judging fighting cocks."

He left the shop. Alex started to follow and then changed his mind. Something was wrong, something was missing, and it took him a moment to realize what it was. He let the door close behind Prester Gamecock. "Matthew?"

"Yes?" the barber responded.

"What happened to your gold-headed cane, the one that was leaning against the wall here yesterday?"

"Cane?"

"I thought it belonged to your customer in the chair, but he grabbed his coat and hurried out the door."

"You mean this cane?" he asked, lifting it from behind a cabinet.

"That's the one, Matthew. The one you used to bludgeon Pierre Facon to death this morning. Don't try it with me. I can move a great deal faster than a limping man with a missing toe."

"I know nothing about his death."

"You knew enough to say he might have been whacked by one of the girls, when I hadn't mentioned how he died. You have a cane that could be the murder weapon, and the necessity for a cane in someone your age implies a foot or leg injury. It was you who lost a toe on board the *Boston*, wasn't it? You told the story to Facon and he stole it as his own, writing to Adams to ask for compensation. When I told him last night that you needed an assistant barber, he wrote you a note and left it in your door. Whatever he said in that note made you realize what he'd done. In your fury, you sought him out at Mrs. Blithe's, knowing he'd be with Estelle, and split his skull with your cane."

"I have no accent, yet you accuse me of being a French barber on board the *Boston?*"

"Facon described you as a fellow countryman and your name is certainly French. If it's not you, take off your left boot and let me count your toes."

He sighed, realizing that further denial was useless. "He stole my story to get money from Adams! I went there full of anger, to beat some sense into him, not to kill him. I never requested payment from the United States and I never would. I am proud to be part of this new nation." He was silent for a moment, finally adding in a quiet voice, "Now what is there for me?"

"I am not the police," Alex told him. He considered his courses of action. "I will report back to the Vice President. The decision will be his, but I can tell you he is a just man and a fair one. I believe he will leave the investigation to the local police without involving himself."

Matthew Dijon nodded. "Thank you, sir."

Alex touched the hair on the back of his head. "As long as I'm here, could you give me a trim before I leave?"

The barber smiled. "It would be a pleasure, sir."

SWIFT AMONG THE PIRATES

Christmas of 1799 was a bleak season for Alexander Swift. His good friend and mentor, George Washington, the new nation's first President, had died on the night of December 14, less than three years after handing over the reins of government to John Adams and retiring to Mount Vernon. Swift and his wife Molly had attended the funeral and burial in the family vault four days later.

With the dawn of a new century, he tried to think of the future, of their son George and the young country into which he'd been born. But his thoughts always returned to Washington, and to the traitor Benedict Arnold. One evening Molly asked what was troubling him. "I suppose the fact that Arnold is still alive, living free in London. Washington should have had at least the satisfaction of knowing he'd died."

"It's over. There's nothing you can do about that now."

"I could go to England and kill him myself."

"But you wouldn't," she said. "You're a good man, Alex. You couldn't kill someone in cold blood, not even Benedict Arnold."

And of course she was right.

Still, through the year that followed, as he went about his government duties, his mind kept returning to it. Not a cold-blooded killing, perhaps, but a duel. He knew they were still legal in England. Occasionally at night he'd waken from a dream, having imagined himself on a grassy meadow, dueling pistol in hand, facing off against Benedict Arnold at last.

John Adams served only one term as President, and the 1800 election brought Thomas Jefferson into the new presidential mansion following a bizarre tie vote between Jefferson and Aaron Burr in the Electoral College. The election was finally decided by the House of Representatives, with Burr becoming Vice President. It was some weeks after taking office in March 1801 that Jefferson summoned Swift to his office for an informal meeting.

"Washington always spoke highly of you," he said. "You never let him down when he called on you." Jefferson was a tall man with freckles and sandy hair beginning to turn gray. At times a bit more awkward than Washington in his speech, he still conveyed a commanding presence.

"I let him down once. I was never able to bring Benedict Arnold to justice."

"Perhaps someday that can be remedied," he told Swift. "Meantime, there is another matter. Since our nation won its freedom from Britain, we have been paying an annual tribute to the Pasha of Tripoli to protect our commercial ships from attacks by pirates. The Pasha has now informed me that the tribute must be raised to two hundred twenty-five thousand dollars a year, and I refuse to pay it. Next week, on May twentieth, I am dispatching a squadron of six frigates—all that we can spare—to cruise the Mediterranean and blockade the port of Tripoli, defending American vessels from attacks by Barbary pirates. I would like you to accompany them."

Alexander Swift smiled at the thought of it. "Twenty years ago I would have eagerly accepted such an assignment, sir. Now I fear my fighting days are past."

"For God's sake, no one is asking you to fight! You would act only as an observer, reporting back to me. Any fighting would be carried out by the crew and by detachments of Marines on board each ship."

"I don't know. It would mean leaving my wife and son for an extended period."

"Two months at most, perhaps less. If our ships have to remain longer, we'll find a way to bring you back."

Swift smiled at his words. "Maybe by hot air balloon?" But he knew he'd accept the assignment from President Jefferson, just as he had so many times from President Washington.

Molly wasn't pleased at the news of his forthcoming absence. "What about little George?" she tried to argue. "He looks forward to your bedtime stories."

"I'll be back before he knows I'm gone."

"But pirates, Alex!"

"Not as bad as facing an entire army of redcoats. And it'll give me lots of good stories for George."

"You're hopeless!" she decided, and perhaps she was right.

A week later Swift was at sea, aboard the U.S. Navy's three-masted frigate *Saratoga*, bound for the Mediterranean. He found it somewhat ironic that the ship bore the name of General Benedict Arnold's greatest victory over the British, before he changed sides in the war. The Atlantic waters were relatively calm in May, and the six frigates rarely lost sight of each other through the voyage. They were under the command of Commodores Richard Dale and Edward Preble, but neither was aboard Swift's ship. His captain was Jonathan Flace, an ugly man whose scarred face reflected war at close quarters. His first mate, named Collins, wasn't much better, with a bald head and a twisted lip that gave him a perpetual sneer.

"I'm in this because I like it," Flace told Alexander on their first day out of port. "Our United States Navy is new and untried in many ways. Coming here against the Barbary pirates is our opportunity to prove how good we are. I respect President Jefferson and the mission he has sent us on. Under Dale and Preble we will crush these pirates and send them running."

"I'm sure the President will be pleased to hear that, sir."

"Good. Are your quarters satisfactory?"

"Perfectly so." He was sharing crowded quarters with a Marine Corps second lieutenant named Sam Vantage, but he knew better than to complain. A man like Captain Flace might easily have tossed him overboard.

In truth, Vantage was a pleasant enough berth-mate. A handsome and knowledgeable young man still in his twenties, he'd won his commission only months before. On their second day at sea he'd taken Swift on a tour of the ship, showing him the impressive sails in their full rigging. "You'll note that all our main cannons are on the upper deck. Older frigates had guns on two decks, but the lower deck now carries no armament and functions as berth space for the crew. Our berths are actually below the waterline."

"I would have thought that two decks of cannons would offer greater firepower."

"True, but in rough seas, the two-deckers had to close their gun ports on the lower deck to avoid being swamped. This way our guns are always ready for use, even in rough weather. Our long hulls and low upper works make for a sleeker, faster vessel."

"What size are these cannons?" Swift asked, patting a rough metal barrel. "They seem quite large."

"They're twenty-four-pounders, as large as those the Royal Navy carries. This ship is one of our newest and largest, carrying thirty-eight guns, nineteen on each side. The main batteries are twenty-four-pounders, the rest are eighteen-pounders. We can blast any pirate ship out of the water." He spoke with the confidence of youth.

"Do you think we'll encounter any of them?"

"We'll be ready if we do."

Swift bent down to lift one of the cannonballs from its stacked pyramid. "These could make a few nice holes in any pirate ship."

"They are solid, but they're working on some that break apart after they're fired and do even more damage."

He took Swift on a tour of the galley and even climbed with him up the rope ladder to the crow's nest. Molly would have been horrified, Swift thought as he clung to the swaying ladder. They went on to meet the helmsman who steered the vessel. "The captain rarely does it himself," Vantage explained.

They were met by a naval lieutenant, Quincy Pitt, to whom Swift had been introduced the previous day. "Enjoying the view, Mr. Swift?"

"Very much so. Lieutenant Vantage has just been giving me the ship's tour. You have a fine vessel here."

"We'll know soon enough," Pitt said. He was the gunnery officer, in charge of those thirty-eight cannons.

By early June they had passed the Rock of Gibraltar and sailed into the Mediterranean. Within days the squadron reached Malta and turned due south toward Tripoli. The ships took up their stations as the harbor came into view. At first there seemed little reaction on shore, but at dawn the following day Swift was awakened by the sound of cannons. The city's shore batteries had opened fire. Spouts of water showed that the balls were landing short of their targets, but there was still reason for concern.

"Action stations!" Captain Flace commanded, rousing the men with a trumpet call to arms. Within moments the crew had manned their guns, ready to return fire. Swift stayed under cover as the water spouts seemed to move a bit closer. He was beginning to regret taking on this assignment for Jefferson.

But the shore batteries were no match for the navy's twenty-four-pounders. As Quincy Pitt and Captain Flace rushed back and forth, urging the gunners on, cannonballs and gunpowder were being reloaded for the next round. There was a moment's silence and then when the silence stretched out, the captain ordered, "Hold your fire!"

Sam Vantage explained to Swift, "The enemy's taken a break to elevate their cannons, so the balls will travel further. They'll probably use more gunpowder to increase the velocity, too. It's not over yet."

However, the day passed uneventfully. Peering through his telescope, Flace reported that all seemed quiet on the shore batteries. "I believe we have delivered President Jefferson's reply to their demand for tribute," he concluded.

Night settled slowly over the anchored squadron of frigates. A cool breeze had blown in, creating a light mist that turned the moon into a fuzzy ball far above their heads. Swift retired to his bunk with a certain uneasiness, but the gently lapping water lulled him to sleep almost at once.

He was awakened suddenly by the sound of cannon fire from the shore batteries. Sam Vantage was already out of his bunk and nearly dressed. "What time is it?" Swift muttered.

"Daybreak. But there is a heavy mist over the water."

Swift followed him topside where the gun crews were already at their stations, loading gunpowder and cannonballs while Pitt shouted sharp commands. It was Captain Flace who issued the order, "Fire at will!"

All up and down the line fuses were lit and within seconds the cannons began to thunder their message, each one recoiling on its wheels as it let loose its fiery blast. The return fire from shore was still falling far short of its mark, and Swift wondered what they expected to accomplish.

Then suddenly he knew. A cannonball flew overhead, crashing into one of their masts. Another followed, not from the direction of shore but from the open sea. The deck was alive with shouts and confusion until Swift and the others turned away from shore and saw a small frigate materialize from the mist not a hundred yards away. It was flying a red banner with a crescent moon, one of the flags of the Barbary pirates.

"To starboard!" Pitt shouted. "They're trying to ram us!"

Loading and firing the starboard cannons took valuable minutes. The pirate vessel headed directly toward them but then turned at the last moment, as if preparing to fire another volley. Swift seemed to realize the true danger before the others. "They're going to board us!" he told Vantage, catching a glimpse of their foes holding scimitars for close combat.

The two ships came together before the *Saratoga* could return fire. Instantly the pirates were upon them, swinging over on ropes to hit the deck with weapons ready. Swift was relieved to see that the detachment of marines was prepared for them. Within minutes the frigate's deck was awash with blood. Judging by their weapons and garb, Swift guessed the attackers to be Turks, as many of the Barbary pirates were. One of them fell before him, hit by a bullet from a Marine musket, and Swift grabbed up his scimitar to defend himself.

He brought down one of the attackers and saw that some marines were swinging over to the pirate ship, taking the fight to the enemy. Cannons were useless at such close range, and might do as much damage to the *Saratoga* as to the enemy. Another round of fire from Marine muskets drove back some of the pirates, but the fighting was soon at such close quarters that no clear shots were possible. It was cutlass against scimitar and dagger.

The battle lasted more than thirty minutes, and in the end the entire pirate crew had been killed or captured. The Americans suffered six dead and eleven seriously wounded. A search of the pirate frigate revealed a young female captive half crazy with fear. Quincy Pitt brought her onto the *Saratoga*, his comforting arms holding tight around her as he guided her along the plank bridge between the vessels. Swift stood to one side watching the crew clean up after the dead and wounded. The slain pirates were unceremoniously dumped overboard, while the wounded were given minimal medical attention by the ship's surgeon on board.

"What happens to them now?" Swift asked Captain Flace.

"We've signaled our flagship to come alongside and remove the wounded. I'll keep a few prisoners here in the event we need them for bargaining. Their captain is dead, but the first mate was uninjured and I will question him personally. Their ship is badly damaged and we'll scuttle her."

"What about our own damage?"

"The mast needs repairing, but I think we can handle it. I don't want to limp back to port with it like this."

"Is there any possibility of another pirate attack?"

Flace scowled at the thought. "The weather was right for it this morning, with that mist to obscure their approach while we were busy with the shore batteries. That won't happen again. And they've lost a ship and crew. They might think twice before risking another one."

Swift was more interested in the woman who'd been rescued. She was an Egyptian named Abden Said, dressed in torn pants and a bloodstained silk blouse. She was still in her twenties, but with sad brown eyes that seemed to reflect a lifetime of pain. Her English was good enough to be understood and Swift sat in while she was questioned by Captain Flace and Pitt. She told them she'd been sailing on a small boat near Alexandria when they were seized by pirates a month earlier. The man with her had been killed and she'd been taken captive. "They say I will be sold into slavery," she told Captain Flace. "I cry and beg but it does no good."

"Were you mistreated?" he asked delicately.

"I am mistreated all my life."

"Who is this man we captured?" he asked, indicating a prisoner seated in irons across the cabin.

The man, with a scarred face and a black bandanna around his head, spit on the deck. He answered in a language none of them understood.

"What is your name?" Quincy Pitt asked.

It was the woman who answered. "His name is Dread, but I do not speak his language. He may be from the Greek islands. He is a gunner's mate."

Captain Flace waved the prisoner away. "Lock him up in the brig with the other prisoners," he told Pitt. "And bring me the key to their leg irons. They are not to be freed except by me."

"What about the woman?" Swift asked Flace after the prisoner had been removed.

He turned to her. "We have no separate quarters for you. I will arrange for you to sleep in the galley and you can help with the meals. If we learn of a ship bound for Alexandria we can transfer you to it."

"Thank you," she murmured. "I will work for you."

Later, toward evening, when the flagship had come alongside to transfer the wounded and prisoners, they gave a respectful burial at sea to the six dead Americans. Swift had never been present at this ceremony before, and he said a silent prayer as each of the bodies slid off into its watery grave.

It was young Sam Vantage who came to him on deck later that night as he stood gazing at the stars. "A beautiful sight, isn't it, Mr. Swift?"

"It is indeed," he agreed. "It's difficult remembering that men died here today under that sky."

"Did you fight in the War of Independence, sir?"

"I was not in the army, but I undertook a number of missions for General Washington, and later for President Washington, including some involving Benedict Arnold."

"I read about him. Did they ever catch him?"

"Not yet," Swift replied.

He didn't think anyone slept well that night. The excitement of the battle, and the fear that it might happen again, had everyone on edge. Shortly before midnight he walked around the upper deck and saw Captain Flace bending over a cannon to examine it. Flace heard his footsteps and whirled around, hand on his sword. "Good evening, Mr. Swift. You startled me."

"Sorry. I couldn't sleep."

"Can't be too careful when there are prisoners aboard," the captain remarked with his familiar scowl. "I have to check everything myself. It's my ship. I am responsible."

"Your men did well today. I will report as much to President Jefferson."

"Thank you, Mr. Swift. I only hope I am able to return to Washington and report to him personally."

They parted then, and Swift returned to the cabin he shared with Sam Vantage. The young officer was not in his bunk, but Swift heard him come in sometime later, undressing in the dark and sliding beneath his blanket.

It was Quincy Pitt who awakened them before dawn with the shocking news that Captain Flace had been found dead on the upper deck, his skull crushed by one of the ship's cannonballs.

The first mate, Collins, took charge of the *Saratoga*, ordering the signalman to notify the flagship of the event. Gathering the crew on deck, he spoke briskly. "Aye, there's a killer among us. The captain's death was no accident. I want you first to check and make certain none of our prisoners could have escaped. After that I'll be talking to every member of this crew until I find the guilty person."

When the crew members returned to their stations, Alexander Swift stepped forward and introduced himself to Collins. "Perhaps the captain told you about me. I am aboard this ship at the direct request of President Jefferson, reporting on the success of our mission against the Barbary pirates. I would like to assist in your investigation."

He smirked at Swift through his twisted lip. "You can do the whole thing, for all I care. I came here to kill pirates, not find a murderer."

"Might any of the crew have reason to kill Flace?"

"He was a stern master. No man can be a good captain without bruising some feelings—and some bodies."

"Whose, for instance?"

He shook his head. "That's not for me to say. I don't implicate innocent men."

"Was there anything in Flace's pockets that might be a clue?"

"Come and see for yourself."

Swift followed him to the frigate's makeshift hospital, where the surgeon was tending the wounded from the previous day's battle. In one corner he saw Flace's body, wrapped in a sack that hadn't yet been sewn shut. The back of his head showed evidence of the terrible blow that had taken his life. A cloth bag next to his body held the contents of his pockets. "Is this everything?" Swift asked, glancing through the few coins, a handkerchief, a pocketknife, and a small compass.

"That's all."

"Didn't he have a ship's manifest?"

"That would be on the bridge along with his log book."

"Could I see it?"

Collins hesitated, then said, "Follow me."

The men on the bridge were silent when they arrived, barely nodding to Collins. The ship was still at anchor and there was little activity. They seemed to be awaiting the burial of their captain, which would come later in the day. The ship's log and manifest yielded no new information, only the note on dead and injured, and the transfer to the flagship. Eight prisoners remained on board, along with the rescued woman. "Is Abden Said still in the galley?" he asked Collins.

"The woman? We've put her to work there."

Swift found her working with the cook on the crew's evening meal. Like the Royal Navy, the Americans had mastered the art of brewing beer and baking bread on shipboard, and the days of insect-infested biscuits were behind them. Abden worked in one of the marine uniforms, a small size but it was still too big for her. "What happened to your captain?" she asked at once, removing a loaf of bread from the oven.

"Someone killed him, crushed his skull with a cannonball."

"One of the pirates?"

"That seems likely, but they were supposed to be locked up. How are you doing here?"

"Very well. It is good to be free again—with the Americans instead of the pirates."

He wasn't sure how safe she'd be as the only woman on a ship full of sailors and marines; he could only do his best to protect her until she could be transferred to another vessel. He left her and headed below deck to the brig. There were two guards now instead of the usual one, and the sullen prisoners were crowded into a single cell. One who spoke English called out to Swift. "Get us out of here!" he demanded. "Some are seriously wounded!"

"Our captain is dead," Swift told him. "You will probably be transferred to another ship soon." He turned to one of the guards and asked, "Were any of these men allowed out of the brig during the night?"

A marine guard answered his question. "We took them to the head one at a time around midnight."

"Were they out of your sight?"

"Just for a minute or so, and they still had their leg irons. They weren't going anywhere."

Swift stared at the man named Dread, wondering if he could have pulled it off somehow. But before he could ask another question there was a sound like distant thunder that sent the frigate rocking. The shore batteries had commenced firing again.

Swift ran up on deck and found Quincy Pitt shouting orders to his men. Well-trained teams took up their positions at each of the port cannons, while the officers stayed alert for another attack from the starboard side. But this day was clear and only their flagship was on the horizon. The shore batteries were still firing and Swift counted a half-dozen water spouts from cannon-balls landing precariously close to them. Then, as he watched, the ship's cannon-balls and powder were loaded, the fuses lit. At Pitt's command, the *Saratoga*'s guns replied to the shore batteries. Swift saw one battlement torn apart by a direct hit from a cannonball.

Suddenly their ship shuddered as one of the enemy cannonballs scored a direct hit. Swift was thrown to the deck, and for a moment he feared the hit had been a fatal one below the waterline. Then Sam Vantage appeared in the hatch and shouted, "It hit near the brig. We've got injured men!"

Swift followed him down the steps while Pitt directed the others to remain at their stations and reload. Another cannonball from the shore batteries hit the water within fifty feet of the ship as the acting captain gave the command to weigh anchor and pull back to a safe distance.

Below deck, all was a frenzy. The cannonball had sliced through the wooden hull, injuring several of the pirate captives and their two marine guards. Vantage was lifting a shattered piece of timber off one of the marines while others unlocked the door of the brig and tended to the injured prisoners. Swift saw Abden Said hurry down from the galley, helping to treat the injured. As Swift made his way to her she was trying to comfort the one called Dread. "He has bad chest pains," she told Swift. "He thinks something is broken."

"I'll get the surgeon."

Swift was aware that the ship was in motion, pulling back out of harm's way. He stayed below for a while longer, until he was sure the ship was in no immediate danger, and then hurried up to the bridge. Collins and the helmsman were at the wheel, struggling to head the ship further out to sea. "I've signaled Commodore Dale that we've been hit," he said. "He's coming aboard personally to inspect the damage."

"At least they've stopped firing."

Collins nodded. "We're out of range now. These ships are no good against cannonballs. We have one named the *Constitution*, a much larger frigate with wooden sides seven inches thick and strong as iron. Cannonballs actually bounce off it. That's in the West Indies now, but if this mission goes on it will probably be sent here as our flagship. It can carry fifty-four guns and has a crew of four hundred and fifty, including fifty-five marines."

It was some hours before the flagship anchored near them and the long-boat was dispatched carrying Commodore Dale and several others. Collins welcomed them with dignity, explaining that he was the first mate and acting captain. "You say that Captain Flace was killed by a cannonball?" Dale asked. "Was it fired from the shore or the pirate ship?"

"Neither, sir. Someone on our ship dropped it on his head."

"My God! You have pirate prisoners, don't you?"

"We do, but they were confined to the brig in leg irons at the time."

"You suspect someone in the crew? I can't believe that."

"It's hard to believe," Collins told him, "but the captain may have made some enemies. He could be a brutal man at times."

"I'll want to see the log, especially regarding punishments." He glanced at Swift, as if noticing him for the first time. "Who might you be, sir?"

"Alexander Swift, special emissary from President Jefferson. I am to report on this first mission against the Barbary pirates."

"Yes, I was advised that you would be aboard the *Saratoga*. Now let us inspect the damage to the ship."

Below deck, crewmen had already covered the gash with canvas and wood. Commodore Dale inspected the repair work carefully, running his hand along the canvas. Finally he gave his verdict. "This is a good temporary patch, but it would never stand up in battle or in heavy seas. Given that, and the earlier damage to your mast, plus the loss of your captain, I must order the *Saratoga* back to port."

"Yes, sir," Collins said. "I understand."

"You will sail tomorrow for the island of Malta, where more temporary repairs can be made. Then you will return home with a skeleton crew. The rest of your men and the marine detachment will be shifted to other ships in our squadron."

Collins was in no position to disagree. "Very well, sir. I'll give you a copy of the roster. What about the prisoners?"

"We'll hold them aboard one of the ships. They may come in valuable as trade."

"We have an Egyptian woman they captured near Alexandria."

"She can come along too. We'll see that she gets home safely."

Collins turned to Swift. "What about him? Do we take him back with us?"

Dale considered it for a moment. "You can stay aboard with the skeleton crew, Mr. Swift, and sail with them to Malta for repairs, or I can put you on the British frigate *Bombay* bound for London. From there you should find an American ship to transport you home."

London. Alexander Swift remembered his unfinished business with Benedict Arnold. "London, sir," he decided without hesitation.

"Fine. We expect to encounter the *Bombay* within a day or two. Its captain has instructions to sail close to our position as protection against the pirates."

"Then everything is settled," Collins said.

"Everything but the killing of Captain Flace. I'll want to examine that punishment log. The killer's motive may reside there."

Swift cleared his throat. "That may not be necessary, sir. I grant that in a crime such as this, motive becomes most important. But the killer may have had a different motive entirely. I was aware that Captain Flace had especially good hearing. He was immediately aware of anyone approaching him from behind. Even if Dread or one of the other captive pirates had managed to escape briefly, they could not have sneaked up on him without his knowing it. Captain Flace appears to have been crouched down, inspecting one of the guns, when the killer dropped the cannonball on his head. It had to be someone he trusted, someone he didn't fear."

"One of the crew."

"But there's something else to consider—the motive. Would he have felt safe with a crew member he might have beaten or abused? I thought about another possible motive, and I remembered the contents of Flace's pockets."

"Nothing unusual there," Collins said.

"No, but there was something unusual missing. I was present when Captain Flace ordered the prisoners placed in leg irons and the key brought to him. The key was not among his possessions when his body was found."

"Who would steal it?" Collins asked. "Certainly none of the crew would try to free the pirates."

"No, but suppose one of them was still free."

Commodore Dale frowned and turned to Collins. "Is it possible that one of the pirates is hiding on your ship?"

The acting captain bristled at the notion. "Mr. Swift just told us no one could have sneaked up on Flace without his knowing it. There's no other pirate here."

"You forget one person," Swift told him. "Abden Said, the supposed pris-oner we rescued from the pirates. There are historical records of women pirates, you know. She was present when Flace told Lieutenant Pitt to bring him the key to the prisoners' leg irons. After dark she followed Flace on deck and spoke with him. When he stooped down to inspect one of the cannons she lifted the cannonball over her head and brought it down on him, killing him instantly. Then she went through his pockets and took the key to the leg irons. I suspect she planned to free the eight prisoners in an attempt to take over the ship, but there were two guards on duty by that time and she couldn't do it."

"A clever explanation," the commodore agreed, "but you need something to back it up."

"How is this? Immediately after her supposed rescue, she told us she could not speak to the pirate Dread because she didn't understand his language. But after the shore battery hit the ship and injured him, she conversed quite well with him."

"Still—"

"Search her," Swift told them. "She wouldn't risk trying to hide the key somewhere on the ship. She'll still have it on her."

Abden Said fought like a fury, but they found the key under her pants, tied to her thigh with a length of string.

Alexander Swift never learned of the young woman's fate. She was to be tried by a U.S. Navy court on the day he was transferred to the H.M.S. *Bombay*. He arrived in London during the last week in June, learning there would be a ship to America leaving in five days' time. It took him only two days to discover the address where Benedict Arnold and his wife resided.

It was Peggy Arnold who opened the door to his knock. "You are Alexander Swift," she said softly, recognizing him at once.

"You remember me."

"You attended our wedding as Washington's representative."

He stared at the woman in front of him, barely able to connect her with the lovely girl who was the belle of Philadelphia. "You have a good memory."

"I remember the happy days, not what came after. What has brought you here, Mr. Swift?"

He glanced around at the shabby furniture, the tarnished dream of a life that might have been something different. "I have some unfinished business with your husband, Peggy."

"Then I fear you have arrived too late. Benedict passed away two weeks ago. He is buried at St. Mary's Church in Battersea."

Swift was stunned at the news—at the thought that he'd arrived too late for the vengeance he'd sought for so long. "What happened?" he asked—a question that took in the whole of their lives. "I thought the British had rewarded him."

"They did at first, but he loaned money to friends who did not repay him. His business ventures failed, and the government lost interest in us. My children and I are barely surviving."

They talked for a bit longer, and he declined an offer of tea, saying he must be on his way. At the door he paused and asked, "What was the date of his death?"

"June fourteenth."

He nodded, seeing some sort of symbolism in it. "The Continental Congress passed the first Flag Act on that date in seventeen seventy-seven, making the Stars and Stripes the official flag of our new nation."

"He should never have turned against it—his flag or his country," she said with a touch of sadness in her voice. "We were both so wrong."

"I wish you well, Peggy," he told her, and went down the steps to the street. It was time to go home.

LADY OF THE IMPOSSIBLE

It had been months since I last saw Sir Gideon Parrot, and his appearance that afternoon in my Manhattan office was certainly a surprise. His slender, bird-like figure always drew attention, and my secretary announced his arrival with a mixture of wonderment and apprehension.

"He's an old friend," I assured her, and went out to greet him personally. "Gideon! It's good to see you again! Are you in New York for a visit?"

He followed me into the inner office before replying. Then he held out a large cream colored envelope. "I received this invitation a few days ago."

I took the envelope. "Are you invited to a wedding, Gideon?" But the carefully handwritten card inside was no wedding invitation. It read, "Sir Gideon Parrot and friend are cordially invited to dinner at the Southampton home of Mrs. Vangie Hope, at 7:30 on Saturday, June 7th." I looked up at Gideon. "That's tomorrow."

"Indeed it is. Will you accompany me?"

"You don't get many dinner invitations, Gideon. When she says to bring a friend she means a lady friend."

Gideon brushed that aside with a wave of his hand. "Do you know who Vangie Hope is?"

"She's the actress who's played a number of character parts on Broadway. For the past few years she's conducted an all-night radio program here in New York. Bills herself as the Lady of the Impossible and interviews the usual late-night kooks—witches, seers, flying-saucer nuts. She should be interesting to meet."

"Then you'll join me?" he asked.

I decided I deserved a night out. "Sure, why not?"

The house in Southampton was one of those rambling mansions with turrets and leaded-glass windows, where rumors of weekend orgies among the wealthy always made good newspaper copy. The evening was warm and humid, and my first impression as a dour butler admitted us was relief that the place was air-conditioned.

"Sir Gideon Parrot?" the butler inquired.

"Correct," Gideon said, "but I use the French pronunciation, with the *t* silent."

"This way, please," he said quietly. "Madame is expecting you." He led us to a high-ceilinged room where several people already waited, and announced in a formal manner, "Sir Gideon Parrot and friend, Madame."

A shimmering beauty in a floor-length silver gown rose to greet us. "Thank you, Diener." She approached with a hand held out to each of us. "I have so looked forward to meeting you, Sir Gideon! We've all delighted in your exploits."

"Which exploits are those?" Gideon asked modestly.

"Your solution to the aardvark murders, and the crime in the catacombs, and the killing on the Stamford express! England's loss has been our gain. I tried to contact you last year, to be a guest on my radio show, but you were out of the country."

"I am frequently out of the country."

Her heavily made-up face relaxed into a smile. "Then I'm pleased I was able to reach you for our little dinner party."

One of the men who'd been lounging on the sofa stood up and extended his hand. "Vangie is a bit slow on the introductions. I'm Carter Hope."

I shook his hand and introduced myself. "You're Mrs. Hope's husband?"

"Ex-husband," Vangie corrected. "And now I'm trapped with his name for the rest of my professional career."

"It's happened before," Gideon murmured. "I believe Agatha Christie had a similar problem."

"Do you read detective stories, Sir Gideon?" she asked.

"If one lives them there is no need to read them."

The others had stood now for introductions. The only other woman present was a girl in her twenties whom I took at first to be the actress' younger sister, though her blond hair contrasted with Vangie's coal-black tresses. She stood very close to a tall young man in a three-piece suit. When Vangie Hope introduced them I realized my guess about the relationship was mistaken. "This is my lawyer, Martin Brockton, and his new fiancée, Lisa York."

"I've heard a great deal about you," Brockton said to Gideon. "Vangie always finds the most fascinating dinner guests."

One other man remained to be introduced—a portly white-haired chap dressed in black. I guessed him to be a preacher of some sort, and this time I was correct. "This is our minister, the Reverend Joshua Sloane," Vangie said. "I imagine Joshua and Sir Gideon can talk a great deal about crime and punishment."

Joshua Sloane was a man with a twinkle in his eye. "You know you only dredge me up when you want to impress someone, Vangie. Why don't you come by church some Sunday and allow me to impress people?"

"Stop that, Joshua!" she chided. "You're always after me about that! You know I'm up all night doing the show. Tonight is special because the station's running a repeat."

I'd hardly said a word since our arrival, and I looked around for someone to chat with while the butler passed cocktails. I settled on Lisa York, since she was young and attractive. "Have you known Vangie Hope long?" I asked.

She shook her head. "I only met her tonight. Martin is her lawyer and he's been here before, of course. A lovely home, isn't it?"

"Beautiful," I agreed. "You know, you and Vangie could be sisters. You're the same height and coloring, except for the hair."

"This comes out of a bottle," Lisa York confessed. "I used to be a brunette too." She gestured toward a framed photograph of Vangie Hope on the wall. "My hair was like that."

Vangie noticed our interest and said, "That was taken five years ago when I starred in a revival of *Anna Christie*." A little plaque beneath the photo confirmed her words.

"I saw you in that," Lisa York said, as if confessing to some indiscretion. "You made a perfect Anna."

"Thank you." Vangie Hope gave a little bow, accepting the praise with a casualness that bordered on the regal.

I decided I didn't much like Vangie, and I hoped it wouldn't be too long an evening.

There were seven assembled guests—Gideon and I, Vangie Hope and her ex-husband, her lawyer and his fiancée, and the Reverend Sloane. Eight seemed a more likely number to be invited for dinner, and I guessed there was one late arrival. The thought had barely crossed my mind when the chimes sounded and Diener appeared to answer the door. A moment later he returned to announce, "Mr. Harry Ralston."

The sight of him in the doorway surprised me. Harry Ralston was a writer, and a good one. I'd met him a few times at Manhattan cocktail parties. "Good to see you again, Harry," I said, shaking hands.

He seemed equally surprised by my presence. "I didn't know you were a friend of Vangie's."

"Just met her tonight. I'm here with Sir Gideon Parrot."

"The famous detective?"

Gideon had come over to be introduced. "Fame comes easy these days," he said modestly. "I admired your book on outer space, Mr. Ralston."

"Thank you. Perhaps we can discuss it on Vangie's show sometime."

Now that the party was complete, she summoned us to the dinner table. With only two women, the seating arrangement was far from ideal, but Vangie and Lisa sat at either end, with three men along each side. I was between the hostess and Ralston. Gideon was seated across from me, next to Joshua Sloane.

As the soup was being served, I heard Harry Ralston say to Gideon, "I'd like to write your biography some day."

"It's a long dull story. Murderers are not interesting."

"That's not what I hear."

"What are you working on now?" I asked Ralston.

"A science-fiction novel, about the discovery of a distant deserted planet with geography identical to earth's."

"A fascinating idea."

"I hope my publisher thinks so."

Dinner went well, as the table talk drifted to literature and the arts. The only brief sour note was struck when Carter Hope addressed his former wife during a lull in the conversation. "I understand, Vangie, that the station isn't renewing the contract for your radio show."

She froze him with a glance. "I suppose that news is all over town."

"Then it's true?"

"True, but unimportant."

"I'll admit I've never heard your show," I said, trying to soften the conversation. "I'm not an all-night person."

"I have hundreds of tapes around the house. I should play one for you."

But as dinner ended she had other things on her mind. Over coffee she came to the point of the evening. "I've asked you all here for a reason. I believe I'm going to be murdered tonight."

There were protests of disbelief from everyone except Carter Hope. "Please, Vangie, not another one of your famous scenes!" He turned to us and said, "When we were still married she used to give dinner parties on all sorts of bizarre pretexts. They were usually confined to imaginative bouts with drugs and sex, but this is something new."

Reverend Sloane came half out of his chair. "Perhaps I should be going."

"Sit down, Joshua. No one's going to defile you." Vangie Hope seemed nervous as she spoke. "This is nothing like that, Carter. I invited you all here because I think one of you wants to murder me. I'm going to give that person an opportunity.'"

Martin Brockton spoke up. "As your lawyer I must advise against this. What do you hope to gain by it?"

"Gain?" Vangie Hope considered her reply. With the candlelight playing on her face she might have been a girl in her twenties again. "If I am murdered I have Sir Gideon Parrot, the world's greatest detective, on the scene to bring my killer to justice. Maybe that's enough gain for me."

"This is foolishness," Carter Hope declared. "None of us wants to kill you, Vangie. Some of us may not like you very much, but none of us wants to kill you."

"We'll see."

"I have no connection with the police," Gideon informed her.

"I know that."

"Just when is this murder to take place?"

"Very shortly now. I will go up to my room and lock the door."

"How is the killer supposed to get at you?"

"Locked rooms never stop them in mystery novels," Vangie Hope replied. "And in a sense this is a mystery novel. Haven't you noticed the skill with which I chose the eight of us?"

We looked at one another, and I for one had no idea what she was getting at. "I am the victim," she continued. "Then we have Sir Gideon Parrot, the great detective, and his Watson."

"I'm hardly a Watson," I grumbled.

"For tonight you are. Then we have the prime suspect, my former husband."

"Vangie, for God's sake—"

"And we have the young lovers, Martin and Lisa." At the opposite end of the table Lisa blushed prettily. "No good mystery novel is complete without them. We even have the least suspected person, don't we, Reverend Sloane?"

"I certainly hope I'm the least suspected!" the minister replied with a chuckle. "But I don't think murder is anything to joke about."

"Where do I fit in?" Harry Ralston asked.

Vangie Hope smiled. "You're the author, of course! Every book must have an author."

I was beginning to think she'd had too much wine. But then she stood and announced she was going to her room. "I will remain there for thirty minutes with the door locked. That should be time enough, if one of you really wants to kill me. Come along, Watson, and escort me to my door."

"Stop this foolishness, Vangie!" Carter Hope demanded once more.

But she left the table and headed for the stairs. I tagged along, not knowing what was expected of me. Upstairs she opened the door of her bedroom and turned to me. "Don't let them come in for thirty minutes. Go back down and sit with them." She gave me a last smile. I turned and started down the stairs as the bedroom door slammed behind me. But Martin Brockton was already on his way up, followed by the others. He went to her door and knocked.

"He knows where her bedroom is," Carter Hope said to me, as if to prove a point.

"Vangie, come out of there," the lawyer demanded. After a moment's silence her voice came through the door. "Go away, Martin. Leave me alone for thirty minutes."

Brockton stopped knocking and we stood looking at one another. Carter Hope tried the door but it was indeed locked. "Another trick of hers," he said.

"What shall we do?" Lisa asked. "Just wait for her to come out?"

Gideon came up to me and stood silently by my side. Joshua Sloane pressed forward. "Perhaps I can talk some sense into her. Vangie! Can you hear me?"

But this time there was no answer from the room.

"Let's go back downstairs and wait," Harry Ralston suggested. "If she said she'd come out in a half hour, she will."

But Brockton had an idea. "Lisa, go downstairs and find one of the servants. Ask them if there's another way into Mrs. Hope's bedroom."

Lisa went off on her mission and Carter Hope tried the doorknob again. "Vangie, come out of there!"

Silence.

Gideon Parrot started opening the other doors in the hallway, looking in on a stairway, a spotless guestroom, a broom closet, a bathroom. Then he came back and we waited some more.

After ten minutes Ralston drifted away, followed by Carter Hope. Joshua Sloane spoke of going home, but decided to wait out the half hour. He went down for his pipe tobacco and then rejoined us. Presently Lisa returned from her mission. "It's spooky down there," she reported. "I couldn't find anyone but Diener the butler. He says this is the only door to her room."

Martin Brockton was staring at her, his forehead creased in a frown. He started to say something but was interrupted by a scream from inside the bedroom.

"Help!" Vangie Hope shouted. "My God, help me! He's killing me!" Then there was the sound of breaking glass.

Brockton and I hit the door together, battering it with our shoulders. It was stout oak, and it took three tries to split it from the frame. By that time the others had come running from downstairs.

I didn't know what to expect—Vangie Hope sprawled lifeless in a pool of blood, or a crazed killer coming through the broken window, or the two of them still struggling.

But the reality was even more of a shock.

The room was empty and undisturbed.

There was no broken glass, no sign of a struggle.

And no Vangie Hope.

"She's gone," Ralston said, stating the obvious.

Martin Brockton cursed. "She can't be gone! We were outside the whole time." He ran to the windows to check them, with Gideon right behind. They were all latched on the inside, and the big panes were unbroken.

Brockton busied himself searching the closets while Gideon examined the lock on the broken door. The bolt had been set to lock automatically when the door was closed. "She must be here somewhere," the lawyer muttered, continuing his search.

But she wasn't.

We looked under the bed, and in her private bathroom, and even in the oversized laundry hamper.

Vangie Hope, Lady of the Impossible, had joined the impossibilities of so many of her radio guests.

"She's not here," Joshua Sloane concluded. "Will you all join me in a prayer for her?"

"It may be too soon for prayers," Gideon said. He started opening drawers, checked the bedside radio, went to the closets, even lifted the mattress.

"What are you looking for, Gideon?" I asked.

"Something that should be here."

"Something besides Vangie Hope?"

"Something instead of Vangie Hope."

"I'm calling the police," Harry Ralston decided.

"No police," Carter Hope said. "It's just another of her melodramatic tricks. She'll turn up laughing at us. Wait and see."

Suddenly Diener, the butler, appeared in the doorway. "What seems to be the trouble here?"

Brockton whirled around. "Your mistress has disappeared."

"Disappeared? Oh, certainly not! She's dozing in the sunroom downstairs. She may have had a bit too much wine."

We all hurried down, with Gideon Parrot in the lead. The sunroom off the dining area was almost in darkness, but I saw her on the couch and breathed a sigh of relief. However she'd got out of that bedroom, it hadn't been by magic.

Carter Hope switched on the overhead light and Gideon lifted her arm gently to waken her.

A slim dagger was thrust deep beneath her left breast.

"How long has she been dead?" Gideon wondered aloud.

"The body's still warm," I observed. "It must be less than an hour."

"Of course it's less than an hour," Carter Hope said with a scowl. "An hour ago she was sitting at the dinner table with us!"

Harry Ralston was already on the phone to the police.

"How did she get out of the room?" Reverend Sloane asked. "Some of us were up there all the time."

"We heard breaking glass," I pointed out.

"But no glass in the room was broken!"

While we awaited the police Gideon and I went out through the French doors to the lawn. We walked around the house and he stood looking up at the lighted windows of Vangie Hope's bedroom. "How was it done, Gideon?" I asked.

"Which—the disappearance or the murder?"

"Aren't they the same thing?"

"We have to understand the nature of Vangie Hope's mind. She constructed the dinner party like a detective hovel, with—as she carefully pointed out—a victim, a detective and his Watson, a prime suspect, a pair of young lovers, a least suspected person, and an author. Did she really know one of these planned to kill her, or did the murderer simply take advantage of the unexpected opportunity?"

Before I could respond we saw the police cars arriving and we hurried back inside. The formalities of questioning were conducted by a gruff detective sergeant named Nims, who made notes of everything in a labored handwriting. "We don't like this sort of thing in Southampton," he said. He ignored the disappearance of Vangie Hope from her upstairs bedroom and concentrated on the killing itself.

"What do you think of him?" I asked Gideon at one point.

"He won't solve it. He's ignoring the state of Vangie Hope's mind, and that's the key to the puzzle. In a sense she wrote the script for her own murder, and we have to know whom she had in mind for the villain's role."

"The least suspected person?"

Gideon Parrot shook his head. "By calling him that she paradoxically made Joshua Sloane a prime suspect."

"Who else is there? Carter Hope? Martin and Lisa?"

"You forget the writer, Harry Ralston. After all, in any detective novel the ultimate killer is not the fictitious character on the page. The ultimate killer is the author."

At that point Sergeant Nims came looking for us. "They were lifting the body and her wig fell off. Did you know she wore a wig?"

"We'd never met her before tonight," Gideon reminded him. "You should ask her former husband."

Gideon and I followed along as the detective brought Carter Hope to view the body. Oddly enough, Vangie's hair was blonde beneath the dark wig and her face appeared younger without it. Her former husband stared down at the body and shrugged. "The lady was an actress, Sergeant. She was forever wearing wigs and changing her appearance."

"The testimony of the others is that she said you'd be the most likely suspect in her murder."

"That was just talk. She was playing her games."

Nims made more of his careful notes. "Do you profit by her death?"

"Of course not! We were divorced! Besides, she was almost broke—worth more dead than alive, with all her insurance."

"One more thing," the detective said. "Wigs always make me suspicious. Is there any doubt that this is really Vangie Hope?"

"Not the slightest. Check her fingerprints if you want. She had a cabaret permit once to sing in a nightclub, and they fingerprinted her."

"Who are her next of kin?"

"Both her parents are dead. There's a sister someplace but I never met her."

"New Orleans," Martin Brockton said, coming in to join the conversation. "An older sister who's quite ill, as I understand it. She's the beneficiary of Vangie's insurance."

Gideon Parrot tugged on my sleeve, and I followed him out of the room. "We've heard enough here. We should follow another line of inquiry."

"How she got out of that locked room?"

"No, no—I've known that for some time."

"What? Then you must know who killed her!"

"I told you earlier they were two separate problems. No, the thought just struck me that when Vangie ran down her list of mystery novel stereotypes who were at the dinner party, she omitted one person—perhaps the most stereotypical of all."

"Who's that?"

"The butler."

We found Diener lurking in the kitchen, nervously smoking a cigarette. "I have some questions," Gideon Parrot said.

"The police already asked them."

"Not these. Where are the rest of the servants?"

"I'm the only one. The dinner was catered. I merely served it."

Gideon nodded. "Now, suppose we learn the whole truth. Diener isn't your real name at all, is it? It's merely the German word for butler."

He seemed to slump a bit in his chair. His voice changed and he said, "Look, my name is Greg Dunning. I'm an out-of-work actor and I met Vangie while I was making a TV commercial. She offered me fifty bucks to do this butler bit tonight and I took it. I don't know who killed her and I don't care. I hardly knew her."

"All right," Gideon said. "Now tell me this—while you were downstairs, during the thirty minutes Vangie Hope was locked in her bedroom, did you see anyone at all?"

"No. I stayed in the kitchen."

"And you didn't see Vangie before you found her in the sunroom?"

"Of course not! Do you think I killed her?"

"Now I know who killed her," Gideon said simply. "And I know how she escaped from that room."

"Shouldn't you tell Nims?" I suggested.

"Vangie Hope wanted this to be like a mystery novel, and I'll go along with that. We'll assemble everyone in the living room and I will expose the murderer."

We sent Diener, or Dunning, to round them up. He caught Brockton and Lisa at their car, about to depart, and found Ralston helping himself to more wine in the dining room. We didn't have to seek out Reverend Sloane. He found us. "What is this business, Sir Gideon? Diener says you're going to reveal the murderer."

"Correct."

Sergeant Nims came into the room with Carter Hope. Everyone else was there, including the butler.

"What are you trying to do?" Nims asked Gideon. "I'm conducting this investigation."

"The investigation is over. I can tell you what happened."

"You can start by telling us how Vangie got out of that locked bedroom," Brockton said.

"That's as good a starting place as any," Gideon agreed. "And the answer is quite simple. She walked up those stairs, opened her bedroom door, pushed the button on the bolt so it would lock automatically, and then—when my friend turned his back—she pulled the door shut from the outside and disappeared through a door across the hall. I noticed one of them led to a stairway."

Ralston had an objection. "But how was she able to talk to us through the locked door? She answered Brockton when he spoke to her, and later she screamed."

"Vangie told us she had hundreds of radio tapes around the house. What we heard was a specially made tape. The machine was probably sound-activated, starting to play when she slammed that door. It was so timed that her answer, and her later scream, came right on cue."

"What about the breaking glass?" I asked.

"That was on the recording too. Obviously glass was meant to be broken, and it was on the tape to make sure we'd hear it. Since the glass wasn't broken we can assume Vangie was meant to break it. She couldn't follow through on the plan because she was dead."

"What plan?"

"To throw a rock through her bedroom window from the yard below, so it would look as if she fell or was pushed through the window."

"Wait a minute, Gideon," I challenged. "Vangie Hope didn't just talk through that door. She specifically answered Martin and called him by name."

Gideon Parrot turned to the young lawyer. "Exactly. And the only way she could have timed the tape to speak his name is if she knew in advance when he would speak and what he would say. In other words, Martin Brockton had to be a willing accomplice to—*grab him, Sergeant!*"

Brockton made his move, but Nims was on top of him, pinning him in his chair.

"Hold it, young fellow! Let's hear the rest of this."

"I didn't kill her!" Brockton shouted. "I didn't!"

"I have more objections, Gideon," I said. "We searched the room and didn't find any tape player."

"You'll remember Brockton searched the closet before the rest of us reached it. He simply hid the small tape machine under his coat and carried it from the room."

"What about the rock that was supposed to have broken the window? We would have seen it, and every mystery reader knows there would be glass inside the room. And there was no glass."

"Brockton was the first to rush in, you'll remember. If the window had been broken he would have hidden or pocketed the rock and kicked the larger pieces of glass under the bed. Vangie could have spread other broken glass outside, creating the illusion the window was broken from within."

Sergeant Nims was still holding Brockton. "She did this all for a joke?" he asked.

"Oh, no. Vangie Hope had a deadly serious purpose. We've learned about her hard times and the cancellation of her radio show. And we've heard about the large insurance policy that made her worth more dead than alive. She planned to cash in by faking her own murder and collecting the insurance."

"For a fake murder you still need a body," Nims protested.

"Yes," Gideon agreed.

"Whose body was she going to use?"

"That should be obvious. The only other woman present is Lisa, and we've already noted her resemblance to Vangie. It wouldn't have been too difficult for a character actress like Vangie to kill Lisa York and take her place among us for a few hours. The insurance money would have been paid to a mythical sister who would have been Vangie in another disguise. I imagine you're the executor of the will, Brockton, so you'd have made sure everything went smoothly."

All eyes had turned to Lisa York, who sat white-faced on the sofa. "I—" She started to speak and then burst into tears.

"Why didn't you tell us you killed her, Lisa?" Gideon asked. "Any jury could see it was self-defense."

While Reverend Sloane tried to comfort Lisa York, Gideon pressed on. "You see this picture that Vangie Hope mentioned earlier? She told us, and the caption confirms it, that the picture shows her as Anna Christie in a revival of the Eugene O'Neill play. But she's a brunette in the picture, as she was tonight with her dark wig. The part of Anna Christie is played as a blonde, following O'Neill's specific stage directions in the printed text of the play. Vangie Hope substituted a different picture for the one that usually hung here, and I asked myself why."

I began to see it now. "Because she looked like Lisa York."

"Exactly! You noticed the resemblance and so did I. If we had seen Vangie with her blonde hair, as in the stage role, the resemblance would have been even more pronounced. That's why she changed the picture."

"I remember she looked younger by candlelight, and when the wig was removed."

Gideon nodded. "Young enough so she could kill Lisa, change clothes with her, and leave her body beneath the broken window. Lisa would become a dead Vangie Hope, and Vangie would become Lisa for the rest of this evening. They were the same size, remember, so the clothes would have fit well enough."

"Wouldn't we have known the difference?" Harry Ralston asked.

"Vangie was betting we wouldn't. None of us had met Lisa before tonight—except Brockton, who was her accomplice. The only danger was Vangie's ex-husband, and she gambled on fooling him for the necessary few hours. With the uproar of the murder she probably could have pulled it off."

"But Vangie's fingerprints are on file," I reminded him.

"If she'd been found beneath her broken window, stabbed and thrown to her death, no one would have questioned her identity. We saw her enter the bedroom, we heard her speak through the door, we heard the window breaking. We would have seen the body, with black wig and heavy makeup applied after death, and no one would have doubted it was Vangie. I imagine she and Brockton had already established that Lisa had no close relatives to question her sudden disappearance after tonight's events. In fact, Lisa's availability and her resemblance to Vangie probably suggested the whole scheme in the first place. Brockton romanced the girl and even became engaged to her, in order to lure her out here for tonight's murder."

On the sofa Lisa shuddered at his words. Then she began to speak, staring at the floor. "I went downstairs—"

"Where Brockton conveniently sent you, into Vangie's waiting arms," Gideon said. "If he knew which was her bedroom, he probably knew there was no other entrance or exit. He didn't need to send you off to find out."

The girl nodded. "I went downstairs and she came at me with that dagger, covering my mouth before I could scream. We struggled and I killed her. I wanted to tell everyone, but the whole thing was so bizarre I was afraid no one would believe me. So I kept quiet."

I remembered how Brockton had frowned when she reappeared in the upstairs hall. He'd known it was the real Lisa and that something had gone wrong with the plan. "How'd you know it was Lisa who killed Vangie?" I asked Gideon.

"The scheme depended on Vangie killing Lisa and trading places with her to collect the insurance. So I knew Vangie would have sought her out downstairs. And Lisa said she saw the butler but he said he saw no one. Her lie, plus Vangie's plan, added up to Lisa as the killer—even though it was self-defense."

Sergeant Nims stood up. "I'll have to book you, Miss York, and let a grand jury take it from there." He cast a baleful eye on the lawyer. "I'm sure there'll be conspiracy charges placed against you, Mr. Brockton."

Martin turned to Lisa. "I didn't know she meant to go through with it. I thought it was all a practical joke."

"We'll see if anyone believes that," Nims said.

Later, riding back to the city, I said to Gideon Parrot, "It was a story out of The Golden Age—like one of those mystery novels Vangie Hope compared it to. Murder at a dinner party, a locked room, impersonations, a plot to collect insurance money—I could be home reading about all this!"

But Gideon Parrot shook his head. "No, you couldn't. They don't write them like this anymore."

THE MAN WITH FIVE FACES

Sir Gideon Parrot had been absent from New York for some time when I received an enigmatic summons by messenger announcing his return. It gave the address of a Mott Street hotel in lower Manhattan and cautioned: *Come for me here at seven Tuesday morning. My very life may depend upon you!* It was, as they say, a summons I couldn't refuse.

Mott Street was something of an oddity even by New York standards, running south from Bleecker Street in Greenwich Village through the Bowery, Little Italy, and Chinatown before coming to a sudden halt just a few blocks from City Hall. Though the street is mentioned in a song about Manhattan, relatively few New Yorkers have been there. As I sought out the number Sir Gideon had given me, the buildings seemed strange even to a native New Yorker like myself.

Finally I found it—a rundown hotel that catered to the fringes of society. A few years back it might have been called a flophouse, but one didn't hear that word much any more. As I entered and climbed the rickety stairs to the sleeping quarters on the second floor, a burly man in a dirty T-shirt suddenly blocked my path.

"You don't belong here, mister," he said, surveying my three-piece business suit. "What are you, a cop?"

"Hardly! I'm looking for a friend."

"You a lawyer? Somebody gonna sue me?"

"Not that I know of. Please step aside." When he didn't move, I added, "Unless you'd like me to call the cops, Mr.—?"

"Milt Quirk's the name. I'm the manager here. I gotta keep things under control, you know?" He stepped aside to let me pass.

When I reached the second floor my sensitive nostrils detected the remains of a sweetish odor—marijuana, perhaps, or some other narcotic. The place was divided into little cubicles, each one doorless but curtained, with common toilet facilities at the end of the hall. I couldn't imagine finding Gideon Parrot in such a foul place, but I tried calling his name anyway. "Gideon! Are you here?"

When no answer came I moved down the line of curtained doorways, glancing inside at the unshaven men just coming awake. I tried calling his name again, and this time I was rewarded by a rasping sound in reply. I yanked open one of the curtains and found Sir Gideon, barely recognizable, seated on a lumpy cot. His clothes were of the shabbiest sort, and had I not been seeking him I doubt if I would have taken this slender bird-like tramp as my old and dear friend.

"Gideon—thank God I've found you! But what are you doing in a place like this?"

"Get me out of here!" he croaked. "The narcotics fumes have affected my throat. I fear I'm both hoarse and dizzy."

"Here, lean on me. Do you have any belongings with you?"

"Only a tiny camera in my pocket. I brought nothing else."

I helped him down the stairs, but now the burly man named Quirk had been joined by another, smaller man. "What are you doing now?" the big man asked.

"Taking my friend home. He's ill."

The smaller man slipped a menacing hand into his pocket, but Gideon cleared his throat and rasped, "It would be a mistake to harm us. We are known personally to Sigmund Llama."

The name had its desired effect. Quirk put a hand on the other's shoulder. "We'd better check on this," he decided.

That was all the hesitation we needed. Before they could change their minds we were out the door, hailing a passing cab. "Now tell me what you were doing there," I demanded when we were safely away.

"That hotel is the modern equivalent of an old opium den," Gideon explained, his voice stronger as he gradually recovered his composure. "Every type of narcotic is sold there, including opium. I disguised myself in these old clothes and spent the night to see what I could learn of the operation, but I sent you the message in the likely event I would need help of some sort to escape."

"Why concern yourself with an opium den, Gideon? In the past your criminal investigations have centered around a nicer class of people, to say the least."

He turned to me, his bird-like eyes bright with excitement. "For almost a year I have been on the trail of a master criminal named Sigmund Llama, sometimes called the man with five faces because he is said to maintain five separate identities in New York, London, Paris, Berlin, and Rome. I believe Llama controls fully half the drug traffic into New York and a substantial share in those other cities as well. That seedy hotel is one of his latest innovations—a modern variation to replace the old time opium den, just as massage parlors are replacing houses of ill repute. I observed a number of well-dressed men—and even a few women—enter the place during the night. I believe one of them might have been Sigmund Llama himself, since he's known to make inspection tours of his establishments when he's in the city."

"He's in New York now?"

Gideon Parrot nodded. "I have it from a reliable informant."

"Have you ever seen his face?"

"Never. I came close last summer in Paris, when I accompanied a police raid on a private airfield. He escaped in a private plane as we closed in, and the police opened fire on it. The plane crashed in flames about a mile away and we recovered a charred body. I thought it was the end of Llama, but a week later I heard he had turned up in Rome. The devil had somehow managed to escape from that plane."

"If he was ever on it."

"In any event, he's now in New York." He dipped a hand into the pocket of his shabby coat and produced a small camera. "I used an especially fast color film to photograph the comings and goings during the night. I believe a light at the top of the stairs provided enough illumination to capture their faces."

"Then you have a picture of this mysterious master criminal?"

"I'm sure of it. The problem is in determining which of last night's visitors was Llama."

Today was the first time I'd heard Sigmund Llama's name, but the stark cruelty of the man was made abundantly clear by a report on the evening news. Three hours after Gideon and I left the hotel on Mott Street it was destroyed by an explosion and fire that killed two employees.

Sigmund Llama was covering his tracks.

I joined Gideon for breakfast the following morning at his hideaway apartment on the Upper East Side. He was studying enlargements of the color photos he'd shot at the Mott Street hotel. I always enjoyed visiting his apartment with its spacious den overlooking the river, with walls bearing framed mementos of his past glories. Here I could relive the murder on the Stamford Express, or the mysterious affair at Larchmont, or the murder of Roger A. Kroid. I could thrill again to the excitement of the chase.

"Those two men who were killed at the hotel, Gideon—"

He nodded sadly. "No doubt the two who tried to stop us. Sigmund Llama does not take kindly to failure. He destroyed the evidence, and two possible witnesses against him."

"He must be a ruthless man."

"He is that." As he spoke he removed the color enlargements from his desk drawer and spread them out for me. "You'll note there are four well-dressed men shown quite clearly. I believe one of them is Llama."

"Have you identified any of these people?" I asked.

"Only one. This man with the black beard is a fairly well known actor, Sam Matters. He's had parts on Broadway and also in London. I'm hoping he can identify the others for us."

"Could Matters himself be Llama?"

"Nothing is impossible. He makes frequent trips between London and New York, and could have visited the other cities under different identities. We must question him this morning."

Gideon and I found Sam Matters rehearsing for a new play at an off-Broadway theater located in a converted garage. He looked exactly like the photo Gideon had secretly taken two nights earlier. He was a man in his mid-thirties, though the beard added ten years to his appearance. We approached him during a rehearsal break as he chatted with an attractive young woman in the cast.

"Could I speak with you in private?" Gideon said after introducing us.

Matters and the young woman exchanged glances. "I'll wait for you," she said and disappeared backstage.

The theater seats were narrow and uncomfortable, apparently salvaged from an old movie house. I sat on the edge of one as Gideon told the actor, "I am investigating the explosion and fire at a Mott Street hotel yesterday. Perhaps you read of it?"

"I may have seen something on the late news," he admitted.

"You were at that hotel on Tuesday night."

"Not me! You've got me confused with someone else."

Gideon produced the color photo from his pocket. "Do you deny this is you, sir?"

"What are you—police or something?"

"I am an independent investigator working on behalf of several governments," Gideon informed him. "I believe you know the reason for my inquiry. The Mott Street address was a modern version of an opium den, and you were one of its customers."

"You can't prove a thing!" Matters insisted.

"Are you trying to say you took a bed there for the night, dressed as you were? That's hardly likely."

Matters tugged at his beard, perhaps seeking a way out. Finally he said, "All right, what do you want?"

"The man at the top—the man who controls Mott Street and much of the other narcotics traffic in this city. I believe his name is Sigmund Llama."

"Never heard of him," the actor answered promptly.

"He travels widely in Europe, as you have done. He maintains several different identities, which might call for disguises. An actor like yourself could easily play that role."

Gideon's words struck home. The actor mumbled, "I just went there for a little coke sniffing, with a friend. I don't know anything about the narcotics traffic, and I never heard of this man Llama!"

Gideon pointed a bony finger at a second man in one of the photographs. "Is this your friend?"

"Yes. Hal Andor. He works for a Wall Street investment firm."

"How do you know him?"

"His wife Barbara is in this play with me. I was talking with her just a few minutes ago."

He called Barbara from backstage and she rejoined them, carrying a Styrofoam cup of coffee. Up close I could see the lines of middle age beginning to appear, but she was still lovely to look at, with golden hair framing a well-formed, intelligent face. "I was telling these gentlemen I was out with Hal on Tuesday night."

She nodded. "I can't imagine what they find to do all night, but I guess I'd rather not know."

Gideon produced one of the other color photographs. "Do you know either of these two men?"

Barbara Andor and Sam Matters both shook their heads. "Never saw them before," she said. "But I don't know too many people outside of show business."

"I'd like very much to meet your husband," Gideon said. "Can you arrange that?"

"I'll take you to his office right now. We may be able to catch him before lunch."

We left Sam Matters at the rehearsal and took a taxi down to Wall Street with Barbara Andor. Her husband's investment office, high up in one of those elaborate bank buildings that dated from the 1930s, seemed a busy enough place on this Thursday noon. We found Andor alone in his office, just finishing a phone conversation. He was a tall dark-haired man in his forties, and he smiled as his wife introduced us.

"They want to ask you some questions about Tuesday night," she told him.

"The hotel on Mott Street," Gideon said. "We're investigating the bombing there."

Andor was suddenly on the defensive. "Who told you I was there—Sam?"

"Yes."

"We went there for a little fun. I'm not involved in any bombing!"

Gideon produced his pictures again. "Can you identify these two men? They were also at Mott Street on Tuesday."

"I know them both slightly. Cedric Lane is a specialist in international law and Anton Legorian is a European trade representative."

"How do you happen to know them?"

"I had a brother who died last year. He was involved in a real-estate deal with them."

"Can you give me their addresses?"

"Legorian has an office at the World Trade Center. Lane is at One Liberty Plaza."

Gideon noted the addresses. "Thank you. I may be calling on you again."

We left Barbara with her husband and walked to Cedric Lane's Liberty Plaza office. He was a stout man in his fifties who gave us very little time. He was on his way to Berlin the following day, he said, and had to finish up some business first. "I wasn't violating any law by just being at the Mott Street hotel," he snapped. "And you can't prove from this photograph that I used drugs of any sort."

"You travel a great deal overseas?" Gideon asked.

"It's necessary in my line of work. But I think that should be enough questioning. You do not represent the police, Mr. Parrot."

"The police of several nations are involved," Gideon informed him. "Perhaps your friend Mr. Legorian will be more cooperative."

"Then go badger him," Cedric Lane suggested. "Good day, gentlemen."

We found ourselves back on the street and Gideon remarked sadly, "He was most uncooperative."

"You think he could be Llama?"

Instead of answering, Gideon tapped my arm. "I believe we're being followed. I noticed that little foreign car earlier."

How anyone could follow us by car through the traffic-choked maze of lower Manhattan streets was beyond me, but as we strolled the short distance to the World Trade Center it did seem as if the little car managed to remain in view. Once it came close enough for me to catch a glimpse of the driver. He wore a scarf around the lower part of his face, though the day was quite balmy for April.

We rode the express elevator to an office high in the north tower of the World Trade Center. Anton Legorian maintained an office in a larger suite under the company name of Euro-Trade Associates, and he seemed to be expecting our arrival. "Cedric Lane phoned me," he admitted, speaking with a trace of accent. "There's little I can contribute to your investigation." He was dapper and middle-aged, with slick black hair and a pencil-thin mustache.

"You went to Mott Street to use narcotics?"

The man shrugged. "A little grass, nothing more. Mainly I went for companionship. I can buy the grass down there on the plaza any lunch hour for a dollar a joint."

"Some of your friends were snorting cocaine."

"What they do does not concern me."

"You and Lane had a real-estate deal with Hal Andor's brother."

"That's correct. But he died before the deal could be completed. A heart attack, I believe, in France."

"You all travel a great deal."

"This is the jet age, Mr. Parrot. Our work demands it."

"What do you know about Sigmund Llama?"

"The name means nothing to me."

As we left the building I remarked to Gideon, "Another dead end, just like the others. Are you certain one of those four is really Llama?"

"We might learn more very soon. There's the car again, still following us. Come on, let's set a little trap."

We entered the side door of the new hotel across from the twin towers and waited. "Mind telling me what we're up to, Gideon?"

"He expected us to visit the Trade Center, so he waited outside. This stop is unexpected and he may follow us in." Of course Gideon was correct. Within three minutes our shadow had parked his car and trailed us inside. As he came through the revolving door Gideon reached out and grabbed the scarf from his face.

It was Milt Quirk of the Mott Street hotel—the man we'd believed had died in the fire.

Gideon and I acted quickly together, propelling the startled man through an unlocked door into one of the hotel's deserted conference rooms. "Suppose we talk," Gideon said. "We thought you died in the fire."

"Yeah," he admitted. "A lot of people did. But it was one of the bums who was still asleep from the night before. It's better this way. Pretending to be dead keeps me alive."

"Sigmund Llama wanted you dead, didn't he?"

The burly man eyed Gideon with new respect. "You know a lot, don't you?"

"Why are you following us?"

"Just tryin' to stay alive, is all. Llama figured I bungled, lettin' you get away from the hotel. He had the place blown up, hopin' to destroy me along with the evidence. I figure if I stick close to you it's my best chance of stayin' alive."

"Llama was there Tuesday night, wasn't he?"

"Yeah," the man admitted. "He always comes by when he's in town. But I don't know who he is. I've only talked to him on the phone, and he disguises his voice so's it always sounds different."

"There were four well-dressed men who visited the hotel Tuesday night," Gideon said. "I took photographs of them."

"Yeah," Milt Quirk agreed. "I know the four you mean—Andor, the Wall Street guy, that lawyer Cedric Lane, the actor Sam Matters, and what's his name, Legorian. They've all been there before."

"And one of them is Llama."

"Yeah, I'm pretty sure. Some of 'em have come by before on nights when I'd heard he was in town. I started checkin' on them myself months ago, just to protect my own hide, you know? I figured if I knew who Llama was I might use it to plea bargain if the cops ever nabbed me."

"What did you learn about them?"

"All four have been to Europe lately. You know Llama is into lots of European cities besides New York."

"We know."

"But none of their trips quite match Llama's schedule. He was supposed to be in Paris once last summer and I know for a fact they was all in New York then. But Cedric Lane did go to Rome when Llama was there. And Matters was in a London play while Llama was bringing drugs across the Channel. It drove me wild. I began thinkin' maybe I was all wet. Maybe Llama was someone else altogether."

"Like who?"

"That's the point—there's no one else! You spent the night at that flea-trap. You know we didn't get many uptown swells there. The society chicks would come down to get high once in a while, but they take a look at the dive and decide they'd rather snort cocaine in Park Avenue apartments. Andor brought his wife with him once and I thought she was gonna throw up when she saw the place.

"Anyway, those four were the only uptown regulars that could be Llama. The rest were bums and college kids out for a thrill. Legorian and Lane usually came together. Sam Matters was mostly alone, but the other night he came with Andor. Is that enough to keep me alive?"

"We'll see," Gideon told him. "Where are you hiding out?"

"I couldn't go back to my apartment, in case Llama had one of his men check there, so I took a room in the Village, on Bank Street near the river."

Gideon Parrot stared off into space. I could see an idea forming. After a moment he said, "I believe I have a scheme for luring Sigmund Llama into the open."

"What would that be?" I asked.

"We could tell Llama that Milt here is still alive, and where to find him."

"Hey!" Quirk objected. "Wait a minute!"

"Don't worry, we won't give out your real address."

"How will you know which of the four to tell?" I asked.

He turned to Quirk. "What's your address on Bank Street?"

"Number 212. There's a row of five connected brownstones and I'm in the middle one. Second floor front."

"What are the other numbers?"

"They're all in a row—208, 210, 212, 214, and 216."

"Perfect!" Gideon decided. "We will telephone each of the four possible suspects anonymously and tell them that Quirk is alive and threatening to reveal Llama's true identity. We'll give each of them a different street number—of one of the four brownstones on both sides of your own."

"Why bring them so close to me?"

"Just stay in your room and you'll be safe. We'll be right across the street watching everything. Llama certainly won't come himself, but if we see anyone suspicious sneaking around one of those four brownstones we'll know which of the suspects sent him."

We escorted Quirk to his Bank Street apartment, making certain we weren't followed. Then we found a lunch counter across the street which offered a perfect view of the entire block. Gideon telephoned Legorian and

Matters, telling them Quirk was at 208 and 210 Bank Street. I phoned Lane and Andor, using the numbers 214 and 216.

"Quirk is alive," I whispered into the mouthpiece when Lane's voice came on the phone. "He's threatening to tell the police that you're Sigmund Llama."

"What? Is this a joke?"

"It's no joke. Quirk is at 214 Bank Street." Then I hung up.

Gideon and I sat down to wait, choosing a booth in the front window of the coffee shop. "Those apartments may have back entrances," I pointed out.

He nodded. "But our man will surely case the building from the front at first. We should be able to spot him then. It's most likely he'll check the mail boxes for a familiar name."

And so we waited over cups of coffee.

We waited all afternoon and nothing happened.

One woman with a small child entered the building at 210.

A few school children ran yelling into 208 and 214.

Nobody came in or out of 216.

Even the postman, who appeared at mid-afternoon, only stuffed a few letters into the boxes in each vestibule and hurried on his way. "He could have been checking the names," I pointed out to Gideon.

"It's a possibility. We'll wait and see what else happens."

But nothing did. We were well into the evening rush hour, with traffic picking up as people returned from work, but still there was nothing suspicious on Bank Street.

"Nobody even looks at any of those buildings," I grumbled. "I think we struck out on this one, Gideon."

Suddenly I froze in horror. There was smoke coming out the doorway of 212—Milt Quirk's building. Gideon saw it too, and he was out of the booth at once, leading the way across the traffic-congested street. "Fire!" a woman in an apron yelled, running out the door.

We hurried up the steps and inside. There was a barrel of burning trash by the stairs, funneling smoke to the upper floors. "Hurry!" Gideon shouted to me.

Almost at once we heard three quick gunshots from the floor above. I bounded up the stairs, already afraid of what I would find. Milt Quirk was sprawled in the doorway of his apartment, and this time he hadn't been so lucky. One bullet had struck him in the head and the other two in the chest.

"He's dead," I told Gideon.

We could hear footsteps above us, running to the roof. We followed them up, but the roofs of the buildings were all connected. By the time we reached the top there was no one in sight—and there were four other doors and fire escapes by which the killer might have escaped.

"I bungled badly," Gideon Parrot admitted. "I cost that man his life."

Fire engines and police cars were arriving in the street below. "How could you have been responsible, Gideon?"

"The killer lit that smoky trash fire to lure Quirk out of his room. As soon as he saw him he killed him."

"But how could he have learned the number of the real building from you? We gave all four of them false numbers!"

Before he could answer there were more shots from below. We ran downstairs and followed some policemen out of the back door of the building. A man we'd never seen before lay dead in a connecting alleyway, a revolver near his right hand.

"Who shot him?" Gideon asked, identifying himself to the officer in charge.

"I did," the officer responded. "It was clearly a case of arson and I was checking the back when I saw this man come out of the next building. When I yelled to him he pulled a gun."

Gideon nodded. "You'll find his victim on the second floor. This will be the weapon that killed him."

Quirk's murder had been quickly avenged, but the dead man at our feet was only a tool of the mysterious Sigmund Llama. As we left the scene I said to Gideon, "It's another dead end. Llama sent that hit man, but now he's dead and won't be talking."

The evening had turned suddenly chilly. Gideon Parrot turned up the collar of his coat and said, "He doesn't need to talk. Now I know the identity of Sigmund Llama."

"But how could you?"

"Let us gather the four suspects together tonight and I will make everything clear."

We arranged the gathering for that evening at my apartment. The telephoned summonses were abrupt and urgent, since we knew at least one of the four would be on his way to Europe the following day. Gideon specified they should each come alone, and I wondered if he was ruling out the bizarre possibility that Llama might be a woman—Andor's wife, Barbara.

Anton Legorian and Cedric Lane arrived within minutes of each other, a little before nine. They accepted glasses of white wine from me and settled down on the sofa. The next arrival was Sam Matters. "I should be at rehearsal," he announced. "This better be important."

When Hal Andor had joined them, Gideon said, "I'll get this over with as quickly as possible, gentlemen. I summoned you all here tonight to talk about a man known as Sigmund Llama."

"As a lawyer I find this most high-handed," Cedric Lane grumbled.

"Not at all," Gideon murmured. "You came of your own free will." He looked around at the four in turn. "As you know, the hotel on Mott Street was destroyed by an explosion and fire. As you may not yet know, its manager, Milt Quirk, was murdered earlier this evening in a Bank Street brownstone where he was hiding out. He was killed by a hired hit man."

"What's all this got to do with us?" Sam Matters asked.

"The bombing of the hotel and the murder of Quirk were both ordered by the same person—a master criminal known as Sigmund Llama who controls a large share of European and American narcotics traffic. I believe Sigmund Llama is in this room."

There were gasps of surprise and disbelief from all four men. "You can't be serious!" Sam Matters protested. "You're accusing one of us simply because we were at that hotel Tuesday night?"

Gideon turned to face him. "No, Mr. Matters, I have other pieces of evidence as well. This has been a case bound up in the number five—Llama is known as the man with five faces, and he operates in five cities. And I can offer five clues to his identity."

Anton Legorian snorted. "Don't keep us in suspense any longer, great detective! Which of us is this supposed master criminal?"

And Gideon Parrot answered, "You are."

Legorian started to rise.

"You and you, and you, and you—in fact, all four of you together are Sigmund Llama."

We'd had the police waiting in the bedroom, and when Andor went for his gun they stormed in, quickly overpowering any resistance. Cedric Lane demanded a lawyer, but the others remained silent. Perhaps they realized this was the end of the road.

"Five clues," Gideon repeated when they were handcuffed and about to be taken away. "First, the clue of the five faces. We knew Llama assumed a different identity in each of five cities. What easier way than if he was really five people?"

"But there are only four!" I protested.

"Which brings us to the second clue—the clue of the European schedules. Before he died Quirk told me he'd checked your European trips. None of you was in the proper cities every time Llama was supposed to have been there—and specifically you were all here in New York when Llama was in Paris last summer. I happen to know about Llama's Paris appearance because I thought I had trapped him there. I was convinced he died in a plane crash until he reappeared elsewhere—more evidence that he was more than one person, and that the fifth Llama really did die in that plane crash as I suspected."

"But who was he?" I asked.

"I rather suspect he was Hal Andor's brother, who died in France last year, supposedly from a heart attack. Third was the clue of the telephone voices. Quirk had spoken with Llama several times on the phone, but Llama always sounded different. Why? Because he *was* different!"

"We should have killed you instead of Quirk!" Cedric Lane spat out.

"Fourth, the clue of the four addresses. We phoned you all this noon and gave you four different addresses on Bank Street where Quirk was supposedly hiding. They were 208, 210, 214, and 216. He was really at 212, and that's where you sent your hit man to kill him. I was foolish to bracket the real address like that—but you couldn't have realized what I'd done unless all four of you got together and compared messages."

"You said there were five clues," I reminded him.

"Ah, yes. The fifth is the clue of the initials. I should have realized it from the beginning. Llama has five letters in it, just as this master criminal had five faces. You chose that name because it combined all of your initials. L-L-A-M-A for Lane, Legorian, Andor, Matters, and Andor's dead brother."

That was enough for the detective in charge. "Take them away," he ordered. "It looks as if Sigmund Llama's drug empire is collapsing. Once word of their arrest gets out I'm sure there'll be plenty of two-bit pushers willing to testify against them in return for lighter sentences. We owe you a great deal, Sir Gideon."

"I was only doing my job," he answered.

"My hat's off to you. You're one of the great detectives of all time!"

Sir Gideon Parrot merely smiled. "And these days there aren't many of us left."

THE FLYING FIEND

I've been asked to record another exploit of my friend Sir Gideon Parrot, and it seems to me I must at last reveal certain aspects of the Flying Fiend affair, a case that baffled the best detective minds of two nations.

One of my clients was a large West Coast corporation that maintained a vacation retreat for executives on a small island in the Strait of Georgia, off the northwest coast of Washington State. It was a picturesque region and I'd often wanted to return there after sitting in on a company meeting at the island a few years back. When one of the executives suggested that I might vacation there for a week in August free of charge, I seized the opportunity. I didn't even question him when he suggested I might bring my old friend Sir Gideon Parrot along for the trip.

I'd never been off on vacation with Gideon before but he readily accepted my invitation. We flew across the country to Seattle and hired a boat to take us up through the inlets and straits to the cluster of islands that sat on the American-Canadian border at this point. Some, like San Juan Island, were large enough to have a national historical park. Others, like the company's Cracker Island, were large enough for only a few buildings and a dozen acres of wooded trails.

"I have to thank you for this," Sir Gideon Parrot said as we stepped ashore on Cracker Island. "We have nothing comparable in Britain, except perhaps the Hebrides off the western coast of Scotland. But the weather there is generally abominable."

"I think it can be pretty bad here too, in the winter months," I said. But this August day was beautiful, with a clear sky showing only the occasional vapor trails of high-flying jets bound across the Pacific.

We were greeted at the Cracker Island dock by Seb Wrankler, a fiftyish man with a gray beard who walked with a little limp and was the company's caretaker on the island. "Hello there," he said, shaking our hands. "This your first visit to Cracker Island?"

I explained that I'd been there previously but hadn't really had a chance to look around. "We're looking forward to a week of peace and quiet."

"Well, you might not get much of that," Wrankler said. "Police boats been around a lot."

"How come?"

"Been some killings on the various islands. Bad for business."

"What sort of killings?" Gideon asked. I could see his curiosity was aroused.

"Madman, most likely. But you got nothing to worry about here, long as you don't go roaming about alone after dark."

"When did all this start?" I asked him. A suspicion was beginning to take shape in the back of my mind.

"Well, the first killing was around the end of June, but it didn't cause much of a stir. They thought it might have been done by a big bird of some sort." As he talked Wrankler picked up our bags and started along the path to the guest cottage.

"A bird?" Gideon was fully piqued now. "How is that possible?"

"The victim was a young man who'd obviously been drinking too much and had fallen asleep on one of the small beaches. There were no footprints but his own leading to the spot. They thought a buzzard might have attacked him, believing he was dead."

"Are there buzzards in these parts?" I asked.

"Oh, we get some turkey vultures up this way in the summer, though not usually over the water. Could have been some big gulls for that matter. The face and head were pretty badly cut up."

"But what actually killed him?"

"Throat was cut."

"By a *bird?*"

"Well, stranger things have happened. And as I said, this was only the first of the killings"

The guest cottage was nicely decorated with watercolor paintings of the area. There were two big beds, along with a writing desk, a bathroom, and plenty of closet space. All the comforts of home, and not a mention of the corporation that was paying for everything.

"After you get settled in, come over to the main lodge," Seb Wrankler said. "I'll whip you up something to eat."

"He seems friendly enough," I remarked after Gideon and I were alone.

Gideon sniffed. "He'd never replace an English butler, but I suppose he'll do. We'll know better after we sample his food."

As I unpacked and hung my things in the closet I said, "You know something, Gideon, I'll bet they invited us to spend a week up here so you could investigate these local murders. It wouldn't be very good for the corporate reputation to have someone killed while vacationing here. They couldn't hire an official detective and run counter to the police investigation, but they could invite the two of us up here in hopes you could help."

"I doubt if my fame has spread this far," Gideon said, though he well knew that his recent successes had been widely reported in the press.

An hour later, as the sun was dropping low in the western sky, we strolled over to the main lodge. There was a large room with a mixed decor—everything from moose heads to model planes—and scattered tables that could be grouped for dinners and meetings. Wrankler was in the kitchen when we entered and he called out, "Make yourselves comfortable. I'm just getting supper."

Over plates of tastily prepared salmon from local waters, I asked Wrankler for more information about the local killings. "What happened after the first one?"

"Well, it all died down in a couple of weeks, as those things will. But then around the middle of July a young woman sunbather was killed in the same manner, just before dark. She was camping with her husband at one of the state parks—there are several on these islands—and suddenly he heard her screams from the beach area. He ran there and found her face cut up and her throat cut, just like the first one. There was no one else in sight and no other footprint but the victim's own."

"Did he see any birds?"

"Oh, they asked him that. There were a few gulls and some boats, but nothing close by. They talked to some bird expert at the university, you know, and he said it would have to be a bird with a very strong, sharp beak—like a parrot, I guess. But I suppose you know all about them, Mr. Parrot."

Gideon bristled, as he always did when his name was pronounced that way. "The t is silent, the accent is on the o."

"That sounds French. I thought you were English."

"William the Conqueror was both," Gideon pointed out, bringing a puzzled frown and silence from Wrankler.

"How many killings have there been so far?" I asked.

"Three. The last one was two weeks ago, on one of the Canadian islands about ten miles from here. Same thing. A man alone on the beach, this time at night again, attacked and killed. No witnesses, no footprints but the man's. The Canadian police have been working with our people ever since, but they've turned up no leads."

"What were the names of the victims?" Gideon asked.

"Is that important?" I wanted to know.

"It could be. There was a famous serial murder in Britain some time back in which the killer followed the letters of the alphabet—A, B, C."

Seb Wrankler went into his little office and returned with a bunch of newspaper clippings. I flipped quickly through them, calling out the names and other information. "First victim was Ross Farley, age 24, of Seattle. That was on June 28th. Then on July 14th, Mari Quinn, 29, of Portland, Oregon. And on July 25th, Pierre King, age 47, of Vancouver, Canada."

"No obvious connections there," Gideon admitted. "And the dates don't correspond to the full moon or anything else I can think of." He went back to his dinner.

"This salmon is awfully good," I said, finishing the last of it. "You catch it yourself?"

Wrankler nodded. "I go out in the boat, catch what I can. The corporation is generous with money, but every little bit helps."

"It must get lonely here."

"No. Most weeks someone's around. And I can always go over to one of the other islands."

We were cleaning up after dinner, talking about plans for the following day, which were to include a boat tour around the islands, when we heard a pounding on the door. Seb rose to answer it, looking concerned.

A woman stumbled in. She was dressed in jeans and a faded blouse. "Hel— help me," she stammered. "My husband's been killed!" I was on my feet at once. "What happened?" She was dazed with shock, barely able to speak. "Over on Cabot Island—"

"That's the next one," Seb told us.

"Something killed him on the shore. Just like those others!"

"You've got to show us where," Seb Wrankler said, taking her by the arms. "Did you call the police? The Coast Guard patrol?"

She shook her head. "No telephone or radio. We're staying at a friend's cottage and the phone is disconnected."

"Let's start across in my boat," Wrankler said. "I'll radio the Coast Guard on the way."

It was dark now and a breeze had come up over the water. We climbed aboard Wrankler's cabin cruiser and started across about a mile of open water, leaving the woman's little outboard beached on our shore. She was regaining her composure and told us her name was Maeva Armstrong. Her husband Frank, a Seattle engineer, had brought her along for a few days of fishing and camping. He'd gone out after supper to relax on the narrow strip of beach and when he didn't return, she went looking for him and found him dead.

Even in the darkness we had no trouble locating the body. After finding him dead, Maeva Armstrong had got a flare from the tent and lit it, hoping to attract help. When none came, she'd taken the boat across the water to Cracker Island. But the flare still sputtered and burned next to the body, bathing it in a bright orange glow. Wrankler maneuvered his craft into the shallow water near the flare and tossed an anchor to the shore. We waded the last few feet through the cool shallow water.

Frank Armstrong lay on his back by the flare, his face and throat cut by some sharp instrument. I tried to imagine a bird's claws or beak doing such damage. It seemed possible but highly unlikely. Wrankler had radioed for help on the way across, and we saw the lights of the Coast Guard craft already turning in toward shore.

"Are these your footprints?" Gideon asked the woman.

She nodded, turning away from the body. The only prints were those of the dead man, and then the single track of her sandals coming up to the body, pausing, and running over to where the boat had been beached. "The killer certainly didn't come by foot," I said, stating the obvious.

Gideon bent to pick up something from the sand. This was by his hand," he said, holding up a little card not much larger than a business card. On it were printed the words *The Flying Friend*. A jagged line of blue ink had been drawn through the *r* in *Friend,* so that the card now read *The Flying Fiend.*

It was one of the Coast Guardsmen who immediately identified the strange calling card. "*The Flying Friend.* That's the Reverend Horace Black, an ordained minister who travels around the islands in a helicopter. He's forever giving away Bibles with this calling card stuck in them."

Gideon Parrot grunted and continued studying the card. "Was anything like this found with the other bodies?"

The Coast Guardsmen shook their heads. No one knew anything about it. "You might talk to Sergeant Monticello," Wrankler suggested. "He's coordinating the investigation for the various jurisdictions involved."

I could see that Gideon was hooked. Whether by intention or not, the corporation had invited the very person most likely to get to the bottom of these killings. In the morning, all thoughts of a leisurely week in the sun put aside for the moment, Gideon and I found ourselves in the office of Sergeant Monticello of the Bellingham police. He was a deep-voiced man with a barrel chest and big hands. He kept moving a glass paperweight around his desk nervously as he spoke.

"You realize only the first of the killings—that of Ross Farley—took place in my jurisdiction," he told us. The county lines and national boundaries are a bit confusing out there among the islands, so for the time being I'm coordinating everything. If these killings keep up, though, somebody with higher rank will probably get the assignment. That's the way it usually goes." His flat voice carried just a trace of bitterness toward the system.

I explained how we'd happened on the body of the latest victim the previous evening, and described the card Gideon had found near the victim's hand. Sergeant Monticello nodded, picking up a typed report from his desk. "It was all here waiting for me this morning. This is the first instance where a card or signature of any sort has been left on the scene. It could mean our killer is getting more sure of himself, or a little crazier. In either case it means more murders to come. There'd be no point in leaving that card if this was to be the last of the killings."

"Do you know anything about the Reverend Horace Black?" Gideon asked.

"Oh, he's a bit of a kook, flying around in his helicopter, but he's certainly no murderer. Everyone in these parts knows him."

"I'd like to meet him," Gideon said. "Ask a few questions."

Sergeant Monticello sighed. "I know you've got quite a reputation in London and New York, Sir Gideon, but you might be out of your territory a bit here. These aren't any big-city killings, and you can't use big-city techniques to go after the murderer."

"I could hardly be accused of using big-city techniques," Gideon answered with a slight smile. "I merely want to ask the man a few questions. He may be above suspicion as a mass murderer, but the fact remains he possesses a helicopter—and we're looking for a killer who seems to drop out of the skies."

Monticello dismissed us with a wave of his hand. "Go. Talk to him if you want. Come back and see me when you've got the murderer."

Horace Black was not a hard man to find. We learned that his church, a vaguely defined Protestant denomination, was located on the largest of the area's islands, at a place called Oak Harbor. It was connected to the mainland by a bridge, and when we arrived there by rented car we saw the helicopter just settling down for a landing behind the church itself.

Gideon Parrot got out of the car and strode forward like some official greeter, welcoming Black back to his own church. The minister, wearing aviator's goggles more suited to a World War I biplane, looked very little like a man of God, but he accepted Gideon's welcome with good humor. "All are welcome at my church," he said, smoothing down his long sandy hair. He was younger than I'd expected, probably still in his early thirties, with a thin mustache that heightened the sense of someone from a past era.

We followed him inside where he quickly picked two books from a shelf and handed them to us. They were Bibles bound in imitation leather and probably costing no more than a couple of dollars apiece—the sort one found in hotel-room drawers. Inside the front cover of each was a printed card reading *The Flying Friend.*

"Now what can I do for you?" Horace Black asked, sitting behind a desk piled high with unopened mail and assorted literature. "Interested in our Bible class?"

"We came about the murders," Gideon responded. "I'am investigating them on an unofficial basis."

"Oh, yes. I've already been in touch with Sergeant Monticello about it. I understand one of my cards was found by the latest victim"

"That's correct. The word *friend* had been changed to—"

"*Fiend.* The killer is not without humor, despite his godless depravity. Of course I leave the cards everywhere on these islands. It's like my parish, in a sense."

"Were you recently on Cabot Island?" Gideon asked.

"Yes, I'm sure I was."

"The victim's wife was not familiar with you."

"Well, these summer people come and go. I may have visited the island's previous residents and left a Bible for them."

Gideon seemed to study the man for a moment and then said, "Of course there remains the possibility that the killer didn't leave that calling card, that the dying man struck out the letter *r* himself to indicate his killer."

"You are accusing me of murder?" The thought seemed to amuse the minister.

"Not at all. Just examining the possibilities."

"Sergeant Monticello already examined the same possibilities. He tells me the dead man had no pen or pencil on him. He could not have altered that card before he died."

"Then I guess I've been wasting your time," Gideon admitted.

"Not at all." Black was gracious now. "Look, I have to fly over to Glover Island. Come along with me, you two, and I'll show you a view of these islands you'll never see from the ground."

It was an offer we couldn't resist. We followed him out to the cabin of his helicopter and climbed inside. Though there were four seats we seemed a bit cramped, and when Black took off straight up, I lurched into Gideon, thrown off balance as in a suddenly rising elevator that stops and then starts again.

It was nearly noon, and the sun bathed the entire area in a soft unreal glow. The waters of the straits were unusually calm, and their mirrored surface resembled the glass in some child's diorama from this far up. Horace Black talked without stopping, pointing out and naming the various islands as we passed over them. He showed us the scenes of each of the four killings, swooping low over the rocky beaches to pinpoint these and other spots of interest.

We settled down on Glover Island and watched while he delivered a carton of Bibles to a colony of summer cottages. Then we were off and flying again, "We keep hearing there could be oil under these waters," Black told us as we glided in low over the straits. "But I guess you hear that all up and down the west coast these days. Be a shame to ruin all this beauty with a bunch of oil rigs." He turned to look at Gideon. "That's something I could kill for, to keep God's land as he intended."

"I doubt if our Flying Fiend has quite such noble motives."

"Of course there's always drugs."

I saw Gideon perk up. "Drugs?"

"Sure. A lot of it comes in from Canada this way. Cocaine, heroin, pot— you name it. I see it all the time when I work with younger people."

"Could the killings be drug-related?"

"None of the victims have been regular island residents. And you read in the papers what goes on every day in Miami. Any time there's a rash of killings along the fringes of the country you have to consider the possibility of drug traffic. I told that to Monticello."

"What did he say?"

"Just that he's looking into all possibilities."

We came in over Black's church and dropped gently onto his landing field. It had been a pleasant scenic flight, even if it hadn't gained us any new facts about the murders. We said goodbye to the Reverend Horace Black and drove back to the mainland.

"What do you think about his narcotics theory?" I asked Gideon.

"I think that a hollowed-out Bible would be a perfect way to deliver drugs without anybody noticing."

We went back to the corporation's island and tried to relax. There were no clues to the Flying Fiend except the card left with the latest victim, and that seemed to be a dead end at the moment. Seb Wrankler had one of the minister's Bibles in the main lodge, but it certainly wasn't hollowed-out.

"Oh, the minister's all right," Wrankler conceded. "I'm not a religious man myself, but I don't mind him setting his helicopter down for a visit now and then. Sometimes when I'm all alone here I'm downright glad to see him."

"That helicopter seemed pretty noisy," Gideon remarked.

"Oh, sure. When he comes to call, you know it."

Toward evening Gideon managed to reach Maeva Armstrong at the funeral home where preparations were being made for her husband's service. I heard him say, "I hate to bother you at a time like this Mrs. Armstrong, but I have just one question to ask you. It might help the investigation. Shortly before you found your husband's body, did you hear any loud noise in the sky—the sort of pulsating noise that a helicopter makes? You didn't? You heard nothing at all?"

After a bit more conversation Gideon hung up and turned to me. "She heard nothing, and I doubt if anyone else did. If the killer is using a helicopter he must have some sort of silencing device for it."

"Is such a thing possible?"

"Not that I know of."

Wrankler was pouring our after-dinner coffee. "Maybe the killer comes in on a hang glider, towed behind a boat."

"Or in a scuba diving gear from under the water," I suggested, entering into the spirit of the thing.

"A hang glider would pass too quickly over the victims," Gideon answered seriously. "And a scuba diver would have left footprints between the water and his victims."

Our after-dinner conversation was getting us nowhere, so we soon abandoned it. The fresh salt air had tired both Gideon and myself and we retired soon thereafter, sleeping soundly through the night.

In the morning when we awakened, the sun was already high among the treetops. It was after nine o'clock, and as we made our way sleepily to a belated breakfast at the main lodge Seb Wrankler met us with news of another murder.

The victim this time was an elderly man who'd fallen asleep while fishing off a pier on one of the larger islands. The killing had occurred soon after darkness fell, but there were witnesses to swear that no one had gone out on the pier until a couple of them walked out together to waken the elderly man and found the usual fatal wounds around his face and throat. There was no calling card from the Flying Fiend this time, or if there was perhaps it had *fallen* into the water or blown away. The dead man's name was Herbert Thompson and he was 67 years old.

"Always near the water," Gideon mused. "As if it was a swimming fiend rather than a flying one." This is two nights in a row. What do you think it means?"

He didn't answer, but after breakfast he went to the telephone and managed to reach Sergeant Monticello at his office. They talked for a long time, very quietly, but when he rejoined Wrankler and me at the table he seemed dejected.

"No new leads," he told us. "It seems hopeless."

"Didn't you ever have anything like this back in London?" I asked him. "Jack the Ripper and that sort of thing?"

"I'm not old enough to remember Jack the Ripper," he answered dryly. "But I do have one idea I'd like to try out on you. It involves something Horace Black told us about there being oil under these waters."

Seb Wrankler snorted. "You believe that old story? The only oil there'll be around here is if the pipeline springs a leak."

"Still," Gideon said, "I think it's worth looking into."

We spent the day exploring the island, with Gideon concentrating especially on the area near the water's edge. I couldn't imagine what he was up to. Finally, in late afternoon, he told me, "I want you to go back to the lodge now. I'm going to stay out here alone."

"Won't it be dangerous after dark? The killer—"

"Exactly! I'm setting myself up as a target and I expect the killer to come after me. Here's what I want you to do. Go back to the lodge for supper as usual and tell Seb I've got a clue and I stayed down by the water. Then, after supper, leave him and go back to our cabin alone. Tell him you're going to lie down. But whatever you do, don't drink any of the coffee."

"The coffee?"

"We were drugged last night."

"You mean that Seb—?"

"No time for talk now—do as I say. I want you to sneak out later and try to follow Seb when he leaves the lodge."

Then he was gone, moving away from me down the shoreline. I felt bewildered and a little frightened, but I did what he asked me. Under the circumstances I found it difficult to converse with Seb Wrankler, and I may have been too obvious when I declined his offer of coffee. But later I acted properly drowsy and told him I was turning in early. Maybe he'd decide the drugged coffee hadn't been needed.

I waited in our cabin for about ten minutes and then made my way through the woods to the back of the main lodge. After an uncomfortable half hour squatting behind a bush, my vigil was rewarded. Seb Wrankler came out carrying a large cardboard box carefully in both hands.

I followed him through the woods, staying under cover at all times. It was dusk now, but I could still see him as he reached the dock and went aboard the boat with his strange cargo. Gideon was nowhere in sight, and I assumed he was still on the other side of the island. After a few moments Wrankler started the boat's inboard motor and pulled away from the dock. Before long the darkness would make it impossible to see anything but the boat's running lights.

Quickly I crossed the island, seeking the area where I'd left Gideon. He was still there, sitting on the sand, staring out at the darkness which was quickly enveloping the water. I wanted to run to him and warn him, but I hung back, hidden at the edge of the trees. I thought I heard the noise of an approaching boat, but it died as quickly as it had begun.

So I waited.

After about five minutes I was impatient to tell him of my presence. I was about to yell something when I heard a low humming sound in the sky above the beach. It grew louder but not too loud, and Gideon appeared not to notice.

And then I saw it—a great winged creature circling about ten feet over Gideon's head.

I broke from the trees, unable to restrain myself any longer. But even as I ran out onto the beach, the creature dove and came in straight for Gideon's face. He started to rise, seeing it at last, but the thing was almost upon him.

Then a sudden single shot rang out and the creature seemed to come apart in midair. There were shouts from the water and two more shots.

"Gideon! Are you all right?" I asked as I reached him.

"I think so. It was a close call."

A Coast Guard boat came into view, and I recognized Sergeant Monticello standing in the bow with a high-powered rifle in his hands. "We got him!" he shouted to Gideon. "He went for a gun and we had to kill him."

I looked back at Gideon. "Wrankler?"

He nodded and walked to the water's edge where the thing I'd taken for a creature lay smashed in the shallow water. It was one of the model airplanes from the lodge. "That was the murder weapon?" I asked in disbelief.

Gideon Parrot nodded. "The Flying Fiend will fly no more."

Later, back at the lodge, with Monticello and me as an avid audience, Gideon explained. "Wrankler used model airplanes with propellers sharpened to razor-thin edges. They were guided from his boat by a thin, almost invisible wire. The killings usually took place around dusk or shortly after dark, when he could still see his victims but the small model planes were almost invisible. He could guide them quite accurately with the wire, and he chose victims who were dozing or otherwise off-guard. Before they knew what hit them those razor-sharp propeller blades were slicing up their face and throat. If the plane was damaged after the attack and unable to fly back to the boat, Wrankler could jerk on the wire, flip the plane into the water, and pull it back on board. There'd be no trace on the hard wet sand between the body and the water."

"But what was his motive?" Sergeant Monticello asked.

"I suspect it was oil. Some other corporation—other than the one that employed him—wanted to drill for oil on these islands. They secretly hired Seb Wrankler to scare people away and make the area unpopular, so there'd be less opposition to their buying mineral rights to the islands. I mentioned oil to him today, figuring if that was the motive he'd probably mark me as the next victim just to get rid of me."

Gideon got to his feet. "Meanwhile, Sergeant, we'll be getting a good night's sleep and heading back in the morning." He paused at the door. "You were here right on schedule after our telephone conversation this morning. I believe I asked you something else too."

"About Frank Armstrong's funeral. It's tomorrow morning at ten."

Gideon nodded. "We'll want to stop there on our way to the airport."

"What for?" I asked.

"Simply to pay our respects to one of the victims."

By morning the newspapers had the story of the Flying Fiend's demise and were speculating as to the motive behind the series of bizarre crimes. As he drove us to Frank Armstrong's funeral, Monticello told us he'd discovered monthly payments to Wrankler by an oil company. "It's only a matter of time before we put it all together."

Gideon waited until after the funeral to approach Mrs. Armstrong. She recognized him at once and hurried over to thank him. "You're the man who exposed the Flying Fiend, aren't you? I don't know how to thank you for avenging my husband."

"He hasn't yet been avenged," Gideon said sadly. "Your husband was not one of the victims of Seb Wrankler and his fiendish device."

"What do you mean?"

"None of the other bodies had the Flying Fiend calling card, only your husband's. That was because the killer's murder device, a model plane, could not deliver and drop such a card. It was important in your husband's murder, though, because you wanted to direct our attention toward the sky and away from the ground—which is the route by which his killer really approached."

"Are you accusing me—?"

"It was a copycat killing, something the police often encounter in serial murders. You killed your husband as he dozed on the sand, probably using a razor to make it look like the other murders. And you left that card so we'd look for an airborne killer."

"I hope you can prove these charges, because I'll sue you for every—"

"Oh, I can prove them, Mrs. Armstrong. You told us you got a flare from the tent after finding your husband's body, and lit it to summon help. The flare was by the body, all right, but there was *only* one set of your footprints to the body and then to the boat You never went back for the flare, which means you had it with you all the time. And you had it with you because you knew you'd be needing it when you walked up to your husband with that razor."

Her body seemed to sag then, as she turned to look at our faces all around her. "And this is Sergeant Monticello," Gideon continued. "I'm sure you remember him, Mrs. Armstrong."

THE CAT AND FIDDLE MURDERS

The strange chain of events that carried Sir Gideon Parrot and myself to England in the autumn of last year need not be recounted here. Suffice it to say that upon completion of the business at hand we were invited to spend a few days at a little island off the Devon coast. Our host was to be Archibald Knore, the department store heir who'd spent ten years and countless thousands of pounds assembling a private zoo for the amusement of himself and his friends.

"How do you happen to know Knore?" I asked Gideon as we made our way across the strip of water that separated the mainland from Placid Island. Knore's was one of the largest department-store chains in Britain, and the invitation to spend a few days in such illustrious company was most impressive.

"I did the man a favour once," Gideon explained. "It's not the sort of favour one mentions in polite conversation, and I doubt if he will do so. He was visiting a young lady of dubious reputation and I helped him escape just before her apartment was raided by the police. But this was years ago. I dare say Archibald has settled down now and devotes his full energies to this private zoo of his."

Right on cue there came a loud trumpeting from the island just ahead. The little mail boat bucked in the water as if startled by the noise and I fastened a grip on Gideon's arm. "What was that?"

"Sounded like an elephant to me. We'll see soon enough—there's the dock straight ahead."

I'd expected Archibald Knore himself to be waiting for us at dockside, but although he wasn't there it was no disappointment. In his stead was as lovely a young woman as I'd had the pleasure to meet since leaving New York. She reached down a firm hand to help us onto the dock, then introduced herself with a sunny smile. "I'm Lois Lanchester, Mr. Knore's secretary. Welcome to Placid Island."

"What a nice name for it," Gideon said, bowing to kiss her hand.

She laughed and tossed her mane of yellow hair with one hand. "During the winter storms we sometimes suspect the prior owners chose that name to enhance its value as real estate."

"This is a year-round home, then?" I asked.

She turned, as if noticing me for the first time, and Gideon hurried to introduce me. "Yeah," she said. "Mr. Knore devotes his full time to the zoo these days. The family business is handled by others."

She led the way up to the house, the fit of her designer jeans over her perfectly formed hips snug. When the great house itself came into full view, my gaze was distracted elsewhere. It was a magnificent place, a sprawling English country house that seemed oblivious to its somewhat cramped island setting. And on the lawn to greet us was a strutting peacock, its iridescent tail-feathers erect.

"He's quite a sight," I remarked.

"King Jack is our official greeter. But you'll be seeing more animals soon." As if to confirm her words the trumpet of the distant elephant sounded again.

We entered the house and passed down an oak-paneled corridor to a grimly masculine study where Archibald Knore awaited us. I'd seen newspaper pictures of him once or twice, but they hadn't prepared me for the overwhelming presence of the man himself. He was tall and large without seeming overweight, and his voice seemed to boom across the room. "Sir Gideon! A pleasure to see you again! Come right in!"

He shook my hand vigorously as Gideon introduced me. "He spent a great deal of time in your London store this week," Gideon said.

Knore smiled broadly. "Spending money, I hope. These animals seem to eat more every year."

"We're anxious to see your zoo," I told him. "But isn't a private zoo unusual these days?"

"No. There are privately owned wildlife habitats in several countries. My friend Gerald Durrell, the author, has a very fine zoo on the island of Jersey. Only government regulation prevents many others from existing. I firmly believe that the task of preserving certain rare species could be carried out much more efficiently in private hands. As long as zoos remain dependent upon public funds, those funds are often the first items to be cut in a budget crunch. The point that feeding people is more important than feeding animals is too easily made."

"Why don't I get you two settled," Lois Lanchester suggested, "and then we can show you around?"

"Do that, Lois," Archibald Knore agreed, "and then bring them back downstairs to meet the other guests for cocktails."

On the way up to our rooms Gideon asked about the other guests. "Mr. Knore often has weekend visitors," Lois said. "This weekend it's a cousin, Bertie Foxe, his wife, and a close friend of theirs, the Czech violinist Jan Litost."

Our adjoining rooms were all we could have desired, with comfortable beds and leaded glass windows looking out on the sea. I was thankful the zoo itself was on the other side of the house where the nocturnal noises of the animals were less likely to disturb our sleep.

We'd barely had time to unpack when Lois Lanchester was tapping on our doors with all the exuberance of a shipboard cruise director. "If you're ready I can give you a quick look at the zoo before cocktails," she told us. "Sylvia Foxe wants to come along too."

"It will be a pleasure," Gideon said. "I've always had a great love for animals."

We met the wife of Knore's cousin in the downstairs hall. She was a tall dark-haired woman dressed in riding britches and leather boots. She had no doubt been pretty once but middle age had turned her face hard and stern. "Are there bridle paths on the island?" I asked after Lois had introduced us.

"No," Sylvia replied. "I simply find this costume more suitable for prowling around the animals. I wouldn't want some little creature taking a bite out of my leg."

"There's no danger of that," Lois told her sweetly.

We left the house by a rear door and followed a covered walkway to a low cinder-block building. Already the scent of animals was heavy in the air, but Lois explained that only the smallest creatures and most dangerous species of snake were kept indoors.

Never having been one for snakes, I passed quickly by the glass cages with their traditional tree branch upon which a serpent lay sunning itself beneath the artificial light from above. The lizards I found a bit more interesting, especially when they were in motion. "The temperature is kept at eighty degrees for the reptiles," Lois explained as she walked us through. "Over there is the bird house with its new penguin pond. But let me show you some of the big cats first."

The lions and tigers were kept in large open pits, with plenty of space to roam about and trees for climbing. "In the coldest weather we take them indoors," Lois said.

"Who takes care of the animals?" Gideon Parrot asked, his eyes on a large tiger that seemed to be feasting on its afternoon meal.

"We have a full-time zookeeper on the staff. His name is Taupper. You'll meet him later. He—" She paused, watching the tiger now, along with Gideon. "My God! That looks like a human body in the tiger pit!"

"It most certainly does," Gideon confirmed. "You'd better call for help."

We were above it now, and as the tiger rolled it over with one powerful paw Sylvia Foxe gasped. "It's Jan! It's our friend Jan Litost!"

A burly man in work clothes I took to be the zookeeper came running in answer to Lois's summons. While he was lowering a ladder into the pit Gideon pulled me aside and pointed to a large sheet of paper that had been tacked to a nearby tree. In large child-like letters were printed some familiar words: HEY DIDDLE, DIDDLE, THE CAT AND THE FIDDLE,

"He was murdered," Archibald Knore said some twenty minutes later. "There's no doubt in my mind."

"Murdered by someone on this island?" Lois Lanchester asked.

We were back at the main house, gathered about the big stone fireplace where cocktails were to have been served. Sylvia Foxe's husband Bertie had joined us, a slender man with thinning hair. "It *can't* be murder," he insisted. "Who on this island could have any possible motive for killing Jan?"

"The back of his skull was crushed," Knore argued. "He was hit very hard with a blunt instrument of some sort. And there are spots of blood on the railing surrounding the tiger pit. Someone killed him and dumped him in there. As to who would have a motive, that's for the police to discover."

"Have they been summoned?" Gideon asked.

"I'll do that now."

But his telephone call to the mainland didn't bring the prompt response we desired. The local constable informed Knore that all the boats were tied up with a rescue mission down the coast and with the winds increasing as darkness approached the police helicopter couldn't make the flight over to the island until morning. "Don't touch anything," his voice crackled. "We'll be there first thing in the morning."

Archibald Knore slammed down the telephone. "The old fool! If there's a murderer loose on this island we could all be dead by morning!"

"The winds are picking up outside," Sylvia Foxe said. "It looks like a storm."

"No storm," the zookeeper said. "The animals aren't that restless." It was the first time Peter Taupper had spoken since he'd lifted the body of Jan Litost from the pit. He was a burly, unkempt man with tufts of gray hair protruding from his ears. I wondered if Knore paid him as much as a municipal zoo would, though I had no idea what good public or private zookeepers earned.

At this point Gideon Parrot cleared his throat and the room fell silent. "In the absence of the official police I may be of some service," he announced. "I was invited here as a guest, but Archibald knows I've had some experience in matters of this nature. I propose we take a few moments to examine the facts."

"What facts?" Lois asked.

"Well, if someone on this island is a murderer we need to know exactly how many people are here."

"That's easy," she responded, counting them off on her fingers. "You two, myself, Mr. Knore, Mrs. Knore—"

"Wait a minute," Gideon interrupted. "Is your wife on the island, Archibald?"

"Dora has been crippled for some years now. She never leaves her room."

"I see. Go on, please, Miss Lanchester."

"O.K. Mrs. Knore, Mr. and Mrs. Foxe, Peter Taupper, his assistant Milo Lune who also tends to the gardening, and of course the butler, the maid, and the cook. There is also a nurse who tends to Mrs. Knore, but this is her day off."

"Then there are twelve people on the island at the present time, not counting the unfortunate Mr. Litost."

"That's correct."

"Who tends to Mrs. Knore when the nurse is away?"

Knore answered the question. "The maid does. She's quite efficient."

"Mr. and Mrs. Foxe," Gideon said. "You brought the victim to this island. Suppose you tell me a bit about him."

Bertie Foxe snorted. "No one has to be told about Jan Litost. He was one of Europe's foremost violinists—he wasn't yet forty years old! It's a terrible loss to the world of music!"

"Had he wife? A lover?"

"I believe he was married in his youth, but he'd been alone for many years. We met him in London last season and became fast friends. It was I who suggested he might want to visit Archibald's private zoo."

"When did you arrive?"

"Yesterday afternoon."

Gideon turned to Mrs. Foxe. "And how is it you hadn't viewed the animals until today?"

"I was indisposed when we arrived, Sylvia Foxe explained. "It was a rough crossing by boat just after lunch—my stomach was unprepared for it."

"But your husband and the late Mr. Litost had toured the zoo?"

"I took them around yesterday," Knore volunteered, "and Peter showed them the giraffe and the zebras this morning. They're kept farther out, away from the house."

Another man in work clothes, somewhat younger than Taupper, entered during the conversation. Taupper introduced him to Gideon and me. "This is my assistant, Milo Lune."

The man seemed unusually shy. He rubbed his dirty hands against the legs of his work pants as he answered Gideon's questions. "Did I see Mr. Litost this afternoon? No—well, yes. I think I did spot him strolling by the monkey cages but only at a distance. I didn't speak with him."

"Is something the matter?" Gideon asked. "You seem nervous."

"No, no—it's just I'm worried about the animals is all."

Gideon next produced the crudely printed note he'd discovered tacked to the tree. "Did any of you see this before? I found it on a tree near the scene."

"It looks like the work of a child," Lois Lanchester said.

"Are there any children on Placid Island?"

"No."

Archibald Knore came forward to study the message. "A child's nursery rhyme. What does it mean?"

"The cat and the fiddle could refer to the tiger and Jan Litost."

"The rhyme is believed to be a reference to Queen Elizabeth the First," Bertie Foxe said. "I've made a study of nursery rhymes."

"Notice the location of the commas in the message," Gideon said, holding it up again.

HEY DIDDLE, DIDDLE, THE CAT AND THE FIDDLE,

"What about it?" Lois asked.

"Not many persons would place commas between those two 'diddles,' yet that is the correct version of the rhyme. The person who wrote this was no child. Note too the comma at the end of the line. What does that tell us?"

"That there's more to come," Lois answered quietly.

There was always the possibility of another person on the island, perhaps an escaped convict who'd come out by boat from the mainland and remained hidden back there among the animals. Knore suggested a search party be organized and I readily agreed to be part of it. Gideon, who walked slowly at best, decided to stay behind and question the servants about anything unusual they might have seen.

I found myself with Bertie Foxe, Peter Taupper, and Milo Lune, making a sweep of the far end of the island. There was a dense wooded area here, with only a high fence to indicate the outer limits of the zoo itself. "No one's here," Milo Lune said. "I'm back here a few days a week and nothing's been disturbed. We're wasting our time."

"We should split up," Foxe suggested. "We'd cover the ground much quicker."

The zookeeper, Taupper, agreed readily enough. "Why don't we spread out and keep walking in a counter-clockwise direction? Then meet back at the house?"

I found myself on the far right of the sweep, close to the rocky shoreline with a view of the water. The others were out of sight within minutes and I eyed the setting sun uncertainly, hoping I'd make it back before dark. But the island wasn't as large as I'd feared and it took me only a quarter of an hour to circle around, following the shoreline until the big house was in sight once more.

But now there were only three of us.

Taupper's assistant, Milo Lune, was missing.

"Where in hell is he?" Taupper demanded, and tried shouting his name. There was no reply.

"Shall we go back?" Foxe suggested. "It'll be dark soon."

"He'll show up," Taupper said, a bit uncertainly.

We were standing, uncertain of our next move, when a window high in the house opened and Sylvia Foxe's head appeared. "There's someone in the elephant enclosure!" she shouted. "I can see him from here!"

I took a deep breath and followed quickly after the others. When we reached the elephant enclosure I saw at once what Sylvia had spotted from her window. Milo Lune was crumpled near the fence of the enclosure while one of the smaller elephants nudged the body with its trunk. The back of his head was battered and bloody but I was beyond blaming the injury on an elephant's hoof. I wasn't even surprised a few minutes later when Gideon Parrot joined us and he snatched another message off a nearby tree.

"THE COW JUMP'D OVER THE MOON," he read.

After a dinner eaten quickly in gloomy silence, we gathered in Archibald Knore's study to sort out what few facts we had in our possession. Knore himself had tried to reach the mainland again, but without success. "The phone is dead," he reported. "It may be because of the heavy winds, or—"

"Or the line may have been cut," Sylvia Foxe supplied. "God, we're trapped on this island with a madman!"

"We must all stay together," Knore agreed. He turned toward Gideon Parrot and said, "I think you and your friend had better double up for the night. Bertie and Sylvia will be together and I will be with my wife." He paused, trying to puzzle out the rest of it. "Lois, you'd better share a room with the maid and cook. And, Peter, you can sleep with the butler."

"Old Oakes?" the zookeeper snorted. "He snores so loud he keeps the animals awake! I'll take my chances alone, thanks!"

We'd already been over the timing of Milo Lune's killing and everyone agreed that either Bertie or Peter Taupper could have done it—or even myself, for that matter. But it was just as likely that someone from the house, or a hidden stranger, could have surprised him with that terrible blow to the head.

"But how could he let anyone approach him with a club or anything after what happened to Jan Litost?" Lois asked. "It doesn't make sense."

"The killer might have been well hidden and struck before he was seen," Gideon suggested.

"But he'd have to push the body into the elephant enclosure," I pointed out. "With the rest of us in the area, someone would be sure to see him."

"But no one did," Gideon replied. "So apparently it wasn't such a risk, after all." He turned to Sylvia Foxe. "You were watching from your window. Did you see anything?"

She shook her head. "Not until I noticed the body. But I wasn't at the window for very long. I'd just come up from downstairs. I went to see if Bertie was in sight anywhere and I spotted what looked like a body."

Gideon turned to Archibald Knore. "Where were you during this time?"

"Alone here in the study. You certainly can't suspect *me* of killing them!"

"I suspect everyone. It's the only way. In fact, I must ask you the same question, Miss Lanchester."

Lois flushed prettily and stammered a bit. "Well, I—well, I was using one of the upstairs bathrooms. My stomach's been in knots since Jan's body was found. I wasn't feeling well."

"Perfectly understandable," Gideon agreed.

Knore came out from behind his desk. "The killer is no one here. It's some madman who murders whoever he finds alone. Jan and Milo were simply unlucky."

But Gideon shook his head, like a professor correcting a wayward student. "No, they were the intended victims. We know that from the nursery rhyme. The cat was the tiger, and the fiddle was a reference to the violinist, Jan Litost."

"But how," Knore asked, "does this latest message pertain to Lune and the elephants?"

"Lune is the French word for moon, of course. I noticed some smaller elephants in that enclosure." He turned to the zookeeper. "Mr. Taupper, if male elephants are called bulls, what are the females called?"

"Cows," Taupper answered quietly. "Everyone knows that."

"Thus, the cow jumped over the moon—and crushed his skull while doing it."

"What's the rest of the rhyme?" Bertie Foxe asked after a moment's silence. "Nothing about foxes in it, is there?"

"No," Gideon answered seriously. "In its earliest version the verse reads, Hey diddle, diddle, The Cat and the Fiddle, The Cow jump'd over the Moon; The little Dog laugh'd To see such Craft, And the Dish ran away with the Spoon."

"You remember all that?" Lois asked.

"During this afternoon's search I looked it up in *The Oxford Dictionary of Nursery Rhymes*. There's a copy in the library."

"Where anyone else could have looked it up too," I observed. "That's how they got the punctuation right."

"Perhaps."

"The little Dog laugh'd To see such Craft," Knore repeated. "I don't see how that can apply to anyone here. And there are no dogs on the island."

"We can't have them," Taupper explained. "They'd upset the animals with their barking."

"Then maybe the chain will be broken," Lois said. "Maybe the killer's work is finished."

Gideon Parrot said nothing. He was staring at a photograph on Knore's desk, obviously a portrait of Knore and his wife when they were much younger. "I think we must speak with Mrs. Knore," he said quietly.

"She knows nothing," Knore protested. "She never leaves her room."

"But things can be seen from a window. Sylvia Foxe saw a body from her window. Your wife might have seen the killer."

Archibald Knore was silent for a moment. Finally he said, "very well. You and your friend can see her. But only for a few minutes. I'll take you up."

The upper reaches of the house seemed unusually dark, with only a dim bulb at the top of the stairs to light the way. The maid who'd been sitting with Dora Knore rose as we entered and Archibald dismissed her with a wave of his hand.

The woman in the bed seemed about Knore's age but she was very thin and rather feeble in her gestures. "You've brought me visitors, Archie," she said in a soft voice. "How nice."

"This is Sir Gideon Parrot, dear. He's investigating the trouble I told you about."

"The killings?"

"Yes."

"Terrible things! We moved here to get away from crime in the cities. After my accident I couldn't walk any more—"

"Might I ask what caused it?" Gideon asked her.

"An auto crash. Archie was driving and the car went off the road. I think he was dozing a bit but I've never blamed him for what happened."

"Mrs. Knore," Gideon began, keeping his voice soft to match hers, "I was wondering if you might have seen anything today from your window at about the time either of those men were killed."

"Oh, no. I never get out of bed. The nurse or Winifred—the maid—tells me what I need to know, which is very little. The weather makes no impact on my life and the animals are Archie's hobby, not mine."

"So you saw or heard nothing?"

"Not a thing."

Her eyes closed for a moment and Knore took that as a signal she was tiring. "That's all," he said.

When we were in the hall Gideon asked, "Wouldn't she be more comfortable in a wheelchair, with the rest of us?"

"No, no," her husband said. "She's fine as she is. She wants it this way."

Back downstairs, plans were again made for the sleeping arrangements. Everyone would be safe through the remainder of the night. And in the morning the police would come.

That, at least, is what we thought.

But in the morning, as Gideon and I were arising before breakfast, Peter Taupper brought news of the latest outrage. The island's only boat had been scuttled at its dock and now lay in eight feet of water. Tacked to one of the mooring posts was the expected message: THE LITTLE DOG LAUGH'D TO SEE SUCH CRAFT.

The telephone was still dead and the winds were still high. We were cut off from the mainland with a killer who showed no sign of stopping.

Over breakfast Archibald Knore said, "At least no one was killed this time."

"No," Lois Lanchester murmured. "Not yet. But there's still one line the nursery rhyme to go." She was helping to serve the breakfast and, taking a sip of Knore's hot porridge with a spoon before she placed the bowl in front of him, she said, "Tastes good."

The Foxes were together at the end of the table, looking unhappy, and Taupper stood in the doorway with a cup of coffee, explaining how he'd happened to find the damaged boat. "I went down to the dock to see if any boats were coming over from the mainland. That's when I saw her sunk in the water. Somebody whacked the side of it with an axe—below the water line, near as I could tell. It was probably done last night, before we all went to bed."

"But what sense does the message make?" Bertie Foxe asked. "I understand that the craft refers to the boat, but there's still no dog on the island."

"Nor anyone whose name sounds like dog," Sylvia chimed in.

Knore looked unhappy. "My wife Dora. *Dora* and *dog* start with the same two letters, but that's a bit farfetched."

"It certainly is," Lois agreed. "Your wife is the one person on the island who *can't* be involved. She never leaves her *room*."

"It's obvious the killer intends to complete the verse," Gideon said. "It's important that we anticipate his actions and beat him to it."

"What is it? *And the Dish ran away with the Spoon?* What could that possibly mean?" I asked.

"I think we're worrying needlessly," Taupper said. "As soon as the winds die down, the helicopter will be over from the mainland."

"Can the boat be repaired?" Knore asked.

"Certainly. Anything can be repaired."

"Can it be repaired by you?"

"I think so. I can patch it and pump out the water."

"Then do it, man! Quickly!"

Sylvia Foxe cleared her throat. "Might I suggest that someone should go with him? If he's down there alone the killer might get ideas."

"Good thinking," her husband said.

"Lois, how about you?" Sylvia suggested. "Or would you rather I go?"

Lois Lanchester finished her morning coffee and stubbed out her cigarette. "I'll be glad to go, but I don't know that I'll be of much help. What say, Peter? Do you need me?"

Taupper grinned. "You can hold my tools. Come along."

After they'd left, Gideon and I went for a walk outside. The unsettled weather had made the animals restless, and the camels shied away as we approached their pen. Over beyond it the zoo's young giraffe was romping in the tall grass and two zebras grazed nearby. "A peaceful place," Gideon said. "The peaceable kingdom—even with a killer loose."

"Gideon," I said, "I have got a theory. Suppose the animals really did kill Litost and Lune. Suppose those crazy notes were written afterward by Taupper to protect his precious animals."

"An interesting theory, but hardly a practical one. The rhyme doesn't fit the events perfectly, but there is some connection. It could hardly have been a spur-of-the-moment idea in the first case, and the coincidence of a second killing accidentally fitting the pattern is out of the question."

"What now?"

He'd turned to stare up at the great old house. "I think we should speak to Bertie Foxe."

We found Bertie and his wife upstairs in their room where they'd gone after breakfast. It was a big sunny bedroom, larger than the one Gideon and I were now sharing but similarly furnished. Bertie sat on the bed smoking while Sylvia stared out the window at the animals.

"I want to know more about Jan Litost," Gideon said. "He was the first victim and the key to this puzzle must lie with him."

"Jan was extremely talented," Bertie Foxe said, taking a long drag on his cigarette. "We'd been friends for years and it seemed a natural thing to accept Archibald's kind invitation to visit the zoo after the London concert."

"Did the three of you travel together frequently?"

"Quite frequently," Sylvia answered from the window.

"You'll forgive me but I must ask this next question. Was there any sort of romantic involvement between yourself and Jan, Mrs. Foxe, which might have made your husband jealous?"

"See here!" Bertie barked, jumping to his feet.

But Sylvia answered calmly, "Certainly not. Bertie and I are happily married and always have been."

"There was nothing between them!" Bertie growled, stepping forward. "Take your dirty little thoughts elsewhere, Parrot!"

Gideon walked to the window and stared out across the tiled roof of the zoo building. He seemed to be looking at the tops of the elephants' heads, barely visible in their enclosure, as he said, "We're all like those animals at times. We meet, and mate, and sometimes kill. It's human nature, or the animal side of human nature, for the males to clash over a female—"

His words were interrupted by a sharp scream from somewhere downstairs.

"Come on!" I shouted, breaking for the door.

We found Archibald Knore at the foot of the stairs, holding onto the maid, Winifred. "What is it?" Gideon demanded as we hurried down to join them.

"I lost my head," Knore muttered, releasing the girl at once. "I was questioning her and she told me a lie. When I grabbed her she screamed."

"A lie about what?"

Winifred was sobbing softly. "He accused me of wantin' to run off with Mr. Oakes, the butler. I never would do a thing like that, sir."

"They've been carrying on behind my back. I know they have!"

"*And the Dish ran away with the Spoon*," Gideon quoted. "You thought it referred to your butler and maid."

"What else could it refer to?" Knore said. "They did it and now they're going to run off."

"You think the butler did it?" I asked in amazement.

"You have books on nursery rhymes in the library. Let's check them," Gideon suggested to Knore, "and let this young woman be about her work."

The library, next to Knore's study, was a pleasant room with books reaching from floor to ceiling and the odor of leather bindings in the air. It took Gideon only a few moments' search to find what he sought. "See here—the same theory that links the rhyme to Queen Elizabeth says that the Dish was a courtier honoured by being assigned to carry golden dishes into the state dining room."

"A butler, in other words," Knore insisted.

"Or a custodian of something valuable, at least. And the Spoon was a beautiful young woman at court who was taster at the royal meals, insuring that the king or queen had not been poisoned."

"I know all that," Knore grumbled. "It still adds up to butler and maid in this household."

"If you'll pardon me," said Gideon, "the maid, Winifred, could hardly be described as beautiful. And the duties of taster seem more closely to resemble your secretary, Lois. In fact, I saw her taste the breakfast porridge just a few minutes ago."

"That's right!" I agreed.

"Lois?" Knore repeated, frowning with puzzlement.

The Foxes had come back downstairs, and as we left the library I saw Sylvia emerge from the kitchen carrying a rolled-up newspaper in her gloved hand. "I'm going outside for a little reading," she said. "Call me if anything happens, Bertie."

Bertie Foxe grunted and said to us, "How do you suppose Taupper's coming along with the boat repairs?"

"Want me to take a look?" I said. But Gideon ignored the question. His mind was still on the problem of the rhyme.

"If the Spoon referred to Lois Lanchester, couldn't the Dish refer not to the butler but to the custodian of your most valuable property, Archibald?"

Knore looked puzzled. "I have no gold."

"The animals, man! Peter Taupper is the custodian of your animals! He is the Plate of the rhyme!"

"Taupper and Lois?" I asked. "You think they're running away together?"

"That's the only way the rhyme can work out," Gideon answered grimly. "Come quickly—there's not a moment to lose."

He led the way, with Knore, Bertie, and me following along. We hurried out of the house and down the path toward the boat dock. I was vaguely aware that the morning's strong winds had let up, but right now we were concerned with more important matters than the weather.

It was the note that stopped us, at the final turn before the boat landing. It had been tacked to a tree like the others, and it read: AND THE DISH RAN AWAY WITH THE SPOON. This time the period was firmly in place at the end of the line. A finish had been reached.

"We're too late," I said.

"Maybe not!" Gideon plunged on and I followed, outdistancing the others.

The first thing we saw was Peter Taupper's body sprawled by the dock, and then Lois struggling with Sylvia Foxe. Sylvia's newspaper lay near Taupper. As Gideon and I hurried to pull them apart I said, "What happened? Did Sylvia come upon them as they were about to get away?"

"That's what it was," Sylvia gasped, struggling in my grip. "Turn me loose!"

But Gideon cautioned, "Hang onto her! She was about to add two more victims to her list! Sylvia Foxe is our nursery-rhyme murderess!"

Peter Taupper had only been stunned by the blow, and he and Lois were able to confirm the attack by Sylvia. She'd used the rolled-up newspaper, which she soaked in water and put into the kitchen freezer until it froze into a club of ice. The victims never suspected a thing when they saw her walking toward them with a newspaper. All she needed was a reasonable amount of strength behind that ice club to crush their skulls. And the weapon could be dropped anywhere unnoticed.

"I *saw* her coming out of the kitchen with the paper," I confirmed. "But why did she want to kill them all?"

"I expect Bertie can tell us about the first murder," Gideon said.

Bertie Foxe hung his head. "I always suspected Jan was having an affair with my wife. I spoke to him about it back in London, man to man, and I had the impression he was going to break it off."

"I imagine he tried to," Gideon agreed. "That's why she killed him. Then when she saw Milo Lune working nearby she must have feared he'd seen her. So he had to die too. The fact that Litost was a violinist and Lune's name means 'moon' must have suggested the nursery rhyme to her as a means of putting us off the track. But in truth it put us *on* the track. In the original rhyme and in her messages, there are eight words beginning with capital letters besides the first word in each line. There are Cat, Fiddle, Cow, Moon, Dog, Craft, Dish, and Spoon. She gave each one the meaning of a person, animal, or thing. Cat was the tiger, Fiddle was Litost, Cow was the female elephant, Moon was Lune, Craft was the sunken boat, Dish was Taupper, for reasons I've explained, and Spoon was Lois."

"What about Dog?" I asked.

"It was a clue to her own identity. A fox is indeed a member of the dog family, and when no other meaning presented itself I saw what she meant— *The little Dog laughed*, just as Sylvia Foxe herself must have laughed when the boat sank."

"She was going to kill Taupper and Lois just to finish the rhyme?" Knore asked.

"I imagine she would have weighted their bodies and pushed them off the dock. If they had seemed to run away, as in the rhyme, we would have blamed them for the prior killings."

Lois Lanchester still couldn't believe it. "And you knew all this just because a fox is a member of the dog family? Why couldn't the killer have been Bertie Foxe instead of Sylvia?"

"There were other things," Gideon admitted. "It was Sylvia who persuaded you to accompany Taupper to the dock, where she could kill you both. And remember yesterday when Sylvia called down from her window that she saw Lune's body up against the fence in the elephant enclosure? When I stood at that same window this morning I could barely see the tops of the elephants' heads. The zoo building blocked the view. She could only have known about the body if she'd put it there herself a few minutes earlier."

There was a throbbing in the sky and we looked up to see the police helicopter coming in for a landing. Out beyond the big house one of the elephants trumpeted a greeting.

THE DOOM BALLOONS

Basil Renfrew was at his desk early that morning, puffing on his eternal cigar as he sorted through his mail. The stock exchange hadn't yet opened for the day, so that the phone at his elbow was quiet, but the sound of Miss Jennings' typing came to him clearly through the half-open door.

It was a few minutes before ten, by the digital clock on Renfrew's desk, when the first of the balloons appeared. It drifted in through the partly open door like a living thing, hovering near the floor for just an instant before beginning its steady rise across the room and toward the ceiling. Renfrew watched it with growing curiosity until a second one appeared behind it. Then he called out to his secretary. "Miss Jennings?" No answer. "Miss Jennings, what's going on here?"

But she didn't answer, and he realized her typing had ceased some minutes earlier. A large bunch of balloons floated through the doorway, with a few stragglers following.

Finally, in exasperation at this bizarre practical joke—for what else could it be? Basil Renfrew stabbed out at the nearest balloons with his lighted cigar.

The balloon popped and flared in his face, sending sudden flames shooting in all directions. Then the others were popping too, as a chain reaction of flame and fury seemed to whip across the room like lightning.

As the flames engulfed Renfrew and clung to his clothing, he died without ever realizing quite what was happening.

That, at least, was how I imagine it happened. Sir Gideon Parrot and I were called in on the case a few days later. It had been a hot summer in New York, and as it drew to a close I was surprised to learn of Gideon's return from London. He'd assisted Scotland Yard in a confidential matter involving the royal family, and I'd expected him to stay on as a guest at one of their country estates.

"Are you needed here, Gideon?"

He nodded. "The matter of that stockbroker who burned to death in his office."

"Basil Renfrew. I read about it. A really bizarre accident."

"Bizarre, but hardly an accident."

"You mean—?"

"His partner thinks it was a murder, and I'm inclined to agree with him." Gideon reached into his pocket and took out some small pieces of colored rubber that seemed to have been scorched and puckered by fire.

"What are those?"

"The police found them in the burned office. Note the piece of charred string attached to this one. I believe they were balloons."

"Balloons!"

"The facts seem clear enough. In fact, the dead man's secretary remembers seeing a man with balloons in the hall when she was on her way to the ladies' room."

"Surely a man with balloons would attract attention in an office building!"

"One would think so," Gideon agreed. "In any event, I am assisting the police in their investigation. Do you wish to join me?"

"Of course!"

Our first stop was the brokerage firm of Royal and Renfrew, where Basil Renfrew had come to his untimely end. Simon Royal, the surviving partner, was a tall slim man in his early sixties who wore expensive suits, and a gold watch on his wrist. His office was quietly elegant, with wood paneling, an oriental rug and a private entrance. He seemed saddened and upset by his partner's death.

"I didn't know the police used outside consultants," he said, shaking Sir Gideon's hand, "but I suppose it's no different from using a financial consultant."

"Not at all," Gideon agreed. "I study the techniques of murder as you might study the rise and fall of bond prices."

"Then you're convinced my partner was murdered?"

"Aren't you?"

Simon Royal nodded. "Yes, I am. That's what I told the police. In this business one makes a great many enemies. Give someone bad advice on an investment and he's your enemy for life."

"Who specifically, might have wanted your partner dead?"

"Anyone from his former wife to a man named Lyon who was a partner in the firm until last year. We forced him out and he's resented it ever since. Tried to take legal action, but he had no grounds."

"What are their names?"

"Marie Renfrew was his wife until a few months ago. And Cal Lyon was our partner. I'll write down their addresses."

"I'll want to speak with Renfrew's secretary too."

"Miss Jennings. I'll show you to her office."

Helen Jennings was a tall young woman with dark hair and a good figure. After Royal introduced us and returned to his office, she explained that she'd been Basil Renfrew's secretary for a little over a year. "Did you know the other partner in the firm?" Gideon asked. "Cal Lyon?"

"Mr. Lyon left shortly after I started work here—within a matter of months. I never knew him well."

"Did he show any animosity toward Renfrew at the time?"

"I wasn't aware of any."

"And had he contacted Renfrew any time recently?"

She hesitated and then replied, "He may have. About two weeks ago there was a phone call that could have been him. I'm just not certain. Mr. Renfrew talked to him for a few minutes, and he seemed to be upset afterwards."

"I see." Gideon never took notes, but I could tell he was filing the information away nonetheless. "Now tell me about the day Mr. Renfrew died. Tell me everything that happened that morning."

Helen Jennings ran a nervous hand through her hair. "I hate to even think about it. The whole thing was so terrible. It was a little before ten in the morning and Mr. Renfrew was going through his mail as he always did. Once the market opens at ten I'll swear the phone never seems to stop ringing, but before that it's fairly peaceful—only a few calls from regulars. I'd just finished typing a letter he'd dictated the previous afternoon, and I was on my way out to the ladies' room when I saw the man with the balloons."

"You actually saw him."

"Oh, yes—quite clearly. He was about twenty feet away, just getting off the elevator with two huge bunches of balloons in all colors."

"What did he look like?"

"Tall—taller than me, even—and with a white face and big red eyes. His hair was straw-colored. In fact, it *was* straw."

"What?" Gideon gasped. "He sounds like a clown!"

"Well, of course! He was a clown—a clown in a tuxedo and cape. I thought you knew."

"A clown in a tuxedo and cape, carrying two big bunches of balloons, got off the elevator and you didn't think it was unusual? Instead of following him you went on to the ladies' room?"

"We see them all the time. It's the Clown-O-Gram service. They deliver bouquets of balloons for people's birthdays, anniversaries, things like that. Everyone knows about them."

"Did this man speak?"

"Not that I heard. I just gave him a passing glance."

"So with that getup it might even have been a woman."

"Oh, I don't think—Well I suppose so, but a tall woman."

"Things like a few inches in height can be easily changed," Gideon pointed out. "But go on with your story."

"There's nothing else to tell. When I came out of the ladies' room I could see some excitement down near my office. They told me there'd been a flash fire." Her voice quivered but did not break.

"Did you see the clown again after that?"

"No. I didn't even think about him. What could the balloons have to do with the fire?"

"They may have caused it. Could I see Renfrew's office?"

"I suppose it's all right if you're working with the police."

She opened the door of the inner office and showed us the room where Basil Renfrew had died. There was surprisingly little serious damage, but the floor and walls and ceiling all bore scorch marks. The desk was charred a bit, and behind it there was a large burned area on the rug, apparently where Renfrew's body had lain.

"It's as if a fiery wind had blown through the place," I observed. Then, remembering the little pieces of colored rubber Gideon had obtained from the police I asked, "You think the balloons contained some sort of explosive mixture?"

"Not a mixture at all," Gideon Parrot said, "I believe they contained pure hydrogen."

"Hydrogen! I thought balloons were always filled with helium."

"They are, in this country. But prior to the *Hindenburg* disaster in 1937 hydrogen was favored for both airships and balloons because it was the most buoyant. Helium is now used exclusively in America because it's nonflammable, but some other countries—especially in the Middle East—still use hydrogen. An actor was burned recently by an explosion of hydrogen-filled balloons in Turkey."

"Do you think Renfrew's death might have been accidental, then?"

"Highly unlikely. Whoever brought those balloons knew exactly what they were doing. I think our next step should be the Clown-O-Gram offices."

A slim young man named Steve Shine greeted us at the little storefront office that served as headquarters for the Clown-O-Gram operation. He was tall and agile, moving among rows of helium tanks and balloons of all colors as he came forward.

"What can I do for you today? Interested in our Honeymoon Special? Or the Birthday Blitz using two clowns and four bouquets of balloons?"

Gideon explained his connection with the police and our investigation of the killing of Basil Renfrew. "Did you you deliver balloons to him on the day he died?"

"I doubt it, but I can check the records. Come on back to the office. Careful of the tanks!"

"These are full of helium?" Gideon asked as we threaded our way down the narrow aisle.

"Sure!"

"Ever use hydrogen?"

"Are you kidding? It's against the fire laws."

"I just wondered."

He flipped through the pages of his ledger. "Nothing to Renfrew. I thought I'd remember it because I was doing clown duty that day."

"You deliver the balloons yourself?"

"Sometimes, if we're short-handed." He pointed to a white-faced, red-lipped clown mask hanging on the wall behind his desk. "When I get a call on short notice and don't have time to apply the clown makeup, I wear that mask."

"How many clowns work here?"

"We generally use part-time college kids. There are four, not counting myself."

It was clear enough that the murderer could easily have imitated a Clown-O-Gram type of delivery, launching the balloons into Renfrew's office while keeping clear of the danger area himself. Chances were Steve Shine had nothing to do with it, but Gideon wasn't ready to let him completely off the hook.

"We may have further questions. Here's a phone number where I can be reached. If anything unusual happens—anything suspicious involving yourself or your deliveries—I want to know about it right away."

"Sure," Shine said, taking Gideon's card.

We drove across town and visited Marie Renfrew next. The dead man's former wife was a stout middle-aged woman whom Gideon found difficult to question. She met us at the door of her apartment and wouldn't allow us over the threshold. "If you're detectives, show me your credentials. If you're not, be on your way!"

Gideon cleared his throat. "I work with the police in a private capacity."

"Sure, you do! And the minute I let you in, the two of you will jump on me and rape me!"

"My dear lady—"

"I can vouch for his identity," I said. "He really is Sir Gideon Parrot."

"You! So who are you?"

"I assist him unofficially in his investigations."

"Oh, I see! He assists the police unofficially, and you assist him unofficially! You're either a couple of rapists or a couple of nuts, and either way you don't get in!"

Gideon sighed and began again. "We're investigating the murder of your husband."

"My former husband, and I don't know that he was murdered. He probably got so hot under the collar he just burnt up."

"Was he an excitable sort?"

"I don't talk about him any more. I don't even think about him if I can help it."

"Did he have any enemies?"

"There you go asking me more questions! I'm not answering questions from you two. Do you think you're Batman and Robin or something?"

"Hardly," Sir Gideon replied, drawing himself up with dignity. "I only recently completed an investigation involving the royal family."

"What royal family is that?"

Gideon saw that it was hopeless. "We may return later," he warned.

Back in the car I tried to console him. "Maybe the police should issue you an identity card."

But he was having none of it. "Thank heaven one does not encounter people that foolish very often. I must keep my unofficial status and deal with it the best I can."

"Who do we see next?" I asked, hoping things would improve.

"Cal Lyon, the former partner. I have his address right here."

As chance would have it, our route took us back through lower Manhattan. We were passing about a block from the offices of Royal and Renfrew when I pointed out the car window. "Look at that, Gideon. It's one of the Clown-O-Gram trucks."

"And there goes the clown himself rounding the corner with his balloons!"

"Do you think he's going to Renfrew's building again?"

"Hurry! Park the car! There may not be a moment to lose."

Finding a parking space in that part of the city was no easy task. I dropped off Gideon, circled the block, and finally settled on a nearby parking garage. I caught up with him as he was boarding the elevator. "I lost sight of the balloons," he admitted, "but I think they came in here."

We got off at Renfrew's floor and immediately were engulfed in pandemonium. People were running in every direction, and a fire alarm bell had started its shrill ringing. "What is it?" Gideon asked, grabbing Helen Jennings as she ran past.

"A fire in Mr. Royal's office!"

We hurried toward the doorway, but the heat and flames were too intense for anyone to enter. A fire extinguisher proved useless, and someone finally pulled a fire hose from its cabinet near the elevator. They hosed down the doorway and were beginning to contain the flames when the firemen arrived.

It was a half-hour before the last of the fire had died and the rubber-coated firemen could search among the charred, smoking remains of the office. We watched from the doorway as they uncovered the blackened body by the desk. I could see the remains of the gold watch on his wrist, and I knew the balloons had claimed the second partner of Royal and Renfrew.

Gideon spent the next couple of hours closeted with the police, telling them what little his investigation had uncovered. When he joined me later he was depressed. "A dozen witnesses saw the clown get off the elevator and enter Simon Royal's office with two big bunches of balloons, but once the fire started no one saw him. Obviously he removed his tuxedo and clown mask, perhaps even burning them in the fire, and mingled with the others in a more normal costume, or else escaped through Royal's private entrance."

"Didn't anybody think to stop him before he reached Royal's office?"

Gideon shook his head. "Remember, the police never announced our theory about hydrogen-filled balloons. The office employees had no reason to be alarmed. Helen Jennings might have remembered our questions about the balloon man, but apparently she didn't see him arrive today. She knew nothing until the fire broke out."

I shook my head, unable to comprehend the horror of it. "Did Royal have a family?"

"A wife up in Stamford. The police are checking with her now."

"Surely the same person killed both Royal and his partner."

"That seems more than likely. The murder method had not been announced and it's not the sort of thing two killers stumble upon accidentally."

"I think we're overdue for a visit to Cal Lyon," I said.

Gideon agreed. We returned to the car and resumed our interrupted journey. Lyon was living in a converted loft near the financial district—a big, high-ceilinged room which he'd elaborately divided into living and working space. If he'd arrived home just before us, he put on a good act, telephoning buy and sell orders for clients while his eyes scanned the stock exchange printouts on the little computer screen at his elbow. He gave every impression of not having budged from the spot since the market opening that morning.

"What is it?" he asked gruffly, hanging up the phone and twisting his big body to face us. "More police business about poor old Renfrew?"

"More than that, I'm afraid, Gideon Parrot told him. "Now Simon Royal has been killed in exactly the same manner."

"Simon! My God! Who are you—a private detective?"

"I assist the police."

"They think the same person killed both of them?"

"That's right," Gideon said. "Someone who had a grudge against the firm and its two partners."

"Meaning me."

"The possibility was suggested by Royal before his untimely death."

"I was about to settle all my claims and drop my lawsuit against the company. My lawyer will verify that. I had no reason for wanting either of them dead."

"Except revenge for being forced out of a highly profitable brokerage business."

Cal Lyon smiled. "Did he tell you it was highly profitable? If he did, he was a liar. During my final months there I began to suspect that Renfrew was cheating the company, diverting commissions to his private account rather than splitting them with us. More than that I think he handled some very shady stock transactions. It was one of the reasons I left the partnership."

"Simon Royal said you were forced out."

"Forced out because I wanted him to investigate Renfrew's accounts!" he countered, suddenly angry. "I left and told them I was suing. But that was a year ago. Passions cool in a year's time."

It didn't seem to me that his had cooled too much, but I let it pass. Gideon did too, seeming more interested in facts than passions. "Could I ask where you were around noon?"

"Where? Right here, of course!"

"Any proof of that?"

"I talked to several people on the phone."

Gideon pointed to an answering machine prominently positioned beside the desk. "The glowing red light indicates your machine is on."

"It's a busy day on Wall Street. I've had it on to intercept incoming calls so I could complete some transactions."

"I see. So you have no alibi for earlier."

"Have it whatever way you want. Got any witnesses who can identify me as the killer?"

"It seems the killer wore clown makeup or a mask."

"Like the Clown-O-Gram people?"

"Exactly."

"A friend sent me one of those on my birthday," Lyon said. "They are fun."

"Not when the balloons are filled with hydrogen."

"Yeah? Is that what the killer used to start the fires? A clever idea. I hope the cops are checking on their delivery men."

"They are," Gideon assured him. "But it sounds as if you admire the killer."

"I always admire clever ideas, in business or in crime. That doesn't mean I approve of murder. They were still friends of mine, despite our bad times."

"And you had no reason to wish them dead?"

"I told you the lawsuit was being dropped." A new set of stock quotations began moving across the screen and he grew preoccupied. "Call me again if I can be of further assistance," he said, clearly dismissing us. "The market's closing now and I'm busy."

Outside, I grumbled to Gideon. "Further assistance! He wasn't any assistance at all!"

"Perhaps not. We shall see. Right now it's important that I call in to Headquarters. I suggested they question Steve Shine and find out if any of the Clown-O-Gram drivers were at Royal's office this noon."

When he stepped out of the phone booth his face was grim. "What is it, Gideon?" I asked.

"They tell me Steve Shine has disappeared. He may have skipped town."

The disappearance of Shine was only one more piece of the puzzle. For the first time we began to seriously consider the possibility that Shine was the killer after all, that no one had faked the Clown-O-Gram deliveries. But if that was the case, what could his motive be?

"The firm might have cheated him out of some money," Gideon speculated. "Or given him some bad investment advice."

"If that was the case, why didn't he kill Cal Lyon too? He was one of the partners until last year."

"He may have tried!" Gideon answered, suddenly excited by the idea. "Remember, Lyon told us he'd received a Clown-O-Gram recently for his birthday. Perhaps that was a death trap that didn't work."

"Why wouldn't it have worked?"

"The balloons are safe until the hydrogen is ignited. Something has to set them off. I suppose a cigarette is the most likely thing, and Lyon doesn't appear to smoke."

"How do you know that?"

"There was no ashtray on his desk."

"What about Renfrew and Royal?"

"I believe Helen Jennings could best answer that. Let us pay a return visit to their office."

The death of Simon Royal had thrown a pall of gloom over the brokerage firm. The offices were closed for the rest of the day, and most employees had already left for home. Police and arson investigators were still sifting through the ashes of Royal's gutted office, where virtually nothing had escaped destruction. We found Helen Jennings cleaning out her desk, filling a box with personal effects from her drawers.

"I wouldn't work here another day," she told us. "Not with some madman trying to kill us all!"

"The killings may be at an end," Gideon Parrot said. "But I must ask one more question. Did Basil Renfrew smoke?"

"He was never without a big cigar, from morning to night. I used to kid him about it."

"And Simon Royal?"

"I don't think he smoked. I never noticed."

That news troubled Gideon. I could see it didn't fit with his theory. "May I use your telephone? I must call Cal Lyon again."

I stood close enough so I could hear Lyon's response in the receiver. "I told you I was busy now, Mr. Gideon. No more questions."

"Sir, I have only two questions for you. Earlier you said you'd received a Clown-O-Gram for your birthday. Who was it from?"

"The card was signed *Your former co-workers at Royal & Renfrew.* I never found out just who sent it, but it was nice of them."

"How long ago was this?"

"My birthday was a week ago Monday."

"And what happened to the balloons?"

"There were two big bunches of them. I was going to keep them for a while, but I really had no place to put them here. Finally I opened the window and just let them float away over the city."

"That may have saved you life," Gideon said.

"You mean they were filled with hydrogen like the others?"

"Exactly."

"My God!"

"Be very careful, Mr. Lyon. If there are any future deliveries, please report them to the police."

After Gideon had hung up I asked him, "Do you really think Lyon's life is in danger?"

"It's a possibility. Of course a clever killer might make up the story of the balloon delivery so he'd appear to be one of the intended victims."

We spoke briefly to the chief arson investigator before we left. He was a bright-looking man named Lieutenant Tragger, but he was the first to admit his lack of experience with hydrogen fires. "If you hadn't told me about the balloons I'd say it was a firebomb of some sort—a bottle of gasoline with a wick in it. Did a hell of a lot of damage, to the office and the body both."

When we returned to the Gideon invited me home with him, to the luxury apartment overlooking Central Park that he used when he was in New York. It belonged, he said, to a wealthy Middle Eastern personage for whom he'd once done a considerable favor. There was an answering machine hooked up to the telephone, as there had been at Cal Lyon's place, and Gideon turned it on to see if there'd been any messages.

Surprisingly, the voice we heard was that of the missing Steve Shine. "Sir Gideon, you asked me to phone this number if anything unusual happened involving my deliveries. You've only been gone about a half-hour but I just received an order to deliver a double Clown-O-Gram to Simon Royal at his office. I'm about to leave now and I thought you should know about it."

"That's it!" Gideon exclaimed, hitting the table with his hand. "The missing piece of the puzzle!"

"You mean that Shine killed—?"

"Come on! We've not a moment to lose!"

"Where are we going?"

"Back to Cal Lyon's loft."

It was after five when I parked the car about a block away from Lyon's place. I was about to get out, but Gideon held me back. "Let's wait here a bit. The streets are crowded."

And indeed they were, as people finished their day's work and hurried toward the subway entrances. "But Lyon won't be leaving," I pointed out. "He lives right there."

"I know."

"You think Lyon killed them to force the company out of business? So he'd get all their clients?"

"No, I think Lyon is about to be killed. If the murderer failed once, last week, he may want another try before he leaves the city."

"Leaves the city? We're back to Steve Shine again. He's the only one who's left."

"There is one other."

"Someone who left? You mean today?

"I mean today."

The crowds were thinning now, and as we talked the shadows grew longer. In another hour this old loft neighborhood would be almost deserted. "Marie Renfrew looked as if she might be going somewhere. Is that who you mean? I suppose a woman could wear the clown outfit as easily as a man could."

Gideon Parrot suddenly gripped my arm. "Over there," he said softly.

I followed his gaze and saw someone on the side street getting out of a parked car. It was a tall person wearing a tuxedo and a clown mask, and he was pulling two large bunches of large multi-colored balloons out of the car after him.

"There's our killer," Gideon announced. "We must hurry."

"Those balloons are deadly, Gideon. Let's call the police."

"No time for the police. Come on!"

I followed him reluctantly across the street, remembering our similar chase just a few hours earlier, when we'd been too late to save the life of Simon

Royal. But this time luck was on our side, if you could call it that. We entered the lobby of Lyon's building only a moment after the clown with the balloons. He was still there, waiting for the slow-moving elevator, when he saw us.

He released his grip on one bunch of balloons, letting them float free to the ceiling. Then with his empty right hand he pulled a cigarette lighter from the pocket of his tuxedo. He shoved the other balloons toward us and flicked on the lighter.

"Get back!" Gideon shouted to me.

There was a sudden flare of fire shooting out in all directions, scorching the walls and ceiling. Gideon and I dropped to the floor as it passed overhead like a roar from a blast furnace. The clown had grabbed for the other bunch of balloons just as the doors slid open and the empty elevator, but he'd underestimated the radius of the flames. Suddenly one of his balloons flared, and then the rest went with a terrible whoosh. He screamed as the searing flames drove him into the elevator.

"Don't let him get away!" Gideon yelled, diving through the flame and smoke to reach the elevator doors before they slid shut.

We reached them just in time, and pounced upon the fallen figure on the elevator floor. Already the fire had burnt itself out against the tile and marble lobby, finding nothing to feed upon, but it had done its job on the murderous clown. The fight had gone out of him as Gideon reached for the mask that still hid his face from us.

In that final instant I thought I knew the answer. Yes, there was one other person who'd been going away that day. Helen Jennings was quitting her job at the brokerage firm, and we'd watched her clean out her desk.

But the face behind the mask didn't belong to Helen Jennings.

It was the face of Simon Royal, back from the dead, but just barely.

We turned him over to Lieutenant Tragger and the homicide detectives, who placed him under arrest while they waited for an ambulance to get him to the hospital. Then I demanded an explanation from Gideon. "You couldn't have known it was Simon Royal," I insisted.

"I had a pretty good idea. The first thing that struck me was the physical evidence—the appearance of the two murder scenes. Basil Renfrew's office was badly scorched but otherwise intact. Simon Royal's office was totally gutted. Lieutenant Tragger even remarked that it seemed more like a gasoline firebomb to him. And that's exactly what it was. Basil Renfrew was killed by hydrogen balloons, and those were obviously hydrogen balloons that went off here earlier, but none went off in Simon Royal's office. He had to be certain the body couldn't be identified after the fire, if he wanted people to believe he was dead. So he used a powerful gasoline bomb like a Molotov cocktail."

"Gideon, if that wasn't Royal's body in his office, whose was it?"

"The man who entered the office with the balloons and the clown mask— Steve Shine, of course."

"Shine! You mean it wasn't the killer we spotted going into Royal and Renfrew's building this noon?"

"Not that time. It was Steve Shine making what he thought was a legitimate delivery. The balloons contained harmless helium, but when he walked into that office, Royal was waiting. He hit him over the head, placed his gold watch on Shine's wrist for identification purposes, and then set off a firebomb of inflammable liquid. While the office blazed and people came running, he escaped through his private entrance. He'd lured Shine there with the balloons, of course, so that his supposed murder would be linked with the killing of Renfrew, and the later killing of Cal Lyon."

"But why did he want them all dead?"

"Because it wasn't Renfrew who was defrauding the company and its clients, it was Royal. When Cal Lyon filed his lawsuit, Royal feared the court procedure would reveal the truth. He failed to kill Lyon last week, but when Renfrew began to suspect him he succeeded in his second attempt. Then he decided to fake his own death and take off for South America with the money he'd milked from the company. Shine was the logical victim to substitute for him. They were both tall, about the same build, and he was relying on the fire to make positive identification impossible. Since the body was in Royal's own office, wearing his watch, no one would have bothered to check dental records. There'd be no questions it was him."

"How did he know Shine would deliver the balloons he ordered."

"I imagine he checked on the company's practice. It was no secret that Shine made the deliveries when no one else was in the office, and the lunch hour was the most likely time for that. If someone else had arrived with the balloons, who bore no resemblance to Royal, he'd merely have postponed his plan."

"And Lyon?"

"I realized Royal was the killer after I heard the message Shine left me. He never would have phoned to tell me he was on the way to commit murder.

And I figured Royal might have one more try at killing Lyon before he left town. He couldn't risk Lyon putting everything together and realizing the embezzler was Royal rather than Renfrew."

"You told me the killer was leaving town today. I thought it was Helen Jennings. I didn't think about Royal having left anywhere."

"We thought he was dead, and death is about as long a journey as anyone takes," Gideon said.

I thought it was an especially long journey to take by balloon.

SOURCES

The Revolutionary Detections of Alexander Swift

The Hudson Chain. *Ellery Queen's Mystery Magazine*, September 1995
King George's Gold. *Ellery Queen's Mystery Magazine*, March 1996
The Uninvited Guest. *Ellery Queen's Mystery Magazine*, November 1996
Duel at Dawn. *Ellery Queen's Mystery Magazine*, March 1998
The Broken Chain. *Ellery Queen's Mystery Magazine*, February 1999
Vulture in the Mist. *Ellery Queen's Mystery Magazine*, August 1999
The Sword of Colonel Ledyard. *Ellery Queen's Mystery Magazine*, December 2000
St. John and the Dragon. *Ellery Queen's Mystery Magazine*, November 2001
Constant Hearses. *Ellery Queen's Mystery Magazine*, September/October 2002
The Orchard of Caged Birds. *Ellery Queen's Mystery Magazine*. May 2003
Paul Revere's Bell. *Ellery Queen's Mystery Magazine*, March/April 2004
The Barber's Toe. *Ellery Queen's Mystery Magazine*, June 2005
Swift Among the Pirates. *Ellery Queen's Mystery Magazine*, May 2007

The Classical Detections of Gideon Parrot

Lady of the Impossible. *Ellery Queen's Mystery Magazine*, May 1981
The Man with Five Faces. *Ellery Queen's Mystery Magazine*, January 1982
The Flying Fiend. *Ellery Queen's Mystery Magazine*, mid-July 1982
The Cat and Fiddle Murders. *Ellery Queen's Mystery Magazine*, January 1983
The Doom Balloon. *Mike Shayne Mystery Magazine*, June 1983

Books by Edward D. Hoch
Published by Crippen & Landru

The Ripper of Storyville and Other Ben Snow Tales. Available as a Kindle ebook
The Velvet Touch. Available as a Kindle ebook
The Old Spies Club and Other Intrigues of Rand. Available as a Kindle ebook
The Iron Angel and Other Tales of the Gypsy Sleuth. Available as a Kindle ebook
Hoch's Ladies. Available as a print book and as a Kindle ebook
Funeral in the Fog and Other Investigations of Simon Ark. Available as a print
    book and as a Kindle ebook
Constant Hearses and Other Revolutionary Stories. Available as a print book and
    (forthcoming as a Kindle ebook)

THE PROBLEMS OF DR. SAM HAWTHORNE

Diagnosis Impossible: The Problems of Dr. Sam Hawthorne. Available as a print
    book and as Kindle ebook
More Things Impossible, The Second Casebook of Dr. Sam Hawthorne. Available as
    a print book and as a Kindle ebook
Nothing Is Impossible, Further Problems of Dr. Sam Hawthorne. Available as a
    print book and as a Kindle ebook
All But Impossible, The Impossible Files of Dr. Sam Hawthorne. Available as a
    print book and as a Kindle ebook
Challenge the Impossible: The Final Problems of Dr. Sam Hawthorne. Available as
    a print book and as a Kindle ebook

CONSTANT HEARSES

Constant Hearses and Other Revolutionary Mysteries is printed on 60-pound paper and is designed by G.E. Satheesh, Pondicherry, India. The type is Goudy Old Style. The cover is by Gail Cross. The first edition was published in two forms: trade softcover, perfect bound; and one hundred fifty copies sewn in cloth, numbered and signed by Brian Skupin. Each of the cloth-bound copies includes a separate pamphlet, "A Flash of Red," a short story by Edward D. Hoch. *Constant Hearses* was printed by Southern Ohio Printers and bound by Cincinnati Bindery. The book was published in March 2022 by Crippen & Landru Publishers, Inc., Cincinnati, OH.